'RAINBOWS SELDOM TOUCH THE GROUND'

(The tragic story of a Donegal Tally Girl)

BY
LOUIE BYRNE

A glossary of unfamiliar terms appears at the end of the book

All characters named in this book are fictional

Published by Premier Books
Unit 'R' Cradock Road
Luton Beds.LU4 OJF
Tel: 01582 572727
Fax: 01582 585868

RAINBOWS SELDOM TOUCH THE GROUND

Children of the martyred race
Whether free or fettered,
Wake the echoes of the song,
Where're you may be scattered.
Yours the message cheering,
That time is nearing,
Which will see all men free,
Tyrants disappearing.

A Chanukah hymn.

British Library Cataloguing in Publication Data.
A catalogue record for this book is available from the British Library.

Copyright© 2000 by Louie Byrne
All rights reserved
ISBN # 09524278 7 7

Again to my wife Bridget.

INTRODUCTION

My name is Michael Kearney and I am the illegitimate son and sole heir to the estate of Lord James Simon Kilgarvan of Cardavon Castle situated in the townland of Dungloe in the highlands of Donegal, Ireland. As to how I, a humble Irishman came to take possession of this estate I beg the indulgence of the reader... '

Lord James Simon Kilgarvan, my mother's tormentor and murderer inherited Cardavon Castle and estate together with a substantial bank balance from his late father, Lord James Nicholas Kilgarvan. Through mismanagement, womanising and gambling most of the estate was soon in the hands of his creditors.

My mother Mary Kearney, God rest her soul, was forced to become the reluctant and innocent 'Tally Woman' to the lord of the castle at the tender age of twelve years. I never knew my mother or she me, for she passed from life to mortal dream before the true bond of love and friendship could be entwined. There is no doubt in my mind but that she was a loving and caring mother and daughter. During her short life span she saw both her parents carried to an early grave. She suffered the trauma of hunger and an uncalled for barbaric and premature death. In her dying breath she continued blaming herself for what happened to her mother. In the misery and shame perpetrated on her she sought absolution for sins of which she was innocent. For my part I pray and blaspheme that the black soul of Lord Kilgarvan should rot and burn in Hell forever more.

My land is in the throes of a great hunger perpetrated on it by an occupying power that cares not what becomes of us.

Our country has been pillaged and raped of its people and produce. Our prayers remain unanswered our children dead. Our customs and beliefs sneered upon, scoffed and derided. Our 'Breton laws' far older and nobler than those of the occupying powers treated with contempt. Even the rainbows are reluctant to touch the ground of Ireland for fear of being tainted. God has abandoned us to our fate in this cursed land of ours.
This is my story... '

                    Michael Kearney.
                    Derryveagh Heights
                    Pittsburgh Pennsylvania. A.D. 1865.

A DAY AT THE FAIR

It was a bright summer's day and a long ribbon of turf smoke snaked lazily into the blue sky. Crickets chirped in the morning dew. Blackbirds and Thrushes sang in the crystal clear air. A mother Robin sitting on a branch nearby defiantly defended her territory and challenged their intrusion into her domain with her own chirping.
Tom halted the pony and looked skywards. From the signs he concluded that they were in for a spell of fine weather. His wife Bríge was sitting outside the cottage on the resting stone when the pony and bucket trap came up the boréen.
"You're home early Tom, who owns the fine trap?" She queried.
"I borrowed it from the estate for the next few days. His lordship has gone to Dublin or elsewhere." He smiled.
"Won't you look the dandy sitting in a bucket trap. Would you like a sup of tae?" She rose from her seat and entered the kitchen.
"Do you know what I was thinking of doing?" He suggested as he sucked on his cré duidín some time later.
"No! But I'm sure that I'm about to be told." She looked up from her knitting at him.
"Why don't we go over to Letterkenny to the fair? It would be a break from the chores for you and the children." He offered.
"Letterkenny! How do you expect to get there with three children?" She questioned.
" What do you think I borrowed the bucket trap for?"
"You don't mean to go now, do you? It's far too late."
"No! Of course not, to morrow morning we'll pack a bite to eat and be on our way early." He promised.
"I wouldn't tell the children until the morning, if I were you." She warned.
"Why not? I was going to tell them right away."
"You do just that and they won't sleep a wink with all the excitement."
"You're right as usual, I'll put the pony in the meadow for now."
They rose early next morning and prepared for the journey.
"Bríge, did you ever see such a Heavenly day?" He called as he returned with a pail of water from the stream.
"I'm busy, did you say something Tom?" Bríge was busy preparing a meal of scones and a few boiled eggs for the journey.
"It doesn't matter, I'll feed the hens on my way." He picked up the bucket of

boiled nettles and potato scraps and left the house. Having fed the hens he went down the meadow and called to the pony. The pony was not to be fooled by a handful of fresh grass and tried to make her escape to the far corner of the field.
"Come on Jenny, we're off to the fair." He spoke gently to her as he reached out and caught her by the mane.
As he harnessed the pony, Brige was busy filling the trap with food and clothing for the journey.
"That's enough, there won't be any room for us." He warned as he saw her come from the cottage for the umpteen time carrying a blanket.
As they crossed the ford over the river Swilly they saw the town of Letterkenny spread out before them. There were people on foot and in drays cluttering up the road. All were intent on getting to the fair early.
"We're here children, this is Letterkenny." Their father flicked the whip gentle across the pony's back. The pony switched her tail and shaking her head dug her feet into the bog road and climbing the short incline.
There was a distinct icy wind blowing in from Lough Swilly bay. Tom feeling the chill tightened his home spun jacket around him. Outside of the town a man brandishing a shillelagh stopped the trap.
"Whoa! Whoa!" Tom pulled on the reins bringing the pony to a halt and looked questionably at the man.
"What's the matter? We're going to the fair." Brige looked down at the intruder.
"Sorry about this, but all carts and horses must be parked in the big field yonder." The man pointed with his shillelagh to a field a short distance away.
"It's twopence for the grazing and parking." He reached up a shovel sized grubby hand.
"My youngest is not all that well and needs to be as near as possible to the fair, can you help us please?" Brige pleaded.
"Sure if I let one go then where will it stop. Let me see him?" Lifting his foot on to the step he looked down at Tomás beag cocooned in a heavy blanket.
"Bless the poor cratur, may God give him the health." The man scratched the stubble on his chin and looked down at two blue eyes smiling at him from under the blanket.
"Do you see the far cottage over there where the river joins the bay?" Again he pointed into the distance with his shillelagh.
"I do, I do that." Tom stood up in the trap and looked into the distance.
"Go round to the back of that and you'll find my wife Anne Kilderry, Tell her that her Tom said to let you into the Quakers patch. There you'll be as near to the fair as the *Sagart (Priest)* is to Heaven." He confirmed.

"Thank you and God bless and keep you and yours." Tom reached out the coins to him.

"Yarrah! Will you be putting that away and say a prayer for herself and me." Reaching out he stroked the head of Tomás beag before he alighted from the step.

"Away with you before I have a change of heart." He laughed as he smacked the pony across the rump. By the time they had unhitched the pony the fair was in full swing.

"I'll take a look round the carts, you go off and enjoy yourselves. Here take this." Reaching into the pocket of his breeches he took out a sovereign and handed it to his wife.

"Can we afford this much Tom?" She looked at the coin in the palm of her hand.

"We've come a long way to enjoy ourselves. For this once let us make the best of it. See you later." Digging his hands deep into the pockets of his breeches he went down the road.

A long row of carts and stalls took pride of place along the roadside.

Potatoes and vegetables were spilled out on the road where potential customers were invited to come and take their pick at a price. Stalls filled with bric-a-brac, home made cakes, scones and jams invited the customers to come and buy.

A man stood on a box with a hailer to his mouth calling to the visitors. Tom, curious as to know what his message was about joined the growing throng. The speaker seemed to be in an agitated mood as Tom pressed nearer.

A second man held a blue flag high and waved it aloft. The flag had a Muriel of *'The Maid of Éireann'* impregnated on it. On a scroll at the base of the flag was written '***ERIN GO BRAGH'*** in bold lettering. Two armed peelers were watching the men intently.

"Irishmen and Irish women come rally to the cause, get off your knees. Are you ready to fight for Ireland and Ireland only?" He shouted as he waved an official looking document before them.

"Join the Fenian movement, support Ireland's right to justice." He continued his rhetoric.

A woman with a green and gold sash mingled with the gathering shaking a tin can.

"Support the cause, remember your Fenian brothers and sisters. They rot alone and abandoned in England's prison cells." She challenged in her native tongue. The gathering began drifting away; they had heard it all so often before. Tom sauntered away leaving the patriotic few to pledge their loyalty.

Crossing the street his attention was arrested to a board held securely to an old milk churn. A game of '45' would be held if and when they had enough places filled.
The price of entry would be two pence for each player. The winner would receive two fine laying pullets. Reaching into the pocket of his breeches he withdrew what money he had. Holding the coins in the palm of his hand he counted them out.
There were five farthings, a few pennies, a sovereign and three cut nails. Spitting on four of the farthings he returned the balance to his pocket and entered the premises.
Several men stood in small groups with tankards in their hands chatting. Along the counter was a selection of clay pipes. There was a hushed silence as the door swung open behind him.
A woman in bare feet accompanied by two ragged children crept silently into the premises and stood before the open fire. Her children peeped out from the folds of her ragged skirt like cygnets hiding in the down of a mother swan. Removing her shawl from her head she rested her hand on the mantelpiece and began to sing.
There was a shuffling of feet as the patrons turned their backs on her. The landlord was about to ask her to leave when she burst into song. As her melodious voice began singing a story of Ireland's poverty there was a hush and all eyes settled on the young woman.

The Jolly Beggar man
I have no more a golden store-that sets the world a scorning,
Yet I be happy every night and merry every morning;
Each day my bread I ask of God, he sends me not away,
So I shall always merry be till I be in the clay.
Upon the roads I pray my prayer,
My thanks to God I pour,

Good prayer I have upon my tongue to say at every door.
No fears have I, the night to pass, exposed to winter's rigour,
For every house will welcome me, the merry jovial beggar.
I ask no bed, no sheet, no quilt-a wisp of straw lay down
And I shall sleep as sound and deep as Kings on beds of down.

I dream of Heaven, the glorious home, where angels walk in white;
My guardian angel at my side will watch me through the night.
I seek no gold to have or hold. For riches wear not well,

And countless thousands seeking it have cast themselves to Hell;
For gold must melt like snow in lent, before the breath of spring,
But the soul that counts it, it must die -a low unloving thing.

"God bless you kind Sir's, it's not for me but for the childer." The woman on finishing her lament urged her children forward. A rusting tin can appeared from under her ragged shawl as she stood looking pitifully at the assembly. With pleading eyes that told her story she stood motionless, the can held in her hand.

It would be a hard heart indeed that would refuse her. As she stood before Tom he reached into the pocket of his breeches and withdrew a farthing and discreetly dropped it into the tin.

"Sorry mam! I wish it could be more." He shuffled from one foot to the other and apologised.

"God will reward the generous giver, thank you kind Sir." The woman smiled. Slowly she walked along the line of men accosting each in turn. Poor as the gathering were themselves they would not refuse a poor woman of the road. She in return gave them of her blessings.

Finally having exhausted her pleadings she went to the door and turning she faced them.

"I can only give you the blessing of a woman of the roads and her orphans in return for your charity." She invoked a final blessing on them and the landlord for their generosity. With her two children holding on to the end of her shawl she left.

"Where do I put my mark for the game, Sir?" Tom broke the silence of the room.

"Give it to the landlord over there. Glad you came, we are waiting to start." He pointed with his Pewter mug to a man standing against the counter.

"You're for the game are you? Best have a drink whilst you wait." The landlord took the four farthings and handed him a piece of paper with the number nine written on it.

"How much is the ale?" Tom asked.

"One farthing a mug and a cré dúidín with a measure of tobacco thrown in." He pointed to a row of clay pipes sitting on the counter. Tom crossed to the counter where a large wooded barrel sat on a trestle. "There's a penny recoverable on the mug before I can serve you." He was informed before being given a pewter mug.

Tom paid his money and picking up one of the pipes broke the stem in half and threw the front piece into the fire. He placed the bowl in his mouth before

filling it with tobacco.
Holding his hand over the bowl he sucked on the pipe before he was satisfied with it. Removing his tinderbox from his pocket he struck a light and joined the others that were standing like statues along the wall.
"We're ready now gentlemen and 'good luck.' The landlord called the men to a rough set of tables.
Sometime later he walked down the street carrying the prized two hens whose legs were tied together. The hens squawked loudly, protesting at being carried in such an uncomfortable manner.
"Shut up will you or I'll wring your necks." He swore at them. Coming down the street against him was Bríge and Séan. Mary was walking slowly behind carrying Tomás Beag in her young arms. In his hand Séan held a wooded sailing boat with white sails.
He noticed that her red petticoat was splashed with mud and looked the worst for wear. Then most of the people, if not all, were in a similar situation. If nothing else it eased his conscious knowing that other families were in the same predicament.
"Been lucky at the cards then?" She looked down at the pair of birds.
"Sure, I won them at '45'. Here take them. They are making me look foolish squawking like that." He passed the birds to his wife without further ceremony.
"They don't look all that old." Bríge weighed them in her hand and thought of the fine meal they would make.
"They're not for boiling, they're laying pullets. Don't you know anything woman?" He added as an after thought.
"Fine pullets sure, if we cannot meet our rent you know who will profit by them, don't you? Pity they were not offering a *'Gentleman who pays the rent'."* She sighed.
"I doubt if the money on offer would run to such luxuries. Be grateful for the hens." He good humorously chided her.
"Oh I am, so I am but..." She looked down at the two hens.
"That's a nice boat, where did it come from?" He ignored her remark.
"We won it on the rings, well Mary did." She added seeing Mary's look of disappointment at not getting the credit.
"Would you like to go on the roundabout with the other children?" Instinctively he reached out and took Tomás Beag from Mary.
A man stood in the centre of the roundabout leaning against a handle that controlled a ratchet holding the drive wheel locked. On seeing that the horses were all occupied he tapped his pipe on the wheel and set it to one side.
"That's it then, now hold tight children." He called. Releasing the brake he

took hold of the handle and laboriously turned it. The drive wheel began to turn, the children shouted and waved as slowly the wooden horses gained momentum.

All too soon as far as the children were concerned the man tired and let the roundabout come slowly to a halt.

"Did you enjoy that?" Their father asked as he escorted them down the street. As the evening drew slowly to a close, the fair was handed over to the adults. By the time they returned to the 'Quakers patch' the children were falling asleep on their feet.

"It's yourselves back safe and sound at last." Anne and Tom came from the cottage to greet them.

"How did it go then, did you enjoy our fair? That's a lovely boat" Anne smiled at the children.

"We had a grand old time. Didn't we?" Bríge spoke for the family.

"I've made a bit of supper for you and the children, I hope you won't be offended?"

"Not at all, we owe you our thanks and our prayers." Tom removed his caubéen out of respect to the house.

"When you finish say your prayers and sit over there." Their mother pointed to two stooléens beside the fire. Leaving the adults to indulge in their conversation the children obediently left the table.

It was sometime later when they were into their umpteen-cup of tae and the '*Craic*' that Anne looked across at the settled bed.

"Will you look at them? God bless them." She smiled. The children were cuddled together on the Leaba Suidheachán sleeping.

"I'd best get them to their feet before they settle in for the night." Bríge rose and approached the bed.

"Sure you can stay the night if you wish." Anne their jovial host offered.

"Not at all thanks, we wouldn't dream of imposing further on your hospitality." Tom insisted.

"You've been more than generous to us, so you have. God will reward you of that have little doubt." Bríge added her thanks. Bríge settled the children comfortable in the bucket trap and covered them with a blanket.

"May the Devil set fire to my thatch if ever the day comes when you and yours are not welcome under the roof of the Kilderry's." Tom laughed.

"Safe journey and may God guide you home." Anne sprinkled the trap with the holy water.

"Thanks again for everything you done to make our day, Tom Kilderry." Both men shook hands warmly.

"Away with you, what are good neighbours for?" He called as the trap left the boréen.

Bríge and her children lay sleeping in the well of the trap as her husband listened to the little river meandering its way to the sea over the Rocky River bed.

In a distant field two abandoned cottages stood shoulder to shoulder. They leaned on each other for support as together they slowly decayed. The broken lop sided windows looked out with unseen eyes into the grey dawn.

The rotting thatch hung chagrin from the roof and covered the porch. What stories lay behind the old oak doors? He thought.

The night was dark and foreboding as he listened to the little river singing merrily as it meandered its way through the reeds and stones.

In the stillness he recalled the story his father taught him of the little singing brook that was forever making haste to the sea and calling…'

> *'I cannot wait, I cannot wait,*
> *I must make haste, I must make haste.*
> *Make way big fish, the hour is late*
> *The open sea I have to make.'*

That was a long long time ago and he had forgotten most of it. His father, rest his soul like the past occupants of the cottages was long since gone.

He glanced down at his sleeping family and thanked God for his many blessings.

CONVALESCENCE ON ÀIREANN OILEÀN

Bríge was concerned that Tomás beag was not as strong as he should be. One night as she and her husband sat by the fire she decided to approach him on the subject.

"Tom, don't take me wrong, but I think that a little holiday on the island would do Tomás beag a world of good. He looks so pale and thin. What do you think?"

"Bless you Bríge I was thinking the same myself but I did not wish to disclose my feelings for fear of upsetting you. We could send Mary with him, that would be alright with you I'm sure?"

"You're a good man, so you are, Tom. You'll need to ask your brother John. His wife Nora might not be too happy to find herself burdened with two children out of the blue."

"Sure John is alright, he'll understand that it's only for a short time. I'll take myself off to morrow and ask him." He promised.

"John we can vouch for, but Nora can be a bit contrary as you well know." She warned.

"You leave Nora to me, I'll talk her round, so I will." Nora the wife of John could be cantankerous when the mood took her.

"Not a word of this to Mary until it is confirmed, do you hear me?" She suggested.

"Me! Would I say anything?" He looked hurt.

"You! You are the worst bladder all this side of the Derryveagh stack." She chided.

"I'll go to morrow without fail, will that suit you?" He promised.

Tom rowed his curragh across to Árainn Mhór where he was greeted on the strand by his brother John.

"You're welcome Tom, what brings you here, not bad news I hope?" John came down the slipway to greet his brother.

"No! Thank God, but I have a little favour to ask of you and Nora."

"It will wait until we get indoors and have a sup of tae, will it not? No wedding haste I take it?" John slapped his brother on the back and laughed.

Over a cup of tae Tom disclosed his concern for his son and his feelings that a stay on the island would help him to recuperate after the long winter.

"Sure it's no trouble at all Tom, we are only too happy to oblige, aren't we Nora?"

"How long do you intend leaving them with us?" She abruptly questioned ignoring her husbands offer.

"We were thinking of no more than two weeks at the most, if that is alright by you?"

"If that's all, then I suppose we cannot refuse." Nora was one of those women who spoke their minds ignoring who they hurt in the process.

Tom returned to the mainland with the good news and could not restrain his feelings.

"Know what Mary? You and Tomás Beag are going to stay on the island with Uncle John for two weeks."

"I knew it, you just had to tell them. Keep it to yourself indeed." His wife shrugged her shoulders in resignation as the children whooped in their delight.

"Oh thanks dad, can we paddle in the sea?" Mary, full of excitement asked.

"Now before you go let me caution you. Keep away from the water unless Uncle John or Auntie Nora is with you. You can build sandcastles on the strand but do not go into the sea. Another thing don't forget your prayers and your table manners, no filling your mouth with food and shaming me as if you were never fed." Their mother warned.

"Will you let the child alone, she knows her manners, don't you Mary?" Her father hugged her to him.

"Go on then, spoil them as usual and leave me to pick up the mess." She chastised him in her usual good-natured manner.

"I'll take care of Tomás Beag and I'll make him a necklace of seashells. Oh thanks dad, when can we go?" Mary ran to his side and kissed him.

"Anxious to get away from us are you? I'll take you over to morrow but for now let me have a bite to eat."

"You'd best get up, I can hear Mary in the kitchen." Tom wakened the following morning from a deep sleep to see his wife standing beside the bed.

"What time is it, it's still dark?" Tom rubbed the sleep from his eyes.

"Dark or not, it's your own fault. Mary is ready for the road and you have to take them." Packing a bit of lunch into a satchel she placed it over Mary's shoulder.

"Now remember, no asking for sweets or anything else for that matter. Take what you are given and be thankful. Here are two farthings for pocket money. Don't forget your prayers and take good care of Tomás Beag. Now off you go and God bless you."

"Are you finished yet? It's time we took the road." Tom stood impatiently at the half door holding Tomás beag in his arms.

"God bless you and take care of you on the journey, bring me back a big seashell." She sprinkled the holy water on them as they left.

She would have liked to be with them but someone would have to see to Séan and her few fowl. The drudgery of the harsh life in the hills of Donegal was telling on her. 'A day away from the cottage would do her the world of good', she thought.

Her heart was heavy as she watched them walking away from the cottage. She was despondent and tired and in need of a rest herself. She began to cry and wished her Tom beside her to offer her a little comfort and encouragement. She never did disclose her foreboding as to the future life of Tomás Beag to her husband. She knew as only a mother can that he was not long for this world. Try as she may she could not dismiss her feelings. She prayed for their safe crossing to the island.

"Here they are Nora and I'm sure that they could do with a bite to eat." John introduced the children.

"Outside you two and play with the other children, I have a supper to prepare." Without ceremony Nora shunted them outside.

"Nora! They're only children and have walked a long journey, let them rest will you?" John was not happy with the curt reception she gave to the children.

Mary took Tomás beag in her arms and left the cottage. She made her way to the strand where several children were playing with a number of crabs.

"Hallo! I'm Mary Kearney and this is my brother Tomás beag. We are staying with our uncle up there." Mary introduced herself and her brother.

"If you catch a crab you can play with us, I'm Josephine Kearney and these are my friends." A girl her hair done up in ringlets came forward.

"He's too young to play with us, so he is." A young boy came and looked down at Tomás beag who was sitting in the sand piling it into a heap.

"He's staying with my father and I say he can play, so there." Josephine exercised her authority. Soon agreement was reached and it was decided that they would build a pond and keep as many crabs as they could catch in it.

Tomás beag was too young and delicate to participate in the chasing and capturing of the crabs and was appointed keeper of the pond.

"You mind the pond Tomás beag and don't you dare let any of them escape." Josephine wagged her finger and warned him.

"Come on then, let's see who can catch the most crabs." Josephine cleaned the sand from her hands in her dress and made her way over the rocks to the pools. Most of the afternoon was spent running to and fro carrying angry crabs to their pond.

"That's ten of mine in there now. Stop him Tomas." Mary called as a crab made a vain effort to escape.

Tomás beag with the aid of a stick kept a wary eye on the movement of the crabs. Any that reached the top of the rampart were immediately despatched back inside the sand fortress without ceremony.

"The tide is coming in, we will need to make the walls higher." Mary warned as she returned with several crabs in a make shift can.

The sun set slowly over the bay casting long fingers of golden light upon the water. The waves gently washed the shore and began moving towards their pond. A huge rainbow formed a crescent over the islands without touching the ground.

"We must go home now, the tide is turning and father will be cross if we get stranded." Josephine warned.

"What do we do with the crabs? Look they're escaping." Mary watched as the crabs scrambled through the breached walls of the sand fortress as it collapsed before the incoming tide.

"Come on, we can catch them again to morrow." Josephine led her friends off the beach.

"Where's Tomás Beag?" Mary returned to the strand and began searching for her brother.

"He's here silly and fast asleep." One of the boys laughed and pointed to where Tomás beag lay half covered in sand.

"Come on we must get home, our tae will be wet." Josephine nudged him with her foot.

Mary brushed the sand off her brother and taking him in her arms left the beach.

"Come on children, hurry up." Nora stood at the cottage door waving to them. A supper consisting of a bowl of gruel and home made scones was placed on the table.

Mary feeling hungry dipped her spoon into her bowl and began to eat.

"Stop, you must not eat yet." Nora took the spoon from her and returned it to the bowl.

"We must wait for dad to say the grace before meals first." Josephine whispered.

"Did you have a good time then?" John entered the cottage and hanging his caubéen on the peg took his place at the head of the table. Mary could hardly restrain herself as she waited for the conclusion of the grace before she once again dipped into the gruel.

"They have fine appetites, God bless them." He remarked on seeing Mary pick up her bowl and begin licking the sides.

"Here eat some scone and leave that be." Nora took the bowl from her and handed her a slice of scone.

"You and Tomás Beag will be sleeping in the box bed there. You'll like it beside the fire so you will." Their uncle pulled down the patchwork quilt to reveal a bed with wooden sides. Spread in the centre was a litter made from fresh straw covered with a home spun blanket.

Later that evening they were assembled around the fire where the rosary was said. Then it was time for bed.

The curtain dividing the bed from the kitchen was drawn and Mary listened in the darkness to the hushed voices of her uncle and aunt for a few moments before she fell asleep beside her brother.

She was awakened next morning by the raucous cry of sea birds. Her brother was still sleeping. Rising she drew the curtain and was greeted by the laughter of the other children of the family.

"I'll say this for you two, you sleep well so you do. Now come and have something to eat." John with a smile on his face invited them to join the family.

"Will I call Tomás beag?" Mary asked as she rubbed the sleep from her eyes.

"If you don't call him now he will sleep his brains away." This remark was greeted by peals of laughter.

With breakfast over Mary wanted to return to the strand and collect her wayward crabs.

"To day we are going over to Rinraros Point, you know what that means?" John promised.

"We are going to see the great big fish, the dolphins." They cheered.

"Did you ever see a Dolphin, Mary?" He asked with a gleam in his eye.

"A what, what is it?" Mary looked puzzled.

"A Dolphin is a big fish that lets you tickle it." Josephine informed her.

"Where are you going to get a boat to take you from the point?" Nora questioned.

"We'll get Aidan Grace to take us across in his long boat."

"Aidan Grace! Will you talk sense, don't you know that his wife Susan is expecting her first child soon?" Nora grumbled.

Mary looked across at her aunt and could not understand why she was trying to stop them enjoying themselves.

"Susan is alright, she understands." He dismissed her misgivings.

"Have you all got lunch, come on show me?" The children held up their packs and began cheering.

"Will you take them away from under my feet, John?" Nora opened the half door and shunted the children out into the boréen. John was in luck as on the quay wall he saw Aidan sorting lobster pots.

"Good day to yourself Aidan. How is Susan? Are you by any chance using the long boat?" John greeted his friend.

"Susan is fine, thanks for asking. I'm too busy repairing the nets that got fouled up on a wreck." He looked at the disappointment on the faces of the children.

"Sure why don't you take it out yourself John, I take it that you intend going out to the Dolphins. Who are these two, I never saw them before?" He studied the two children.

"This one is Mary and that one is her brother Tomás beag. They are the children of my brother over in Dungloe." He informed his friend.

"If you are thinking of going to see the dolphins they have moved over towards Torneady Point. They were following the herring shoal into Rosses Bay. They must have a belly full by now and will be in humour to play." Aidan informed him.

"Thanks Aidan, I'll leave the boat on the strand if you are not about." John promised.

"Good luck John. Would you leave the oars and locks under the boat, they have a habit of disappearing." He helped John to launch the boat.

As the boat rocked in the sea John jumped aboard as Aidan gave it a final push. John sat on the centre seat and taking the oars in his hands he was soon making headway in chase of the elusive dolphins.

"Look, look over there I can see them." All eyes were cast to where Josephine was pointing.

"Sit down and stay in your seats, you'll see them in time enough." John warned the excited children.

There was no need to row nearer to the great mammals. On hearing the children they began leaping and swimming towards them.

The children stroked the friendly mammals and laughed aloud when one of them reached up to the boat and nudged them.

As the time came to say good bye to the Dolphins Tomás Beag began to cry.

"Don't cry Tomás beag, we will come back another day to see them. Won't we Uncle John?" Mary comforted her brother.

John told them the fairy tale of how the dolphins once lived on land and were recruited by the sea God to roam the seas searching for drowning sailors in order to rescue them.

As they returned to the island they saw a man waving to them from the strand at Torneady Point.

"Is that Aidan on the strand?" He asked his daughter as he shaded his eyes and looked into the distance.

"It's Aidan Grace dad, he must have walked to the point." She informed him.

John pointed the boat towards the small cove and rowed towards the strand.

"Hallo Aidan, we didn't stay away too long, did we?" John apologised as he beached the boat.

"No! I was thinking that the children would be tired and unable to take the long road back to Leabgarrow. We can row the boat around there saving the long journey by road." Aidan was aware that Tomás beag would not be fit for such a journey.

"That's more than generous of you Aidan, you're a considerate man, so you are." John thanked him.

The men took the oars in their hands and were soon making headway back to the east shore.

The children laughed and giggled as the dolphins followed the boat leaping and splashing. Diving under the boat they came up on the other side and nudged the boat drawing the children's attention to them.

"Say good bye to the dolphins children." They waved as Aidan rowed the boat back to Torneady Point accompanied by the friendly dolphins.

"Oh look! Will you look, they are jumping through the rainbow." Mary pointed to the dolphins as they moved out into the bay. A rainbow formed a large arc that seemed to span the horizon through which the dolphins were swimming and leaping.

There was so much to do and so much to see that the time on the island passed all too soon. They were disappointed when they saw their father coming up the strand one afternoon with his bundle. They knew that it was time to say goodbye to their relatives and friends and the dolphins.

TOMÁS BEAG IS TAKEN BY THE FAIRIES

It was the first day of February, Saint Bridget's feast day and the day of the preparation of the crop. Intercessions were made to the great saint to protect the crop and to give a good yield. Saint Bridget was the patron saint of farmers. She was born the daughter of a rich noble lord. Her hand was pledged to the son of a nobleman when she came of age. She had promised herself to God and would marry no man. This act of defiance brought shame on her father and he banished her to the kitchen. In order to make her see the folly of her action she was ordered to scrub the pots and feed the swine.

The sick and poor would come to the dairy where she worked and beg scraps from her. She always provided them with a parcel of food. It mattered little how many called all were given a generous amount. Her father could not understand where all the food was coming from. In her innocence she told him that the food did not come from his bounty but from God's. He wondered and could not understand who this bountiful God was, he being a pagan. He was so impressed that he went to see Saint Patrick and to seek an explanation for this phenomenon. On hearing it explained was converted.

On another occasion as she was walking along the banks of a river she stopped to pray. God came and told her that she must build a church on the spot where she knelt. This land belonged to a rich pagan landowner. He had had no belief in this new religion called Christianity. When she asked him for a piece of land to build a church he laughed.

"You may have all the land that your cloak can cover." He promised her.

She spread her cloak on the bank and began to pray. Her cloak grew until it covered many acres. Seeing that a miracle had taken place the landowner willingly gave her the land. Her cross hardly resembles a cross, it is made from picked and platted reeds. It is usually hung over stables and doors to ward off evil. When there were brighter times in Ireland the young men would dress up on her birthday and carry her effigy through the villages.

Tomás beag was not with the family for more than four years and a day before he was taken back to Heaven by Saint Bridget or so the family claimed. Mary was heart broken and could not understand why he was called back to heaven that stormy night.

"God could have waited until the primroses and cowslips were in bloom. I promised to take him to the fairy fields when the flowers were springing, Why did he have to take him, Ma?" She questioned through her tears.

"It's Gods' holy will and who are we to question him" Her mother sighed.

"But Ma! God has so many babies, what did he need little Tomás beag for?"

She cried.

Her mother's eyes again filled with tears but she did not reply. What could she tell her daughter? Mary was not too happy with the way God had taken her brother from her. She couldn't be consoled and cried herself to sleep.

Next day they placed him in a little box filled with straw and took him to Crohy Head and laid him down with his curly head facing the wild Atlantic. His father filled in the grave as their mother took her children to a green sward overlooking the ocean swell and sat down. She watched the crew of a *'Pookaun'* collecting seaweed from between the Crags and inlets. This they would sell or barter to the smallholders for food and clothing. The seaweed they would use as fertiliser on their small allotments.

She listened as they sang in the *'Gaelic'* the story of *'The Maiden who lived on the Rill.'* This story had been handed down to her family in song and story from way back...

The maiden had inadvertently wandered into their fort on the top of the hill and was captured by the fairies. As punishment she had to become a nanny to their children. Once a year she was allowed to venture out from the Rath into the world of mortals and sing her lament. If her kinfolk should hear her lament and come to her rescue then the spell would be broken and she could go free. Year after year she ventured to the same spot and sang her lament hoping that a mortal would hear it and come to her aid, thus breaking the spell. Unaware that many, many years had passed she continued with her pleading for her kinfolk to come and rescue her, alas without success...

> *'O maid that standest down by the Rill,*
> *Shó hó ló, Shó hó ló.*
> *Oh dost thou know my grief and my ill?*
> *Shó hó ló Shó hó ló.*
> *A year and a day I was snatched from the hill,*
> *Shó hó ló, Shó hó ló.*
> *From my love to the* **Lios** *on the little green hill.*
> *Shóhéen, shóhéen, shóhéen, shóhéen.*
> *Shó hó ló, Shó hó ló.*
> *Shóhéen, shóhéen, shóhéen, shóhéen.*
> *Shó hó ló, Shó hó ló.*

One day as she stood on the Rill singing a stranger passed by and curious as to know who was singing so beautifully came forward to listen. As he approached she stepped into the world of mortals and aged a thousand years. The stranger fled from the spot in fear. She had stepped out from *'Tír-na-nÓg'* and entered the world of mortals; there would be no returning. The maiden unaware of what had happened to her continued her song as she sank to the ground. There would be no redemption for *'The Maid who lived on the Rill'*. She would have to continue singing and pleading without any hope of redemption. All her kinfolk had long since passed away. There was nobody left to rescue *'The Maid of the Rill'*. The fairies took pity on her and removed the spell. They would not let her grow old so they turned her into a lark to sing forevermore in the blue skies.

"My Tomas is now with the *'Fairies of the Rill'*, he will never grow old nor will he be burdened by the harsh grinding poverty of Donegal." She sighed as the boat moved down the coast leaving the haunting music in its wake.

"I wonder if he will play with the dolphins?" Mary interrupted her day dreaming and looked out to sea hoping to see the Dolphins playing.

"He'll play with them as they will with him. He has all day now to play, so he has." Her mother predicted as she looked out on the endless ocean. She watched as a fish or was it a dolphin rose from the depths and returned to the ocean with a splash.

"Look Ma! There is a great big rainbow coming in off the sea." The children pointed to a rainbow settling down deep in the Atlantic Ocean. They watched the dolphins leaping through it and were happy.

"It's the dolphin's Ma, they have come to play with Tomás Beag. They are taking him with them." Mary jumped up and down in her excitement.

Brige, her heart breaking turned away and wept, she wished her children wouldn't go and leave her if only for a day. Composing herself she gathered her children to her and told them the story about the fairies that carried the rainbow out to sea. They set it down between the vast Atlantic Ocean and Gweebarra bay. This was a special tribute to Tomás beag. It would rest high above the spot where they laid him down. Whenever little Tomás wanted to, he could slide down the rainbow and play with them.

"Will it touch the ground where he sleeps?" They challenged.

"No, mo cúhlas, regrettably rainbows seldom touch the ground of Ireland anymore." Wiping the tears from her eyes she continued looking out into the vast expanse of ocean.

Turning she saw the disappointment on the faces of her children.

"Oh don't worry, mo cúshlas, he won't be alone, the Maighdeáh Mhara *(Mermaids)* and the dolphins will come every day and play with him. That is why we left him here so he can help them count their gold." She hugged her children to her.

"Can we come to Crohy Head too and play with him. Can we please Ma?" They begged.

"Of course, but for now let's go home." She tightened her shawl around her and rose to her feet.

"Slán leat Tomás Beag" (*Good bye little Tomás*) The children kissed the rough wooden cross they erected over his grave and ran to join their parents.

"Tá brón orm agus mo cróide briste." (*I am so lonely and my heart is sorrowful*) Bríge took her husband's hand in hers and began to cry inconsolable. She looked back at the lonely grave and tried to retrace her steps. "Just one more time Tom, just this last calling." She pleaded as her husband placed his hand round her waist.

"No Bríge, let him go. His playmates are now from another world." He paused and looked into her sad eyes. He could not console her.

"Let's away home now." Placing his slán on his shoulder he called his children to him. The family, in bared feet, hungry and in ragged clothing took the long boréen back to the family cottage in Dungloe.

SÉAN GOES TO THE HEDGE SCHOOL

Bríge sat one evening beside the fire knitting an Aran sweater for her husband and saying the *'Trimmins of the Rosary.'*
It was their belief that whatever prayers they said as they worked would benefit the wearer. She continued invoking all the blessings she could think of on the sweater when the door opened and her husband entered.
"I was praying for you just now, there's a little gruel in the pot. I'll warm it up for you."
Putting her knitting to one side she pushed the pot over the coals.
"No hurry, no hurry at all for when the good Lord made time he made plenty."
Having arranged the cushions to his satisfaction he sat down in the sugan chair. Removing his cré dúidín from his pocket he took a spleen from the ashes and lit his pipe.
Smacking his lips he drew long breaths encouraging his pipe into life. For some moments he concentrated on getting the pipe going before he sat back and closed his eye.
Bríge studied his features in the glow of the turf fire and smiled to herself. This was her Tom; a good man if ever there was one. He was doing his best for her and their family and never grumbled nor did he raise his voice in anger.
She lifted the lid from the pot quietly so as not to disturb him and stirred the contents.
"Are you awake Tom?" She gently called.
"Sorry Bríge, I must have dozed off." He apologised as he moved his outstretched foot out of her way.
"Oh I am sorry did I waken you, I was just stirring the pot?" Bríge replaced the lid.
"No need to apologise Brige, sure I was only resting my eyes."
Taking his pipe he knocked it against the toe of his boot. Placing it back in his mouth he pressed the cup with his thumb and once again began sucking on the stem.
As wafts of blue smoke came from his mouth he again removed the pipe.
"Do you know Bríge, I was thinking on my way home that Séan could benefit from the learning." He replaced his pipe and sitting back in his chair waited her response.
"What may I ask brought this about and we with no money to pay for it?" She placed a bowl of hot gruel on his lap.
"Thanks Bríge, would you ever pass me a spiúnóg?"
"Is trom an tuala an leisge" (*laziness is a heavy load*). She smiled as she

handed him the spoon and returned to her knitting.

"Thanks! Séan is now of age and he should be for the learning. It is no load to carry. When the time comes for him to leave and leave he must this God forsaken land then the learning will stand him in good stead. You mark my words, it is for the best." He prophesied.

"I agree Tom, but how could we afford it? Then there's Mary to think about." She replied without lifting her eyes from her knitting.

"The girl will be no problem, when the time comes I'll go and see the matchmaker and make a good deal." Having finished his gruel he picked up a glowing ember and relit his pipe.

"I agree, still I ask again could we afford it? It would be futile sending him for a few lessons and then find out the we could not continue paying." She insisted.

"We have the few sovereigns saved and God is good for the rest. It will be a good investment, you'll see." Tom Kearney was philosophical with life if with nothing else.

The matter was settled there and then and on the following Monday morning bright and early Séan was despatched off to the hedge school. Under his arm he carried the four sods of obligatory turf for the school fire. The school, such as it was, was situated some miles along the Crolly road.

Tired, weary and apprehensive from the long journey he entered a lean-to covered in rushes.

A large turf fire was burning in the centre of the room and several boys were sitting on round stones that had been procured from the seashore. At a rough desk sat a tall man dressed in strange clothing and beside him sat an austere looking woman in a long one-piece dress with a white ruff collar buttoned at the neck.

"That's Mrs Hoctor, watch out for her she'd twist your ear in a flash." One of the boys nudged him and whispered.

Séan was called forward to hand over his turf and money for his lesson. Mrs Hoctor took his farthing and entered his name into a hard-backed book.

"What are you waiting for? Go and sit down." She dismissed him with a wave of her hand. Looking round for a rock to sit on he could find none.

"You get your own rock from the beach." Mrs Hoctor eyed him suspiciously from the corner of her eye.

In the meantime he was obliged to sit on a gathering of ferns.

The gentleman called the assembly to order by banging the sallac slat (*Sally rod*) on the rough desk. This made the scholars jump. Then he began speaking in a strange tongue. One that Séan had seldom heard before.

"I'm Eoin Hoctor and this is my wife Joan. We are here to teach you English."

The man adjusted his rimless spectacles as he spoke. Sean did not take to his hawk like features any more than he did to his wife.

When all the fees had been collected Mrs Hoctor closed the book and took her place beside her husband.

"I'm Mrs Hoctor and at all times you will address me as 'Madam' do you understand? I will speak to you in your native tongue and my husband will repeat what I say in English. You will then repeat after him the English meaning. Now do you all understand?" She smiled benignly.

"Yes Mrs Hoctor, Madam." Came the half-hearted response in Irish.

"Good, now that we understand each other let's begin." Mrs Hoctor opened a book and read a passage in Irish. Her husband translated it into English.

Parrot fashion the scholars tried to respond but were making poor if any progress.

Séan was pleased when the lessons ended and it was time to go home. It was a waste of a good farthing that could be put to better use as far as he was concerned.

"Before you go I want each and every one of you to take your slates home and memorise all my husband taught you this day." Mrs Hoctor looked down at the assembled scholars.

"How did you get on at school to day?" His anxious parents questioned him that evening.

He explained as best he could all that happened and of the strange man and woman speaking in a language that he did not understand. He also told of the man beating the boys with the sallac slat.

"That must be the English that they are learning, you will need to know that when you go out into the world." His father encouraged him.

Later that evening when the children had retired to bed Brige again brought up the subject of Séans schooling.

"Why must he learn the English? Is the language of his own country not good enough?" Brige felt rebellious at her native language being demoted.

"Will you look around you woman, what is there here for our son? A cruel land that's as stubborn as it is unyielding.

Fit only for goats and sheep and the amadáns trying to make a poor a living from between the barren rocks." Tom felt annoyed at being chastised for trying to do the best for his son.

"I don't like to see my son with the 'Beata Scóir' tied around his neck like a tethered sheep. What's it all for anyway?" Brige was a true Fenian.

"It's to make them aware of the English and how important it is, don't you understand woman? Every time they speak in Irish a mark is put on the stick and at the end of the day the notches are counted and the pupil punished accordingly." He explained.

"Don't you address me as *'Woman'*, Thomas Kearney. Are you seriously telling me that my son is being treated like a felon in his own land? Punished for speaking in his native tongue. Is it little wonder that he is so rebellious? English indeed. Huh!"

"Sorry Alannah. It's for the better, He'll thank us one day, you'll see." Tom apologised.

"Thank us? From what I am hearing it will drive him stone mad, so it will."

"We'll leave it for now and see what come of it later." Tom tried to ease the tense situation.

"I'll say this Tom Kearney and you mark my words, your son will not forgive you for tying a foreign yolk around his neck." Bríge in her temper knitted faster.

Although Seán would have preferred to stay at home and help his father he was compelled to continue with the schooling.

He repeated as best he could whatever his teachers taught him. What it all meant remained a mystery to him. If his parents and his playmates could not understand the language why was he forced to learn it? He wondered.

One day as he sat listening to all the chatter going on round him Mr Hoctor pointed to him. He rose to his feet and asked him in Irish what he wanted and for his pains he was dragged across the floor and given a thrashing.

Some days later he was once again called before the master and questioned.

"What does he want of me?" He called to the assembled pupils in his native tongue.

The teacher realising that he could not speak or understand English addressed him in his native language.

"Ná labraiam an Gaedeala, búacaill gan tabirt."*(Don't speak in Irish you illiterate boy)*

He was warned that he must avoid speaking Irish if he wanted to get on in life. This was what his parents were paying for. To remind him Mrs Hoctor twisted his ear and gave him a beating with the sallac slat. Being beaten by a man was bad enough but by a woman and in front of his friends was humiliating and more than he could bear.

He could not understand why he was being beaten for speaking in his native tongue. The other boys in the village spoke in Irish and they never got beaten for it. Reluctantly he continued with the schooling but was making little if any progress with the strange language.

One day frustrated by his lack of effort to learn the master dragged him before the class.

"You are deliberately refusing to learn and causing disruption to the others, bend over." He ordered. Séan was given such a chastisement that he began to cry out. With the punishment completed he was ordered back to his rock seat.

"I cannot speak your language and I don't want to." He stood impertinent some distance from the teachers and stubbornly replied in Gaelic.

This defiant stand did nothing to appease his tormentor. The master banged the sallact slat on the desk and demanded that he should come before him. Séan left his seat and was away down the mountain road as fast as his legs would carry him to the safety of his home in Dungloe.

Much as his father tried by beatings and persuasion to get him to return to school he would have none of it.

"Leave him Tom, if he does not want to learn the English then we cannot force him." His mother was tired of all the beatings and arguments.

LOST IN THE DERRYVEAGH MOUNTAINS

Spring came late to Donegal as it did every year. The snow was slow in clearing the tops of the Derryveagh Mountains. The little stream that gently meandered its way down the mountain in the summer to replenish Lake Craghy was now a roaring torrent.
The watery sun had descended below Crohy Head leaving the dark night without twilight. The nights slumber was torn apart by the roar of thunder and the incandescent flashing of lightening.
Bríge looked apprehensively towards the little window. She tried to collect her bearings but her mind was elsewhere. Her thoughts were those of a cornered beast seeking some refuge. Her Séan had not as yet returned home from the cursed mountain. She knew that it was trying to destroy her and her family. Where was her God? Why didn't the almighty hand of her God return her child to her? Her faith and endurance were being tried and tested. A calm overtook her and she resigned herself to a terrible gnawing homesickness. She readily cried as the music from the mountain mocked her.
Perhaps she could find a quiet spot where she could lie down and wait in silence for her God. She was depressed and angry for there was no respite from the daily drudgery.
These were dangerous times to be on the mountain. Time and time again Séan was warned of this hazard. Little notice did he take for it seemed that the mountain or someone in the mountain kept calling him back. His parents were heartbroken from searching for him time and time again.
"What he needs is something to occupy his mind, Tom." Bríge insisted one night after another protracted search on the mountain for their wayward son.
"I suppose you are right Bríge, leave it to me." Tom returned to his pipe.
It was some two weeks later when the door was opened one evening and in its frame stood his father with a bundle hidden under his coatamore. He had a grin on his face that would do justice to a five-barred gate.
"Could you ever guess what I got for our Séan?" He beamed making no effort to cross the floor.
"No! Let me guess, would it be a puppy?" Bríge looked down at the wagging tail sticking out from between the buttons of his coatamore.
"It is indeed, I was given him by Chris Logue from Ailt an Chorrain (Burtonport). He tells me that he has the makings of one fine sheep dog and he never asked for one penny, not even a Luck Penny." Tom hoping for a compliment looked towards his wife.
Opening his coat he gently placed a brindle pup on the floor. He was all excited

as he tapped the pup on the rump and tried to encourage it to run towards his wife. The pup wandered into the middle of the floor and relieved himself. She looked down at the pup with that cross look of hers that said it all.

"Chris Logue gave you a Sheep dog. I suppose Pauline told him to get rid of it? What would we be doing with him and not a sheep to our names? What in God's holy name prompted you to take that, Tom Kearney?" She pointed to the pup who had taken a sod of turf from the cisceán was sitting in the centre of the floor tearing it to pieces.

"Will you look at the cratur? Sure I got him for Séan. They'll take to each other like ducks to water, so they will, and he cost us nothing" He predicted.

"A duck to water is it and how do you intend to feed it? Did that not cross your mind?"

"Sure there will be no need to worry about feeding him. There are more rabbits in the Derryveagh Mountains than there are stars in the sky."

"God owns the stars in the sky but Lord Kilgarvan owns the rabbits in the mountains. Did you ever once give that a thought? Oh! Never mind, he is here now and we could not insult good neighbours like Pauline and Chris Logue, now could we?" Bríge on seeing his determination to keep the pup capitulated.

When Séan returned home he was delighted to be greeted by a yapping pup. The dog's whole body shook in excitement as he wagged his tail in greeting.

"Where did he come from and who owns him? Come here you beauty." The pup jumped into his open arms and began to lick his face.

"What did I tell you, sure as the good Lord made them he matched them." Tom looked across at his wife with a contented grin.

"He's a present for you son, we hope you'll like him? Take good care of him now and when you meet Chris or Pauline Logue don't forget to thank them. Do you hear?"

"Like him! I love him and will look after him and take him hunting in the mountain."

Bríge looked across at her husband, this was not what she wanted to hear.

"Be careful son you know what the mountain is like. See that you do not catch his Lordships rabbits." His father warned.

"What are you going to call him?" His mother asked.

"I'm going to call him Óisín after the Fenian who was taken to Tír-na-nÓg." It was a foregone conclusion that master and dog would take to rambling in the mountains and valleys around the cottage.

As the dog grew in strength he proved an asset to the family as his father predicted he would. Thanks to his ability to hunt they could now enjoy the occasional rabbit or hare stew in place of the monotonous few boiled potatoes.

"I'm worried Tom that they will be caught one day poaching on his Lordship lands. What would happen to them?" Brige confided in her husband.

"Will you not be worrying girl, nothing will happen to them."

As the family grew so the cottage became overcrowded and it was decided that Séan would have to be moved.

His father with the help of his neighbours built a snug extension at the rear of the cottage. Séan could hardly wait to get his own room, for now he could have his Óisín by his side.

He took full advantage of his new freedom and became a law unto himself as he spent more and more time hunting in the mountains. The family would often sit outside their door and listen to him and his dog calling to each other from deep in the Derryveagh Mountains.

His sister was jealous of his lifestyle and often complained that she was doing all the housework whereas he spent his time in leisure.

"Don't worry about Séan, Mary he will have to come down to earth soon." Her mother assured her.

Much as he enjoyed his new found freedom it could not last as his mother predicted. Adulthood came early in the harsh environment of Donegal. He was soon told that his rambling in the mountains had come to an abrupt halt. He would be required to work on his lordship's estate to earn his keep. The following morning as the early sun burnt the mist from the mountains he was rudely awakened by his father.

"Wake up Séan, it is time." His father called as he rapped the door.

Óisín on hearing the knocking cocked his ear and rising from his litter began to bark in excitement. This was to be another day on the hills and a new adventure to be looked forward to.

"Not to day Óisín, you must stay home for a change." Tom caught hold of the excited dog and tied him with a rope to a post.

As father and son went up the boréen towards the castle the dog let out such howling and lamenting that half the countryside must have been aroused from their sleep.

"Hush Óisín! I'll be back to you soon." Séan tried to pacify the worried and excited animal. The dog would not be placated and continued to howl and moan long after they had left. Unable to withstand all the caterwauling Brige untied the rope and let him run free. The dog ran round and round the yard trying to pick up the scent of his master. Unable to find him he lay down with his head between his paws and began to moan.

Late into the evening he sat facing the boréen waiting and worrying for his lost master.

Then he heard a voice calling him and rising to his feet he began to bark and was away like the hammers of Hell up the boréen.

"That dog knows who his master is." Remarked his father on hearing Óisín barking in the distance.

"Take it easy Óisín." Séan called as his pet with a leap jumped into his outstretched arms.

"Sorry Óisín, you will need to get used to waiting for me." He apologised to his dog.

Side by side they rambled down the old boréen. He stopped occasionally and looked across at his beloved mountains silhouetted in the waning light. Then with a sigh he continued on his journey to the cottage. To morrow would be another arduous day working for a pittance.

Weeks went into months and he was showing more and more reluctance to carry out the tasks imposed on him. This led to constant friction and beatings by his taskmaster.

"I fear Bríge that Séan has no heart for the work involved. He gets beaten frequently for being disobedient. It breaks my heart to see my son treated in this manner." Tom complained.

"It's that dog so it is, every time he comes home the dog demands to be taken into the mountains. The mountains of Derryveagh keep calling to them, I'm convinced that there's a charm on it." Leaning over the half door she looked across at the mountain.

"I know how you feel about the mountain, but what about Séan?" He insisted.

"There's only one thing that you can do and you know what that is, get rid of the dog."

"The dog go! I could never be so cruel to our Séan, they love each other, and it would break their hearts. Whatever would Chris and Pauline say? No! The dog stays."

"You asked for my opinion and advice and I gave it. It is now for you to decide."

"But who would want a grown dog?" He pleaded.

"Who indeed. Ask Chris and Pauline to take him back. The folk around here have problems enough feeding themselves without taking on the responsibility of a useless dog."

"Very well then I agree. Would you talk to Chris and Pauline when we are at the castle?" Tom shuffled from one foot to the other.

"Me is it? Who may I ask brought the dog here in the first place? The dog and Séan are your responsibility, I have my hands full enough with the cottage. Me! Get rid of the dog, indeed." She sarcastically remarked.

Séan resting in his bed with his faithful dog beside him heard his parents planning to dispose of his companion and began to worry.

"They'll not separate us ever Óisín. I would die before I would let them take you away." He promised as he affectionately stroked his pet.

That night he took Óisín to his bed to protect him. He spent a restless night and the least sound put him back on guard. As the dawn rose in the Irish sky he awakened from a broken sleep. He now knew what had to be done.

Calling on his dog to remain quiet he packing his few belongings. Then opening the door he slipped out into the open countryside with Óisín by his side.

He looked back nostalgically at his homestead and knew instinctively that this would be for the last time. Óisín ran ahead of him and gave the occasional glance back to reassure himself that his master was following.

They were now free, free from the cruel landlord and his lackeys. Free from the cruel ocras and the constant beatings.

The wild hills of Donegal would be their hunting grounds and the fairies their companions. Should fortune answer their call then they may be lucky and find Tír-na-nÓg.

His father was taken aback the following morning when he found his sons room vacant and Séan and the dog gone.

"Bríge, they must have heard us talking and have gone into the mountains, what should we do?" He pleaded.

"There's little that we can do for now, you get off to your work. When they are hungry and tired they will come home, mark my words." She told him showing little concern.

They had not returned by nightfall and his parents began to worry.

They made a frantic but futile search of the surrounding countryside hoping to find them but without success.

"We are wasting precious time looking alone Tom. They will be in the mountains and we will need to call on the neighbours to help. Let's go home and have a bite of supper then we'll go into the mountain and renew our search."

Seven long days and nights were spent searching over and over again through the valleys and mountain. Of Séan and his dog there was no sighting. It was as if the mountain had swallowed them.

"I told you Tom, I told you time and time again, you wouldn't listen. The mountain and its fairies have taken our son of that I have no doubt." She cried despondently.

The fruitless search was abandoned and the neighbours returned to their homes. Bríge and Tom returned to their cottage.

Entering the little bedroom facing the mountain she opened the old drawer and removed the Connail Mhór (*Big Candle*) and kissed it. Lighting it she said a silent prayer. Having made the sign of the cross with its light she placed it in a jar facing the mountain.

"Séan! Séan avic, it's your sorrowful mother calling to you. Wherever you are look! Look at the Connail and follow its light home. We all love you and miss you. You can keep Óisín forever but please son, come home." Again she lifted the Connail Mhór and made the sign of the cross with its light.

Her heart beat violently when she heard the calling of an animal. She listened carefully, she prayed that it was Óisín. Alas it was only a lost vixen calling to her mate. The wind from the mountain sang its melancholy music as if mocking her.

The windowpanes shook and rattled. Everything it would seem portended disaster. Outside the snow was falling heavily; Dark foreboding clouds descended from the mountain bringing with them ever thickening flurries of snow.

The flakes plastered the windowpanes like a slowly closing curtain obliterating her view of the mountain. It swirled on the green sward as it slowly consumed the velvet green sheen. It mocked her as it danced and formed high crests before her. Then it leaped impetuously over the rocky land and rattled the latch on the door. She felt the melancholy of the elegy as she watched the storm grow in intensity. The pagan mountain continued to mock her and her God. She knew that it would not give up her son.

Was it not now taunting her pleadings and her prayers? All around her rested the barren landscape. The dead pagan oak tree on which the mountain reined her tears mocked her. Everything it seemed was dead in this forsaken land leaving her alone awaiting the cold hand of death.

"Oh God, why have you deserted me?" She cried aloud in her depressed state. Neither Séan nor his dog was ever found. His mother up to the day she was laid in the clay swore that her son was a free spirit wandering deep in the mountains of Donegal with Óisín by his side. He must have been taken to Tír-na-nÓg by the fairy king she insisted.

Had not the great Óisín, the son of Finn of the Finna returned from Tír-na-nÓg after three hundred years? So too would her Séan return from the Derryveagh Mountains with his Óisín by his side. This was her belief and her goal in life but it never was to bear fruition.

THOMAS KEARNEY GOES ON HIS FINAL PILGRIMAGE

Lord James, as he was known was becoming a tenacious visitor to Tom Kearney's cottage on one pretext or another. Brige noticed that he was paying undue attention to her daughter. This worried her as she was well conversed with his reputation as a philander.
"Tom we will need to keep a wary eye on his Lordship." She informed her husband.
"His Lordship! What would we be watching him for?" Tom looked puzzled.
"Have you not got the eyesight that God gave you? He has taken a shine to our Mary?"
"Mary! Our Mary but she's only a child. Come to think of it he has been more than sweet to me of late." Tom scratched his chin. A sure sign that he was thinking.
"Now will you listen to me Tom Kearney. That man's reputation is well known. I'd put nothing past him." She warned.
"Keep her indoors whenever he comes calling, I might send her over to my brothers place at Leabgarrow (Aran Island) for a time." He suggested.
Within a week Tom had kept his promise and she was sent off to her uncles place on the island. With Mary gone his Lordship lost all interest in the family. All thoughts of Mary's welfare were forgotten when stories of a great famine in the south of the country began to filter through.
It was rumoured that a great blight had struck the land and the potatoes were rotting in the ground. There was a great keening and mourning throughout the land. Whole families were dying in the boréens and in the fields.
Those who survived were so weak that hungry rats and dogs were feeding on them and they still alive. Harrowing stories filtered through causing panic within the people.
The land it was said by the good sagart *(Priest)* had a mallact *(Curse)* put on it by Almighty God as a punishment for their sins.
This calamitous news brought much dread to the people of Dungloe. They were told that the plague was rapidly spreading north. It had already reached the outskirts of Sligo to the south. There was pandemonium in the community as rumour followed rumour.
Something would have to be done to save Ulster. The parishioners went and consulted with their parish priest. They would have to pray again and again seeking God's intervention, to spare the people of Ulster he warned them. If

they failed to acknowledge God's chastisement, they too would become victims of the Ocras Pláig. (*Hungry Plague*) A wary eye would have to be kept on the potato crop, he warned them.

This challenge did not go unanswered for the people took his teachings seriously and made extra novenas in the church and at home.

Early one morning the persistent ringing of the church bell awakened the village. There must be a calamity to report for the only time the Doomsday Bell would be rung outside Church times in such a manner would be when there was a disaster at sea or that there was a message of some importance to the village.

Anxious to know what the news was they assembled in the square. From there they walked in procession to the church. Some prayed, others speculated and some looked traumatised as they anticipated the worst.

As the priest opened the presbytery door a hush fell on the congregation. Slowly and deliberately he mounted the marble steps leading to the pulpit. Removing his cap he opened the service with a short prayer. He then warned his flock of the disaster that was about to engulf them. He could not emphasise enough the urgency of the situation.

"The hand of the Lord has not yet brought its wrath down on the people of Ulster but be warned for we know not the day or the hour. The plague is greater than had been anticipated and is at this very moment eating into Ulster." Like a prophet of doom the priest continued his rhetoric.

He pounded with his fist on the pulpit putting the fear of Christ into his captive congregation. Then he pointed into the assembly.

"Tom Kearney as leader of the fishermen I call on you to lead the curraghs by sea to Glenn Colmcille to make the oilitreat." (*Pilgrimage/Stations*) The priest demanded.

"We will go to night, father, won't we men?" Tom rose to his feet; he like the rest of the congregation was caught up in the euphoria of the situation. He enthusiastically agreed knowing that the others would not refuse the good priest.

"And now I want all the women and children to assemble here at the church this evening to join with me in spirit with our brave men folk in making their own oiltreat." The priest pleased with the response closed the meeting with a blessing.

"Here Tom wear your new Aran geansaí. The blessing is new and the night is cold." Brige blessed the sweater with holy water before presenting it to her husband.

The curraghs and there were fifteen in all set their sails south in a calm sea.

They reached Glen Head without incident and removing the sails took to the oars and pulled for Mailinmore Bay.

They were welcomed ashore by the villagers carrying lighted spleens to light the way. They too had received the message of their impending arrival in advance and were anxious to participate in the Oiltreat.

In bared feet and with a prayer on their lips and hope in their hearts the procession set out for Glean Colmcille. At each of the fifteen stations they halted and knelt on the rough ground.

Our Father, Hail Mary and Creed were told 150 times in all. They circled every turás and reverently handled the stones with religious zeal and affection. Each pilgrim in turn lay in the rock bed of Saint Columba and praying aloud to their God confessed their past sins and promised to atone for them.

As they rose with the sign of absolution on their foreheads and a peace within their hearts they each took a handful of earth from the sacred ground and placed it in the pockets of their coatamores to protect them from adversities.

In a final act of contrition before departing for home they stood in Saint Columba's stone boat and washed their sore and bleeding feet in the blessed blood stained water.

They offered up their suffering to the Sacred Heart and Saint Columcille in the hope that they would be merciful and listen to their pleadings and unselfish sacrifice. Times were harsh enough in Ulster without the cursed blight.

They were content within themselves as they departed still praying. Would God listen to their earnest and sincere Oilitreat? Would he, in his infinite mercy spare the land of Ulster from the Ocras Pláig? They could do no more but wait for his mercy.

Dawn had not yet broken when they once again returned to their curraghs in Mailinmore Bay. The seas were squally and agitated as white horses rode high on the surf. This caused no concern to them for it was not unusual for an Atlantic swell to boil up along the rough coastline.

Further out the sea was a glassy blue and as calm as the water in a holy well. They would soon be out in safe open waters and a calm sea.

Tom led the way in his curragh warning them to be guarded. He was apprehensive as he looked north towards Crohy Head. He felt sure that he saw his son Tomás beag standing on the cliff top looking towards them and said a short silent prayer for the repose of his son's soul.

A rainbow appeared from deep in the Atlantic Ocean and settle over the grave of his son without touching the ground. This was a bad omen that brought a foreboding over the fishermen.

They sat silent for a moment and watched for they knew what such an apocalypse meant. Blessing themselves they prayed for guidance.

As they moved deeper out into the ocean they noticed that a storm was brewing. It blew steadily in from north/north east. Then without warning it increased in intensity with such force that they were compelled to remove their sails and resort to rowing.

Tom realising the seriousness of the situation they were now in was thinking of returning to Mailinmore bay to await an improvement in the weather. If he did so and the curraghs were to capsize on the breakers what would his neighbours think of his leadership? Pride would not allow him to surrender to his instincts.

"Follow me." He shouted encouraging them into calmer waters far from shore. About them the seas roared as it crashed into the breakwater.

He noticed that some of the curraghs were drifting away from the small flotilla. Others were too near the shore and were drifting into dangerous currents.

"Keep together and pray to God for guidance." Tom called loudly over the roar of the wind. Making for the shore was now out of the question. To attempt to ride the breakers crashing on the cliff face would be suicidal.

The families on hearing the roar of the storm and knowing that the little fleet would be on their way home ran to the cliff tops and looked anxiously out to sea.

They gathered at Glen Head, Dawros Head and Crohy Head. Anywhere that there was a vantage point. They watched for a glimpse of the little fleet as it struggled homewards.

"Light the beacons, light the beacons." The cry was heard above the winds. Beacon after beacon burst into life all along the coast.

Soon the light from the fires lit up the night sky and could be seen far out to sea. Sparks caught by the winds raced towards the heavens as if in offerings.

"Look! Look they are praying for our safe return." The fishermen pointed towards the fires and thanked their God. They took comfort in the knowledge that their folk would be waiting anxiously for their safe return.

"Tie the boats together." Tom instructed as they battled against the elements.

"It's them, thank God, Look!" The cry went up from a lookout as the little boats appeared round the headland.

"What are they doing?" Came a questioning response.

"They are trying to make for their home port of Airt an Chorram." Came the reply.

"How many are there?" Again an anxious voice challenged.

"There seems to be fifteen but I'm not too sure, they are tied together." Again came the encouraging response from the cliff top.

"Light the beacons on the strand. Hurry they need the light to guide them ashore." The priest called. The urgency of the situation was denoted in the tone of his voice.

Several of the old women began to keen and croon in sympathy on hearing of the desperate situation that the boats were in.

"Stop keening, stop it at once, they are not lost. Go down on your knees and start praying for their deliverance." Encouraged the priest.

Like corks the little curraghs bobbed about in the raging sea. A cry of despair rendered the air as the tempest swallowed the little fleet. This was followed by a sigh of relief as they were once again vomited back on the crest of the waves. Then above the crashing waves, the boiling seas and the howling wind they heard the fishermen praying.

"Ciúin! Ciúin anois." (*Quiet! Quiet now*) The priest challenged his flock.

"Listen they are saying Na Molta Diada (*The Divine Praise*). Answer as loud as you can. Encourage them by letting them know that we too are praying for their safe return home." The priest pleaded.

They watched and prayed aloud as the little fleet struggled against the odds in their vain attempt to reach the safety of the harbour mouth.

"They're turning away from the shore, why? What is the matter?" Came the distressful message from the lookout interrupting their praying. The assembly rose to their feet as one and looked out to sea.

"They cannot cross the dangerous breakers and are seeking shelter in deeper waters until the storm abates. Tom Kearney knows what he's doing, a wise decision, a wise decision indeed." An old fisherman assured them.

Out at sea the drama continued as several of the fishermen were catapulted from their frail craft into the ocean.

Their curraghs had collapsed and they were unable to right them. They would not and could not seek refuge in any of the other boats. It is totally impossible to board a curragh in the boiling seas. They knew that the frail boat would capsize endangering the occupant should they attempt to board any.

The only possible way of saving themselves was for the occupants to tie a rope to the back of the curraghs and tow them ashore.

"Hold tight to the ropes and we will pull you ashore." The men in the remaining boats let out ropes and encouraged those in the sea to hold on to them.

One by one those holding the ropes released their grips and were swallowed up by the ocean. Tom felt himself being somersaulted into the air as a giant wave capsized his frail craft.

"Tom, grab the rope, grab the rope Tom." He heard his friend Séamus O'Brien call out as he came to the surface. Seeing the rope trailing in the water he swam

towards it. In desperation he reached out and grasping the rope he twisted it round his wrists and held on as best he could.
The cold ate into his body and his heavy homespun clothing hindered his ability to stay afloat. In desperation he tried to instil life into his hands. There was no response; he watched the rope slowly uncoil itself leaving him to the mercy of the ocean. He knew that there was no hope for him.
"I'm lost Séamus, would you say the act of contrition with me?" He called weakly. He tried desperately to regain a hold on to the rope trailing from the curragh of Séamus but there was little if any feeling left in his hands.
"Hold on Tom, have faith. The storm is abating and we will soon have you home safely." Séamus again tried to encourage him.
"No Séamus I'll not make it, I'm finished. Tell my Bríge that I love her and to remember me in her prayers." Slowly he began drifting away from the curragh.
"Tom! Will you listen to me, tie the rope around your hands." Séamus again pleaded.
"It's no use Seámus, please pray for my..."
"Tom! Tom Kearney where are you? Raise your hand Tom; I'll save you I promise." He called as he watched the empty rope trailing behind his curragh.
"God be good to you Tom and all belonging to you." There was nothing more that he could do.
As the dawn broke over the eastern sky the little fleet was once again on the move towards their homeport.
"They're turning for home at last." Came the message from the lookout at the cliff top.
"How many curraghs are there?" Again the question was asked.
"I cannot really tell, they seem to be still roped together and making for Gweebara bay." Came the response.
Following their desperate struggle against the elements the little fleet was finally inside safe waters between Crohy Head and Portnoo.
"Thank God! Thank God they made it." The cries of the anxious families could be heard above the mournful howl of the wind.
Their joy turned to sorrow when they saw that six of the curraghs were upturned with no sign of the occupants.
The survivors related how several of the boats had capsized in the cruel seas. The fishermen were catapulted into the boiling waters by mountainous waves. They tried to save them but this was impossible. The cold and the boiling surf were beyond human endurance. They managed to rescue three who had tied the ropes to their hands.
There was no hope for the others in the freezing waters, they lost their grips on

the ropes and were presumed drowned. Six men sacrificed their lives that night to save the village from the plague. Tom Kearney was the last one to drown. The wild shoreline was searched daily for the bodies of those lost that stormy night.

Within a week most of the bodies had been recovered and returned to their loved ones.

By the following week only the body of Tom Kearney remained missing.

"Don't you fret Bríge, we'll find your Tom and lay him to rest beside his infant son Tomás beag." They assured her.

After a week of searching the body of a fisherman was found by lobster fishermen from Mullaghmore. It was found between the rocks on Inismurry Island. It was badly mutilated and beyond recognition. The priest was sent for to administer the last rites of the Church.

After a short service he instructed that the Aran Sweater be removed from the corpse.

"Take the sweater to the cottage of Bríge Kearney at Dungloe and ask her if it belongs to her Tom. Place the corpse inside the old monastery ruins. There we will hold the *Lyke Wake* until we can ascertain who the poor fisherman is." He instructed.

It was confirmed some days later that the sweater did belong to Tom Kearney. On hearing the sad news John, his brother brought Mary back from Leabgarrow.

Next day the body of Tom Kearney was placed in a coffin and taken back to Dungloe. There the family waited to welcome him home for the last time.

"I expect you want me to take care of the funeral arrangements." John whispered.

"Would you do just that, John?" Bridge thanked him.

John called on Margaret Doyle and Biddy McAvoy to make the shroud and to wash and lay out the corpse for the three-day wake.

John took himself off to Crohy Head where he dug the grave.

Following the wake his coffin was taken on the shoulders of four fishermen. His brother led the cortège to Crohy Head. The sad cortège led by Bríge and daughter Mary wended it's way slowly to the lonely headland.

"Tomás beag will be waiting to greet him." Bríge cried as the cross on the grave of her son came into view. They laid him down in a fresh grave beside his youngest son.

"It is best that Mary stays with you now for comfort." John told his sister-in-law after the funeral service.

"You're right John, it will be a lonely house without my Tom."

"Not at all Bríge, you have your good neighbours by day and God's angels to watch over you at night." John comforted her.

"Two children and a good man taken from me. The light is gone from my cottage and my heart is filled with sorrow. Why is God punishing me so?" She cried.

"Now if there is anything that you need do not hesitate to let me know. You could come and stay at our place on the island if you wished." John unable to give her an explanation changed the subject.

"No thanks John. You have enough on your plate without our burden."

"The invitation is there Bríge and a Ceád Míle Fáilte. There's never a cold hob in our home for you and yours as far as we're concerned Bríge Kearney."

"Thank you John, Tom would be as proud of you as I am. I'll remember your words, so I will."

THE SEDUCTION OF MARY KEARNEY

The widow Bríge Kearney and her daughter Mary knelt on the dirt floor of their kitchen reciting the rosary as outside the cruel wind continued to howl. With the rosary finished she quenched the candle and encouraged her daughter to retire for the night.
"There is little to keep you out of your bed girl, best be off now." She instructed.
Alone now with nothing but the wind moaning in the chimney she sat looking into the fire. Her thoughts and prayers were with her husband and the two sons that she so recently lost.
"Whatever will be the outcome now Tom? We have no money to pay our rent and no crop." She sighed as she riddled the fire.
Looking round the bare cottage she rose to her feet and taking a shovel she filled it with peat dust and smothered the flames. The fire would slowly smoulder and by morning it would be ready to be revamped.
Crossing the room she reached into the old seashell hanging on the wall containing the Holy Water. Calling God's absolution on the souls of her husband and son she retired to the *Leaba Suidheacan*.
Taking her beads from beneath the pillow she began the five sorrowful mysteries. She prayed for the soul of her husband and her youngest Tomás beag.
Looking towards the window she prayed for the return of her son Séan.
"Séan avic, your father is dead and the cottage needs the hand of a man. Please God send my son home." She humbly prayed.
Her candle pierced the dark recesses of the room probing, seeking. Something or someone was calling from the darkness. Was it the love of her Tom assuring her that all would be well?
No! It was not he. It was the cruel wind from the mountain that penetrated the thick walls of the cottage and trapped itself in the chimney.
Long moans followed each other into the cottage and raced up into the chimney trying to escape. The sorrowful moaning interrupting her '*Trimmins*'.
As she prayed and tried to ignore the intrusive winds her eyes slowly closed and she succumbed to sleep.
It was early morning when her sleep was disturbed by incessant hammering on her door.
"Who is it and what do you want at this hour?" She called out.
"Open this door at once Bríge Kearney. I am Frank McLaughlan, bailiff to Lord

Kilgarvan." She heard the raucous voice challenge.

"I'm coming, let me get dressed first." 'This is it then they have come sooner than I expected they would.' She murmured to herself.

On opening the half door she saw before her the bullish form of the bailiff silhouetted in the frame.

"You wasted little time in calling. You know that my Tom is hardly cold in his grave?" Bríge opened the half door and looked out into the grey dawn.

"You and yours are to be off this land by twelve noon, do you hear me. You have not paid any rent. Do you think you can live here rent-free now that your husband is dead? Well do you?" He held his shillelagh in a threatening manner in front of her face.

"Where can we go to? Cannot his Lordship stay his hand until the spring at least. Would you please ask him for a stay of execution?" Bríge pleaded.

"Are you deaf woman or just plain stupid. There will be no reprieve unless you have the rent due. Well do you?" To emphasis his threat he banged his shillelagh against the door.

"You know well that we have no money, but please for God's sake..." She pleaded.

"I'm sorry but I cannot make any exceptions for you."

Mounting his horse he departed vowing to return at noon to ensure they were gone.

Lighting the candle she set about packing what essentials she could carry. Her pots and pans and her delph given to her as a dowry by her mother would have to be abandoned.

"What was all that about, and why are you packing?" Mary entered the room.

"We must leave here at once and find shelter before night fall." Her mother began to gather up what essentials they would need for the hazardous journey over the mountain.

"Come on girl we don't have much time." She encouraged her daughter to pack.

By midday they were ready and about to leave the cottage when down the boreen came a gig. Sitting on the high sprung seat was the bailiff and a stout woman.

"We are leaving now and won't be anymore trouble to you. May God forgive you and the landlord? Do what you will with what's left, for all the good it will do you." Brige slung her bundle over her shoulder and called on her daughter to join her.

"That will not be necessary. I explained to his Lordship your situation and he agrees that you may stay in the cottage." Frank McLaughlan smiled like a

benevolent father.
"Oh thank you Sir. May the good Lord and his blessed mother protect you and yours." Bríge knelt on the ground and joining her hands invoked a blessing on the bailiff.
"He has also offered your daughter employment as a kitchen maid in the castle." The bailiff smiled like a benevolent father.
"At the castle is it?" Bríge hesitated.
"It will be alright Bríge Kearney, I'll look after Mary. My name is Maura O'Reilly." The woman seeing her hesitate assured her.
"You will look after her won't you, she's only a child you know." Bríge pleaded.
"Don't you worry, be assured she's in safe hands with me." Maura smilingly promised her.
"God bless you mam, you're a kind soul I can see it in your face."
"Are you finished gossiping? Come on, up you get." He invited Mary to join them on the sprung seat.
Mary obediently picked up her bundle and approached the cart.
"You won't be needing those." The woman instructed her to leave the bundle behind.
"I'll come home as often as I can. Goodbye ma." Mary promised as she took her place beside the woman on the high seat.
"Get up there." The bailiff snapped the reins across the back of the horse.
"God bless you Mary and come home as often as you can." Her mother hung on to the shaft of the cart as it trundled up the track.
As the cart left the boréen to join the main road she stopped and waved to her departing daughter.
"I'll be praying for you Mary, come home soon."
The cart stopped before an archway guarded by two large iron gates. Two neat stone cottages stood guard one each side of the entrance.
Over the archway she saw two stone animals holding a banner with some foreign language chiselled deep into the granite.
"Come on Jack, open the gates." The bailiff shouted making no attempt to leave his seat.
"It's yourself Frank. Have you no patience man?" From the cottage to the left limped an elderly man supported by a walking stick.
"You're getting too old for the job, that's your problem Jack. Now open the gate I haven't got all day." Grumbled the bailiff.
The old man leisurely approached the gate and lifting the huge bolt swung it open.

"Don't worry about me Frank, look to yourself. Old Father Times is no more generous to you than to me." The old man laughed as the gig moved under the archway.

Mary looked back as the old man pushed the gate to and secured the bolt. Through the tunnel she could see part of the castle balustrade and a circle of granite steps.

"This is it then, get yourself down." The woman called on her to join her in the courtyard.

The bailiff removed his cap and walked slowly backwards towards the castle.

"Why has the bailiff removed his cap and why is he walking backwards?" Mary giggled.

"Stop that at once, do you hear. It is the custom for gentlemen to remove their hats. It is demanded that male servants humbly approach the castle. We must approach it with our eyes down cast and genuflect when we reach the door. Should any of the gentry appear you must go to the corner of the stairs and face the wall." She cautioned.

Mary stood befuddled before the castle. She had never seen such a place before.

"Come on follow me." The woman was half way up the steps.

"It's very big isn't it?" Mary remarked as she quickly followed.

"Don't ask so many questions, genuflect at once." The woman commanded.

The woman took the huge cast iron knocker in the shape of a lion's head in her hand and rapped on the door. A girl in a white uniform opened the door to them.

Mary entered the hall and looked down at the chequered black and white marble floor, then towards the many doors to her right and left. Where, she wondered did all the doors lead? An imposing circular staircase rose above the great marble hall on two broad flights.

A fine balustrade supported by delicate barley turned spindles, three to a step snaked upwards to the first floor and beyond. This led on to an ornate whispering gallery that done credit to the other surroundings. Fine tall arches supported on marble columns divided the outer and inner halls.

A man in a smoking jacket tied with a silken cord stood with his back to the balustrade looking towards the bedrooms.

"Come on hurry up." The woman encouraged her to climb the stairs.

As they crossed the hall at the head of the stairs the man looked towards her and smiled.

She followed the woman to a bathroom at the end of the great hall. The walls were tiled in white glazed tiles with the occasional Grecian floral design

breaking the monotony of the white. In the corner stood a large iron bath standing on four cast iron legs. Each in the form of a lion's leg holding a ball.
"Now get those rags off you and get into the tub." The woman ordered.
The young girl that she had met previously at the door entered carrying a large pail of hot water.
"Come on. What are you waiting for?" She again ordered Mary into the bath. Mary found herself sitting in the bath being showered with hot water. She began to relax as the woman washed her in a sweet smelling soap.
"There now doesn't that feel better? Come on out you get" The woman held out a large towel and wrapped it around her as she left the bath.
"Now dry yourself well, I'll be back in a moment."
The woman returned carrying a heavy bathrobe and invited her to put it on.
"Now my girl let's have a look at that hair of yours." Opening the door she again called on Mary to follow her.
As they passed down the hall the man was still leaning against the balustrade. They entered a large bedroom in which there was a four poster bed over which hung a servant pull call. The windows were covered in heavy drapes that hung in an inverted 'V' from ceiling to floor.
The walls were covered in green wallpaper on which were embossed large clumps of red climbing roses. Several large paintings hanging on chains graced the walls. In the centre of the room hung an ornate chandelier that was set in an embellished centrepiece that matched the dado rail.
"Come sit yourself down here." She was invited to sit at large dressing table with three matching mirrors.
The woman combed and platted her hair and told her to remove the dressing robe and get into the bed. Mary was by now of the opinion that working as a servant was not as bad as she was led to believe.
'Why! She thought, I'll like this position.' She relaxed in the feather bed and played with the servant call cord.
"Leave that alone, you mustn't touch it." The woman again entered the room carrying a tray. A plate containing cold meat and buttered scone sat in the centre and beside it stood a glass of milk.
"What is it for and what will happen if I touch it?" She let go of the cord as she spoke.
"Don't be so inquisitive, it is a servant call chain and it will not be answered for you. Eat up now and rest." She ordered.
With the meal consumed she snuggled down into the feather bed and soon succumbed to sleep.
She awakened from a deep sleep to feel someone stroking her breasts and

fondling her intimately. She felt the body of a man trying to mount her and moved away.

"Leave me alone, get out of here. *Maura O'Reilly! Maura O'Reilly.*" She called in desperation through her nightmare.

"Come here you little hussy." The man grabbed her round the waist and dragged her to the centre of the bed.

She soon realised that this was no nightmare.

"*Maura O'Reilly! Maura O'Reilly*". She screamed again and again as she caught hold of the servant pull cord and began pulling it in desperation.

"Leave that go, there's no one going to answer you." The man slapped her face.

The more she struggled the more the brute seemed to enjoy it.

"Please leave me alone. I want to go home." She pleaded.

Weak and exhausted from the struggle she found that she could no longer fight him off. Rising above her the man forced her legs apart and mounted her.

She screamed as his manhood tore through her virginity causing her intense pain. Her pain excited him all the more as he drove his manhood deep inside her virginal body.

With no consideration of the pain and distress he was causing her he continued to rape her. On the contrary the more she resisted the more it excited him.

His heavy body was smothering her and she fainted in distress.

She awakened to feel his manhood tearing at her very soul and again cried out. Screaming obscenities and holding tightly to her breasts he forced his lips on to hers.

She smelt the rancid alcohol on his breath and tried to move her lips away but again he overpowered her. In desperation she bit his lip and scratched his back.

"You Fenian bitch, I'll teach you a lesson you'll not forget." Wiping the blood from his mouth he left the bed.

Picking up his riding crop he pulled the coverings she was clinging to off her and dragged her on to the floor. Grabbing her he turned her over and trashed her naked body several times.

"Now behave yourself or I'll kill you here and now." Throwing her back onto the bed he began to suckle her breasts and maul her before he again mounted her and continued to abuse her.

There was no escape she was exhausted from her ordeal and could nothing but lie there and let the brute abuse her as he pleased.

Quickening the strokes of his penis he forced it deeper and deeper inside her.

"God in Heaven please help me." She prayed as she felt that she was being torn apart.

Finally as if in answer to her prayers she felt him stretch full length on top of her and grunting and groaning he held her close to him, he shuddered as his sperm entered her womb. He lay on top of her for some time panting. Finally he rolled off her and leaving the bed he took the chamber pot from under it and without shame relieved himself.

"Behave yourself from now on and you'll have nothing to fear." He told her as he returned to the bed and was soon sleeping soundly.

Mary crept from the bed and crawling to the door she gently turned the handle. There was no escape. The door had been locked and the key removed.

Seeking some hiding place from the brute she crept to the window. She silently lifted the sash seeking an escape route but the drop was too far. She closed the window and continued her search for a secure hiding place. Seeing a recess behind the drapes she rolled herself into a tight ball and remained still.

She was awakened when she heard the man again using the chamber pot.

"What are you doing there? Come back to bed at once." Pulling the drapes aside he picked her up in his arms and threw her on to the bed.

"Please! Please let me go home." She cried.

There was to be no reprieve as once again he held her down and abused her in the most humiliating and bestial manner.

Having again satisfied his lust for her he rose from the bed and retired to the bathroom.

Mary lay on the bed sobbing. There was to be no escape.

"You look disgusting." She looked up and saw the man standing over her with the riding crop in his hand.

"Please, not again." She cried as she cowered in the bed.

"I'm not going to touch you, that is if you learn to behave." He sniggered as he ran the riding crop across her body.

He continued with his sadistic game of cat and mouse for some time. Tiring of his brutal and sadistic game he dressed and opening the door went out into the hall.

"Maura O'Reilly, Maura O'Reilly where are you?" He called as he slapped the riding crop against his leather leggings in annoyance.

"Coming Sir, what is it you want?"

"See that she is dressed and has something to eat." He pointed towards Mary. She was rolled up in a tight ball in the bed whimpering.

"What are you staring at? Get on with it woman." He shouted as he left the room and strolled down the hall.

"Oh you poor child, come with me." Gently she encouraged Mary to leave the bed and accompany her to the bathroom.

"Oh no! Not back there." Mary began to shiver as on leaving the bathroom she was led back into the bedroom.
"It's alright, he's gone now." Gently she guided her back into the bedroom.
"What is to become of me, why can't I go home?" She sobbed.
"Mary my child, don't you know that if you don't do as his Lordship demands then you and your mother will be banished into the countryside. You must realise that with no money to pay for the cottage there's little alternative. You are now his '*Tally Woman.*'"
"Oh my God! Is there nothing that can be done?" This news came as a shock to her.
"I'm afraid Mary that there is no alternative. I'll do all I can for you. Now sit down and I'll fetch your new clothes. Then we will go and have breakfast." Maura consoled her.
There was to be no respite as night after night he came and ravaged her.
She tried lying in the bed impassive as he indulged in his orgies of the most humiliating and bestiality on her body. This conduct on her part made him angry and he had no hesitation in inflicting his own punishment.

THE BIRTH OF MICHAEL KEARNEY

Twelve months had passed and reluctantly Mary had reconciled herself to a life of drudgery and humiliation. The alternatives for her and her mother was too horrendous to even contemplate. As the summer gave way to autumn she was feeling nauseous in the mornings.
"I'm not feeling too good." She approached her good friend Maura O'Reilly and told her of her problem.
"What ails you, have you got a fever?" Maura placed her hand on Mary's brow.
"It's my stomach, I keep wanting to vomit." Mary held her stomach to denote where the pain was.
"You don't know what the matter is then, do you?" Maura smiled.
"No, please tell me, I feel awful."
"You are with child."
"You mean that I am going to be a mother, Oh God! What is to become of me?"
"You'll be alright, better in fact than some of the girls in the village. You should be grateful indeed for a very benevolent master." Maura O'Reilly assured her.
"Grateful to that brute, I don't want to marry his Lordship. I want to be out of here." She cried.
"His Lordship marry you? Will you talk sense; he could not even if he wanted to. You are a *tally woman* and a Catholic. There is no place for you here now."
"What will happen to me then?" Mary pleaded.
"Happen! You wanted your freedom did you not? Now is your chance."
"You mean I can go home at last?"
"No! You will be taken to another estate somewhere down the country and married to one of the farm hands. He will be obliged to accept you and your child as his own."
"I have no intention of being bartered like a beast, I'll return to my mother. She will care for me and my child." Mary indignantly replied.
"Mary, listen to me, you will not return home, his Lordship will see to that. What do you think his Lordship would do if you disobeyed him?" Maura O'Reilly warned.
"What can he do to me that he has not already done?"
"He can and would evict you and your mother from his cottage. You wouldn't want your mother to die on the mountain, would you?" This form of blackmail

once again brought her into line.
Late one evening Maura O'Reilly came and told her to pack her belongings.
"Where are we going to?" Mary asked.
"I'm not going anyplace. Remember I told you that you would be married off to a servant in a far county. You are going to Cork to a place called Rathcormac. You are to be married off there before the baby is born."
"I'll not go! I won't do you hear me? I want to go home to my mother." Mary insisted.
"We had this argument before. Go home to your mother indeed. I never heard such nonsense. Don't you know that as soon as you leave here, your mother will be evicted? I'm warning you for the last time behave yourself." Maura O'Reilly shouted.
"No, I don't believe you anymore, you done nothing but tell me lies. He would not evict my mother. I am carrying his child." She insisted.
"Carrying his child, you and a dozen others I've no doubt. He will not accept the baby as his. He can and he will evict your mother. I should know; I never told you this before I too was a tally woman and I know what he is capable of."
"You a tally woman to who?" Mary looked shocked.
"To his lordship who else."
"Why then did you not try to escape and why are you helping me?"
"Because I love him and cannot bear to see him with another woman?"
"Love! Love that animal. Whatever is wrong with you?"
"Never mind what is wrong with me. I'm only helping you out of the goodness of my heart. Now do you want to escape or not?"
"Of course I want to escape. Oh I am sorry, please help me?" Mary desperate to escape to escape held on to her arm.
"Very well then, you get your belongings together and wait in your room."
Mary in deep shock returned to the room and picking up her portmanteau she began packing. As the light faded she trimmed the lamp and continued with her task.
"Why am I packing this lot? What am I doing?" She threw her portmanteau from her. Sitting on the bed she tried through her tears to contemplate what would become of her. She turned her thoughts to her mother for consolation. These were interrupted as the door slowly opened and her heart gave a leap.
"O God, not this night and me with child." She cried as she anticipating a final visit from her cruel master.
"How are you feeling now Mary?" To her relief Maura O'Reilly appeared in the doorway.
"A little tired but I'll be alright. When can I leave?" She sighed with relief.

"Good! Now be patient it will take a day or two but no more." She was assured.

It was two days later when Maura O'Reilly was sitting in the kitchen having a cup of tae that her day dreaming was interrupted. Looking up at the callboard she noticed the bell leading to Mary's room was ringing urgently.

"What's wrong with that girl?" Putting her tae to one side she rose and left the kitchen.

"What's the matter with you now?" She called before she had fully entered the room.

"Oh God, please help me, I'm in agony." Mary lay on the bed in a state of agitation and sweating profusely.

"It's alright relax. You are about to give birth." She approached the bed and taking the pull call from her hand she began pulling it.

"Is something the matter?" A young maid entered the room.

"Go and fetch some towels and hot water immediately" Maura informed her.

Late that afternoon her son was born.

"Mary Kearney will you just look?" Maura held her new born infant up for her to see. The infant's head was covered with the caul.

"Well Mary, what do you think of your lucky son?" She carefully removed the caul and washed the infant before laying him down beside her.

Mary looked bewildered and confused at the bundle lying beside her.

"Now Mary, you must be tired. I'll take the baby, you get some rest."

Two days passed and all thoughts of escape had left her, her motherly instincts were concentrated on the welfare of her infant son.

One dark night she was awakened from a deep sleep by Maura.

"Wake up and get dressed, wake up girl." Mary sat up in the bed with a start.

"Where's my baby? She looked up to see Maura O'Reilly standing over the bed.

"Come with me, we must hurry." She held her finger to her lips.

"Where are we going to? Where is my baby?" She demanded to know.

"Will you hurry and for God's sake keep quiet." Maura stood over the bed throwing Mary her clothes. There was a note of urgency in her voice.

"But where are we going to? I'm not leaving here without my baby?" She stubbornly sat on the bed refusing to leave without her son.

"Your baby is safe, now don't make matters worse, get dressed will you?" Maura insisted.

"Where! Where is my child?" She rose from the bed and in an agitated state began searching the room.

"Your baby is waiting for you, down by the lych gate. I'm going to help you

and your child escape from here. It will mean that you and your mother will have to flee the cottage before morning. Do you understand?"
"I don't care, so long as we escape from his Lordship." She tightened her cloak round her and picking up the portmanteau followed her.
Down the ornate staircase they crept and opening the hall door went out into the night.
They followed the drive until they reached the lych gate leading to the Protestant church. Seeing her son lying on the bench she ran and picking him up held him close.
"I left the gate unlocked after service this evening. May God protect you and go with you and your family Mary Kearney. You and your mother must get out of the county this night. Here are a couple of sovereigns and a bundle of food to help you on the road. Remember, if you are caught don't under any circumstances involve me." Gently she pushed her through the lych gate and on out into open country.
"May God reward you Maura O'Reilly."
"Here wear this always for luck." She handed her a small leather pouch.
"What is it?" Mary asked.
"It's the caul from your son, never be parted from it. Now get away before it's too late." Maura warned.
She turned to see the large oak door closing. She looked at the door and heard the turning of the key.
She was now outside the confines of the castle and on the road to her home. Making all haste she reached the cottage of her mother as the dawn was breaking in the east.
"Open the door mother, it's me" She tapped the window of the cottage.
"Good God it's yourself at last. Has something happened to bring you here at this hour?" Her mother looked down the boréen for her mode of transport.
"How did you get here and why so early? O God! Of your mercy be good to you my poor child" She looked down at her daughter holding the baby close to her breast.
"Oh mother, we have to leave at once." She fell into her mother's arms crying.
"Mo cúshla, what have they done to you?" Releasing herself from her daughter's arms she held her hands open to receive the baby.
"Mother, Maura O'Reilly helped me to..."
"Relax, sit yourself down and I'll make you something to eat, Don't worry so, we will manage." Her mother invited her to sit on the stooleen.
"We have no time mother, we must leave at once." She pleaded.
"Don't upset yourself, have a bite to eat." Her mother tried to encourage her.

"I told you that we must leave now. They will be coming looking for me. I am to be married off to a servant in the county Cork. They are coming. Oh please hurry."

"Alright let me put a few things together." Her mother noting the urgency in her voice began picking up bits and pieces from the dresser.

" Pack what you think you'll need and no more. Let us away from this place." Mary warned her.

"Come on then it is a long road that we have to follow." Her mother hoisted her bundle on her back and led the way away from their cottage home.

"Where are we going to go?" She asked.

"I have a sister over in Drumfree. She will take care of us until we find a cottage of our own." By noon they found themselves deep in the Derryveagh Mountains.

By late afternoon Mary was showing signs of fatigue and her mother decided that they should seek refuge and a bite to eat.

"I have a bundle of food that Maura O'Reilly gave to me." Mary opened her portmanteau and handed the parcel to her mother.

As they sheltered under an outcrop of rock they looked anxiously into the distance.

"Can you ever forgive me? I never in my wildest dreams thought that he would abuse you." Her mother interrupted her dreaming.

"You were not to know, mother. We should be thanking Maura O'Reilly for making my escape possible."

"May God and his blessed mother watch over her and protect her." She invoked a blessing on Maura.

"We cannot stay here any longer. Time is getting on and we must reach Gartan Lake before nightfall. Are you able to continue?" Her mother asked.

"I'll be alright mother, don't fret for me." She went to pick up the case.

"Here, I'll carry that. You see to your child." She picked up the portmanteau and took the rough road down the mountainside.

"We must be careful from now on. The Red Coats will be on patrol in the glen." Her mother warned. No sooner had she uttered this warning than they heard the rattle of sabres in the distance.

"Whist mother! Listen there are horses out there." Hiding in the heather they waited until the horsemen passed. Rising from their cover they saw a troop of horse passing along the outskirts of the wood and enter the glen.

As the troops passed out of sight Mary rose and looked into the distant valley.

"There's nothing out there, where's the lake?" She asked her mother.

"I suppose I was thinking ahead. I was hoping to reach it sooner rather than later. However it is getting late and we will have to find shelter before nightfall. Don't worry there is bound to be a cottage near by." She assured her.

Her mother led them down into the valley and on towards the little brook.

"We'll find shelter soon and then ask if we are on the right road." She optimistically predicted as she looked to the left and right trying to find her bearings.

"There's a cottage over there on the hillside." Mary pointed to a small cottage peeping out from the shelter of a crop of rock.

"We don't know if it is occupied or not but we will have to take shelter in it. Come on let's not waste precious daylight." Mother and daughter walked slowly across the green sward of the valley floor and within the hour found themselves climbing the hillside.

Sharp stones bit into their bare feet and they slipped on the wet moss and loose stones.

"God in heaven whatever possessed anyone to build a cottage here?" Panted Mary as she struggled to protect her child.

"Are you alright? Do you want to stop and rest?" Called her mother who by now had made it to the boréen leading to the cottage.

"No, you go on ahead, I'll catch up soon." She panted.

MOLLY CULLHANE TELLS HER STORY.

Mary watched anxiously as her mother approached the cottage. She was delighted when she saw the door opening and hastened her steps. Her mother stood beside a jovial woman in the doorway waiting to greet her.

"Thank God we made it." She lay her child down and removed the hood of her cloak from her head.

"This is my daughter, Mary meet Molly Cullhane." Her mother introduced them.

"You're welcome I'm sure, come in and take the weight off your feet. You came a long ways then?" The owner of the cottage reached out her hand in greeting.

"All the way from Dungloe and it's glad we are to bid *'Good Bye'* to it I can tell you."

"This is my infant son, Michael." Mary opened her shawl revealing the face of her smiling son.

"I can only offer you a drop of goats milk and a piece of rough scone, God help us all. When you have eaten you can tell me what the Craic is all about."

"That's more than generous of you and God will reward you. Of that have little doubt." Mary thanked her generous host.

"Amen! Amen, no truer words were ever said inside these four walls." The woman filled the corcan with milk and pushed it over the fire.

"Sure it won't be long on the boil for what there is of it. Now you were saying Mam." The woman sat on a stooleen before the fire stirring the pot with a blackthorn stick.

Brige told her story and how her daughter was taken to the castle of Lord Kilgarvan under the pretence of employment and of her seduction.

"These are sad days, sad days indeed in Ireland. Come on now have this when it's still warm." She rose and went to the dresser and returned with several tin mugs. What was in the pot she divided equally between them.

"It wasn't a lot, was it?" She apologised on seeing Mary draining the last of the milk.

"It was fine thanks, without you we would have perished out there." Brige laid her mug to one side.

"My man died out there, beyond Lough Barra it happened." Molly looked towards the window with a far away look.

"Did you say Lough Barra?" Brige interrupted.

"I did that, where did you think you were?"

"I thought we were at Lake Gartan."

"Wishful thinking on your part, what would you be doing going that far?"
"I've got a sister up at Drumfree and we were hoping to find a vacant cottage there."
"From what you tell me, I would be making my way to the far counties away from Lord Kilgarvan and his bailiffs. The gentry have long arms as you well know. Still it is none of my business." Molly warned.
"You could be right Molly, but we know nothing of the far counties and less of their people." Brige replied.
"Well you come to the right cottage to find that out, so you have. You see I came here from Cooraclare in the County of Clare. We too had to leave the land but not for the same reason as you. Then what reason do the landlords need?"
"My late husband Michael, God rest his soul, was a faithful servant to Sire Walsh. Never was he one to neglect his duties nor would he be part or parcel to any felon band. Not mind you but he loved ould Ireland, don't get me wrong. There are many of our own kin I can tell you who pretending to love the ould sod who would sell the pass (*Betray their country*) for a spoonful of porridge. Not so my Michael. It was always himself who was called upon to strike the bargain at the fairs. His word was his bond and having struck a deal he would seal it with the usual handshake and the luck penny. There would be no reneging on the deal once it was struck no matter how much more was on offer afterwards. He always called money obtained from a broken word '*Judas Money*'. It was his honesty that led to his downfall." Molly let out a sigh.
"Sure I remember it well and how could I forget...?
It all began over at a fair in the town of Kilrush one Tuesday morning." Molly looked nostalgically towards the distant hills. "He had struck a deal with a knacker from Galway for the sale of a dry cow. The price was agreed and the luck penny exchanged. Michael thought no more about the sale as he continued bargaining for the rest of the cattle. That was until he was approached by a stranger."
"What are you asking for the dry cow over there?" The stranger asked.
"I'm sorry that beast is long spoken for, I have others in far better shape. Would you like to make me an offer?" He rightly informed the stranger.
"Not at all, I was only interested in that one." He pointed to the dry cow.
"Well as I said it is spoken for." Michael insisted.
"What was the deal then, I never heard the bidding?" The stranger demanded to know.
"Sorry, you should know better than ask me that question. That's between the buyer and me. I suggest that you ask him."

"Don't you know who I am you insolent wretch? I'm of the opinion that there is some shenanigan (*underhand deal*) taking place here. Why won't you tell me how much you sold the beast for?" He demanded to know.
"I can assure you that the sale was above board. Now will you excuse me." He walked away from the insulting brute. The fair continued and my husband had all but forgotten his encounter with the dealer. That evening he returned to Sire Walsh and handed over the money from the sale.
"Michael, how much did you get for the dry cow?" Sire Walsh asked.
"It's all written down, why do you ask, sir?" Michael questioned.
"It has been brought to my notice that you may be doing deals for your own benefit. I wouldn't like it if you were." There was a warning in his voice.
"You know me Sir, I would never betray a trust."
"I hope not, for your own sake Michael, It would be the sorry day for you if it were otherwise." Came the veiled threat. That night he sat on the stooleen in a sombre mood and I knew that there was something the matter.
"What ever ails you Michael? You're not yourself at all, so you're not" I gently tried to get him to tell me what was worrying him.
"It was that dealer, I'm sure it was. Do you know that Sire Walsh more or less accused me of pilfering from the sale money?" He then told me all that happened.
"Take no notice Michael. Sure the world is filled with jealous people. I doubt if the squire took any real notice." I comforted him.
"I suppose you are right Molly. Still I'll not forget that dealer's face and I'll have sharp words with him at the next fair. I didn't like the tone of his questioning."
"That dealer seems to have some powerful friends and you should forget all about it." I tried to warn him but he insisted on having the matter resolved. I thought it best to leave him to get it out of his system. After all there wouldn't be a fair in Kilrush before Lady day. By then it would have long blown over. The next big fair day was in Miltown Malbay and Michael and two other drovers set out with a fine mixed herd for the fair. I packed him a bite to eat and blessed him at the door as he left. I had forgotten all about his previous encounter with the dealer. He didn't come home that night and Squire Walsh sent one of his henchmen to our cottage to find him. There was neither sight nor sound of him. The squire was of the opinion that he had absconded with his money. He cared nothing for the welfare of my husband or to the fact that he was missing.
He went to the constabulary and accused my husband of stealing his money and absconding with it. A detachment of Royal Irish Constabulary and Red Coats

were sent out into the '*Burren*' and the surrounding countryside to apprehend him. Should he show any resistance they should take no chances but shoot him dead. Another dead Fenian would be a blessing.

Next morning he was found in a ditch bloodied and as near to death as was possible and with empty pockets. Robbers had ambushed him on the return journey. They had beaten him, robbed him and left him for dead. I can tell you that the squire was more annoyed and worried for the loss of his blasted money than for the welfare of my husband. When he somewhat recovered he was called to the peelers barracks and questioned at length as to how he lost the money. They said that they had a witness who saw him drinking heavily and in congenial conversation with a ruffian. They believed that money had changed hands. Not alone that but this vagabond was a known Fenian. Did he let the Fenian rob him to use the money to buy arms for the nationalist cause? The question was asked supposititiously. Eventually, unable to convict him of any wrongdoing he was released. As he left the barracks he saw the dealer in deep conversation with the sergeant.

On his release Sire Walsh made it clear that he had no further time for my man. He was called to the manor and dismissed without a word of explanation or wages. We were of course evicted from our cottage and forced to build a scalpeen in the surrounding hills.

Now branded a thief and a liar he could find little work and spent most of his time wandering from one fair to the next seeking work where possible as a drover for a pittance. He put it all down to his encounter with the dealer and was determined to bring the matter to a head.

It was on the Wednesday of the following week that there were ructions in the village. The body of the dealer had been found lying by the roadside with a musket ball between his eyes. The Fenians got the blame for it of course. It was common knowledge that the dealer was an informer. May God forgive me but I thought he got what he deserved.

My Michael and two others were arrested. They were interrogated and tortured in the barracks. I tell you mam, in all truth that you could hear the screams of them above Cree village. My man had been home all that Tuesday and Wednesday, he could no more have shot the blackguard than you could. It was doubtful if any decent person was out and about at the time. The weather was so bad that one wouldn't put the dog out.

I went to the barracks and told them my story but my assurance was not enough to convince them. I was told that the felons had confessed of their own free will to the murder and claimed that they done it for Ireland.

The outcome was that they were taken to Ennis to a summary trial without the rudiments of truth. Their confessions were read out in court. Written of course by the sergeant who claimed that they were illiterate and that he had written down their confessions word for word as they dictated. This was another blatant lie for my Michael was full of the learning and everybody in the village, including the sergeant was aware of this. All too often he was called upon to read and reply to letters for friends and neighbours including the Red Coats. The sergeant swore that he read their confessions to them before he asked them to put their mark on the document.

What defence could they muster against the forces of the crown?

I heard the words as they echoed around that grim courtroom.... 'Guilty as charged.'

"My husband and the other two were taken to the gallows. He looked at me longingly as they placed the black hood over his head, still pleading his innocence." Molly let out a deep sigh and wiped the tears from her eyes.

"I witnessed the hangman pull the lever and I shut my eyes and said a silent prayer. When I opened them I saw his body dangling beneath the trap door. Some moments later I saw the body of his comrade appear below the second trap door. It jerked in the last spasms of death and then all was still." There was a silence in the room.

"Hard times indeed Molly and it's sorry we are to hear of your troubles. We will remember you and Michael in our rosary, so we will." Bríge took her hand in hers and broke the silence.

"Whatever happened that you are living here on Glendower Mountain?" Mary asked.

"It's not by choice I can assure you. Did you ever hear of the Fight for Killmallock town in the County of Limerick?" Molly continued her story.

"No! But then we've never been out of the hills of Donegal". Bríge apologised.

"My eldest brother Dan was an active member of the Fenians and a *Peep O' Day Boy.*"

"A Peep-O-Day boy. Whatever are they?" Bríge interrupted.

"They are Fenians who attack the estates of the gentry." Molly informed her.

"Sorry for the interruption whatever happened?" Bríge apologised.

"I told you that Dan was a Fenian. One of them had been arrested on the word of a lackey for the gentry. He was taken to Kilmallock barracks on a trumped up charge, brutally flogged, tortured and condemned to hang. All the landed gentry had to do was point the finger and some poor soul found themselves on the prison ship bound for Van Deemens land or swinging from the gallows high. The local Fenians took it upon themselves to attack the barracks in an effort to free their comrades. Attack the barracks they did and their bravery will be told in song and story long after their Fenian bones are mingled with Irish soil. It was the hardest fight of all. Although outnumbered and outgunned they managed after a long struggle to breach the outer walls and gain access into the square. Once in the open they were met with a hail of musket shot. They fought their way to the prison compound and released their comrade but not without loss of life. My brother was one of those left dying in that compound.

'I can tell you that when the Red Coats came in numbers from Limerick there was a Hue and Cry for anyone connected with or related to a Fenian. We knew well enough what the outcome would be. Those with cottages would be evicted and their homes put to the spleen. Then we would be whipped out of the county or worse. Myself with four other women were warned to get out of Clare that very night or else we would find ourselves incarcerated in the women's jail in Limerick. There we would be left to rot with our children. Heeding their warning we took our children and ourselves across the Burren and climbed the Aughty Mountains, avoiding the Red Coats who were in hot pursuit. There were ten children with us. They ranged from two infants to a boy of nine years of age. One of the infants still suckling at her mother's breast died on the second day. We dug her a little grave with our bare hands and having said a prayer marked her grave with a rock. At Kilconnell Abbey some of the women and children felt that they were now safe and left the company. We continued on into the great bog. A week later what remained of our little band arrived in the town of Boyle.

"This is as far as we go Molly, I lost one of my children and by God I don't want to lose the other. We don't care anymore." One of the women, her youngest had died the other side of Loughrea spoke up.

"I'm with you Josephine, enough is enough. I'm too old for wandering around the mountains. Come to think of it, we done nothing wrong and why then should we be on the run?" Another spoke out.

"Ah! Who could blame them, sure we did not know where we were going to settle. I continued on alone until I found this abandoned cottage and settled in. I've managed to survive, Thank God. I can tell you that you are the first visitors to my door this year. So there you have it."

"I suppose we should be on our way by first light." Brige broke a long silence.

"You cannot possible move on so soon, look at your poor daughter?" Mary was lying on the floor close to the fire sleeping.

"I expect you're right Molly and God will reward you for your generosity."

MOLLY BECOMES A GODMOTHER.

Bríge and her daughter stayed at the cottage of Molly Cullhane throughout the rest of the long winter.
Mary reluctantly related the story of her ordeal at the hands of Lord Kilgarvan and swore that should her God spare her she would have her revenge.
In the spring against the advice of Molly, Bríge decided that they would finally leave and take the long road to Drumfree.
"Bríge Kearney will you show a little sense and consideration for your daughter. There's no way that she could make such a journey. Do want her and her child to die on the mountain?
"We've imposed enough on your generosity and really we should be moving on." Bríge insisted.
"You're no trouble at all, Should anything happen to them and God forbid that it should, could you live with yourself?" Molly advised.
"Molly we are beholding to you for all you done for us. We are not the ones to take advantage of your generous hospitality." Bríge again insisted on leaving.
"I'm more than grateful for the company of a fellow human being. This is a lonely place. Just stay for a few more days until the snow leaves the mountain; then by all means go to Drumfree if you must." Molly pleaded
"For Mary's sake we'll stay then and thanks." Bríge finally agreed.
"I know it is none of my business, but did you ever get the child baptised?" Molly asked one evening.
"Mary was the child baptised, do you know?" Bríge looked anxiously towards daughter.
"No mother, there was no time."
"Well we had best put the matter to right, God forbid but one never knows what might happen." Molly advised.
"What name are you going to call him after?" Molly took the infant and wrapped him in an old piece of sheet.
"I was going to call her Bríge should she be a girl. Seeing that he is a boy I'm going to call him Michael." Mary informed the gathering.
"Michael! Please are you calling him after my Michael, say you are." Molly rocked the infant and hugged him as if he was her own child.
"Yes indeed Molly. It is the least that we could do to remember your kindness to us."
"We had best baptise the child now just in case. I'll fetch the holy water. Brige would you fetch the bit of a candle." Molly took charge of the proceedings.
"Here Mary take hold of your son and Bríge will you hold the lighted candle

near to his little face. Would you ever bring the pinch of salt? Are we ready then?"

"As ready as we will ever be." Mary smiled down at her infant son.

"I baptise thee...' Go on Mary name your child," Molly called out and she as excited as a cat with a mouse.

"Michael Thomas Kearney." She replied.

"Then I baptise thee Michael Thomas Kearney in the name of the Father, and of the Son, and of the Holy Ghost. Amen." Molly invoked the strength of the Blessed Trinity on the child. She made the sign of the cross on the forehead of the infant with the Holy water.

Bríge took the pinch of salt and having smeared a lick on the child's lips sprinkled the rest on the threshold to deter the Buacaill Míocumta (*Deformed Fairy Boy*) from stealing the baby.

"Now Mary could I be impertinent and make a suggestion?" Molly looked round at the company.

"Go on, you seem to have everything in hand." Bríge agreed.

"Well! Wouldn't it be better not to tell people that the child was Mary's? You know how gossips spreads?" She looked deep into Mary's innocent eyes as she spoke.

"Do you know that is a grand idea. We could not disclose that he was the son of Lord Kilgarvan. God only knows what would happen if he found out. No, you're right Molly. I'll take responsibility for the child for now." Bríge agreed.

All too soon, as far as Molly Cullhane was concerned they packed their bags and were once again on the road to Drumfree.

"We'll be beholding to you Molly and you can be assured of our prayers." Bríge stood by the threshold. Michael wrapped up in the warm folds of her shawl was sleeping peacefully unaware of the drama unfolding around him.

"You take good care of my Godson and when he is of age tell him of Molly Cullhane of Slieve Snagh." She spoke to the baby through her tears.

"Don't worry Molly, Michael will come strolling up the old boréen to your door one day, please God. We had best be making the road now that the weather is in our favour." Bríge looked across at the feathery clouds passing over the valley.

"Wait for a minute will you?" Molly went back into the cottage and returned with an old pair of *scapulars* and placed them around the neck of the infant.

"These belonged to my mother and her mother before her. They are my most precious possession and I want him to have them." Kissing them she placed them round the neck of the child.

"Tá an grian a soillsiuad, act mo cróide briste. Labraím dtí an bárda aingeal óir

mise."
(The sun is shining but my heart is broken. Speak to your guardian angel for me.)
Molly spoke in her native tongue as she clasped the baby's hands in hers. Seeing their determination to be on their way she called a final blessing down upon them.
"Go gcuirid Dia ar beala do leasa tú agus go bfágaid Dia an tsláinte agat."
(May God direct you and spare you the health)
They could still see Molly waving to them as they entered the valley below Slieve Snagh.
"Come on now, if we put one foot before the other we should reach Letterkenny by nightfall." Bríge wrapped the shawl tighter around Michael and led the way across the valley floor.
"We should follow the river Finn and the Swilly. The ground is fairly soft going and will not cut our feet." Mary suggested.
"If we follow the Finn we will find ourselves in the twin towns of Ballybofey and Stranolar, that would be miles out of our way. Should we reach Breenagh before the light fails then we are but a stretch of the feet from Letterkenny." Her mother suggested.
By midday the weather was showing signs of deteriorating. A cold sleet was sweeping along the valley floor. Gusts of biting cold winds penetrated their sparse clothing.
"We have to find shelter, keep looking for a suitable refuge." Molly struggled on ahead holding the infant close to her breast.
They could see the vast sweep of the valley before them and the towering Derryveagh mountain peak to the west.
"We cannot go on mother, we must rest." Mary called above the wind and sleet.
"We mustn't stop, it's too exposed we'd perish out here." Her mother warned.
"Look! There's a big lake over there." Mary pointed to a vast expanse of water some miles distant.
"God has answered our prayers, so he has. It has to be Lake Gartan. It just has to be." Her mother was willing and praying for it to be their refuge.
Moving east along the lakeshore they crossed into the bog. Through the mist they saw the outline of a bog cutters scalp (Hut).
"This is a God send, so it is. We will rest here until the weather mends." Pulling the rough door to one side they entered and saw that three steps had been cut into the side giving access to the bog floor some feet below.
Mary breast fed her child and found that she could hardly keep her eyes

opened.

"I'm so tired, I'm going to have forty winks." Without waiting for a reply she went to a dry corner covered in bracken and ferns. Making her infant son comfortable she lay down and fell into a deep sleep.

Bríge sat by the makeshift door looking at the heather as it blew to and fro. Occasionally a squall of rain and sleet cascaded down the surface leaving little droplets of jewelled crystals that were trapped for a time in the thatch before escaping.

As they dropped to the ground they made a musical sound and formed into a pool of water that grew as the rain continued to fall. Her eyes began to close and her mind began to wander. She was back in her own cottage with her knitting on her knees. Her Tom was sitting in the sugan chair reading.

She heard her son Séan playing with his dog, Oisín. Mary was sitting on a stáca straw making Saint Bridget crosses. Tomás beag was lying in the cradle of straw gurgling and talking to the angels. Life although harsh and cruel to them could at times be bountiful and for this she thanked her God.

She listened and she smiled as she heard Mary singing the song of the Coolin. She wanted to participate but for some unknown reason she could not respond. Mary finished her singing and rose from her stooléen. Lifting Tomás Beag from the cradle she kissed him. Without looking back she lifted the latch and went out into the night.

"Don't take Tomás beag away from me please." Bríge pleaded.

She reached out hoping to take the child from her daughter, only to find that she could not rise from her stooléen.

Mary was leaving with her infant son and she could not stop her. She cried out to her Tom to come to her aid. He continued reading his paper oblivious to her desperate cry for help. Mary turned and smiled as she wended her way down the long boréen.

She awoke with a start from her dreaming and looked towards her daughter. She lay sleeping peacefully in the corner with her infant beside her. Tears filled her eyes as she looked at them both and wondered what was to become of them. Would she find a safe haven for them in the dark bleak moorland of Drumfree?

She knew of the hardship that they would have to endure. She prayed alone to her God that he would witness her misery and distress and come to their aid. Not wishing to disturb their sleep she rose and lay down beside her daughter and slept.

TRAPPED IN THE BOG

They slept long into the morning and were awakened by the calling of a vixen to her cubs.
"I wonder what time it is?" Bríge rose stiffly from her makeshift bed and moving to the door looked out into the empty bog.
"I'll go to the stream and fetch some water. You get a fire going." Her mother picked up the tin can and left the scalp.
"God but it's foggy out there, I can hardly see my hand before me."
"You had best be careful now, remember to stay on the path." Mary warned her.
There were so many paths leading in different directions that she was unsure which led to the stream. She could hear frogs croaking some distance ahead of her. She listened carefully and gambled that the path to her right led to the stream. Treading carefully she soon found herself standing beside the stream.
"Thank God I made it." She silently prayed as she reached down and filled the can.
The mist began to thicken obliterating the path. The only way she could keep to the narrow path and away from the dangerous mire on her return was by carefully retracing her steps. That was easier said than done. She looked for a marker but there were none. She could no longer see the scalp and became disorientated. Escape was impossible and having lost her way she began to panic. She wandered deeper into the bog losing all sense of direction. Her feet sank deeper into the mire and movement was becoming impossible. Soon she found that she was unable to move in any direction. She was now trapped in the moving bog. She stood still and began to shiver uncontrollably. In her terror she could not call out. She felt herself sinking deeper into the quagmire. The mist rose and she saw the glow from the fire. Regaining her composure she began calling.
"Mary I'm sinking in the bog. In God's name please help me." She continued pleading as the mist again slowly obliterated the light from the fire.
"Where are you mother, keep calling?" She heard the comforting voice of her daughter echo in the distance.
"I'm sinking in the bog please get help." She cried in desperation.
"I'm coming, I can hear your voice." Mary reassured her.
"No Mary. Don't try to find me, run and get help."
"Lie down flat in the bog and remain still." She advised her mother.
"You cannot save me on your own, don't risk the lives of us both. Get some help." Her mother again pleaded.

"There's no one here to help only me, keep calling I'll find you. Is there a path to the left of the fire?" She questioned.
"I don't know, in God's holy name run for help." Her mother cried out in terror as she felt herself slowly being sucked deeper into the bog.
"I'll light a spleen, I'll find you have no fear." Mary tore dry rushes from the inside of the scalp and bound them tightly round a stick with a piece of calico from her shift.
Setting the rushes alight she held it above her head and began searching for the path.
"You're going the wrong way, keep to your left. Please hurry, I'm sinking fast." Her mother cried out on seeing the light going away from where she was trapped.
Mary ignoring her mothers warning held the spleen high above her head and continued on down the path.
"Where are you mother? Keep calling, keep calling?" She insisted.
"Oh Mary it's too late, you'll never be able to save me on your own."
"I can hear you, keep calling. Are you lying on the bog?" She held the spleen higher hoping to see her mother and to encourage her.
"I cannot lie down for I'm trapped up to my waist."
Mary, throwing caution to the wind followed the path to where she presumed her mother was trapped.
"Call to me mother, please let me hear your voice. If you can see the spleen tell me how near I am to you." She pleaded
"I'm over to your left but I don't know if there is a path. For God's sake tread carefully Mary." Her mother warned.
The mist began to rise from the surface of the bog as quickly as it had descended.
"I can see you mother, I'm over here." She waved the spleen in the air.
Coming to the edge of the swamp she looked across at her mother and was shocked to see her trapped waist deep in the quagmire.
"How am I going to get out?" She pleaded.
"Now don't panic, follow my instructions. Take your shawl off and tie it round your waist." Mary stuck the spleen in the ground and removed her own shawl. Her mother tied her shawl as best she could round her waist as instructed.
"Now I'm going to pass you mine and I want you to tie them tightly together." She threw the end of the shawl to her mother.
"Can you reach it?" She watched as her mother tried to retrieve the shawl.
"It's not long enough, I cannot grasp it." She tried in vain to reach out for the end of the shawl but the suction from the bog held her fast.

"Don't worry I'll make it longer." Her daughter assured her. Removing her long skirt she tied it to her shawl and again threw it towards her.

"That's it. I've got it now." Her mother caught the end of the skirt and tied it to her shawl.

"Please! I don't want to die here. Get me out, please! " She began to struggle. Mary felt herself being dragged deeper into the bog as her mother panicked and began pulling on the makeshift rope.

"Stop struggling, you are making matters worse, relax and I'll pull you out." Mary promised. Once again she took a firm grip of the makeshift rope and tried to pull her mother from the mire. She knew that she alone would not be strong enough for the task.

"Hold on Mother, I'll lie down on the bog and hold the rope until help arrives." She prostrated herself on the surface of the bog hoping that it would keep her mother from sinking deeper. It was to no avail, was she to become a victim of the bog? Slowly she felt herself sliding nearer to where her mother was trapped. In order to escape from her entrapment she released the rope.

"Stay still, I'll be back in a minute. Whatever you do try and keep calm." Slipping and sliding Mary dragged herself from the bog and on to the path.

"Mary, go back and see to Michael. There's little hope for me, before you go say the act of contrition with me." Her mother challenged on seeing her daughter coming back down the path carrying a tree trunk.

"I'll pull you out, you'll see." She dragged the tree trunk towards where her mother was and slid it on to the bog.

"It's no use I cannot reach it." Her mother cried in despair.

Mary continued pushing the trunk towards her mother. When she reached the makeshift rope she tied it round the log and retreated from the bog dragging the log behind her.

"How are you Mother?" She called when she reached the path.

"Hurry Mary, Oh God I fear I'm lost."

Ignoring her mothers pleas she rolled the log down the opposite side of the path and into the cutting. Crawling down she straddled herself across the log embedding it into the side of the bog at the same time.

"Is it holding?" She called to her mother as she pushed it into the side of the cutting.

"It's holding Mary, but what use is it. I will soon drown or die from the cold and exposure. When I'm no more go back to the cottage of Molly Cullhane. That's the only hope for you and Michael beag." Her mother pleaded.

"Save your strength, it's morning and I'm sure that there will be sleadors coming on the bog early." She encouraged her mother.

She began singing and encouraged her mother to join her. The song echoed in the still air as the morning sunburnt *'Jack-O-Lantern'* off the bog.
"Quiet mother, I thought I heard something." They listened and hoped.
"It's only a fox calling." Her mother despondently replied.
"That's no fox, that's a dog. *HELP! HELP! HELP!* Mary called into the dawn. Her mother began to cry.
"Look! Will you look mother it's a dog, it's a dog I tell you. *HELP! HELP! PLEASE HELP US."* Mary knew that where there was a dog there would be people.
From out of the mist came two sleadors with their sláns over their shoulders. They were running to where the calling came from.
"Over here, over here, please hurry." Mary climbed back on to the path and began to wave and call.
"Whatever is the matter?" The elder of the sleadors called.
"We are trapped in the bog, over here." She again cried.
"Jesus help us how did this happen? Paul run to the cutting and get a pole ladder, hurry man." The elder man called to his companion.
Pulling the log up from the cutting he opened the knot holding the shawl.
"Don't do that, she'll slip deeper into the bog." Mary warned.
"It's alright girl we know what we are doing." The sleador assured her.
"That's it Paul slide it out towards me." The elder man instructed.
Crawling out on the rungs of the ladder he soon reached her mother.
"We'll soon have you out of there, can you lift your arms?" There was no response.
"I think she's unconscious " He placed his hand on the woman's forehead.
"Do as I say and be as quick as you can, then come back here. Do you understand?"
Having secured the skirt to the ladder he returned to the bank and joined his son.
"Now Paul you and the girl go to the back of the ladder. Rock it gently when I tell you to." His father retired to the centre of the ladder and sat on it.
"Now Paul start rocking." He shouted to his son.
"It's no good dad it won't move. She's trapped too deep."
"Get down into the cutting and pull as hard as you can on the rungs." His father encouraged them.
"That won't do. Here girl you sit here and tell us if she moves?" Mary was directed out across the ladder to her mother's side.
"Now Paul, one two, three, pull. One two three, pull." Both men kept a steady motion on the end of the ladder.

As the ladder began a pendulum motion they put all their weight on the end of it forcing it to rock.

"She's moving! She's moving! Thank God she's moving. Come on, come on try harder." Mary encouraged the men as her mother was dragged slowly from her grave.

Reluctantly the bog released her mother until with a suction movement she was catapulted on to the surface where she lay still.

"She's out, she's safe. Thank God, thank God." Mary prayed aloud.

"Don't go out there, come back." Paul, on seeing Mary moving towards her mother warned her.

"Isn't one of you trapped in the bog enough, stay where you are." His father shouted in annoyance.

"Now Paul lets get her out." The men pulled the ladder with her mother attached to it out of the bog and on to the path.

"She's dead, Oh God she is dead." Mary cried as she hugged her mother.

"Paul bring a hand sleigh from the bog. You girl, go back to the 'Scalp' and light the biggest fire that you can. Then boil lots of hot water." The elderly man instructed.

Mary continued piling turf on the fire as she watched for the two men. She waited for what seemed like hours but was only a matter of minutes before she saw them appear out of the bog dragging the sleigh.

On reaching the fire she was delighted to see her mother lying on it.

"Come over here and get her clothes off, quick as you can and place her as near to the fire as possible. Then get some dry cloths and straw and rub her down." The man ignoring the nakedness of the women ordered.

"Come on give her a hot drink, don't just stand there." He ordered Mary who was standing in a trance some distance away praying.

"You may as well stop son, she is gone. May the Lord have mercy on her soul." The elderly man looked into her eyes.

"She is not dead, she cannot be." Mary dropped the can and ran to the side of the sleigh.

Fumbling through her portmanteau she found what she was looking for.

She withdrew a piece of broken mirror and rubbed the surface of it. Holding it close to her mother's mouth she tried encouraging her to breathe. All her efforts were in vain, the mirror remained clear. She knew that her mother had passed from life to mortal dream.

She knelt on the clod sodden bog and blessing herself recited the final act of contrition on behalf of her mother. Again the mist slowly obliterated the watery sun. A rainbow began creeping over Derryveagh Mountains and came to rest high above the bier where her mother lay. She noticed that although it hung over the bog it never touched the ground. She heard her mother's voice crying in the wind.

"Mo cushla, Rainbows seldom touch the ground of Ireland anymore."

"O God in heaven what is to become of me now?" She held her mother to her and began weeping.

"Come on girl, go back to the fire, we will get her dressed." A sympathetic hand was laid on her shoulder.

Mary was in the scalp rocking her baby to and fro when the men returned. They rested in silence for some time looking into the fire.

"Should we bury your mother in the little graveyard yonder?" Paul, breaking the silence gently asked.

"No! No you'll not bury her here in this God forsaken place." Mary cried.

"What do you want us to do then?" He asked.

"I will give you two sovereigns if you take her to Dungloe to lie beside my father."

"Should we agree, will you be coming with us?" The elderly man asked.

"I must take my son back to the cottage of Molly Cullhane first. I will meet you in Dungloe. That is if it is alright with you?"

"Of course, of course we will, won't we dad?" Paul looked towards his father for confirmation.

"My name is John Murphy and this is my son Paul. You know Molly then, do you?"

"I do that, she was a very good friend to us." Mary nodded.

"Molly Cullhane is the salt of the earth, tell her that we were enquiring as to her health."

"On your way then Mary, your mother will be in good hands, God rest her soul."

"We'll wait for you in Dungloe, and don't worry." Paul encouraged her to leave.

THE OLD WOMAN OF THE ROADS

Oh to Have a little house!
To own the hearth and stool and all!
The heaped up sods upon the fire,
The pile of turf against the wall!

To have a clock with weights and chains
And pendulum swinging up and down!
A dresser filled with shining delph,
Speckled with white and blue and brown!

I could be busy all the day
Clearing and sweeping hearth and floor,
And fixing on their shelves again
My white and blue and speckled store!
I could be quiet there at night
Beside the fire and by myself,
Sure of a bed and loath to leave
The ticking clock and the shining delph!

Och! But I'm weary of mist and dark,
And roads where there's never a house or bush,
And tired I am of bog and road
And the crying wind and the lonesome hush"
And I am praying to God on high,
And I am praying Him night and day,
For a little house- a house of my own
Out of the winds and rains way.

PADRIC COLUM

RETURN TO GLENDOWER

Mary wrapped her infant son in a warm blanket and took the long road back through the wind swept mountain to the home of Molly Cullhane.
The crying wind and the lonesome wailing of the wild mingled with the occasional clatter of falling rocks off the face of the Derryveagh mountains mocked her. Darkening clouds raced over the peaks carrying with it cutting sleet. They swept across the rock face licking the settling snow from its surface.
The mysterious ever-calling voice of the mountain came closer to her as she entered the final stages of her journey. It came first in a sobbing cry and when ignored then in threatening outbursts. It did not always roar and moan for at times it was hushed, silent, quiet, waiting. The clouds parted like the curtain of night to reveal a haunting moon on the stage of life. Raising her light above the dark mountain it disclosed the infinity of the bog road. Slowly the curtain of night again closed hiding the moon. She knew that the mountain was mocking her as it had her late mother and brother. It had put aside her love and buried it in the foreboding bog. This is indeed a cruel and lonely place, she thought. She had plenty of time to remember her short life and her family. The occasional hush and stillness of the valley seemed to awaken long cherished memories.
Memories she gladly accepted. The times she spent with Tomás beag and her parents. The little surprise gifts her father would bring home, perhaps a rag doll for her, a rattle that he made with his own hands for Tomás beag and a camán (Hurley) for Séan. She remembered too when the autumn came and he brought home a handful of rosy apples from the big house. There was great excitement when her mother took the apple cake from the griddle pan and set it on the table. She continued to recount the more pleasant incidents in her life.
"Shure if nothing else it will pass the time." She spoke as her tears clouded her vision.
She was deliberately trying to suppress all the dark sorrow she had endured. Ahead of her lay the steep climb to the home of Molly. Time was moving on and fatigue was taking its toll. She watched the watery sun sinking slowly below the Derryveagh Mountains and hastened her steps.
"Muise, go dtugaid Dia ciall dúinn go léir agus go bf égaid Sé an tsláinte aguinn."
(May God give us sense and leave us the health). She intoned.
"Here am I dandering and day dreaming when I should be hastening my steps." She chastised herself as she tightened her shawl round her infant son.

She knew that Molly would be sitting by her fire numbering her beads and praying for them. The rain penetrated her shawl as the mist began to obliterate the valley floor. Ignoring the stones cutting deep into her bared feet she covered her infant son and made haste up the old boréen.

"Nac gcuirfead sin fearg ar naom." (Wouldn't that vex a saint) She cried out as she slipped on the moving shale cutting her feet in the process.

Seeing the welcoming door of Molly's cottage she began calling.

"Molly, Molly Cullhane will you open the door in God's holy name. My mother is dead." She cried as she tightened the wet blanket around her infant son.

The door remained tightly closed and why not? It was there to protect the occupants from the cruel rain and cold.

"Oh Molly open the door. In the name of God open the door or we will perish." She slapped her palm against the unyielding door and fell on the threshold weeping. Her task was completed; she had brought her son to safety through the mountains. A watery red blood permeated from her feet staining the resting stone. She felt herself falling.

Molly tossed and turned in her sleep. The distant dull sound of calling and the rapping on her door disturbed her.

The wind had now subsided, its rage spent. No longer did the sleet seek refuge on her window only to be licked off by a greedy gust of wind. All was calm yet there was something or someone outside besides the night. Unable to sleep she rose and going to her door called through the stout oak.

"Who's there?" She paused and listened. Did she hear a child? Drawing the stout bolt she lifted the latch and opened the door.

As the door opened Mary wrapped in her shawl fell backward into the kitchen and remained still. Her infant son began to cry as he rolled from her numbed arms.

"Oh God be good to us all what has happened Mary?" She opened the door wider and looked out into the darkness hoping to see her mother.

Hearing the infant crying she picked him up and placed him next to the fire. Dragging Mary clear of the door she closed it against the night.

Returning to the threshold she again opened the door and looked into the darkness. Where was Bríge?

"Bríge Kearney, answer me where are you?" She called into the night. Her voice echoed through the mountains before fading into the valley floor. "God in heaven whatever happened this night?" She continued to call as she searched outside the cottage.

Returning to the cottage she closed the door. Dragging Mary nearer to the fire she riddled life into it. She went to the dresser and instinctively took out the 'Connail Mhór' and lit it. She placed it in the window recess.

"Jesus, Mary and Joseph guide your feet Brige Kearney to the home of Molly Cullhane." She prayed as she blessed herself. Brige would see the light and be assured her daughter was safe. Turning her attention to the child she removed his clothing and placed him in a ciscéan filled with clean straw and lay him beside the fire. She filled a stán pigín (tin mug) with warm water from the corcán and held it to Mary's lips.

"Wake up Mary, come on wake up will you?" She pleaded as she encouraged her to drink.

Mary opened her eyes and began to cough.

"What happened? Where is my baby?" She called between a bout of coughing.

"Your infant is well Mary, where is your mother?"

"Mother! Mother is dead. She is dead. It is so..." Mary collapsed into her arms. Removing her wet clothing she dressed her in a clean shift and placed her in the 'Leaba Suidheacán' (Settled Bed) beside the fire.

It was late morning when Mary was awakened by the crying of her infant son.

"There mo leanb, hush! Hush, your mother is resting." Molly spoke quietly to the child

"Oh Molly, what ever is to become of us? Mother is dead." Mary sat up in the bed and again began to cry.

"Thank God you are alright Mary. Were my ears deceiving me last night?" Molly wrung her hands in sorrow.

"No Molly, I wish to God that it were otherwise. Mother perished out in the bog."

"God rest her soul. I had best get some help to bring her body home."

"There's no need." Through her tears Mary related what had happened to her mother.

"John Murphy is a good man. If he promised to return your mother's body to Dungloe then as sure as there is a fire in the grate he will." She assured her.

Next morning she awoke early and fed her child. Molly noticed that she had her bag packed.

"I'll leave Michael with you Molly if you don't mind and take the road to Dungloe. I'll come back as soon as possible." Mary rose from the bed and began dressing.

"Perhaps you should rest a little longer. However, if must be then it must be, Michael is in safe hands here." Molly assured her.

MARY IS REUNITED WITH HER NIGHTMARE

It was early spring in Donegal that morning when Mary led the sad cortège to the burial plot at Crohy Head. The sward leading to the graves of her father and brother had never before been so crammed with cowslips and primroses.
She searched the ocean and she looked towards the island where her uncle lived. She was hoping to see the Dolphins again. Alas there was no sign of them; the water was a pale blue with hardly a ripple on the surface. On the cliff face Guillemots, Puffins and razorbills fought for nesting places.
"Don't disturb the long sleep of Tomás beag and my parents." She pleaded as she saw the slán of the sleadór turn a fresh sod near to her father's grave.
Mindful of her concern they moved a few paces away and dug the fresh grave near by. Once again she left the graveside and went alone to the edge of the cliff and began looking out across the vast ocean.
She saw, as she knew she would the rainbow rise above Aireann Mhór and settle over the grave.
"When will the rainbow touch Talab na hÉireann?" She addressed the waves.
"Whatever are you going to do now Mary? I suppose you will be returning with us to Molly's cottage" John Murphy invaded her solitude.
She heard him calling to her but could not understand what he said. Her heart was heavy and tears rolled down her cheeks.
Retreating to the headland she picked a mixed bunch of primroses and cowslips and lay them on the fresh grave of her mother.
"Mary! What are you going to do now?" John Murphy came and lay his hand on her shoulder.
"Do! What can I do? I'll be taking my ease in Dungloe before I return. I'm in no fit state for the journey. Would you tell Molly that I'll be home within a day or two God willing."
"We understand and will to be sure to tell her, Bail Ó Dia ort." (God bless you)
"Go mbá h-amlaid duit." (The same to you) She replied.
Slowly she retreated from the graveside and took the boréen back to Dungloe. There she would seek shelter before returning to the cottage of Molly Cullhane to collect her son.
She was grateful when a good neighbour let her have the Leaba Suidheacán for the night. For that she would be offering up the indulgence.
Refreshed and anxious to be reunited with her son she rose early next morning and left the village.
Some Irish miles outside the village she stopped and sat down on the resting stone outside an abandoned cottage. She felt alone and despondent and was

fatigued. Her eyes grew heavy and leaning against the threshold she succumbed to sleep.
It was dusk when she was roused her from her slumber by someone shaking her roughly
"Wake up! Wake up there!" She opened her eyes and saw the figure of Frank McLaughlan towering over her.
"Was this a nightmare that had come to haunt her?" She thought.
Rubbing her eyes she saw standing some distance away a jaunting car and on the high seat sat Maura O'Reilly and another woman. This situation was disastrous and more loathsome than any horrendous nightmare she began to panic.
"Jesus, Mary and Joseph help me, what do you two want of me?" She asked.
"We heard you had returned. Tell me where have you hidden the infant?" The bailiff entered the abandoned cottage and began searching.
Mary seeing her chance of escape began running down the boréen.
"Come back here you little bitch." Looking round she saw Frank McLaughlan gaining on her.
Overpowering her he dragged her back to the gig and forcibly lifted her off the ground.
"Come on will you grab her." He called to the women.
"Let me go! Let me go." She screamed as the two women roughly dragged her towards the gig. After a brief struggle she was finally hauled on board.
"Hold her down, sit on her if you must." Frank McLaughlan instructed. The women pinned her in the well of the gig as the bailiff took the reins.
Once again she found herself incarcerated inside the walls of Cardavon castle. She was questioned time and time again as to the whereabouts of her infant son. Defiantly she refused to tell them for she knew that he would be sent away from her to a far county.
"Never mind, we have her back. As far as I'm concerned that's all that matters. Take her upstairs." His Lordship instructed.
Once again Mary was incarcerated in the castle. His Lordship was determined to install her as his *'Tally Woman'* again.
Mary was having none of it and refused all platitudes.

THE MURDER OF MARY KEARNEY

Mary cursed Lord Kilgarvan from her heart. It was he who was responsible for the death of her mother and for that there would be no forgiveness.
She swore to her God that at the first opportunity she would see him dead. It was he who was responsible for the death of her mother. It was he who now deprived her of her son. An only son she was reluctantly forced to abandon into the care of Molly Cullhane.
Would she ever see him in this life again she wondered?
She continued to resist her captors and was intent on causing as much mayhem as possible.
"Take her to the east wing and put her in the tower." Instructed his Lordship. He was no longer able to manipulate her or force her into submission.
They frog marched her out of the main building and incarcerated in a small room on the first floor of the tower.
"You can shout and scream all you want to now, nobody will hear you." Lord Kilgarvan slammed the door shut and turned the key.
"Here! You see to her, and when she's chastised return her to the castle." He handed the key to Maura O'Reilly and left the tower.
"You took from me my immortal soul. You condemned me to everlasting Hell fire for my sins. I'll see you burn in Hell, Lord Kilgarvan." She screamed her curses at him as he left.
Maura O'Reilly tried to appease her but without success.
"I thought that you were my friend, why did you betray me?" She challenged her.
"I never betrayed you, you came back to Dungloe and were seen. Tell us where the child is and it will be alright." She promised.
"Go to Hell you Judas, you will never learn where he is. *Never*, do you hear me, *Never.*" She stood rebellious before her tormentor.
"Very well then, you will stay here until you come to your senses."
She continued to refuse all platitudes, swearing that she would die rather than submit.
Mary worried more for the welfare of her baby son than for her own.
She pleaded with Maura to release her.
"If you behave yourself you can be reunited with your son." Maura O'Reilly promised one evening.
"Oh thank God, thank you Maura. Where is my son, is he here? Please I beg of you." She pleaded
"Your son is being brought to the castle and should be here within the week."

Maura O'Reilly promised.

"What of Lord Kilgarvan, where is he?"

"His lordship is away in Dublin and is not expected back for at least two weeks."

On hearing this and the assurance of Maura O'Reilly that she would be reunited with her son she agreed to return to the castle peacefully.

As the weeks passed and with no sign of her son she became suspicious of their motives and again became rebellious.

Matters came to a head some weeks later when his Lordship returned and learnt that she had been moved back into the castle. That night he came to her room in a drunken state.

"So you came to your senses Mary, my blood boils in my veins to possess you here and now. I'll not leave this room this night, do you understand?" Reaching out her took hold of her and began tearing at her clothing.

"Leave me alone or as true as there is a God in Heaven I'll swing for you." She swore as she fled from his grasp.

"We'll see about that, now come here this instant." Lifting his riding crop he lashed out at her. Staggering across the room he lunged at her and fell heavily to the floor.

Mary retreated to the casement and found herself trapped between the window and Lord Kilgarvan.

"Now I've got you, come here." Reaching out he took her by the arm and pulled her towards him.

Throwing her heavily on the bed he once again began tearing at her clothing. Most of which were now in shreds and exposing her nudity. This encouraged and excited him. Opened his breeches he held her down and forcing her legs apart tried to seduce her.

"I said that I would swing for you and by God I will." She spat into his face. As he tried to remove the spittle she drew her fingernails down his cheeks. She felt her nails dig deep into his flesh and felt the hot blood seep between her fingers.

She did not care. This was the fiend that raped and sodamised her when she was but a child. This was the brute that sent her mother to an early grave. The more she thought about what the brute had inflicted on her and her mother the more satisfaction she gained from her treatment to him.

He began screaming in agony and fell to the floor holding his hands to his face.

"I'm blind, I'm blind" He staggered around the room screaming in a demented state.

The door was opened and Maura O'Reilly entered the room.

"What is going on here?" She looked at his lordship wreathing in agony on the floor.

"Get me some help, She tried to kill me." He screamed.

Maura O'Reilly ran from the room and returned carrying a basin of hot water and a flannel.

"Hold steady Sir. When you are cleaned up I'll take a good look." She began to wipe his face.

Mary sat on the bed ignoring her nakedness. In a trance she watched Maura O'Reilly wash the face of her tormentor.

"You will need to have the surgeon look at your wounds." She informed him.

"How could you do such a thing to him?" She turned on Mary.

"I warned him that I would kill him and you too. You had for your own sakes best release me here and now." She demanded.

Staggering from the bed he went to the mirror and was shocked on seeing his reflection. A watery blood covered his face and deep scratches disfigured his features. He looked in horror at the watery blood running down his face.

"Look at me? I'm disfigured for life. I'll…" Before he finished the sentence Mary came off the bed and picked up the basin. She threw the contents over him before attacking him with it.

A fierce and bloody struggle followed before he finally overpowered her and threw her heavily back on to the bed.

Ignoring the presence of Maura O'Reilly he pulled her forward by her legs. As she fell back in the bed he once again attempted to rape her. Mary tried to rise and as she did he punched her full in the face.

She lay in a stupor unable to defend herself as blood poured from her broken nose. She began to cough as her blood entered her mouth and began to choke her.

"I said I would take you and by God I will." He screamed as he sadistically and unashamedly abused her again and again.

"Please! In God's name help me, please." No longer able to resist him she weakly pleaded with Maura O'Reilly. The look of horror and shame on her face told the story.

"Release her Sir, you don't know what you are doing, I beg of you listen to me." Maura O'Reilly was now in a state of agitation.

"Release her! The Irish bitch, I'll make her pay dearly for what she did to me. Hold her down." He demanded.

Maura O'Reilly as in a trance took hold of Mary's hands and pulled her across the bed and held her face down. She was unaware that his intentions were to take his revenge on her in the most obscene and bestial manner. Having satisfied his lust he again ran his hands over his scarred face and let out a demonic scream. Grabbing his riding crop he began brutally beating her. Her screams echoed throughout the house then all was silent.

"Stop now Sir, that's enough. Please you are going too far." Maura O'Reilly let go of Mary's hands and ran round the bed to the side of her master. She pleaded with him to stop and tried to restrain his hand.

"Stop! I'll stop when I'm good and ready," He panted as he paused for breath before resuming the vicious beating. He had lost all sense of reasoning in his drunken frenzy for revenge. There were no more cries of protest from Mary; she lay in a crumpled heap on the bed.

" In God's name stop. Can't you see she's unconscious." Again Maura O'Reilly went to his side and again tried to stop him.

"Get away, I'm not through with her yet. This is one chastisement she will not forget in a hurry." He pushed her across the room as in his demented state he continued beating at the unconscious body.

Maura O'Reilly found herself crashing against the casement. She looked in horror at her master. The look on his face told her that he was insane.

A watery blood oozed from the wounds on Mary's back and buttocks. She no longer cried out. Her body lay crumpled on the bed oblivious to the pain.

Having exhausted his revenge on her he sat down and threw the riding crop across the room. The crop landed beside Maura O'Reilly.

"Look! What's got into you?" She picked up the riding crop and rising to her feet she approached the bed. Rocking backwards and forwards he collapsed into a sadistic laugh.

"Look at this? What sort of an animal are you? Are you mad?" She held the riding crop before him. Blood soaked flesh hung in shreds from the leather binding.

"Mad! I'll show you who's mad. Get out of my way before I give you the same." Wiping the spittle forming on his mouth he rose and adjusted his breeches that were round his ankles. Reaching above the bed he tore the silken pull cord from the ceiling and twisted it in his hands.

Pulling Mary's head back with the cord he tied it around her neck and pulled it tight. She heard the crack as he broke her neck.

"Let go, In God's name let go. You've murdered the girl, are you possessed of the Devil?" She screamed at him.

"Never mind her, look at my face?" Unconcerned as to what he had done he untied his hands from the cord and threw it on top of her body. Again he approached the mirror and tenderly inspected his injuries.

As there was no movement from Mary, Maura O'Reilly approached the bed and looked down at her.

There was no clean flesh that she could see. She had been beaten to a pulp. "I think you killed her. Oh my God, come and look." She held her hands over the body unwilling to touch the mangled flesh.

"Killed her, what are you talking about?" Grabbing a decanter he took a deep drink and staggered towards the bed. Again he took a long drink before looking down at the carnage he inflicted.

"Help me to turn her over and let me see." He muttered as he placed the decanter on the side table.

Together they turned her over; Maura O'Reilly looked in horror. Mary's lifeless blood soaked eyes were open and staring at them.

"What can we do? We will have to send for the constabulary?" She distanced herself from his side.

"There will be no constabulary calling here. She has nobody belonging to her." Again he took a deep drink from the decanter before flinging it across the room. "What do you mean? What do you intend doing with her?" Maura O'Reilly moved further away as he made to approach her.

"You're not frightened of me, are you? Now shut up and let me think, she brought this on herself." He added without remorse, trying to justify his conduct.

"She is dead. Don't you understand, what are we to do?" Maura O'Reilly covered Mary's body with a blanket.

"We will take her to the crypt and lock her into one of the coffins. This will remain a secret between you and me. Do you understand, we will hide her in a coffin." He muttered incoherently.

"You cannot do that, we must report the matter. I will tell them that she attacked you, but we must inform the constabulary." She pleaded.

"Cannot! Cannot, I am the law here, do you understand? Tell them, tell them what? That you were an accomplice to her killing, you know that they would hang you."

"But I done nothing wrong I pleaded with you to stop. You cannot blame me, you cannot." She pleaded.

"And who would believe your story tell me, you an ignorant Irish peasant? Don't make me laugh we will dispose of her body quietly and nobody will be any the wiser, do you understand?" He insisted.

Mary's body wrapped in the blood soaked blanket was taken that evening by Maura O'Reilly and the bailiff to the family mausoleum. His lordship went before them and opened the iron door.

"Where should we put her, Sir?" Frank asked as they lay her sagging body on the floor.

"I'll open this one down here." He pointed to a large oak coffin gathering dust on a stone slab.

Removing the brass thumbscrews he removed the heavy lid and lay it against the wall.

"Come on lift her up and put her inside." He called.

"I cannot do it, I just cannot." Maura O'Reilly stood some distance from the body nervously wringing her hands.

"Never mind her, come on help me to lift her." His Lordship called to his bailiff.

They placed Mary's body on top of the skeleton inside the coffin and secured the lid.

"Nobody will ever think of looking in that coffin. Keep quiet about this both of you, do you understand?" He warned as he replaced the lid and screwed it back on the coffin.

Pushing the iron door to he turned the key. Through the darkness they returned to the castle.

Next day they let it be known that once again Mary had left the castle of her own free will.

A ROUGH RHYME ON A ROUGH MATTER

The merry brown hare came leaping
Over the crest of the hill,
Where the clover and corn lay sleeping
Under the moonlight still.
There's blood on your new foreign shrubs, squire;
There's blood on your new pointer's feet;
There's blood on the game that you sell, squire,
And there's blood on the game that you eat!"

Leaping up late and early,
Till under their bite and their tread
The Swede, and the wheat and the barley,
Lay cankered, and trampled, and dead.
A poacher's widow sat sighing
On the side of the white chalk bank,
Where under the gloomy fir-woods
One spot in the ley throve rank.

She watched a long tuft of clover
Where neither rabbit nor hare never ran;
For its black sour haulm covered over
The blood of her murdered man.
She thought of the dark plantation
And the hares and her husband's blood
And the voice of her indignation
Rose up to the throne above.

You have sold the labouring man, squire,
Body and soul to shame,
To pay for your seat in the house, squire
And to pay for the feed of your game.
You made him a poacher yourself, squire,
When you'd give neither work nor meat;
And your barley-fed hares robbed the garden
As our starving children died at your feet;

When packed in one reeking cabin,
Man, maid, mother, and little ones lay;
While the rain pattered in on the rotting bride-bed
And the walls let in the day;
When we lay in our burning fever
On the mud of the cold clay floor,

Till you parted us all from our mothers, squire,
At the cursed workhouse door.

We quarrelled like brutes, and who wonders?
What self-respect could we keep,
Worse housed than your hacks and your pointers,
Worse fed than your hogs and your sheep?
Our daughters with base-born babies
Have wandered away in their shame;
If your misses had slept, squire, where we did,
Your misses might do the same.

You may tire of the gaol and the workhouse,
And take to allotments and schools,
But you've run up a debt that will never
Be repaid by cunning and ruse.
In the season of shame and sadness,
In the dark and dreary day,
When scrofula, gout, and madness
Are eating your race away;

When the kennels and liveried varlets
You have cast your daughters' bread;
And worn out with liquor and harlots,
Your heir at your feet lies dead;
When your youngest, the mealy-mouthed rector,
Lets your soul rot asleep in your grave,
You will find in your God the protector
Of the freeman you fancied your slave.

She looked at the fresh bit of clover,
And wept till her heart grew light;
And at last, when her passion was over,
Went wandering out into the night.
She died that night on the hill, squire
Beside the fresh grave of her man
Her rosary lay silent beside her
There's a curse on you and your clan.
But the merry brown hare came leaping
Over the uplands still,
Where the clover and corn lay sleeping
On the side of the white chalk hill.

MOLLY ADOPTS MICHAEL KEARNEY

John Murphy and his son came to the door of the cottage of Molly Cullhane and lifting the latch entered.
"Well bless my old eyes, if it's not the pair of you. Mary Kearney told me you might call. Will you have a sup of tae?" She rose from her stooléen beside the fire.
"Sure we will and thanks." Paul removed his coatamore and hung it behind the door.
"God bless all here." John crossed the floor and turning his back to the fire lifted the tail of his coatamore against the heat.
"Come on now tell me how you fared in Dungloe." Molly pushed the crane holding the iron kettle over the coals.
"A sad day Molly, a sad day indeed. We buried her mother next to her husband and son as she requested. I expect Mary told you all about it. God be good to them all." He added as an afterthought.
"No, she hasn't come home yet. I expect that she is staying with her uncle over on the island. Did she say when she'd be coming back?" Molly lifted the lid from the kettle and placed two eggs inside.
"The poor cratur was so exhausted by the time she reached Crohy Head that she decided to take a rest in the cottage of Brenda Webb. She told us that she would be returning to Glendower before the weekend. "I'm surprised that she is not here yet. She seemed very anxious to return for the child." John informed her.
"So am I, if the truth be known. Sure she is only a child herself." Molly had no intentions of telling anyone that Mary was the mother of the child.
"I suppose you will take care of them for a time at least?"
"They're as welcome as the flowers in May to stay in the cottage of Molly Cullhane for as long as they want to. She's been away a long time I hope that she has not fallen ill. To tell you nothing but the truth I'm worried for her safety." She returned to the fire and poured boiling water into the tae pot and scalded it.
"Molly, do you know the Nuns missed a good one in you so they did." John complimented her on seeing her preparing the meal.
"Come on now the pair of you and less of the sweet talk, sit yourselves down."
"Sure a sup of spring water would have been just as welcome so it would. You're by far too generous to us." Paul watched her take the two boiled eggs from the kettle.
"It's a long hungry road to Finntown and you deserve better. You'll not be

forgotten in my prayers so you won't." Molly set the meal before the men and sat down beside the fire. She waited patiently hoping to learn all the gossip and how Mary fared in Dungloe. By the time the men had finished telling their story the light was fading.

"We had best be making our way down the mountain Paul. We'll bid you good night Molly. Thanks again for the supper it was appreciated."

"Before you go, would you ever say a decade of the rosary with me for the safe return of Mary?" Molly removed her worn beads from the back of the chair.

"Molly give me the beads, not alone will we say a decade for her but a whole rosary for the repose of the souls of Bríge, her husband and her son." John volunteered.

All too soon Molly was once again alone in the cottage. She watched as the two men made their way down the mountain path before they were swallowed up in the mist.

"Come on child, let's get you nursed before we settle down for the night." Picking up the infant she sat looking into the fire.

Next morning she awakened early in anticipation of Mary's arrival.

"It won't be long now, mo Cúshla, your mother will soon be home." Sitting on the resting stone she spoke to the child as she waited.

Several months passed and with no sighting of Mary she was very concerned for her welfare. "I hope to God that nothing has happened to you, Mary." She spoke aloud as she looked towards the valley and beyond. After a further month without any news or sighting she decided that she would have to take the rocky Derrydruel road to Dungloe. The mountains were snowbound after a week of heavy snow. If the weather permitted it she would cross the old bog road to Dungloe. Wrapping the infant in a warm blanket and placing her heavy Galway shawl around her shoulders she locked her cottage.

"If only I had a pair of stout boots then the journey would be all the shorter." She remarked as she looked down at her bare feet.

"A prayer would not go amiss, now would it Michael?" She smiled down at the child.

Two days later she saw the village before her and hastened her steps.

"Go soirbigid Dia duit An Clocán Liat (God prosper you Dungloe)" She prayed.

Knocking on the open half door of a cottage she sought refuge. A jovial woman opened the door. Molly held the child close to her and appealed to her host.

"Tá ocras orm. Tabair dom rud eicínt le n-ite má's é do toil é? (I am hungry could I have some food please.)

"Tar istaec agus céad míle fáilte romat. Tá atas orm tú feiceál." (A hundred thousand welcomes to you. I am glad to see you.) The woman greeted her in her native tongue.

"Dia 's Muire duit is Pádraig" (May God, Mary and Saint Patrick bless you) This was the custom in the Irish countryside. Molly took her place by the fire without further apologies or ceremony.

"I expect you have been long on the road?" The Bean-ó-Tig took the bellows in her hands encouraging life into the fire.

"A long ways indeed. I crossed the Derryveagh Mountains above Lough Muck no later than this morning." Molly informed her.

"God help you, a rough road so I'm told." The woman pulled the creel over the coals.

"Rough, why there's little need for me to climb Cnoc Pádraig in order to enter the kingdom of heaven. I done my penance on the climb here." Molly laid the infant down beside the fire.

"That's a fine healthy looking child you have there, God bless him. Will I put him in the Leaba suidheacán when you have a sup of tae. It is a boy I presume?"

"He is indeed, his name is Michael Kearney. My name is Molly Cullhane from Glendower."

"I'm Mary Culligan, come on sit nearer to the fire and lets have the craic. There's a fine sheep's head sitting in the corcan and we will have a sup of broth before bedtime."

"I'm looking for the cottage of Brenda Webb, it was there that his mother stayed after the burial of her mother. Do you know of her?" Molly asked.

"I do indeed. So she's the daughter of the woman that drowned in the bog. God help the poor orphan. Here get this down you." Mary placed a bowl of hot broth on the table.

Molly sat beside the fire making a vain effort to stay awake as Mary continued gossiping. Slowly her eyes closed.

"My trouble is that I don't know when to stop talking, let's get some rest, you have a long journey before you to morrow." Mary shook her awake.

Mary awakened Molly the following morning, in her hand she held a mug of hot milk.

"You must have been tired, I thought you were never going to wake up. I've seen to your child. He has a great appetite, thank God." Mary smiled benevolently.

"You should have called me, I feel shamed sleeping in so long."

"It will do you good Molly, Brenda lives some two miles down the Derrydruel road. It's a long tiring road so it is."

"I've come so far now that another mile or two will make little difference. Like you Mary Culligan I'm thinking I made my heaven on earth."
"Heaven, who was talking of heaven? What I'm looking for is a man to look after my small holding." She laughed.
"That should be little problem to a fine woman like yourself."
"Problem is it, will you look at me, long past child bearing years and with two Irish acres of rocky land to offer as a dowry. He would have to be a saint or an amadán to take me and that dowry on." Mary spread her hands in resignation.
"Away with you Mary, sure you're only having the craic with me. Now I must be off."
Molly found herself on a mud road beside a small lake. She could hear the seas pounding the coast not too far away.
It was late evening and the wind rose from the sea bringing with it squally rain. A few misshapen willows growing beside the seashore bent double like cripples fought bravely against overwhelming odds. A melancholy elegy mourned their demise.
"Would you know where the cottage of Brenda Webb is?" She called to a man crossing a stile.
"You cannot miss it Missus, it's on your right about two hundred yards down by the lake shore."
"Thank you, thank you kindly and God bless you." Molly replied.
"No trouble at all, thanks for the blessing and the same to you." The man lifted his caubéen out of respect before continuing his journey.
"The cottage is farther away than I thought it would be." She panted on seeing it silhouetted in the distant waning light.
"Would this be the cottage of Brenda Webb?" She called to a woman trying to close the door of her coop against the wind.
"That's myself, is there something that I can do for you? Come on up to the cottage. It's a cross looking day is it not, thanks be to God?" She finally succeeded in securing the door.
"I'm a friend of Mary Kearney and was worried when she did not come home. I'm told that she stayed with you." Molly introduced herself.
"She did, she did indeed. It was the occasion of the burial of her mother, God rest her soul. Are you telling me that she has not come home yet? Wherever could she have got to? Come into the cottage out of the cold." Brenda invited.
"I am that, shure I'm worried sick looking for her, so I am. It's as if the earth opened up and swallowed her. God between us and all harm." Molly was getting excited.
"Sit down and calm yourself. I should have offered you a cahir, excuse my bad

manners. I'll pull the ciotal (Kettle) over the coals." Brenda apologised.
"Do you know if she has anyone belonging to her here about that she might have gone to?" Molly asked.
"I know that she has an uncle over at Leabgarrow, but it is doubtful if she has gone there." Brenda continued to busy herself over the coals as she spoke.
"Leabgarrow, how far away might that be?"
"You'll not be going there, not in this weather that's for sure. It's on the Aran Island. She told me that she was returning to Glendowar. I'm sure she would not have gone there without letting me know."
"Perhaps she met her uncle and changed her mind. She was very distressed as you can well imagine." Molly suggested.
"No! She would never go all that way without telling me. She was one sensible girl and was determined to return to Glendowar come what may." Brenda assured her.
"Come on now pull up you chair and have a sup of tae." Brenda called as she placed an egg in a mug filled with sand to hold it firm.
"You'll spend the night here and no argument about it. To morrow God willing when the storm has passed you can decide what you want to do."

MOLLY DISCLOSES MARY'S SECRET

"You were telling me Brenda of her uncle over in the Aran Island. I'm wondering should I go and visit him now that the weather has mended?" Molly asked.
"You could do worse Molly. It's a long road and you would need to get to Ailt an Chorrain. The weather is in your favour and you have a good chance of getting across in one of the curraghs." Brenda looked out from the half door.
"Are the curraghs safe I heard a lot about them?" Molly was feeling apprehensive.
"Safe is it, why they have been using them since long before Saint Brendan came to these shores. Of course there is the occasional accident. But then shure that is the will of Almighty God." Brenda dismissed her fears.
"That's it then, I'll take myself off now that the weather is fine."
"Will you look at that Brenda? A good sign if ever there was one." Molly looked across the valley to where a large rainbow was draping its myriad colours over the horizon.
"I see. A rainbow is it, ah well! At least the weather is on the mend?" Brenda was not about to tell her of the premonition that rainbows brought to that part of the country.
"Do you think I should take the road then?" Molly asked.
"Myself I'd leave it for a day sure there is no hurry." She was concerned about the appearance of the rainbow.
"I'll be guided by you Brenda, I'm sure you know all about the weather here about."
Next morning Molly rose early and was pleased to see a gentle mist rising above the valley floor.
"Brenda, I'm determined to make the journey to day come what may."
"It's as good a day as any I'm sure. Now I'll make a little parcel to keep the hunger away. I hope you find Mary and may God guide your footsteps."
"You're a decent woman Brenda and I thank you. I'll be asking Michael to have word or two with his guardian angel for you."
"Praying for me is it, I suppose it wouldn't go amiss. Go raib mait aguit." (Thank you)
"You don't need praying for Brenda. I'm asking him to pray to his guardian angel to send a man to your hob."
"Well God bless you Molly Cullhane, you are starting him young as a match maker." Brenda went into the scullery laughing.
"We're off now Brenda and thanks again for your hospitality. Perhaps our

paths will cross again."
"I hope so Molly and you never know next time there might be a man to greet you."
"Oh go on with you Brenda Webb, I hope so too. Next time we meet I might be wearing the *Caipín Lása* (Lace cap) *agus an Bunneóg*. (Handkerchief).
"Go ngnótuigid Dia díb." (God speed you) Brenda called out.
"Snuacar cugat". (A good spouse to you) Laughed Molly good humorously as she waved her good bye to her friend, Brenda.
Seeing the seashore and hearing the raucous cry of the gulls she hastened her steps. To her left she saw the small island of Inisfree. This encouraged her and she was relieved when she entered the small port of Ailt an Chorrain.
"Céard is féidir liom a deanam duit indiu?" (Can I be of assistance) A fisherman repairing a fishing net spoke to her in her native tongue.
"I'm looking for a boat to get to get me to the island." Molly informed him.
"Which island are you going to. There are a lot of islands out there?"
"I want to get to Leabagarrow on Aran Island." She informed him.
"Leabagarrow, you know someone there then?" He asked.
"I'm going to see John Kearney, do you know him?"
"Know him, do you see that man down there sitting on the wall? That's John." The fisherman continued repairing his net.
"Go mairid tú."(Thank you.) Molly made her way to where a tall man sat day dreaming.
"Are you John Kearney from Aran Island?" Molly looked up at the weather beaten face of a young man.
"I am that and who might you be?" He jumped down from the wall and stood before her.
"I'm Molly Cullhane but that is of little consequence. I'm here looking for Mary Kearney. I believe that you are her uncle."
"That I am but she is not here, the last time I saw her was at her mothers funeral over at Crohy Head. God rest her soul." John removed his caubéen out of respect for the dead.
"Would you know where she went to from there?" Molly asked.
"Sure, she took the gap through the Derryveagh Mountains to Glendower. You must be the woman she was going to stay with."
"I am that but I've not seen her and that is the reason why I am here."
"Come on over to the island and speak to my wife. This indeed is serious news. The sea journey is not that far. That's the island over there. Not nervous are you?"
"I don't like the sea and I am rather sceptical about travelling in such a fragile

boat." She looked down at the little canvas boat lying upside down on the sand. "Don't worry you get in the boat and I'll hand the child to you."
Molly wondered why she was so nervous as the journey was pleasant enough. "Come on up to the house and meet my wife Nora. Be careful it can be slippery." He warned. Several children came to greet them as they came ashore.
"Dad! Dad what did you bring us?" They called as they ran to greet him.
"Here you are a few sweeties, divide them fairly now."
"My children you know." He apologised.
After a meal they sat around the fire where Molly began telling what she knew of Mary and her family.
"I'm concerned for her, she would never abandon her infant son, would she?" Molly looked towards the bed where the child was sleeping.
"A child! You're not telling us that Mary has a son? Why she never told us that she was wed?" John looked shocked.
"Did she not tell you then. This is her son Michael?"
"Are you telling us that this infant child is Mary's? There must be some mistake, she's not spoken for?" Nora looked towards the child, a shocked expression on her face.
"There's no mistake I can assure you. Of course he's hers. Who did you think he belonged to?"
"Why! I thought that he was your son." He stammered.
"Will you have some sense man. How could the child be mine?" She half laughed.
"What will you do with him, you'll need to find Mary?" Nora seemed worried.
"Why do you think I am here, I'm worried that something might have happened to her?"
"Mary Kearney with a child out of wedlock." John's wife began to pace the floor.
"You are not thinking of leaving him with us, are you?" John fidgeted with the chair.
"From the way you both are talking one would think that she deliberately had the child. You're not the least bit worried that something might have happened to Mary. She could be lying dead or drowned in the mountains for all you care?" Molly was getting annoyed.
"Those are hard words, hard words indeed and without justification. You and the child can stay here for as long as you wish. I have little doubt that she will come here looking for you." John promised.
"Is there something on your mind that you wish to spit out?" She noticed the

knowing glances he made towards his wife.

"As long as you stay here you will need to let the folk think that the child is yours. It's a small community and you know how people gossip?" He warned.

"That's all very well for you to say. What if Mary turns up here and claims her son. Will you tell the neighbours that he is her son or are you more concerned as to what they might think and say?" Molly's temper was getting the better of her.

"Mary will understand the situation, so she will." John looked deep into the fire.

There was a silence in the room that seemed to tell it all. The tense atmosphere was broken when the half door was opened and the children entered.

"Outside and play for awhile we're busy talking." Their mother ushered them outside.

"From what I can gather, you are ashamed of her. It was not her fault if you must know. She is your own flesh and blood, a kin's woman and you disown her out of hand." Molly defended Mary's character.

"Will you not raise your voice so. We know all that but we have to think of our children as well. The stigma would rub on to them." Nora emphasised.

"Is that it then, you are not worried that something might have happened to your niece. All you seem to care about is what the neighbours might think or say about an innocent child. Perhaps it would suit you better if they were both dead?"

"Now Molly don't upset yourself, of course we worry for her. Why didn't she tell us of the child when we came to the funeral of her mother?" John asked.

"I don't know and care less, you can ask her that question yourselves."

"Try to understand, you know this is a small community. No matter what you or I said would make little or no difference." John insisted.

"No Molly! My John is right, we must put our own family first." Nora insisted.

"There is little more to be said then, is there? I'd best take myself off before I say too much." Molly picked up the child and wrapped her in her shawl.

"There's no haste, you should stay the night. We will pray for Mary and him."

"Him! His name is Michael if you don't mind. There is no need to feel ashamed. Keep your prayers from the way you're talking you need them more than she does. If you would oblige and take me back to the mainland I'd be grateful."

"Now Molly let's not be too hasty about this, stay awhile and let us think what is best for the child." John tried to excuse their conduct.

"There's nothing to think about, you have made your position perfectly clear. What is best is that I get away from here, I feel thoroughly ashamed of you

both. Do you know the trouble I took coming here seeking your help?"
"We are grateful for your concern and thank you but…' John seemed lost for words.
"Oh come on get me back to the mainland, you've made your position clear." Molly interrupted him.
"But where will you go with the child?" John asked.
"Where will I go? I'm sure you're worried or care little where we go."
"Don't leave with bad blood, give us a chance to explain." He half apologised.
"Very well then, I'll leave Michael with you and should I meet up with Mary I'll tell her he is in the safe hands of his folk on Aran Island." Molly called his bluff.
"Now you are being unreasonable, we told you why we cannot have the child here."
"There's nothing more to be said then. If you won't take me back to the mainland now I'll find someone who will."
"Very well then I'll take you back. Would it be asking too much if we asked you to keep in touch with us." John shuffled from one foot to the other.
"I'll make no such promise. I'll not tell Mary what happened here to day. I'm not the one to make bad blood between families. She can make her own mind up."
"Will you take a little food with you on the journey home?" Nora asked.
"No thank you, we'll not be beholding to you. Your food would choke in my craw. I'll bid you good day and sorry for troubling you. Here take a last look at your nephew." The child began to cry.
"Don't take on so Mo cushla, Molly Cullhane still love you." She sarcastically remarked as she held the child up for them to see. Wrapping him in her shawl she left the cottage.
Back on the mainland John accompanied her up the slipway and again tried to make peace with her.
"John Kearney would you ever go home and stop trying to ease your conscience, Go and leave us in peace." She hastened her steps to outpace him.
"You'll keep in touch won't you Molly?" Stopping he removed his cap and called after her.
Molly ignored him and continued on up the boréen.

A SAD RETURN

"Don't fret Michael, we will soon be home in Glendower where your mother will be waiting to greet you." She addressed the child as he began to cry.

"Mary! Mary we're home." She called as she entered the boréen leading to her cottage. She stopped and looked at the closed door expecting to see Mary open it at any moment.

"Mary, where are you? Will you open the door." She rattled the latch. The door remained locked. She knew that there had not been any callers in her absence. Lifting the slab beside the resting stone she removed the key and opened the door.

"There's no one at home Michael, I'd best get you comfortable." Placing her child on the bed she lit the fire and set to preparing a meal.

"Mary Kearney where are you?" She was now very worried indeed.

That night she lit the Connail Mhór and placed it in the window recess. Should Mary be on her way she would see it and know that her son was waiting for her. The years passed and she abandoned her constant vigil by the half door. She knew that something must have happened. As Michael's Godmother she had an obligation to care for him. His own people did not want the stigma. Although it was several years since Mary Kearney left the cottage for the last time Molly kept hoping that she would return some day. No Irish mother would abandon her child. One afternoon as she dozed in her chair she heard the catch on the door rattle.

"Mary, thank God you are back. Whatever happened to you?" Anticipating the arrival of Mary she threw the blanket off her legs and ran and opened the door.

"Good day to you Molly, I was passing and thought I'd call in." Before her stood John Murphy. His caubéen sat jauntily on his head and a cheerful smile greeting her.

"Oh Good God I hoped it was her." Disappointed she retreated back inside the cottage.

"Hoped it was who? Whatever is the matter Molly, you look as if you saw a ghost?"

"I wish I had John, I really do." She spoke quietly.

"Is there something the matter, can I be of some help?" John was showing his concern.

"Sit yourself down, it's a long story that I fear will never end." She crossed to the fire and pushed the creel holding the kettle over the coals.

"Who owns the boy sleeping by the fire? Have you some relatives staying then?"

"No John, you remember the woman that got drowned and the daughter and baby?"

"Remember, how could I ever forget them. Are you seriously telling me that she never came home? Is it little wonder that you are worried."

"No! She's not here and that is what is troubling me." She went on to tell him all that happened and her search on Aran Island for Mary.

"That type of hypocrisy makes me sick. Molly you deserve a lot of credit for going to so much trouble for complete strangers." He sympathised.

"I don't deserve any credit John, sure I am his Godmother and now it seems his adopted mother." She sighed.

"I hate to say this Molly, but say it I must. I cannot help it but I have a bad feeling that something happened to that girl. I saw how distressed she was at her mothers funeral, she would never abandon her mother's child."

"They are my sentiments too John. Come on the tae is getting cold." As they sat by the fire Michael woke up and looked curiously at the stranger.

"Do you remember me telling you about the sleadors who tried to save your grandmother from the bog? This is one of them. Now come here and meet John Murphy," Molly introduced them.

"Pleased to meet you Michael, you sure have grown into a fine boy."

"Thank you Sir, I am pleased to meet you." Michael extended his hand in greeting.

"You have a fine mannerly boy Molly. A credit to your upbringing." John gently tossed the boys curls.

"I'm glad you mentioned that John, I need a favour from you. I'm taking him to the far counties. He needs to go to school and there is no hope of finding one around here. In my absence would you oblige and keep a watch on the cottage. Feel free to use it whenever you need. If by chance Mary should turn up then tell her to wait for our return. Will you do that for us please John?"

"Of course Molly, you know that there's no need to ask. Tell me where were you thinking of going to?"

"Galway seems as good a place as any, what do you think?"

"May God keep the Galway road open before you Molly. Your cottage will as safe with John Murphy as in God's blessed hands so it will."

"Here's the key then and if by chance I fail to return, will you see to it that Michael Kearney inherits the ould place. Not much to leave him I agree but ah well who knows..." Tears began to dim her eyes.

"Stop that Molly, there's no need to feel so. The day Molly Cullhane leaves Glendower will be the sad day indeed." John sympathised.

'Tis the tearful road that I'm taking John. God be good to Mary Kearney she is out there someplace of that I have little doubt." She looked across at the heather covered hills rising above the valley floor. Again tears dimmed her eyes.

"Dry your tears Molly, you're a good soul so you are. When do you intend leaving?"

"I'll be away first light to morrow morning, God willing." Molly dried her tears.

"Is there anything that I should know of before you go?" John asked.

"Nothing, nothing at all apart from keeping your ear to the ground. If Mary does come home tell her to wait and not to worry. I'll bring her son home to her safe and sound."

"I'll make sure that she gets the message." He promised.

"That's it then John, you'll see to the hens and the goat. There's a ridge or two of potatoes to be dug and a few vegetables in the garden, help yourself to them."

"I expect you will be long gone by the time I get back to morrow. Good luck to you and Michael in the far county. God guide your feet." He shook her hand warmly.

As he left the cottage, she watched him enter the valley. As he crossed the stream he turned and looked back at the cottage. Raising his shillelagh he waved it in a final salute. She waved back and continued waving until he disappeared from view.

TOSSING THE CUP

Over the peaks of the Croaghgorm (Blue Stack) mountains a watery mist hung that cold autumn morning as Molly and Michael crossed the valley floor.
"Wouldn't it be a great surprise to us both if we were to come across your mother and she on her way to meet us?" She asked by way of conversation.
"She's never coming home, I know she isn't." He grumbled.
"Of course she'll come home, your mother would never abandon you. You must have faith, Michael." She endeavoured to encourage him.
"She didn't abandon me I know that. She died someplace out there on her way home as did her mother."
There was little to see as a mist covering the valley floor floated to and fro like the swell of a lapping tide. The long feathery clouds followed each other and cascaded into the side of the mountain. It was as if they were committing suicide. There was a murmuring in the valley. It was the mysterious whisperings of the phantoms of the mountain. She felt the fullness of it all as it grew louder and louder in her ears. Yet it was but a whispering like ghosts calling from a distant shore.
"Come on then Michael, I'm not going to get too much conversation from you." She shivered as she looked at the overpowering mountain. She smiled as she adjusted his scarf around his neck.
"I'm perfectly alright, thanks all the same." He loosened the scarf.
"Suit yourself then, but don't complain to me of the cold later." She chastised him.
By noon they had crossed the ford on the river Eske and entered Donegal town.
"It's market day Michael, come on we'll go and get a bite to eat and a rest. Afterwards if you want you can go and enjoy yourself at the fair." She tried to cheer him up.
Having eaten their meal and rested they went down the street and entered the large square. The square was crowded with sellers and buyers. Molly sat on the shaft of a cart and looked out onto the street.
"Michael there's a fair down by the shore, here's a penny go and enjoy yourself."
"Oh thanks Ma, can I go now?" He seemed to be in better humour.
"If I'm not here when you return I'll be in the tae house. Away you go and take care."
She smiled to herself as she watched him racing down the sloping street to where the fair was in progress.

As she sat day dreaming she noticed a gathering in a discreet corner of the square. Curiosity getting the better of her she went to investigate.

"Before you; ladies and gentlemen you see for the first time in Ireland two of the most talented birds known to man. They were brought here from a foreign land far over the seas. Their power of fortune telling is incredible, now who would like to try their luck?" A weather beaten man dressed in a seafarers cap and sporting white whiskers continued his rhetoric without stopping.

On a long perch two budgerigars kept walking to and fro from one end to the other. The owner held a little stick in his hand and occasionally he would place it under the bird's feet and encourage them on to it.

"How much will it cost me?" A potential customer called out.

"I'll not be taking the shirt off your back, I'm only asking a farthing. I'll ask the bird of your choice to pick out your fortune, what is your name?"

"Very well then, my name is Joseph, ask the green one to tell me my fortune."

" You Sir have picked Cleopatra, she is the queen of all the Pharaohs. Show me your money Sir and let the bird decide your future." Picking the bird up with the pointer he took it to a small wooden box. In the box were rows and rows of small blue printed cards.

"Now Cleopatra draw the card that will bring good fortune to this worthy gentleman." As if in acknowledgement the bird chirped and reaching into the box retrieved a card. The bird held the card in his beak.

"Go on Joseph take your card from Cleopatra and keep it to yourself." Joseph retrieved the card and going to the rear of the gathering began to read it.

"Now who is going to be next. What about you madam?" He pointed towards Molly.

"Is it me you are talking to?" Molly looked round her and then pointed to herself.

"Sure and why not, it's only a bit of fun." The smile on his whiskered face grew larger.

"Who me! Oh go on then it might be my lucky day." She handed over her farthing.

"Now which bird do you fancy to tell your fortune?"

"I fancy the blue one, I'm sure I saw her wink at me." Molly laughed.

"You madam have picked Caesar. The wisest of all the Romans."

Once again took the bird to a box this time containing pink cards and encouraged it to pick out one.

"Blue for the boys and Pink for the Ladies. Now Caesar will you pick out the Lady's good fortune." He encouraged the bird.

"Thank you Caesar." Molly genuflected before the bird as she took the card

from its beak.
She read the card and smiled to herself. Fortune it read would answer her call and she would soon meet with a tall dark gentleman who would marry her and that they would have many children and live to a ripe old age.
"Ah well it is only a bit of fun." She spoke to herself and smiled.
Molly browsed through many of the stalls in the square before she returned and sat on the wall.
As Michael had not returned she retired to the roadhouse for a meal.
"Did you go anyplace then?" She looked up to see Michael standing before her.
"No! Not really I had my fortune told by a bird though." She laughed.
"I saw him too, he's still there with his birds. I wonder why they don't fly away?"
"I expect that they are tame and well used to being handled. Come on let's find a bed for the night."
"Why can't we stay here, it's as good a place as any?" He grumbled.
"For the simple reason that it is too dear. We'll try for a place out of town."
Taking the road to Laghy, they soon found a shakedown with a *Leaba suidheacán* more suited to their modest means.
The cottage though humble was clean and was occupied by an elderly couple.
"Would you care to share a sup of tae?" The old man asked as he pulled the iron kettle from over the coals.
"Of course we would and thanks." Molly joined the old couple at the fire.
"What about himself?" The old woman asked, nodding towards Michael.
"Leave him be, he is young and has little time for us old folk. My name is Eammon Welsh and this is my wife Ita" The old man smiled.
"Where have you come from yourselves?" He queried.
"We came from Glendower on the other side of the Derryveagh Mountains." Molly informed him.
"A long road you came then, no doubt you stopped over at the fair in Donegal town?"
"We did that and I had my fortune read by a bird. Here it is." Molly took the card from her pocket and presented it to them.
"That's all trickery, now if you really want your fortune read, ask my Ita." He challenged.
"Would you like me to toss your cup for you?" Ita wrung her wrinkled hands and like a soothsayer looked deep into her eyes. There was something in her looks that worried Molly.
"Sure and why not. It's a long time since I had my cup tossed I can tell you."

Molly accepted the challenge. The kettle was placed on the crane and swung over the turf fire.

"Won't be that long before it comes to the boil." Eammon twisted another sod of turf deep into the red embers. Sparks and flames raced up the wide chimney obscuring the kettle before it settled down once again.

"Ah! There she goes." The old woman rubbed her hands together. The kettle lid began to lift up and down ejecting spouts of hot water that sizzled on its sides.

Ita left the fireside and returned carrying a china taepot. Pouring boiling water from the kettle into the pot she swirled it round and round slowly and deliberately. She felt the sides of the pot occasionally to ensure that the pot was good and hot.

"Now for the sup of tae. There's one for himself, one for myself, one for you and one for the pot." She counted the spoonfuls of tae into the pot. Satisfied she filled the pot with boiling water and replaced the lid.

"Now five minutes to brew and all will be fine." Raking a few hot ashes from the fire she placed the pot on top and sat down.

"That was as fine a cup of tae that I ever drank" Molly smiled on finishing her cup.

"Will you toss your cup then and throw the dregs into the ashes and call on God's blessing." Ita invited her.

Molly swirled the tae leaves round the inside of her cup and tossing the dregs into the fire called on the blessed Trinity to bless her and Michael.

"Here's my cup then, let's hear the worst." She smiled as she handed the cup to Ita.

"This is serious business my girl and not to be treated with flippancy." Ita with a look of chastisement took the cup from her and placed it upside down on the saucer. Then she twisted it three times to the left and three times to the right. Turning it right side up she examined the contents quizzically. Again she raised her eyes and looked across at Molly.

"You're sure you want me to read what I see?" Ita looked sympathetically at her.

"It's not good news by the looks on your face, is it?" Molly sighed.

The tae leaves were scattered hieroglyphically inside the cup. Ita handed the cup to her husband Eammon for verification. He looked seriously at Molly and again at the contents. He shook his head in a knowing way and handed the cup back to his wife.

"It's a heavy burden that you carry child, a heavy burden indeed. Look at that Eammon?" The old woman holding out her index finger pointed to something in the cup. She held it close to Molly and again pointed out something that the tae leaves were telling her. Molly unable to understand what was so exciting nodded her head in agreement.

"I see two barren roads, mo cushla and there's nothing but sorrow on both of them. Look at the top one, look it has clean teeth (hunger) not even a bush in sight. It's the road to poverty and despair. Below it is the boréen leading to the three crosses and the rainbow. There's a great plague on that road and you may walk it in the near future. I'll tell you no more, I've said too much already, so I have." Like a soothsayer the old woman sat silently with the cup in her hands looking deep into the fire.

"What else can you see on the road, I may as well hear you out?" Molly insisted.

"It's a cup of sorrow that I am looking at, so it is. There's a man and a woman on a mountain road and they are going on a journey. There is a great Ocras on the land but they are not trying to escape from it. Something keeps driving them on to a sorrowful awakening. I see a great building that is in ruin and in it lies what they are seeking. The woman will not see the end of the road, so she won't. If you look over here the woman is no more and the man has reached his goal. Be mindful to what I tell you, why do you think our paths crossed this night? You must not walk that road for this cup is for you and is a warning. When the time comes and come it will as sure as night follows day make sure you do not cross that mountain." Ita again warned.

"Take the cup and smash it, then it may never happen." Advised Eammon.

" Jesus! Did you not see the rainbow and hear the calling when she spilled the dregs on the hot turf. Eammon will you talk sense?" The old woman who seemed to have the wisdom of a soothsayer spoke out. She seemed to be in an agitated state and her hands shook as she held the cup tight.

"Think hard on what I say and keep it in your heart for one day what the tae leaves foretold may save your life." She warned.

"The time is late and the candle is almost burnt out, will you be saying the rosary with us?" Eammon rose from his chair and removing his rosary beads from around his neck began to pray.

Molly lay in the Leaba suidheacán that night her mind in turmoil. She was worried by what the old woman had foretold. Michael interrupted her thoughts.

"What did mother look like?" His voice penetrated her dreaming.

"Your mother! Don't talk as if she were dead. She is ever so pretty. Did I tell you how she tried to save her mother from drowning in the bog?"

"Yes, I heard all about that, do you know any more stories about her?" His inquisitiveness regarding his mother knew no bounds.

"Did I tell you that she had a brother named Tomas beag? He was taken to heaven at an early age. You see Michael, God takes all sick children to Heaven."

"Perhaps he has taken my mother too, there is no other reason for her to abandon me."

"Abandon you? Whatever gave you that silly notion? I left a message with John Murphy to give to her when she calls to my cottage. Would I do that if she were dead?"

"You've been telling me that for years now and still there is no sign of her. No! She must be dead." He grumbled.

"For the last time, your mother is not dead, she will find us, I promise. Now go to sleep." Molly insisted.

"Táim a' tuitim 'moodlad. Ní féidir liom úile aongbáil ar oscauilt." (I'm falling asleep and cannot keep my eyes open.) She gave an encouraging yawn.

"Good night mother." He tightened his blanket around his shoulders and soon succumbed to sleep.

She smiled; satisfied that he was now calling her, *Mother.*

MAURA O'REILLY MAKES HER CONFESSION.

Maura O'Reilly fell victim to the Curse (consumption) a wasting decease that cruelly ate away at the body. One day she was the picture of health and the next morning she found that she was lethargic. She accepted that it was the will of God and that she had no alternative but to accept it. Lying in her bed despondent she prayed to her God for the cure. But there would be no cure. She knew that as soon as her condition became known she would be ostracised from the community. It was only a matter of a short respite before she succumbed to death. Not wishing to suffer the agonising shortage of breath or to be found dead without the sacrament of confession on her soul, she decided to make her peace with her God before it was too late.
Firstly she went and collected clean rushes from *Tobar Brigit* (Saint Bridget's Well) and wove them into her cross. She burnt the corners and placed the cross under her tick (mattress). Tearing a piece of *Brat Bride* (unwashed cloth) from her shift she washed it in the water of the well and placed it on the old Hawthorne bush overshadowing the well. In the dark of the night and long before the dew had risen off the fields she collected the cloth and tied it round her neck. She would now be spared the agony of suffocating from the mucus strangling her lungs.
Walking through the grounds one morning she began coughing without respite. She knew that her time had come. Fatigued she returning to the castle and went to her room where she slept a restless sleep. Rising early she looked at herself in the wardrobe mirror. Her shallow eyes, deep dark patches and sunken jaws told the whole story.
"Perhaps a raw egg taken in milk would prolong my life that little bit longer." She spoke into the mirror, then she smiled.
Prolonging her life for what? To die alone gasping for the last breath in her pain raked body. No forget the cure best get it over and done with. She would now go and see her confessor and seek respite for a happy death.
Dressing herself she opened the door and took herself off down the garden. Looking across the bay she saw the sun rise in a gentle pink glow. The crystal branches of the trees creaked before surrendering their gentle slivers of ice. They lay there awhile before melting into the sod as the sun heated the landscape. The grass noisily protested as her feet bent its stiffened white stems. She shivered in the cold morning air.
Going up the incline to the presbytery she felt short of breath and pausing placed her hand on her chest to regain her composure. Again she felt the pain in her chest and a raking cough in her throat. She again held her hand to her

chest in an effort to ease the raking pain and regain her strength. Gasping for breath she struggled to the door and raising the iron knocker and let it fall with a slap.

The priest opened the door and looked out with horror at the wretch standing before him. A trickle of blood oozed from the side of her mouth. He knew from experience her reason for calling outside confessional hours.

Removing his handkerchief he placed it over his mouth and not wishing to embarrass her he pretended to wipe his mouth. Yet he made no effort to return it to his sleeve, instead he kept it firmly against his face. He was horrified when she reached out and laid her hand on his sleeve.

"Father, I am aware that I am not too long for this world and I would like you to listen to what I have to tell you." She finally gasped.

"Would you like me to hear your confession then?" The good priest asked keeping a safe distance between them.

"Not as such father, for what I am about to tell you is for the putting right of a terrible wrong."

"Surely you should be telling the authorities, if a crime has been committed?"

"Father this crime was committed by those in authority. Telling them would only result in yet another crime being committed. Can I sit down please." She paused for breath before continuing.

"Very well then but I hope it has nothing to do with the Fenians. Sit yourself down here." He pointed to a chair near by.

"No father, it hasn't got anything whatsoever to do with them...'

"It came about shortly after the great disaster when Tom Kearney and all those fishermen were drowned off *Airt an Chorram...*"

"God give them rest and be good to them." The priest remembering the tragedy intoned a blessing on their souls.

"Amen, amen. Father." She weakly replied.

"Lord Kilgarvan wanted Mary the daughter of Tom Kearney, one of his tenants as his tally woman. He seemed besotted with her and she only a child. When Tom drowned, his widow Brige could no longer pay her rent for the cottage. It was then that he decided he would take Mary as his *Tally Woman* in exchange for the rent. He sent Frank McLaughlan, his bailiff to the cottage of the Kearney's on the pretence of evicting them for non-payment of rent. He told Brige Kearney that they would have to vacate the cottage by midday leaving all their goods and chattels behind them. This was a ruse to catch Brige off guard and get her confused. Frank went early the next morning and ordered her and her daughter out of the cottage as arranged. Then collecting me as planned we returned to the cottage and told her that his Lordship felt benevolent towards them. They could stay on in the cottage providing that Mary came and worked at the castle in lieu of rent.

Brige; knowing his reputation was hesitant at first but I assured her that I would be looking after her daughter's welfare. When we got to the castle I helped Mary to wash herself, I took the innocent child to his Lordships bedroom and told her to get into bed. She was naked and asked about her clothes and I told her not to worry, I would have new ones ready for her by morning. That evening I brought her a meal and told her to get a good nights sleep before she started work next morning. I returned to the kitchen and removed the pulley to the call bell leading to his Lordships bedroom. This was the room that Mary was sleeping in. I was aware what was about to take place that night and did not want them disturbed. Next morning I returned to the room and found her in a distressed state and I knew then that he had his way with her. She kept pleading with me to return her home but there was nothing that I could do about it.

He had a sadistic obsession for her and gave her little peace day or night. The more she resisted him the more he was sexually aroused. I tried to tell her to submit to him and make it easier on herself. She stubbornly refused and was beaten all the more for it.

Twelve months passed and she found herself with child. As she was only a child herself she did not realise that she was pregnant, she thought that she was very sick and about to die. I was glad she fell pregnant for now she would be banished from the castle and married off to a cowman down country. He could not be any worse to her than was her master.

One evening as I was returning from the cottage of Nancy O'Flaherty I took my rest on one of the seats under the great archway. Now there are eye windows on either side of the archway to allow light to enter. As I sat there I heard voices outside. I listened and heard his Lordship and Frank McLaughlan in deep and hushed conversation. What I heard that night made my blood run cold.'

"I'll not let her go Frank, she has me bewitched." I heard his Lordship say.

"You have no choice in the matter Sir, you have to banish her and the child." He advised.

"No Frank! By God I'll not part with her, there must be another way."

"You cannot keep the infant in the castle. You are not thinking straight, if I may say so, Sir." Frank warned.

"Listen to me Frank McLaughlan, she is mine and will stay mine, do you understand what I am telling you?" His voice rose in anger.

"Then you must get rid of the infant, there is no other way." Frank advised.

"You're right Frank, why did I not think of that?"
"The problem is getting hold of the infant and disposing of him, Sir."
"There's always Maura O'Reilly, she would help me." I tell you I felt a shiver down my spine on hearing my name being used in their treachery.
"She could take the infant to the piggery, nobody would be any the wiser. Now would they?" Frank proposed.
"Good God I thought, they're planning to murder the infant and feed him to the pigs. Returning to the castle I decided there and then that I would help Mary to escape with her child. I never disclosed my reason to her, I smuggled her and her infant son out through the Lych gate."
"I'm glad to hear that you done good by the girl in the end. At least you atoned for your sins, God will forgive you." The priest anxious for her to leave as quickly as possible absolved and comforted her.
"Father, there is more to it than that."
"More! How much more is there to tell? God in Heaven protect us." The priest mopped his sweating brow.
"One day I was over in Dungloe when who should I see but Mary Kearney. Making further inquiries I was informed that she was home to bury her mother. When I returned to the castle I foolishly told Frank McLaughlan that she was home. He wasted no time in informing his Lordship.
He was delighted and ordered us to harness the gig at once and go looking for her.
"You will not be welcome back here without her." He warned us as we left.
We found her asleep on a resting stone outside a deserted cottage and kidnapped her.
There was no sign of the infant. We returned to the castle with her. We told him that the infant was not with her and this seemed to please him.
She fought us like a tigress all the way to the bedroom. Finally exhausted she lay on the bed sobbing and cursing us all to hell.
The crux came some two weeks later when I heard his Lordship screaming. Rushing to the bedroom I opened the door and saw his Lordship with his hands over his face.
On seeing me he took his hands from his face and cried out...'
"I'm disfigured, I'm blind." I went to the bathroom and poured water from a jug into a basin. I returned to the bedroom to find him staggering in a drunken state round and round the room. I encouraged him to sit down and I cleaned the wounds and thankfully discovered that they were not as bad as he suspected. I assured him that the surgeon would put matters right. He sat there mumbling to himself with his hands covering his face. He kept drinking from a whiskey

decanter on and off.
Mary; her clothing in rags sat on the bed as if in a trance looking into space. "Why did you do this Mary?" I shouted at her. It was then I saw the teeth marks on her breasts, One nipple had been bitten so badly that it was severed from her breast. Her body was covered in bites and scratches.
"Enough! Good God in Heaven are my ears deceiving me?" The Priest looked in horror at her.
"I'll not stop father, not until you hear the full story. You don't know the nightmares I have suffered all those years. My sleep is disturbed night after night listening to her ghost screaming to be released from the tomb. I don't want to go to my maker with this mortal sin on my soul. You must listen and forgive me. I want to die peacefully without the mark of Cain on my soul. You must hear my confession for you are my confessor." She demanded.
"I am bound by my sacred oath to listen to your confession. Good God! How could you be part and parcel to such a crime?" The priest wrung his hands in shock.
"His Lordship approached the bed and stood before us without shame or decency. Mary sat before him showing no emotion." She continued her confession ignoring the troubled priest.
"He slapped her across the face time and time again with his open hand. Then he punched her full in the face. I saw the blood ooze from her half-open mouth and nose. Oh God I'll not forget that night. Then he pulled her forward by her legs and again he raped her. I was shocked and confused. He was acting worse than a beast in a field.
Somehow, how I'll never know she managed to get off the bed and attacked him with the basin that I brought the water in to wash his wounds with."
"Hold her down, will you?" I heard him shout as if I was dreaming. I didn't know what I was doing and obeyed him." Burying her face in her hands she paused…'
"Mary was lying face down on the bed and not moving, how she came to be in that position I could not understand, she must have lost consciousness. Not thinking straight I took hold of her hands and held on to them. Why I held them I'll never know nor forgive myself for doing so. Oh God in heaven why did I do it?" She collapsed sobbing and coughing. Regaining her composure somewhat she continued…'
"His Lordship began brutally beating her and beating her with his riding crop, she did not cry out or move. I knew then that she was unconscious. I released her hands and ran round the bed and tried to take the riding crop from him but he pushed me roughly across the room and continued beating her. I fell heavily

into a corner of the room. I don't know what really happened. I was confused. It wasn't my fault, Father. I tried to save her, honest I swear before God that I tried." She banged the sides of the chair with her clenched fists. A trickle of blood appeared from the side of her mouth. This she quickly wiped away with her handkerchief.

"It's all right relax and take it slowly, would you like to rest now?" The priest comforted her.

"No Father, please let me finish my confession before God..." She wrung her hands in agitation...'

"Finally tiring he threw the riding crop across the room and sat down on a chair. I looked with horror at the riding crop; it was covered in blood and raw flesh. I held it up before his face and tried to make him understand the gravity of his action. He would have none of it. In a temper that defied belief he rose and tore the pull cord from above the bed and strangled her with it. I heard her neck snap as he jerked on the cord.

I crawled from where I fell and approached the bed. I knew at once that she was dead.

It was then that he decided he would hide her body in the family crypt. With the assistance of Frank McLaughlan we rolled her in the bloodied blanket. That night we took her body to the family crypt and placed her in the coffin of Lady Jane Symour-Kilgarvan, the wife of Lord Simon Kilgarvan who was his mother. As far as I am aware she is still there." She looked wild-eyed at the priest.

"I cannot find peace within myself, her ghost haunts me day and night without respite. It was her spirit that inflicted the curse on me. Why is she doing this to me? In God's name, why? I tried, I did; honestly I did. I tried to save her but her spirit wants revenge on me and will not let me rest as day and night she haunts me." Rising from her seat she began pacing the hall...

"Her spirit came into my room one night and I promised it that if she left me in peace then I would find her son no matter how long it took me. I heard that a Clare woman by the name of Molly Cullhane who had a cottage over in Glendower on the other side of the Derryveagh Mountains was looking after him. I went there and found the cottage, but I was to be disappointed. The cottage was occupied by a sleador by the name of John Murphy..."

"Good day to you mam, are you looking for Molly?" He greeted me.

"I am that, would you tell her that I would like to speak to her please?"

"She left here some years ago, she was going to Galway to find work and a school for her adopted son." He told me.

"Did she tell you who the child's mother was, or did she know?" I asked him.

"Sure she knew, he is the son Bríge Kearney who perished in the bog yonder, God be good to her soul. She keeps in contact with me; she is hoping that Bríges daughter Mary Kearney will return. I thought for a moment that you might have some news of her whereabouts. Why do you ask"?
"No reason at all. I don't know any Mary Kearney." I denied her as Judas did Jesus.
"Ah well I'm doubtful myself if she is still alive, I saw her last at her mothers funeral over at Crohy Head in Dungloe. Where might you be from?" He asked.
"I come from the village of Ramelton outside Buncranna." I again lied.
I realised at once that they were trying to conceal the true identity of the boy in order to save him. I was pleased to know that her son had escaped and hopefully was still alive. I wanted to continue my quest but I fell ill with the curse." She was now calm.
"What do you want me to do, I cannot disclose what you told me in confession?" The priest looked shocked.
"Would you, for the sake of my immortal soul father, try and find them. Give the boy this letter and tell him that he is the rightful heir to Cardavon castle and estate?" She pleaded.
"I find it hard indeed to comprehend your story, but I have no doubt that it is the truth. I will make inquiries as to the whereabouts of Molly Cullhane and the boy. Now go and may God grant you peace." The Priest took the letter from her and absolved her.
Maura O'Reilly returned to Cardavon Castle and going to her room made her peace with her God that night. She slept peacefully undisturbed by the spectre. She was discovered next morning covered in a pool of blood. The curse had claimed another victim.

THE DEMISE OF LORD KILGARVAN

With total disregard for his captive tenants and the upkeep of his estate Lord Kilgarvan continued to squander what assets he had in the banks and elsewhere. Whenever his funds were exhausted he systematically plundered the vast estate of valuables to meet his gambling debts.

His father, the late Lord James Simon Kilgarvan aware of his sons gambling and womanising had, on his death- bed entered a codicil in his will. The castle, its contents and the home farm were to be held in trust and could not be sold or mortgaged.

Desperate for funds to meet his rising debts and a stake at the tables of the gambling fraternity he devised a clever plan. There were several valuable paintings within the castle, if he could find a good enough reason to remove them then his money problems would be solved for the present. With the connivance of his faithful bailiff, Frank McLaughlan he concocted his plan. Two of the paintings would be removed from their frames and shipped to London. He let it be known that they were going there to be cleaned and restored. Once in London two copies were made of the originals and returned to the castle. The originals were sold to a dealer for a handsome profit. This paid off his gambling debts and left him enough over to buy a place at the gaming tables in Dublin, Belfast and London.

As the switch of the paintings was not detected he continued to strip the castle of its other valuables, replacing them with fakes. Finally with nothing left of any value to dispose of he was unable to honour his debts. His promissory notes to pay were returned without being honoured and he soon found himself ostracised from every gaming house in Ireland and England. As his reputation as a man without honour became known he was no longer made welcome to the great houses.

He was now spending more and more time away from the castle. The affairs of the estate he left in the hands of his bailiff.

Tradesmen calling for payments of debts long overdue were fobbed off with promises of payment when his lordship returned.

Matters came to a head when the annual wages were due to the servants.

"Where are our wages, the year is finished and we want to return home?" They demanded.

"His Lordship is detained on business in London. You will be paid in full on his return." The bailiff promised time and time again.

"He has no money to pay us, no more than the tradesmen." Tempers began to fray and discipline broke down.

"We know that he has systemically plundered the castle of its assets, he has nothing left. What does he intend to pay us with?" Desperate workers besieged the office.
"You will all be paid in full, I assure you, just be patient." Frank McLaughlan pleaded for tolerance on his behalf.
A week passed and with no sign of any wages the workers were in a rebellious mood.
Rumours soon spread that his Lordship unable to meet his debts had fled the country.
"Where is he and why cannot you find our wages?" They demanded to know.
"I cannot pay you, I've not been paid myself. You'll need to be patient a little longer." The bailiff again pleaded.
"Patient, my wife and children are starving and I need my money now. If he cannot pay me then by God I'll take its worth, so I will." One of the men servants pulled a heavy drape from one of the banqueting hall windows and filled it with silver and pewter ware from the large sideboard.
"I'm taking no more than what is due to me, now get out of my way." Brushing the bailiff to one side he hoisted the bundle on his back and left the castle. Soon there was a free for all as his creditors and workforce began systematically stripping the estate of what assets were left. Cattle and sheep were driven from the fields and sold. Bed linen, drapes, curtains, pots and pans were confiscated. Anything saleable that would recompense for the year's work. There was nothing that Frank could do to stop them. He could but watch as the castle was denuded of most of its furniture and fittings.
His lordship returned to his castle from yet another fruitless search for funds. Seeing his fields emptied of cattle and sheep he knew that he had nothing left to live for. He was confronted by the reality of the situation when he entered the castle.
He was surprised to find that his entire household had absconded, taking with them what possessions they could pilfer. Hearing footsteps coming from beyond the great archway he went to investigate.
"Your Lordship, what will you do? His bailiff came from the shadows.
"Do Frank! What can I do but accept the situation?"
"There was nothing that I could do to stop them Sir." He apologised.
"I know Frank, I know and I cannot blame them. Is Maura O'Reilly still with us?
"Maura O'Reilly, have you forgotten Sir, she is dead and buried?"
"Sorry with all of my problems I had forgotten."
"Whatever will you do now Sir, you cannot possible stay here alone?"
"I take it that you too will be abandoning me, Frank McLaughlan?"
"I'll not abandon you Sir, but what purpose could I serve here alone?"

"I understand, do you know that the great doors have never been bolted from the day the castle was built?"

"I am sorry Sir, really I am."

"You were always a loyal servant Frank and I know you were always fond of my twin bore and hunting garb. I'm sure that you could put them to good use."

"Are you going away then Sir?"

"No Frank, I'll not be going away, but I'll not be doing any more hunting or riding."

"Will you help me to lock the security shutters before you leave?"

Together both men entered the castle and closed and bolted the heavy wooden security shutters. As they closed the shutters the castle was slowly plunged into darkness.

Leaving the great hall they stood outside for some time talking.

"Here Frank! You have been my most loyal servant. You deserve a lot more but it is all I have left to offer you." He placed the reins of his horse in his bailiff's hands.

"Not your horse and saddle Sir, whatever will you do?"

"Good bye Frank, I wish you luck wherever you go. I have no further use for a horse."

Crossing the gravel path he closed the great doors and placing the key in the keyhole turned the lock. He watched as his bailiff rode his fine chestnut mare down the long drive. Going through the great archway he stopped and looked into the empty cottages. There was nobody now to close the wrought iron gates against intruders. Lifting the great bolt he pushed first one gate closed and secured it with the second. Then dropping the bolt into its socket he walked back to the castle.

At the family mausoleum he ran his hands over the family crest and looked down at the iron door.

"Sorry I let you down father." As he walked up the steps he turned and again looked down at the black door of the crypt.

"Mary! Can you ever forgive me? I was willing to sell my soul to the devil for you and in all probability I have?" With a sigh of remorse he returned to the long drive.

All was now silent as he vaulted the fence and entered the meadow above the great lake.

Stopping at the lakeside he turned and looked back at the castle.

With a sigh he removed his clothes. Turning his back to his castle he faced the lake and continued walking.

A CASE OF MISTAKEN IDENTITY

Frank McLaughlan rode high and proud in the saddle on the back of Lord Kilgarvan's chestnut mare. As he entered the home farm on his way to his cottage the rain came on again.
Stopping the mare he dismounted and reached into the saddlebag. He removed the hunting garb and placed it over his shoulders. Placing the hat at a jaunty angle on his head he continued on his journey home. He wondered who the new lord might be and if he would be as kind to him as Lord Kilgarvan had been. In a spinney some distance down the bridle path two Fenian Volunteers sat concealed. One was Gerry Brosnan holding a cudgel in his hands; the other Tony Finn held a loaded musket in his sweating palms.
"Do you think he will come to night?" Gerry asked his companion as he shivered in the cold and rain.
"He'll come alright, have no doubt about that, Tony. He always calls to see Frank McLaughlan on his return. "
"What do you think he will do when he finds his castle has been looted?"
"His castle looted, don't make me laugh. What of the poor wretches he left destitute without a brass farthing for their years labour. Don't tell me that you are feeling sorry for him?"
"No I'm not, I could never forgive him. When I think of how my infant son died from lack of nourishment. Had he paid me the wages due my son would be alive this day." Tony gripped the musket tightly in his sweating palms.
"I think I hear someone coming" Gerry whispered.
"Now remember, don't do anything hasty, we don't want to kill an innocent person." Gerry looked out from his hiding place.
"There's someone on horseback coming over the ridge." Tony warned.
"Go up to the hump backed bridge and see if you recognise who it is." He instructed.
"Should I take the musket with me?" Tony asked.
"No, I'll take care of it, you might trip and disclose our whereabouts."
After some time Gerry heard a rustling in the undergrowth.
"Is that you Tony?" He whispered holding the musket at the ready.
"It's alright, where are you?" Tony came out into the clearing and approached him.
"Did you see who it is, is it him?"
"It's him alright, although I didn't see his face."
"Are you sure now Tony?" He tried to look into the distance.
"It's him I tell you, how could I mistake his hunting gear and his chestnut mare? I recognise them as well as I know you."

"Come on then get ready and may he rot in Hell." Gerry placed his musket in the fork of a tree facing up the road. Cocking the hammer he dug the butt of the musket deep into his shoulder and stood waiting. They heard the clip clop of the horseshoes as the rider came closer to their hiding place.

Gerry waited until the horseman was within range. He looked out at the rider, the reins were slack in his hands. His head was down protecting him against the driving rain. There was no mistake, the rider was Lord Kilgarvan, who else owned such a fine mare and wore such outlandish clothes?

Blessing himself he tucking the musket deeper into his shoulder he took aim and slowly pressed the trigger.

There was a flash and he was catapulted backwards. As he regained his balance he heard the horseman cry out as the bullet entered his temple. The horse took fright and bolted into the mist. They watched as the horseman fell from the mare. As he did his foot got caught in the stirrup and he was dragged upside down along the road.

They came out of the cover of the spinney and followed the mare. Some distance down the road the stirrup broke and the body of the rider was catapulted into the hedge. The mare relieved of her burden stopped short and began chewing grass from the bank. Cautiously with his musket at the ready, he approached the rider.

"Is he dead?" Tony asked with a tremble in his voice.

"I've got a loaded musket don't you move" Gerry warned the motionless corpse.

Seeing that the rider was not moving he came closer. Tucking his musket under his arm he looked down at the mud covered coat. The hunting coat completely covered his face making identification impossible.

"Tony come over here and find out if he is still alive, I'll cover for you." He again pointed his musket at the prone figure, warning him not to move. Tony reluctantly approached and pulled the coat from the face of the rider.

"Jesus! It's not him. It's Frank McLaughlan." Both men stood looking down at the dead face.

"What is he doing dressed in his Lordships clothes and riding his mare?" Tony questioned.

"I suppose like ourselves he knew that he would never get paid and took what he felt was his due."

"Whatever the reason he was no worse and no better than his master. He'll not be missed."

Leaving the corpse where it lay in the mud, the Fenians entered the woods and vanished into the night.

A MEETING OF MINDS

Having bid good bye to their generous hosts Molly and Michael wended their way down the old bog road. It was noon when they had reached the town of Bundoran where they once again rested.
"We'll not spend too long here Michael, I was hoping to reach Sligo before the light fades."
"Come on then don't let me hold you up." Michael rose from his seat and began walking down the road.
Passing through Tullaghan they saw a large dray drawn by two shire horses with a tall gangly man sitting in the sprung seat. The dray was heading south and passed them at a leisurely pace before stopping some yards down the road.
"Where would you two be going to?" The driver asked when they came beside him.
"We're going to Galway in the far county." Molly informed him.
"Galway is it now, well I'm not going that far but I can take you as far as Sligo."
"God bless you and keep you in good health. Come on Michael." Molly thanked him.
" My name is Terry Davenny, I'm a miller by trade. Whatever would be bringing you to Galway?"
"I'm Molly Cullhane and this here is Michael Kearney from over Dungloe way." She introduced them.
"You have come a good journey then, so you have. There are always drays travelling between Galway and Sligo. I might be able to arrange a passage for you both."
Slowly the dray rounded Sligo bay and entered the town.
"This is it then, far as I go I fear. If you intend staying in the town for awhile I'll make some enquiries."
"Enquiries! What enquiries?" She looked questioningly at him.
"To find out if there's a dray going to Galway of course."
"Thank you. You are too kind? Isn't he Michael?" She felt embarrassed and wondered if he noticed her curt remark.
"Good luck then, I'll look forward to meeting you again. That is if you are still in town." With a wave of his hand he vanished into one of the side alleys.
Molly and Michael retired to the coach house where they had a meal. They were disappointed to learn that there would be no transport leaving the town until the following morning.
Resting on a seat by the bay they watched the hustle and bustle of the busy little town. Slowly she closed her eyes and was about to doze off when she

heard a voice calling.

"I see you had no luck then." Looking up she saw Terry coming towards them.

"No I'm afraid not, we will stay here the night and with any luck get a lift in the morning. Thanks for all your help and consideration."

"You're not thinking of sitting here all night, are you?"

"Not really, we'll find a shake down some place later on." She shrugged her shoulders and thought that he was being a bit too brazen.

"Tell you what as you have plenty of time on your hands, why don't you come along to the hooley."

"To a hooley at my age. I'm a bit long in the tooth for a hooley. Do you want to go Michael?"

"Where is it being held?" Michael asked.

"One of my relatives from out of town got married this morning and we are having a bit of a party. You're more than welcome." Terry invited.

"Thanks! Thanks a lot how could we refuse such a generous offer." Molly smiled.

"Come on then. It's not too far." Terry walked ahead of them up the dark street and on into the countryside. Looking back he saw Molly hesitate.

"Come on it's only a stretch of the feet. Just up the road." He again encouraged them.

They heard the 'Craic' long before they reached the bend in the road. Before them they saw set into a field a thatched cottage with a welcoming open door. Bull rush torches lit the boréen outside to guide the guests.

They followed him into the cottage and stood with their backs to the white washed wall.

A woman was standing in the centre of the room singing a song. Her bared feet and ragged hessian skirt denoted that she had little if any of the worlds wealth. She was singing a love song of her native land and clenching her fists with feeling.

A Youth and an Irish Maid

As I rode out one evening
In the summer time
To view the fields and meadows,
All nature seemed delight
The thrushes and the blackbird's notes
Invited and I stayed,
To hear the conversation
Of a youth and an Irish maid.

The young man broke the silence first
And to his love did say;
Oh Molly! Lovely Molly,
No longer can I stay.
For the ship is waiting at Queenstown
And her anchor now is weighed.
But where're I go I'll think of thee
My lovely Irish maid.

When you go o'er to Yankee shore
Some Yankee girls you'll see,
They'll all look very handsome
And you'll think no more of me.
You'll forget your vows and promises
That to me you have made,
You'll forget them all you left behind
And your lovely Irish maid.

When I go o'er to Yankee shore
Some Yankee girls I'll see,
Shure they'll look very handsome
But to remind me still of thee;
For there's not flower, nor a shady bower
Or a place where we have strayed,
Where're I'll be, I'll think of thee
My lovely Irish maid.

These two fond hearts together drew
Into a last embrace,
And tears like falling dew drops
Came rolling down each face.
There's not a day when you're away,
But I'll visit this dark cool glade
Where first you stole my heart away
My lovely Irish maid.

As she wound down the song she spoke the last line...
"And Sheila and Joseph their love did pledge. That's it now." Looking at the

assembly she shyly genuflected and returned to her stooléen.
"Joe Hennessy will you wake up and give the pipes a blasting." The host dressed in rough tweed trousers the legs of which were tied with hemp half way up called to an old man sitting deep in the chimney recess. Joe, a well-respected piper from Limerick sat dozing beside the fire. Between his legs sat his faithful dog and on his lap lay a set of battered Ulilian pipes.
Puffing contentedly on his cré dudéen he picked up the pipes and placed the bellows under his armpit. Removing his pipe he spat into the fire and looked at the gathering. Placing his fingers on the pipes he fired up the bag and began playing the sweetest notes of a lively tune that caressed the gravest heart.
A young couple in bare feet, their arms crossed took to the centre of the flagged floor and tapped out the time with their toes. They danced across the flagged floor, their feet tapping out the rhythm as they went. The floor space was soon filled with anxious dancers, intent to show their prowess in the space provided. Those not participating were either forced against the walls or out the door, where they stood encouraging the dancers by clapping in time to the tune.
The piper was in great fettle and kept the dancers on the floor longer than they intended. Molly watched for the next couple to vacate the floor.
"Come on Michael, now it's our turn." Seeing a couple tiring and about to leave the floor she encouraged him to join her.
All too soon the floor was emptied and the guests returned to the cottage. Their host took to the floor and with his hands deep in the pockets of his tattered waistcoat called for a 'Sean Scéal'...
"I'm sure the woman from Clare knows one that we never heard, come on now missus let's hear from you." He called to Molly.
"Well I suppose it is the least that I can do, I'll try but don't hesitate to stop me if you heard it before." Molly volunteered.
"My mother, God rest her soul told this story many the time *'In the glow of the Turf Fire'*
Now there lived in Watergate in the city of Limerick one John Dwyer. He was a malicious debaucher and feared neither God nor man. It was one night after a heavy bout of drinking and gambling that it happened, God between us and all harm...
John had spent the day with a woman of ill repute, leaving his good wife to fend for their family as best she could. He was a blackguard if ever there was one, God forgive me.
The hour was late when he left her bed and began his return journey home."
"Shame on the blackguard." Came chastisement from the gathering.
Molly looked into the gathering and smiled for the story was being well

received. She continued...'
'Passing the old city walls at Watergate he turned into the old graveyard intending to take the shortest route home. The old graveyard is situated on the north side of the milk market in the city, so it is.
On a path inside the graveyard what did he see but a skull lying on the ground. In his drunken stupor he took a kick at the skull sending it deep into the undergrowth.
"You are welcome to come and join me to morrow." He laughed as he left the graveyard.'
"God between us and all harm." An old crone crossed herself and called for a blessing on the gathering. "Sorry for the interruption, go on." She apologised. Molly continued her story...
"The following night as usual he was away to partake of a game of cards and a heavy night of drinking and the comfort of a woman's bed should she be willing.
On his way home that night he again entered the old graveyard. He was more than surprised I can tell you when he was accosted by a tall gentleman. The gentleman was attired in a costume of an age long past and on his head he displayed a silk top hat.
"Who do you think you are? Get out of my way?" He was in an offensive temper and tried to deliver a vicious blow on the gentleman. He was shocked and surprised when his hand went through him.
"What are you, in God's holy name tell me?" The coward called as he shrank away from the spióradh, (Spirit) for that is what he had encountered.
He soon sobered up I tell you and was now fearful of the dark stranger standing before him.
"I sir, am the gentleman that you invited to join your party." Boomed the tall stranger.
"Go away! Go away at once. This is not real I must be having a nightmare." The blackguard screamed.
"You are not dreaming, John Dwyer, *Look?*" Removing his tall hat the spirit pointed to a large bruising on his forehead.
"This was done by you to me last night and you are now welcome to join my party."
"This cannot be happening to me, go away leave me in peace." A cold sweat appeared on his forehead. He tried to run but his feet were like lumps of lead.
"Little peace did you give to others, including the dead. Now you plead for peace for yourself." The ghostly voice boomed out.
"What is it you want of me, anyway?" The snivelling wretch pleaded.

"There is nothing that I seek of you, John Dwyer not at present. Come the feast of Samain (All Souls Night) we will meet at this spot again." With that the spirit vanished into the night.
John returned home and threw himself into bed; there he slept long into the afternoon. He remembered what took place the previous night but foolishly dismissed it as a nothing but a bad dream.
Time passed and the incident with the spirit was forgotten as far as he was concerned.
The feast of Samain came and John was away with his cronies for another night of drinking, card playing and debauchery.
It being all souls night it would have been better had he gone to church and said a few prayers for the repose of the souls of the dead.
It was a good night for him; the cards had fallen in his favour. His pockets were filled with sovereigns and his belly with finest poteen. In the crisp air he began singing an old commallie as he staggered towards the old graveyard. At the entrance he saw the gentleman standing swinging an ebony cane.
"You have arrived then, John Dwyer?" The spirit spoke.
"So I have, and I don't give a curse for you." John showing his drunken bravado tried to look into the face hidden under the tall hat.
"Come! Follow me John Dwyer, I have something for you." The spirit began to glide out of the graveyard.
John had no choice but to follow for he had no control over his movements.
"Come here." The spirit stopped at the gate and raising his hand beckoned him forward.
"This is for you John Dwyer." Opening his cloak he withdrew a brown '*Connáil na Marab.*' (Candle of the dead)
"What need have I for a candle?" He laughed.
"Take it John! Take it and remember when it is spent so will your life be spent." John found that although he had not taken the candle it was now in his hand. As the spirit vanished the candle lit.
He held the candle for some time not knowing what to do with it. Then blowing it out he put it in the pocket of his coatamore and returned home.
Time passed and he had forgotten all about the candle and the ghost. He had more pressing matters to attend to, drinking and card playing.
The candle lay deep in the pocket of his old coatamore throughout the summer and on into the autumn.
On the feast of Samain his wife was alone in the house fending as usual for her children as best she could. There was no fire in the grate and no food on the table. The sparse candle flickered as she tried to replace the missing buttons on

her husband's old coatamore. Finally with a last gasp it burnt itself out and the room was plunged into darkness.

'I'll finish it to morrow in daylight, please God.' She thought to herself.

She began returning the buttons and patches to the pocket of his old coatamore for safe-keeping. In the pocket she was surprised to find the *'Connail na Marab.'*

She was puzzled as to what a candle for the dead was doing in his pocket. Happy to find a light with which to finish the patching she placed it in an old saucer and lit it.

"May God's light show mercy to all the poor holy souls this night." She prayed as she lit it.

Meanwhile far away in the city her wayward husband continued his drinking and card playing.

Mary, his wife sat beside the cold hob putting the final patch on a tattered jacket for one of the children by the light of the flickering candle. The candle burnt slowly nearer and nearer to the base of the broken saucer.

Midnight came and passed, John continued gambling and drinking long into the night. As the dawn broke in the east he left the den of iniquity.

He had lost all his money and was in a foul mood. He staggered towards the graveyard where once again the spirit was patiently waiting.

"What is it now, I've just about had enough of you?" He swore at the spectre and tried to pass.

"I've come for you John Dwyer, where I am taking you to you will have no need of money." The spectre opened his black cloak wide.

Mary put the jacket to one side as the candle spluttered and died.

"God be good to all the dead this blessed Halloween night." She prayed and blessing herself she retired to her cold bed. John Dwyer at that moment collapsed at the feet of the spirit and drew his last breath. The gathering remained silent as Molly returned to her seat. Then the host again came forward and congratulated her on a fine story.

"I heard many the good story under this roof and many others but I'll say this I never heard the likes. Now who is going to match that one?" He encouraged the gathering.

As the night deepened the participants having made their apologies slowly dispersed to their respective homes. Molly and Michael were invited to stay behind and take their ease in the Leaba Suidheacan.

ON THE ROAD TO GALWAY

Molly was awakened by the noise of the housewife riddling the fire and the noise of a cart in the boréen.
"Good Morning, so you are awake at last, you must have been jaded by the way you slept. There was enough noise here and outside to awaken the dead." Mary, their host looked across at Molly sitting up in the bed.
"Whatever time is it, I'm still tired?" She sat on the side of the bed and stretched herself.
"It's long past milking time but if the fancy takes you then go back to sleep. Sure there is no hurry, now is there?" Mary offered.
"Much as I'm tempted to accept your generous offer, we must be making tracks. Come on Michael time to hit the road."
"There's hot water in plenty in the kettle and a basin in the scullery." Mary called as she left the house with a bucket of mash for the fowl.
"Will you get out of that bed and fold it back into place." Molly insisted.
"Where will I put the blankets?" Michael more asleep than awake looked at the dishevelled bedclothes.
"Fold them up and put them on the bed, now hurry up will you." She instructed.
"I see you have been making yourself useful then, come on I'll make you a bite to eat." The woman returned and looked at the Leaba suidheachain.
"Here get that down you, you have a long road to follow, believe you me." Mary set two generous plates of food before them.
"You're far too kind, isn't she Michael." Michael was already sitting at the table eating and waved his fork in acknowledgement.
"God bless the house and all within." Molly looked up from the table to see the frame of Terry Davenny leaning over the half door.
"Come in there's no need to stand on ceremony. There's tae in the pot for the asking." Mary picked up the pot and shook it.
"Mary Allanah, you know all my failings, so you do. I should have made an honest woman of you long ago." He joked as he entered the kitchen.
"Enough of that now Terry, don't let my Danny hear you talk like that."
"So the two sleepy heads have made it at last, I thought you were going to dream your brains away." He took his place at the table.
"Was that your cart making all the noise this morning?" Molly asked.
"None other and it is that cart that is going to take you to Galway. So don't insult it."
"To Galway indeed, do you know how far that is?" Molly asked.

"It's a good stretch I'll admit, you weren't thinking of walking it, were you?" Terry joked.
"Will you not mind him, he makes that journey regularly." Mary intervened.
"What of the horses, they surely could not travel all that far without rest?" Michael asked.
"You're right, we change the horses at appointed stops and replace them with fresh. On the return journey we again change them for the first pair of rested horses. So long as the cart stands up to the roads there never is a problem. Now, whenever the fancy takes you we will hit the road." Terry rose from the table.
"Here before you leave take this with you." Mary came from the scullery with a parcel of food.
"Mary, you shouldn't have. There's no need for this; you have been so kind to us. However we are grateful and thanks." Molly picked up the parcel.
"Will you not be thanking me, sure it's only a mouthful. God bless you on your journey and I hope you find what you are seeking."
"I'll call in on my return and drop in the new scythe. Thanks for the tae and the Craic. Come on you two get a move on." Terry took his place on the high sprung seat up front.
It was dark night when they entered the village of Claregalway. Terry halted the dray on the main street and invited them to dismount. Entering a dimly lit roadhouse he invited them to join him.
"Peggy me darling, is Pat about?" He addressed a fat jovial woman standing behind a make shift counter.
"I'm sure he heard you and should be here in a minute. How are things with you?"
"Oh! So and so you know." Terry shrugged his shoulders.
"Here's Pat now." Peggy looked back towards the kitchen.
"Well Terry; here again and I see you brought company, I didn't know you were one for the ladies." Pat came from behind the counter.
"It's nothing like that, would you ever fix them up for the night and take them to Galway to morrow morning." Terry looked embarrassed.
"That's a tall order Terry Davenny, are they relatives or something?"
"Nothing of the sort Pat but... I'll tell you the whole story another day so I will. For now will you trust me?" Terry pleaded.
"Sure he's only teasing you, it's no trouble at all. How many favours have you done for us with no questions asked." Peggy interrupted.
"And many the jar of *'Potéen'* you smuggled in under the noses of the excise men." Pat slapped him on the back and began laughing.
"This is where we part company Molly, I have to pick up a load from the

village of Athenry. You'll be right for a lift into Galway. This is Peggy and her husband Pat, they will look after you both." Terry introduced Molly to his friends.

"Now should you get the chance would you ever leave your new address with them. You never know I might find out something of Mary in my travels." Terry suggested.

"You're one good soul, so you are and God will reward you." Molly thanked him.

"She's right you know there's not many Terry Davenny's to be found. Here is my hand." Michael shook his hand warmly.

"There's many the person called me worse than that, so there are." He laughed as taking his seat on the dray he turned left on to the Athenry road.

"Pity there aren't more Terry Davenny's in this ould world." Molly sighed as she looked after the cart as it faded into the distance.

Next morning true to his word Pat harnessed the mare to the trap.

"Good luck to you both and may God bless you. Now don't forget to send us word when you get settled. I know that Terry will be anxiously waiting for results." Peggy called as the trap slowly moved down the road.

After an uneventful journey Pat set them down in the square in Galway and once again having reminded them to keep in touch took the road home.

"This is it then, someone must have been praying for us to get this far." Picking up the portmanteau Michael followed Molly down the narrow street.

She began making enquiries regarding work for housekeepers in the town. There were a few but none were willing to accommodate Michael as well.

"We can give you a situation but the boy will need to go to the hiring fair." She was told. The hiring fair was where boys and girls went seeking employment.

"He'll not be going to any hiring fare, you can be assured of that. Where I go he goes also." Molly insisted.

"Come to think of it, the old rector from Menlough was over at the hiring looking for someone to look after him." She was informed.

"Is he still looking, do you know?" She asked.

"I should think so. What he pays in wages wouldn't keep you in leather." The informant laughed.

"Where is this place, not too far away I hope?" Molly asked.

"No! If you have a mind to it. It is on the road by Tirraleen Castle, so it is. You cannot miss it if you follow the river Corrib." She was informed.

"Come on Michael, it's worth the looking " Molly without waiting was making strides out of town. They travelled some distance without finding any sign of a house. They were about to believe that they had taken the wrong road when

Michael who was walking some distance in front stopped.
"That must be it over there." He pointed to a large detached stone house set back from the road.
"It looks the worst for wear but solid enough." She continued up the drive as she spoke.
As they reached the portal the door opened and a stooped gentleman came forward.
"What can I do for you people?" He asked as he rubbed his hands together.
"Are you the rector who is seeking a housekeeper?" Molly dropped her bundle and came nearer to the door.
"I am that, but I don't need any labour on the farm. Are you a good housekeeper and can you cook?" The old rector studied them both.
"I can do both and much more but where I go the boy goes too." She insisted.
"There is little that I can pay you and that will not be paid until I receive my stipend at the fall of the year. I'll let your boy stay with you." He offered.
"What salary is on offer then?" Molly asked.
"There's full board with your own room and a room for the boy. Then I could let you have six guineas."
"Six guineas is it, not a lot for a years work I'm thinking. What I'm looking for is a decent living and a good school for the boy." Molly began to bargain.
"I agree with you Missus, the wages are not attractive nor is the house. I can arrange a good schooling for the boy. There's a fine farm of land here that needs a strong back to break it. Should he be willing then I'll share the profits from it in return for his labour." He suggested.
"What do you think of that offer Michael?" She asked.
"It suits me fine, so it does," Anxious to rest his head Michael would have agreed to any suggestion. He looked round at the badly neglected farm.
"There's your answer Sir. Now when can we move in as we are homeless?"
"My name is Canon William Bougham, most people call me Canon or Bill. If you feel easier calling me Bill then I have no objections. I'll show you to your rooms and then you can look over the house. I'll not be making any demands on your time. I'm sure you know how to manage a house better than I can. You see my good wife died some six months ago. The house has been neglected ever since."
It did not take long for Molly to get her feet under the table. She soon had the house to her satisfaction and running like clockwork.
She made it her business to go to Claregalway and leave her new address for Terry Davenny.

TERRY DAVENNY DOES THE CALLING

One morning as the rector was sitting down to his breakfast Molly approached him.
"There's a fine run out there behind the bawn crying out for a few hens to fill it. Would you ever consider letting me have a few shillings to go to the market in Galway?"
"How much would you need?" He asked without question.
"I don't know off hand, say a florin, is that too much?" Molly asked for a florin hoping to get one shilling at least.
"A florin indeed, very well then I'll let you have it. The market day is on Wednesday."
"You'll let me have the florin then?" She looked surprised.
"I said so didn't I. I'm sure that you will spend it wisely, won't you?"
From that small beginning Molly never looked back as she prudently invested her small purchase.
With good management she began to build up her flock of hens and geese and in time she added a milch goat.
True to his word the rector arranged for Michael to have tuition in a fine school in the city. He also allowed him free access to his library.
Molly returned from the market one day full of excitement and went to see the rector. Knocking on the door to his study she entered without invitation.
"Whatever is the matter? You look as excited as a bag of bees." He looked up from his book.
"As you know I went to the market as usual to sell a few eggs and chickens." Holding her chest to regain her breath she paused.
"Will you sit down before you have a heart attack and tell me what happened."
"Well! There was an auction in the square and I got carried away. God help me, I did so I did. I spent all the money I got for the chickens and the eggs and more besides."
"So you spent more money than you had, is that what you are saying? Whatever did you buy that cost so much?"
"I bought a cart and a horse, so I did. They looked so strong that I could not resist the temptation." She blurted.
"A cart and horse. Got carried away did you and how much did you bid on them?"
"Four pounds for the two and I promised that I would give the money to the drayman when he delivered them here." She rose from her seat and looked out of the window.
"What else did you buy with the money you got from the sale of the poultry

and eggs?"

"I bought a cow, you see a farmer over near to Salthill is selling out and emigrating to America. It was a chance in a lifetime so it was. Whatever can I do?" She pleaded.

"Do Molly! Go and make us a nice cup of tae. We'll soon make a good return on our horse and cow, won't we?" He smiled as he returned to his papers.

"But Sir, They will be here soon and how will I pay them? Bad cess to that blabbering tongue of mine." She rose from her chair and once again looked out on to the road.

"I told you that I would pay, now go and make the tae will you and stop your snivelling."

"God bless you Sir, you're so understanding."

"Molly I hope the cow is as generous to us as you were to the auctioneer with my money." He smiled and returned to his book.

Contented that all would be well she placed the iron kettle on the *crann tógála (crane)* and prepared the tae.

In time Michael took the cow to the bull and slowly the farm came back to life. When the horse was not needed to pull the cart he was used to work the fields. One fine morning as she was digging in the quarter acre field behind the kitchen she heard a dray coming up the drive.

"Now who could that be?" Putting her slán to one side she came round the house.

"Good heavens it cannot be, is it yourself Terry?" Wiping her hands on her apron she ran to greet him.

"It's me right enough Molly, I should have been here sooner, but, ah well! Better late than never". He jumped off the cart and with a grin on his face that would do justice to a churn of cream approached her.

"Times are good to you by the looks of things and where is Michael?"

"He's away at school, however don't stand there on ceremony. Come on in, come in and take the weight off your feet. Is there any news?"

'If it is about Mary then I'm afraid that I must disappoint you. It is as if the earth opened and swallowed her up. I was over your way and met the sleador John Murphy, he was asking for you. He wants to know when you are coming home. The only caller to the cottage was a woman from Ramilton but she was of no consequence."

"Did you tell him where we are?"

"I gave him all the news and told him that you were settled in Galway. He would love to come and visit you but the journey is too far. Still your house looks fine and he seems to be taking good care of it and the garden."

"Like yourself Terry, John is one great soul so he is."
"I'm really pleased to hear that you are getting on so well with the Protestant gentleman."
"He's a good old soul, so he is. Not in the best of health if you must know, but he never complains."
"Never mind him for now, I've come a long ways to hear all the news and gossip. I must see to the horse though, he had a long journey. I'll be back in two shakes of a lambs tail for the sup of tae and the craic."
"I'll put the tae pot on a bed of *gríosach* whilst I'm waiting for you to return." Molly scooped out a shovelful of hot ashes from the fire and set the taepot in the middle to brew.
They sat one each side of the fire sharing a pot of tae when the door was opened.
"Is it yourself I'm looking at?" Terry rose to his feet and looked at the figure of a tall youth standing in the doorway.
"It's me alright, how are you keeping? I see you are still your old self, a bit heavier you'll agree." Michael came forward his hand held out in greeting.
"I suppose you'll suggest that I walk to Galway to lose weight next." Terry laughed as he patted his midriff.
"There's a strange horse in the meadow, don't tell me that you have been to the mart again?" Michael addressed Molly.
"Wherever it came from I can assure I didn't buy it, where is it?" She rose and went to the window.
"That's my horse, I let him off to do a bit of grazing before I return. No problem is there?" Terry informed them.
"No trouble at all, it's just that Molly has the habit of coming home with one surprise or another." Michael laughed.
"I do not, whatever I buy is for the good of the farm." She replied rather hurt.
"Time passes quickly when one is having a good time, I must be off. It will be all clocks before I reach Tuam." Terry looked up at the clock and decided that it was time to leave.
"I'll give you a hand to harness the horse." Both men left the house with Molly following behind.
"I'll let you go now, don't leave it so long next time. Don't forget to put the *stopallán* back in the gap. Good bye and safe journey." She watched as they vaulted the stone wall and disappeared from view down the long meadow.

THE OULD HAG FROM LIMERICK

Molly spent most of her time planning and scraping as to how she might return the farm to respectability. The canon had reneged on all responsibility for the house and farm. She knew that he was in a lot of pain and tried to comfort him in any way she could.
Mostly he liked to be left alone in his study writing. She would bring him the occasional cup of tae for which he was always grateful.
One evening as the sun was sinking below Galway Bay he heard the cart trundling up to the back door. He knew instantly that she had bought something or other from the market. Curiosity got the better of him when he heard her calling to the mare in no uncertain terms to stand still.
Rising painfully to his feet he went to the back door and looked out. There she was trying to manipulate a dash churn from the back of the cart. The mare tormented by horse flies kept moving and scraping the ground much to her annoyance. It seemed that every time she got a grip on the churn the mare decided to move.
"Hold on there, I'll take hold of her winkers as you remove whatever it is you bought." Bill limped out the door and approached the mare.
"Thank you, I was beginning to think that I would have to churn on the cart." She laughed as she got her hands round the churn and lifted it off.
This was followed by a collection of accoutrements necessary for the production of butter. There was the plunger together with cover, a separator, a couple of butter pats, a butter marker, a butter worker and a collection of large earthen ware vessels to cool the milk in.
"Don't you want to know what I bought?" She challenged as he retreated to the house.
"It's a milk churn for a start, I suppose you know what you are doing." He hobbled back to his study showing no interest whatsoever.
"I'll be making a sup of tae in a minute, would you like a rasher and egg or two with yours?" She asked.
"No Molly, a few slices of scone with honey would not go amiss though, thanks." Closing the door behind him he left her to her chores.
Having made the tae she took a tray to Bill in the study and once again tried to justify the purchase of the churns.
"We'll have our own butter and cream now. You'll let me know how much salt you like in yours, won't you?" She again tried to instil some interest but without success.
"I will of course, now would you please let me be. Sorry, thanks for the tae and

scones." He apologised for his abrupt behaviour. She knew that he was in pain and from previous experiences she found it best to leave him alone on such occasions.

She was now the proud owner of two churns; one was screwed with thumbscrews securely to a table in the scullery.

The other called a dash or barrel churn sat on the floor and stood as tall as a milk churn, both were made of wood with brass bands to keep the wood watertight. She scalded and scrubbed them until the wood gleamed white before she was satisfied with their condition.

Not having enough milk to justify the labour involved in butter production she went to an immediate neighbour and bartered for a half churn of fresh milk. Her first efforts were a complete failure for she spent too long in the churning. She went to see Bill and ask his advice.

"Molly, don't you know that *'Long Churning makes bad butter'?* The faster one churned the better the butter. He advised.

On seeing that she was insulted by this advice he asked her if she had seen any strangers hanging about.

"What kind of strangers and how would that affect the butter making?" She asked.

"Did you never hear tell of the *Ould hag?*" He looked deep into her eyes.

"No! Who might she be? What has she to do with my churning?"

"Who is she you may well ask. I advise you to show her a little respect. Down in Munster and more especially around Limerick lives the *'Ould hag of Limerick'*. She has special charms and is usually about at this time of year, it being springtime. She'll come in the form of a hare sucking the teats of the animals as she goes. If she's about then you will get no more butter, nor milk for that matter for the rest of the year." He assured her.

"Are you telling me that I'll not see a scraping of butter on account of some ould hag from Limerick, bad cess to her?" She stamped her foot to show her annoyance.

"Now Molly be careful how you behave towards her, she won't take too kindly to your tantrums." He warned.

"Tantrums indeed, all I want is to be left alone to make my own butter. Is that asking too much? How can I get rid of the ould witch?" Placing her hands on her hips she again stamped her foot.

"Here's what you must do. Check that there's an ould horseshoe fixed to the bottom of your churn. Then go down the meadow to where the cow and goat are and see if a hare or a strange ould woman is lurking in the field. If so return at once to the house making sure that she doesn't see you. You must then get

Michael to make a spancel by the light of the full moon. He must make it from hair off all the animals on the farm. As he makes it he must utter these words..."

'There's butter in my churn
The hare has got to turn
Saint Bridget prayed on the first of May
That evil spells be cast away'

As the dawn breaks over an Irish sky he must go down the field. Ignoring the cries of the hare and any other distraction, which the hag will no doubt put in his path. He must *'Walk the field'* brushing the dew up with the spancel as he goes. On his return to the house he must place the spancel on the fire and call up the chimney...

'Here I place this spancel
The Ould hags curse to cancel
I pray to God my hand to guide
Saint Bridget's cross I'll weave this night.'

Repeatedly making the sign of the cross on your forehead and invoking the blessing of the *Blessed Trinity*. You must gather up a drop of milk from the neighbours and place all in the churn. Go to your poorest neighbour and beg a piece of her butter and place that into the milk. Gather a handful of rushes weave them into the *'Cross of Saint Bridget'* and wash it in her holy well. Place the cross under the churn and both you and Michael must take turns in churning and at the same time recite this prayer 'Thanks Saint Bridget for all your blessings.'

Having observed this part of the cure he must then place a *'Saint Bridget's Cross'* over the scullery door and to the rafters tie a branch of the *'Rowan Tree'* that has been soaked in salted water. When all these customs you have observed then and only then will your churn be filled with butter."

"Now how would you know all this and you not one of us? No disrespect to your cloth"

"No offence taken Molly, I might be a *'Church Of Ireland'* Minister, but I'm still a superstitious ould Irishman." He assured her.

"I see, and you're tell me that this is true. You wouldn't lie to me?"

"Believe what you will Molly. I can assure you that the ould hag will not let you churn. "The ould hag has got into your churn and you will need to get her out." He warned.

"Perhaps that's why they auctioned it. I wonder did it come from Limerick?" She questioned.

"Who knows, you could be right. Where it came from does not matter. You've

got to shift the ould hag from your churn and fast." He warned.
"I'll set the task as soon as Michael returns from school. No ould hag is going to profit from my churn. The cheek of them Limerick folk." Molly returned to her kitchen in a foul mood.
Michael returned to the house that evening and much to his surprise she prepared a meal for him that would do justice to a ploughman. A sure sign that she had something in mind.
"I'll never eat all this." He looked at the overbrimming plate and the large slices of buttered scones.
"Eat it all up I have a very urgent task for you." She told him as she repeatedly filled his mug with sweet tae.
"What is it? I have a lot of studying to do." He was suspicious of Molly's tasks.
She explained all that the rector had told her and of her efforts to churn without results.
"Are you telling me that there is a *Piseóg on the farm?*" Michael looked worried.
"No I'm not, it's just that the rector suspects that the '*Ould hag from Limerick*' might be up to some *Shenanigans*. I'd love to know how she survived in my churn with all the scrubbing I done?" She informed him.
"I'll make the spancel to night for the sky is clear and the moon full." Michael promised.
That night he set about the task and by midnight he had made as fine a spancel as ever came out of Galway.
Next morning before the cock had time to do the crowing Michael was up and about.
Molly on hearing him riddled the fire and set the iron kettle on the crane. Taking the bellows wheel in her hand she put life into the fire.
"Keep the fire going, I'm off down the meadow." Michael picked up the spancel and dipped it in the holy water before leaving the house.
On his return he saw that she had a fire going that would roast an Ox. The crane had been moved from over the coals and the grate cleaned. All was now ready for the exorcising of the '*Ould hag from Limerick*'.
"Is that it, Michael?" She looked with misgiving at the dew soaked spancel.
Ignoring her he took the spancel and placed it on the fire and called her to his side. They repeated the prayer over again up the chimney as the spancel spluttered and burnt. When the spancel was completely burnt they came from inside the chimney and looked at each other before again blessing themselves. By midday they had completed the ritual much to their relief.
"I feel a lot better now, how about you Michael?" She sighed.
"Amen Molly, we must never speak of this again." Returning to the table they both sat looking into the fire.

THE STATIONS AND THE CRAIC

Molly and Michael were taking a leisurely stroll along the banks of the river Corrib one fine afternoon when his attention was drawn to an overgrown meadow on the opposite bank.
"I wonder who owns that land?" Michael drew her attention to the neglected meadow.
"I don't know but it's a terrible waste of a good field. Do you know I could put that to good use" She looked despairingly at the lush grass choking in a field of weeds.
"It must belong to somebody, I wonder who?" He scratched his chin.
By the time they returned to the house he had forgotten all about the field but not Molly.
"How are you feeling this evening Bill?" She inquired as she set a tray before the rector.
"I can't complain, it's the will of Almighty God." Painfully he rose from his seat.
She laid the tray to one side and adjusted the pillows to make him more comfortable.
"There now a nice cup of warm tae and a slice of scone will perk you up some what."
"Where did you go today, not out buying again?" Cautiously he sat back in his seat.
"No! We took a stroll along the river bank and saw a lot of neglected land on the opposite bank." She informed him.
"Oh that, I've not been over there in years. We used to have a *'Droichead Coise'* across to it but it fell into decay and was washed away in the great flood."
"Are you telling me that you own that land too?" Molly looked surprised.
"I do that, but I feel I should not have told you. Next you'll be building a bridge across the river." He laughed.
With Michael away at school preparing for his examinations she was left alone to look after the house and farm. Bill required more and more of her attention as his health continued to deteriorate. She had little time to dwell on other matters and the subject of the field passed out of her mind.
The Stations were coming rapidly upon them and the holy well would need a coat of white wash. Then there were the prayer sticks to prepare. She noticed that the *Bean-Ó-Shéidhe stepping stone stile* was in need of urgent attention. Why, she thought did they have to have the Stations in the middle of the

cropping? This period would be devoted to praying and fasting in atonement for their past sins. To add to her problems she was informed that the Stations would be held at the holy well the following Sunday.
Molly informed the rector of her need to go to the well and whitewash the covering. She would also have to scrub the kneeling stones and remove the grease and grime of the past twelve months. There was one consolation in that lent would soon be over and Michael would be back home for the Easter break.
"I don't know if I'm coming or going Bill." She complained.
"It's all in a good cause Molly, I'm sure you'll manage." Was his philosophical reply.
Full of her own importance she sat on the resting stone looking at a hen with her new brood strutting ostentatiously up to the door. In the distance she saw a cart moving along the road and wondered where it was going. She followed its progress from between the hedges until it came into the opening in front of the drive. She smiled to herself as she recognised the tall figure of Terry sitting high on the sprung seat.
"Can't stay away from us, but never mind you're more than welcome." Rising from the resting stone she went and greeted him.
"You've come at a time of need Terry Davenny, so you have."
"Don't tell me that you only want me for my labour and not for myself." He laughed.
"You're as welcome as the flowers of May and I'm hoping that you will stay for the 'Stations'" She greeted him.
"Don't tell me that there are stations here too. I attended them over in Monivea not too long ago." He grumbled.
"You'll stay will you not? Sure you need all the blessing that you can get."
"When are they being held then and what about a drop of tae?"
"To morrow morning bright and early over at the shrine. Come on inside, do you like my family of chicks?" She shooed the inquisitive hen and her chicks away from the door.
"The Stations are not being held in the house then?"
"Don't you know that this is a Protestant house and anyhow down here the Stations are held at the shrine. I suppose it is because the cottages are so isolated." She whispered.
"How is the old gentleman, what does he think of the stations?"
"He's indifferent and not himself at all, there's not a bad bone in his body."
"I'll stay but I must be back in Donegal the day after next. I suppose you can let me have the Leaba Suidheacan for the night?" He asked.
"That's it settled then, come on let's have the tae."

Whatever gave her the idea that she alone would have to prepare the well for the stations was soon dispelled. There were more than enough hands repairing broken stiles and whitewashing the well when she arrived. A large slab of Liscannor stone standing on three stone legs sat in front of the well as a makeshift altar. This looked more like a megalithic tomb than an altar.

Michael came home the day before the stations were to be held and was given the honour of leading the procession and carrying the cross to the well the following morning. Catholics from the surrounding countryside gathered long before the service started. There was flurry of handshakes and exchanges of gossip all round. The younger ones eyeing up potential partners. Deals were made for the exchange of goods and animals. For many from isolated districts this was their one and only gathering of the year and they intended to make the best of it. With them they brought their children to be baptised as there were no priests and no churches in the mountains. Many couples who were living as husband and wife came to be married in the sight of God. Two priests from Galway attended the stations and confessions were heard kneeling on the rough ground before the mass was celebrated. Mass was celebrated on the Liscannor slab and a collection or offerings were gathered up for the priests in keeping with the wealth of the participants. The names and amounts donated were read out starting with those who gave the most. The priest blessed the water and invited all to take a container of the holy water home with them. As the slab was cleared of the sacred vessels they were soon replaced with hampers of food. This was a welcome sight to all present. They had fasted from midnight the day before and were famished with the hunger this included the two priests. Towards evening the gathering adjourned to a meadow below the well. Several doors had been borrowed from neighbouring haggards and laid out in a square in the centre of the meadow. It was not long before a spontaneous band began to entertain the gathering. There was no shortage of singers or dancers. As the sun sank over Galway bay the air was filled with music. Couples, their inhibitions put to one side danced the buckles off their shoes. Not mind you but that there were few if any with shoes of any sorts.

Bottles and flasks of '*Potéen*' were passed from hand to hand with a wink and a nod. It was at such gatherings that the '*Matchmaker*' would be called upon to do the talking.

With all the energy being spent on singing and dancing it was hard to believe that these people had walked many miles the previous day over mountains to reach the Stations.

Molly went looking for Michael and found him down by the bank of the river in deep conversation with a girl dressed in a shawl of Galway grey. Without disturbing them she returned to the gathering. A rendering of an ould song was in progress with Terry leading the singing.

Molly waved to him and he waved back without interrupting the song.

Sitting on a gathering of straw she hugged her knees to her and let her mind wander.

"Well, did you find him?" Her dreaming was interrupted by the arrival of Terry.

"Find who? Oh Michael! Yes I found him and more besides." She smiled.

"Come on then, I know you are dying to tell someone." He teased her.

"I guess our Michael is growing up, he's down by the river with a cailín. I wish that I could find his mother." She sighed.

"Come on, we came here to enjoy ourselves." He pulled her from the ground and escorted her to the dancing doors.

All too soon the dawn rose above the mountain and the gathering was slowly dispersing.

Molly and Terry crossed the ladder stile and wended their way back to the house.

"Molly, will you bide here with me awhile?" He took her hand in his and looked into her eyes.

"Whatever is it Terry?" She felt the warmth and unsure quiver in his voice.

"Would you mind if I done the calling. I won't be offended if you refuse me?"

"Are you asking my hand Terry Davenny?" She squeezed her hand into his.

""Sure I am, I have a fine stone cottage and twelve acres of good watered land and..."

"There's no need to go on, I'll wed you for yourself and for nothing else." She interrupted him.

"You'll not regret the day you said '*Yes*' to Terry Davenny so you won't." He promised.

Returning to the house they found Michael sound asleep on the Leaba Suidheacan.

With a fluttering in his heart and the song of the birds in his ears Terry Davenny took the rocky road back to Donegal.

THE EXCISE OFFICERS RAID A STILL

Terry lay slumped across the backrest of the sprung seat leaving his horse to meander slowly along the old bog road. The grey dawn rose slowly over the mountain ridge between the village of Cloonboo and Lake Corrib. He knew that he had more than a generous helping of *Potéen* under his belt.
A mist rising from the lake blanketed the surrounding countryside in a delicate floating cloud. Feeling the discomfort of the hardback rest he removed his coatamore and rolling it into a pillow placed it behind his head. It was a chilly dawn yet he was as oblivious to it as he was to his surroundings.
He felt like singing but his mouth was parched dry. His belly was filled with warm *Potéen* and his dreams were of his Molly. He was content with himself and the world and had good reason to be. Had not Molly Cullhane promised to be his bride?
His horse slowed to a crawl as he rubbed his eyes trying to look through the mist. His eyes grew heavier and heavier, was she thinking of him as much as he was of her? What if she changed her mind?
His faithful horse with his head down slowly and deliberately pulled the cart on into Headford. The reek and smell of newly revived fires filled the morning air as the town slowly came to life. A milk cart trundled down the road on it's way to the creamery.
"Good morning, God bless you." The farmer lifted his cap as the carts passed each other in the opposite directions. There was no reply from Terry, he was dreaming the hours away.
He awakened to the neighing of his horse and the reins being pulled sharply from his hands. Looking round him he saw that his horse had come to a halt and was shaking his head. Rubbing his hands over his face he let out a loud yawn and slowly opened his eyes.
His horse was standing over a trough drinking. Removing his caubéen he scratched his head. Jumping off the cart he went to the trough and shared a drink with his horse, then he plunged his head into the cool water. Removing his cravat he wiped his face and began looking for familiar surroundings.
"Where have you brought us to?" He addressed his horse.
Seeing a woman approaching the pump he waited for her to advance.
"What town is this Mam?" He asked.
"By the looks of you it wouldn't matter either ways, You're in Headford in the County Mayo. Where were you going to if you don't mind me asking?"
"Going to!" Oh I was going on to Sligo." He looked puzzled at her wondering how he got Mayo.
"I see you had a good skinful, was it a good hooley then?" The woman half

laughed.

"To be honest with you I was at the stations in Galway. I should have changed horses at Tuam. Do you know I could murder a mug of tae." He confessed "The stations was it now, we never have stations as good as that here. Come on pump the handle for me and I'll let you have a good breakfast and a mug of warm tae." Placing the bucket on the hook over the spout of the pump she studied him as he operated the handle.

"I've seen you before someplace, now let me think?" Rubbing her chin she continued studying him.

"I know who you are now, you are the drayman from Donegal, Teeeerry." She snapped her fingers as she tried to remember his surname.

"Terry Davenny, how do you know me?"

"Sure I've often seen you over in Tuam, pick up the bucket. My Joseph will be surprised to know that I picked up a new man at the crack of dawn." She again laughed as she walked up the street ahead of him.

"You're away off the beaten tracks, so you are." Her husband remarked as they sat by the fire.

"Not too far, if I had slept any longer I could have wound up in Castlebar." Terry consoled himself.

"Not as bad as my Joseph, he found himself in Limerick at one stage and he was only going as far as Ballyhale. To make matters worse he lost his horse and cart. The horse had more sense of direction than him and found her way to the door."

"There's no need to bring that up again Mary, it was at your sister's wedding after all."

"At my sister's wedding was it and who landed in Limerick with her instead of her husband?" She again laughed.

"It was the bad Potéen I tell you. Never mind her, she's always telling yarns."

"I'll be thanking you now for I must be away, it was nice meeting you both." Shaking hands warmly they parted company.

"If you turn the cart round here and take the road to Belclare on your left, it is signposted Tuam. That will take you back on the Sligo road. God bless you now." Mary instructed as she stood by the half door.

"So much for your directions Mary, is it little wonder that I arrived in Limerick. You'd be far better taking the road to Ballinrobe and then on to Claremorris." Joseph advised.

"It's six of one and half a dozen of the other, so take whichever one suits your fancy." Mary despairing of the situation returned to the cottage.

"I can pick up a fresh horse in Tuam, so I suppose I'll take that road." Terry again took his place on the sprung seat and with a wave of his whip encouraged the horse forward.

It was dark night when he reached the mill at Ballsadare on the outskirts of Sligo. Tired and weary he backed the horse and cart into a siding.

"Well done, my old friend." He addressed the horse as he took him by the winkers to the two-acre field. Opening the gate he took the winkers off the horse and giving him a slap on the rump released him.

He was pleased when he saw the horse doing a *Rinnce Fada* down the meadow.

He walked the short distance to the home of his cousin on the Carrowmore road.

"God bless all here." Lifting the latch he entered the kitchen. He was surprised to find that there was nobody home.

Going into the scullery he removed the linen cloth from the milk jug and filled himself a cup of fresh milk. Returning to the fire he sat down on the sugan chair and removed his boots.

He drank the milk and lit his *Cré Dudéen*.

He was awakened by a commotion going on in the boréen.

"What can we do they've got all four of them?" He heard his cousin Nora crying.

"Come on Nora, come into the house." He heard her husband Brendan consoling her.

Terry was putting on his boots when the door was opened and his cousins entered.

"Oh Terry, Thank God you are here. What are we to do?" Nora ran forward and nearly knocked him out of the chair.

"Whatever is the matter with you?" Terry pulled a boot on by the tongue.

"It's Séan, the excise men have got him." Brendan slumped into the nearest chair.

"Where was he caught? Let me guess up at the still." Terry answered his own question.

"There were three of them and our Séan using the still. I was on my way down the hill to join them when I saw much to my surprise the excise men coming up the hill against me. They were armed to the teeth and seemed to know just what they were looking for."

"Sure why wouldn't they, they couldn't miss the reek and the smell of the Potéen making. Were the boys distilling at the time?" Terry questioned.

"Of course they were, but how did the excise men know? Someone must have informed on them." Brendan questioned.

"Sure Ireland always had informers and Sligo is no exception." Nora spat out the words.

"I have no doubt that they were told to take the boat as they would be seen crossing the hill." Brendan justified his accusations.

"Never mind that for now. What I want to know is, did they take the worm with them?" Terry insisted.

"How the hell do I know or care, I'm more concerned for our Séan and the others."

"Calm down Brendan, it's a civil enough question. Now tell me all that you saw." Terry tried to calm the tense situation.

"When I saw the excise men I lay down in the heather and watched them, there was no time to warn the others. I heard them protesting to the excise officers that they did not know of the still. They claimed that they saw the reek and went to see what it was about.

Then they saw several men running away down the hill. Of course the excise officers did not believe them, would you? I saw them screw the hand irons on Séan and the others. Some of the excise men held on to the chains as the others tipped the wash on to the hill. Then they took the boys away."

"Think Brendan, did you see any of them carrying the worm." Terry insisted.

"You and your bloody worm, what's so important about it anyway? They had enough on their hands dragging four struggling men and their carbines without worrying about trying to carry the worm." Brendan was getting annoyed.

"That's good news, so it is." Terry began lacing up his boots.

"The boys will be incarcerated in Sligo jail by now. You're not thinking of an attempted rescue, are you?" Nora asked.

"No! Whatever gave you that idea? Come on we are going back to Knockarea hill."

"Knockarea Hill! Do you want to get us all locked up. Whatever would we be doing there?" Brendan demanded to know.

"We are going to do them bloody excise men so we are. Come on and you too Nora."

"See if you can spot a boat." Terry instructed. As they reached the shore he began looking in the bulrushes

"I thought that we were going to the still?" Brendan began belting the undergrowth with a stick.

"Will you keep your voice down and get rid of that stick. They may be waiting to ambush us farther on?" Terry warned.

"Nora, go up on the ridge and keep your eyes and ears peeled. If you see anything suspicious give a long hoot. Brendan you go down to the lower shore and see if you can locate their boat." He instructed.

"I told you that they took the boys back in the boat." Brendan protested.

"They'll remember that they need evidence for the court and return for the worm. I have no doubt but that they will use the boat again." He continued peering through the undergrowth.

They searched the bay without finding the boat and were about to climb the hill when Nora let out a long hoot. Terry looked up and saw her pointing towards the bay.

Looking up the bay he saw the long boat silently approaching the strand where they were standing. He waved back to her in acknowledgement.

"Come on Brendan now is our chance." He led the way across the ridge to the site of the still.

He removed the worm and cascaded the drums down the hill. They came to rest in the bracken covered bog.

"That's enough Brendan, come on let's get the hell out of here." He placed the worm over his shoulder and began his decent.

"Look over there, some of them are going for the still." Whispered Brendan.

"A lot of good it will do them, come on let's pick up Nora."

Nora joined them as they began the decent to Ballsadare Bay.

"Look there's their boat." Brendan full of excitement began to run for the boat.

"Get down you fool." Terry ran towards him. As he did he saw an excise man raise his carbine to his shoulder.

Before he could stop him a shot rang out and Terry felt an instant pain in his leg. There was confusion for a moment as he lay on the ground with blood flowing from a wound.

Nora ran down the hill to help as the excise officer was busy reloading his carbine.

"Get him Brendan before he reloads." Terry raised a blood stained hand and pointed to the officer trying desperately to reload his carbine.

Without hesitation Brendan threw himself at the office and downed him with one savage blow.

"Can you walk Terry?" Nora helped him to his feet.

"I think so, it's a flesh wound he missed the bone." He kept a tight hold on the worm as he hobbled to the boat with the assistance of Nora.

Brendan released the rope holding the boat at anchor and pushing it out into the bay jumped aboard.

"Come on grab the oars." Terry already had two oars secured in the locks and was guiding the boat towards the open sea. Brendan took the second pair and joined him.

"Hold the tiller steady Nora." Brendan instructed.

"Where do we go from here, Terry?" Brendan asked.

"We'll go ashore further up the coast and go on foot to Carrowmore."

"This is as good a place as any to land." He instructed on seeing a small inlet.

"What will we do with the boat?" Brendan stood on the strand holding the boat.

"Push it out into the bay, the current will take it across to Carrowreagh beach. When they find it they will think that we came from around that district." Terry instructed.

He was glad when he saw the outline of the cottage, as no doubt were the others who had the task of carrying him and the worm.

"Thank God we made it." Terry slumped down in the Leaba Suidheacan.

"I'll make a pot of tae and then we'll get a good nights sleep." Nora volunteered.

Next morning Brendan and Nora went to Sligo and told the others what they and Terry had achieved.

"It's for the crown to prove their case against you and without evidence that is impossible, even for them." Nora assured him.

Just as Terry predicted there was no visible proof against the four men that they were actually producing illegal whiskey. Without such evidence the crown had no alternative but to withdraw their case.

MICHAEL MEETS THE CISCEÁN MAKER OF ORANMORE

Eugene O'Byrne was known throughout the county and beyond as the 'Willow maker.' From sugan chairs to lobster pots he was the man for the job. James was a widower and the father of Veronica, his only daughter. He was a proud man and over protective of her. It soon became local gossip that she was seen alone with Michael Kearney on several occasions since the day of the *'Stations'*.
It also came to the attention of the Parish Priest who did not take too kindly to such liberties. This was not the way that courting couples behaved in the west. He knew also that the *'Craw Thumpers'* would be putting pressure on the priest and gossiping. His daughter's reputation was at stake and he would have to protect her at all costs. It mattered little how innocent their meetings were. Protocol had to be upheld. He would call on Molly and Michael without delay to iron out the matter. Michael was in the library when he heard a light trap coming up the drive. Curiosity getting the better of him he went to the window and looked out as the driver dismounted. His heart gave a leap when he saw none other that Eugene O'Byrne opening the door of the trap and alighting. He heard the rap on the knocker and the footsteps crossing the hall.
"What brings you here, Eugene O'Byrne?" Molly held the door open.
"I've come to do some straight talking, is Michael at home?" He demanded to know.
"Sure come in and take the weight off your feet." She opened the door wide and invited him to come inside.
"I may not be that welcome when you hear what I have to say. It's about my daughter's reputation." He hastened to add.
"Oh come on in, God help us and our reputations." She led the way into the kitchen.
"Would you fetch the boy?" He asked.
"I'll put the kettle on the hob first, this could take some time." Molly crossed the floor.
"Did you wish to see me?" Michael entered the kitchen.
"I did that and I suspect that you know why." Eugene studied him closely.
"Is it about Veronica? If it is don't you think that she should be here too?" Michael stammered.
"No! Why should she be? It's not right the way you are attending to the matter."
"You have high notions of your daughter, Eugene O'Byrne and I cannot blame you for that, so too have I for Michael. However I must agree that this matter should have been left in the hands of the matchmaker, don't you agree?" She interrupted.

"I agree surely, so I do, now if you approach me through the matchmaker we will discuss terms as to what is for the better" Eugene softened his tone.
"Michael, tell me are you serious about Veronica?" Molly addressed him.
"Of course I'm serious and so is Veronica." He insisted.
"Leave Veronica out of this for the time being. There's nothing that you or she can do for now. If you care for each other and want to do the walking out then you must do it through the matchmaker." She insisted.
Michael stood in silence for a time looking from one to the other. Then he offered a compromise. "If I agree can we still see each other?"
"That's not for you to decide, you have to think of my daughters reputation. You'll either do it right or not at all." Eugene insisted.
"It's sensible and right Michael and I must agree with Eugene." Molly interrupted.
"I'm sorry Sir, I'll bow to your wishes and yours too Molly." He was now contrite.
"You can get on with your studies for now Michael. Will you stay for a sup of tae Eugene?" She offered as Michael vacated the room.
"Sure and why not, we have a lot to talk over so we have." Removing his caubéen he sat down by the fire.
"It's only right that you go and see the *Matchmaker,* Molly. You don't mind me taking the liberty and calling you by your first name do you?" Eugene smiled for the first time.
" Not at all, sure if all goes well won't we be kit and kin?" Molly took her place beside the hob.
"True, true, not a truer word did you ever speak." He rubbed his hands together.
"Pity his mother cannot be here to speak for him." Molly looked deep into the glow of the turf fire.
"Mother! You're not his real mother then. Not that it matters?"
"Sorry to say I'm only his Godmother. His poor mother vanished from this earth on the day of his grandmothers funeral."
"The light of Jesus to her poor soul, I'll not forget her in my prayers." He promised.
"We don't know what happened to her, I'm hopeful that she is still alive and will find her son. He is taking her absence real bad and has now stopped talking about her."
"A bad sign that and I know how you feel. Neither of them have a mother to give them their blessings." He sighed.
"Sure the dead know all about their children here on earth. I'm sure that they are looking down on us now and praying for us and them."
"Together we'll do our best for them, we can do no more. The rest is in their

hands and the hand of God." Eugene blessed himself.

"You know Molly, here we are sitting at a strangers fire making plans for our children and between us we nothing to offer each other." He let out a sigh.

"We have our friendship and if all goes well we could wind up with a houseful of fine grandchildren." She consoled him.

"Come to think of it now, what use have we for the matchmaker? Wouldn't it be better giving the few sovereigns to the young couple?" Eugene suggested.

"You're right, sure what is there to barter?"

"I suppose and there again..." He looked deep into the grate and let out a sigh.

"If that's the way you feel Eugene then far be it from me to object. Give me your hand on it. Whatever will the Minister say when I tell him?" She added as an afterthought.

"Sure there's no haste for the present, let us keep this to ourselves until we are sure."

"I might as well tell you that I'm walking out myself." She blushed.

"Sure that's great news, so it is. Who is the lucky man, would I know him?"

"I don't think so, he's a drayman from Donegal by the name of Terry Davenny."

"Terry! Terry Davenny, the sly ould fox he never told me. Terry delivers my ciscéans all over the counties. Well I never, wait until I see him." Eugene slapped his hand on his lap and laughed.

"Don't breath a word to him, let him break the news when he's ready, promise?"

"Of course, A fine man is Terry and you'll not regret the day you accepted his offer."

"Come on let's have another sup of tae and you won't mind if I make it respectable with a drop of *Potéen?*" Eugene rose from his seat and went to the door.

"Not at all, sure I'll join you, we have a lot to celebrate." Molly went to the dresser and returned with two mugs.

Eugene went outside to the trap and returned with a jug of '*Potéen.*'

That evening sitting by the fire Molly Cullhane and Eugene O'Byrne defied convention and became matchmakers themselves.

Michael happy with the outcome retired to his bed and slept restlessly long into the night. He awoke with a start, gasping for breath and sweating profusely. He looked around his room in the dim light of the dawn, What had disturbed his sleep? He rubbed his upper arms for they ached and were heavy. Then he remembered his nightmare of that night. In it he was in a large garden where his mother lay on a green sward over which a rainbow hung. She lay sleeping and unconcerned as a tall man kept bullying him. The man was fully clothed and soaking wet. He wondered why he was so wet and what had happened to him. He called to her to plead with the man who was holding him by the upper arms in a brutal manner shaking him. Although he was calling loudly there was a distinct silence in the room. He escaped from the brute and entered a room to his left. The room was narrow and the floor was covered in dead leaves. On long slate slabs set along the walls on either side were several people sleeping. His mother entered and climbed on to one of the slabs and went to sleep. He called to her to come and sweep the leaves up but she remained sleeping. He went to a vacant slab at the far end of the room and lay down, feeling drowsy he wanted to sleep. The bully followed him into the room and began pressing down on his upper arms. He was demanding that both he and his mother should leave the room. They had no business to be there, yet no words were spoken it was all done by telepathy. The slab that he was lying on was his by right he claimed.

The man's anger knew no bounds as he reached down and tried to smother him. A bloody sweat oozed from the pores in his body, he gasped for breath. Screaming a silent scream he felt his life ebbing, then he awoke...'

He related his dream to Molly and asked her what it meant.

"Someone need's your prayers Michael." Was her simple explanation?

PISEÓGAS-MALLACTS-LEIGEAS (Superstitions-Curses-Cures)

Molly came down early to set the fire and attend to her chores. She was surprised to find that the study door was ajar and someone was in occupation. Opening the door slowly she looked inside and saw Bill lying uncomfortable in the sugan chair sleeping. Closing the door behind her she retreated to the kitchen and set the kettle on the crane.
"Is that you Molly?" She heard him call.
"It's me alright, I didn't waken you did I?" She apologised.
"Of course you did, don't you know that a woman can never pass the fire without tampering with it." He grumbled.
"Would you like a bit of breakfast, I'm about to wet the tae?" She asked.
"Thanks that would be appreciated, sorry for being so grumpy. I suppose you are wondering what I am doing in the study so early in the morning?"
"No, Not really, I'm sure that you know your own business in your own house."
"To be truthful Molly, I was unable to make the stairs last night."
"Oh I am sorry, Why didn't you call me or Michael?"
"I'm not one to disturb others. You have enough to do without fussing over me."
"It wouldn't be any trouble at all, that is what we are here for. You have been more than good to us and we are not about to forget that."
"Thanks Molly, I appreciate it, so I do."
"Here, drink this when it's hot. Tell me, was it the pains that stopped you sleeping?"
"It was that, I think I'll ask Michael to move the box bed in here."
"No need, I'll see that it's done as soon as he returns from school. Now eat your breakfast and rest yourself."
Later that afternoon Bill was disturbed by noises coming from the kitchen. He could hear a lot of pulling and dragging and the voice of Molly giving instructions.
"Can I be of any help?" He called.
We've got the press bed outside, where would you like it?" Molly entered the room and looked round for a suitable place.
"I'd like it over here near to the window if you wouldn't mind." Rising he picked up his walking stick and moved out of their way.
"In here with it and do be careful." She instructed.
"I thought that there was only you and Michael in the house." He looked at the tall stranger holding on to one end of the bed.
"It's my friend Terry doing the calling, just in time would you say?"
"That's fine, is that where you want it? Oh by the way this is Terry. Terry this

is Reverend William Bougham." She introduced the two men.
"Bill will do fine, I'm pleased to meet you. I hear you are not from these parts."
"No! I'm a Donegal man, I travel a lot of the counties here about."
"I asked Terry to borrow a curing stone from the dry well in Limerick. Here it is." Molly reverently held an oval quartz in the palm of her hand.
"What's that and better still what am I supposed to do with it?" He looked suspiciously at the stone.
"It's a curing stone, don't tell me that you never heard of them? He also turned the cursing stones for you." She added with a look of disappointment on her face.
"Molly I'm sorry, I'm sure that what you done was with the best of intentions but would you tell me what it all means?" Noticing the look of disappointment on her face he apologised.
"It all happened a very long time ago down in a place named Ballynanty Beag in the county Limerick. Saint Leila blessed a well there and promised all those who were pure of heart and prayed at her well would have one wish granted. One day a traveller committed the sacrilege of washing his feet in the well. Soon afterwards the well dried up much to the detriment of the parishioners. The people prayed that the good saint would understand that they were not to blame and that she would restore the miraculous water. The well filled with water again and strange things began to happen. Firstly a fairy thorn grew overnight beside the well. Then oval quartz stones appeared in the water. They soon discovered that they were warm and soothing to the touch. The people were convinced that they were *curing stones* placed there by the saint herself in recognition of their faith. The miraculous curing power of the stones spread throughout the county and beyond. Pilgrims praying at the well and seeking her intervention by placing their hands on the stones at the same time have, if they are pure of heart their requests granted. The strange thing about the stones is that if you borrow them and fail to return them to the well they lose their power and become *cursing stones*. That then is the story of the *curing stones*." Molly reached out the stone to him.
The assembly was silent for a moment as they digested the message of the stones.
"Molly, I thank you for your concern and I most certainly will pray in my own simple way holding the stone. I feel however that there is no miracle cure for me." Holding the stone firmly in his hands he sat down wearily in the sugan chair.
"Have faith Bill, have faith in the stones, we'll all be praying for you." Terry laid a sympathetic hand on his shoulder.

"Do you think that your saint will mind a Protestant praying to her?" He looked up and weakly smiled.
"As long as you believe, that's all that matters, isn't that right Terry?" It would seem that she had convinced him of the power of the stones. He was in so much pain that he was willing to try any cure or miracle on offer.
"If at anytime you need assistance just let Molly here know, I'm your man, of that be assured." Again Terry comforted him.
"There is something that you can do right now. You know I'm all alone now and it does get lonesome, would you ever stay awhile and chat?" He pleaded.
"Terry chat, why he could talk the black feathers white on a crow, so he could." She drew up a chair.
"There's a bottle of *Poteén* on the cart looking for a night of the Sean Scéal did you ever taste it Bill?" He offered.
"*Poteén!* That word conjures memories of the time when I was a young curate in the county of Armagh." Bill picked up the tongs and retrieved a sod of turf that had escaped from the fire. As he placed it on the blaze sparks raced up the chimney. Resting back in his chair he continued...'
"It was at the wedding reception of young Samuel Keating and his bride Alice McGee. I remember it as if it were only yesterday. Minnie the mother of Alice was a staunch Protestant. Whatever was written in the bible she took literally to her heart.
Doctor Keating, the father of Samuel was the very opposite, a sceptic perhaps in a sense. Most of the people were tenants to the big landowners and had little to give in return for his services. Needless to say he was always offered the customary bottle of Poteén, a chicken or a stone of potatoes or a tin can.
Over a period of time he had collected several bottles of the finest Poteén ever produced in the county Armagh.
The wedding reception he knew would be the ideal place to dispose of it. I can tell you that the '*Craic'* was in full swing long before the cock had settled down for the night. What I'm about to tell you happened around midnight...'
Minnie sat in the coal telling all those willing to listen and more besides what a fine bargain the son of Doctor Keating had got in her fine daughter.
Minnie had a fine head of flaxen hair that reached half way down her back. She was as proud as a Peacock of her hair and kept it brushed and platted. The final touch was a green and yellow bow tied to the end of it like the tail of a cow at the show."
"Will someone fetch me a drink of tae before I die of thirst?" She grumbled.
"Here Mrs take a drink of this." A benevolent guest, not knowing her tastes handed her a tin mug. Minnie took a deep drink from the mug before rising to

her full height off her stool. Foaming from the mouth and her eyes staring like a mad person she clutched her throat and for once was unable to utter a word. Pointing to her throat and with her tongue hanging out of her mouth she looked towards the gathering.

"Whatever is the matter with Minnie? Doctor Keating come quickly she is having a seizure?" Someone urgently called.

The doctor ran to her side and looked with incredulity at her. He had never seen a case like it before. Then he looked at the tin mug still held firmly in her hands.

"Whatever possessed you to give that to her?" He chided looking into the mug.

"She wanted a drink, how was I to know?" The guest apologised. In the meantime Minnie had recovered and returned to her stool.

"Which one of you brought this devils brew into my house?" She challenged holding up the mug for all to see.

There was silence in the room as the gathering moved away from where she was standing.

"They'll be condemned to Hell fire before the cock crows, just like this devils brew." She promised. Before anyone could stop her she pitched the contents of the mug into the fire. One would have thought that the Devil himself came out of the fire in answer to her command. There was a roar from the hearth and a ball of fire engulfed Minnie.

It only lasted a minute but when it subsided there stood Minnie as black as the hobs of hell, her golden blonde tresses singed beyond recognition.

Her eyebrows were gone and her face was as red as a turkey cock. She stood before the assembly screaming and raking singed hair from her head.

"Get out, get out of my house all of you." She ordered.

Minny was not seen out of doors for some considerable time after that. Nobody to my knowledge ever told her that it was the good doctor that brought the devils brew to the wedding."

"Do you know you mentioning the crowing of the cock reminds me of a yarn I heard in Castleconnell in the county of Limerick. Would you like to hear it?" Terry asked.

"I'd like nothing better." Bill settled back in his chair forgetting his aches and pains.

"I was taking my ease with one of the locals when we came to a little graveyard at Stradbally, it's just past the bridge at Castleconnell in the County Limerick.

It's an insignificance little village. There was nothing special about the place;

well I say that with my ease, if you know what I mean?" Terry continued. "Going up the drive I came to a headstone covered in lichen and ivy. I saw that it had a portentous carving on it, part of which I could not see. Curiosity getting the better of me I scraped the lichen away to disclose the carving of a cock cooking in a pot and below it the skull and crossed bones. I studied it for some time before my friend came on the scene.

"What are you looking at Terry, do you know the family?" He asked.

"No! God be good to them." I replied. "Will you take a look at what someone has chiselled into this old headstone." I cleaned it a bit more for him to see it better.

"You mean *'The Cock in the Pot' and the Skull and Crossed Bones'?* You're not the first to ask about that and you won't be the last." He answered without looking at it.

"Whatever does it mean it must have some story to it?" I looked puzzled.

"It has, it has indeed." He smiled.

"Go on put me out of my misery and tell me the story." I insisted. He then related the following story...'

"It all happened a long time ago in the Holy Land. Judas having betrayed Jesus returned to his home in a great state of exasperation and was confronted by his wife.

"Whatever is the matter with you Judas? Why are you so flushed and out of breath? You look as if you were up to no good." She chided him.

He remained silent as he watched her cooking a fine cockerel in a pot for his dinner.

"If you're not going to tell me would you get out of my way and let me get on with my cooking." His wife continued pressing the question superfluously.

"Do you remember my friend Jesus?" He finally broke the silence and asked.

"Jesus! The healer that you and the other fishermen go about with, everyone knows him. What about him?" Unconcerned she continued with her cooking.

"The very same. If the others call tell them that I'm not at home." He instructed her.

"What have you lot been up to this time, you haven't been upsetting the Romans again, have you? You'll all be sent to the arena to fight with the lions if you don't behave yourselves." She warned.

"I betrayed him to the Romans. I told them that he was an agitator and stirring up trouble. They asked me what kind of trouble. I lied and told them that he was planning to overthrow the Roman Empire in Jerusalem. I was asked to write down my statement and given thirty pieces of silver for my troubles."

"You never did, how could you betray your best friend. Where is he now?"

"They handed him over to the Jews and they took him to Golgotha, where he was drugged and beaten. I never thought that they would believe me."

"But where is he now? I'm ashamed of you. How could you do this to your best friend? You take that money back to them right now and tell them the truth." She chided him.

"I only wish that I could but cannot for they took him to Calvary Hill. I feel awful for I never thought they would do such a thing to the healer." He was in a state of agitation.

"Calvary Hill! Oh no. What have they done to him?" His wife looked horrified.

"Jesus has been crucified. He will no more walk the road to Damascus than will that cockerel in the pot crow." He wrung his hands and pointed to the cockerel in the pot.

"No sooner had he uttered these words than the cockerel rose up out of the pot and sitting on the hob crowed three times."

Judas on seeing and hearing the cock crowing ran from the house and hanged himself on a tree nearby. From that day the tree became known as *'The Judas Tree'*.

"Why the Skull and Cross bones below it?" I asked.

"That's to represent '*Golgotha*' remember from your school days. '*The Place of the Skull*'. My friend reminded me.

"That is a beautiful story and one that I never heard before. I really did enjoy it. Thank you Terry you made my day. Pity I did not hear that story as a young curate." The minister smiled.

"Why is that?" Terry questioned.

"It would lead me into a wonderful sermon." The old minister lay back on the pillow.

They spent the best part of the night relating in song and story the history and legends relating to their land. That was until tiredness and the drop of *Mountain Dew* took its toll on their weary bones.

A MESSAGE OF HOPE

Terry had returned to Donegal. The school had closed for the holiday and Michael was home once more. It was coming up to the Christmas season and Molly was determined to make it one to remember. She was still worried as to the state of health of the old minister.
He was getting more and more cantankerous but she understood that it was not his fault. It was the will of Almighty God she insisted. She approached the study door and knocked.
"What is it now, who's there? Can't a man get any peace in his own house?" Came the grumbling voice from the other side of the door.
"You know well who it is, who did you expect, Father Christmas? I've brought you a mug of broth." She smiled at her audacious remark.
"Come in girl, I'm sorry but the pain and depression is getting to me." He apologised.
"I'm off to Galway and taking the cart. I want to buy a few groceries for the Christmas."
"I suppose you will be taking Michael too. Whatever do you want to buy now?"
"I need Michael to help me as I'm going to make a pudding and a cake for us. I'll need spices, lemon peel a little Brandy, mixed fruit and ...'
"Will you ever shut up woman I don't want to know. I may not be here for Christmas."
"Why are you intending to go someplace, Do let me know, won't you?"
"Very funny. Oh get out and do whatever you want. You never ask me anyway." He grumbled.
Galway was filled with shoppers and traders from up and down the country. All it would seem were intent on stocking up for Christmas.
"Pull the cart in here Michael and find out how much the grazing is to day." Molly pointed to a long row of carts in the square.
"How much should I pay?" He began releasing the horse from the cart.
"Pay the going rate but try and get a field near to the town. I don't want to find myself traipsing half way to Castlebar carrying a days shopping. Meet me under the hanging window." She instructed.
The market was crowded with shoppers and traders all intent on taking advantage of the festive season. Returning to the square he saw Molly in deep discourse with a farmer.
"I got good stabling and fodder for the horse in the town. How are things going?" He asked.

"I'm looking at that hen turkey over there. With three weeks to go before Christmas I could have a fine bird raised by then. What do you think?" She whispered as she nodded towards the bird of her choosing.

"How much would you be asking for the little hen in the corner. I've not got a lot to spend. Anyhow there are only two of us and a small turkey would do?" She had set the bargaining in motion.

"Ah come on now missus you must be joking. Will you not take the eyes out of my head. Look she's a darling of a bird. Seeing that you have a good eye for a bargain I'll let her go for three florins and that's a sacrifice." With a jovial smile he tucked his shillelagh under his arm and held out his hand.

"Does she sing?" She asked.

"What do you mean does she sing? She's a turkey and turkeys don't sing."

"By the way you were praising her I got the impression that she was some kind of an opera singer. Three florins indeed, did you not hear me right? I only want the little hen and not the whole flock. Three florins, Huh!" Molly looked him straight in the eye and began walking away.

"Now don't be too hasty, tell you what I have another one just as big and to you just two florins." He beguiling smiled.

"If the other one is as good as her why is she three florins and the other two?"

"Well mam! To tell you nothing but the truth she is a bit lame in the foot."

"Lame in the foot, do you take me for some kind of an oinseach. Go on then show her to me." She insisted.

"I would willingly but my woman is bringing her on the other cart and has been delayed." He apologised.

"Pull the other leg will you. By the time your woman makes the market I'll be long gone and have purchased a hen elsewhere. Lame of the foot indeed. Is she walking to the market?" She remarked.

"Very well then seeing as you have set your eyes on the hen and that it is coming up to Christmas, I'll let her go at two and a half florins." Again he tried to sell her the bird.

"Make it two and I'll be willing to take her off your hands. I'll also expect you to be generous with the luck penny seeing as it's near to Christmas." Molly demanded.

"Do you by any chance of the imagination come from Cork. Mam?"

"No, and I don't know that it's any concern of yours. Why do you ask?"

"To tell you the truth Mam, I found them as mean as dyke water. Go on then let's see the colour of your money." He hastily added.

"It's agreed then two florins and a luck penny. What are you offering?"

"I'll let you have a bag of best banner spuds." He offered.

"Now who's as mean as dyke water? I'll be looking for a half dozen large

Swedes as well." She insisted.
"You met a real Father Christmas in me. Mam. Come on son pick out the Swedes for your mother."
"I'll pick my own Swedes if you don't mind. Michael go and help him fill the potatoes and see there are no stones thrown in." She went to a pile of Swedes and made her selection.
"I'll collect them this evening and don't you swap my hen when I'm away. Do you hear me?" She warned.
"Can we go to the tae house now, I'm perished with the hunger. If we don't go now then we will not get anything to eat." Michael pleaded.
"Very well, we'll go over there. It looks as if everyone else has the same idea as you."
Sitting at the long table they were soon joined by others.
"You must have met the hungry grass." Molly watched as a group of men helped themselves to the over brimming dish of boiled potatoes.
"You might say that. We are on our way home to Connemara. We left England last evening having spent the season pratie (Potato) picking in Lincolnshire. What would you be doing here?" One of the young men asked.
"Christmas shopping as usual this time of the year. I just picked up a nice hen turkey at a reasonable price. Your family will be glad to have you home for Christmas I'm sure." Molly replied.
"They will that. The house is always full for Christmas. Will all yours be home?"
"There is only me and Michael. We work for a Church of Ireland minister outside the town." Molly informed them.
"You're a widow woman then and you have a fine son so you have. God bless him."
"No! He's not my son, I'm his god mother, his real mother is missing." Molly related how Mary failed to return following her mother's burial.
"Mary Kearney, now that name rings a bell. Séanin there was a Mary Kearney out of Donegal working with us in Cambridgeshire was there not?" He asked his companion.
"Let me think now, Mary Kearney. There was a May Kearney a little woman that kept very much to herself. Come to think of it she did come from Donegal now that you mention it." His friend replied.
"What did she look like and what age would she be?" Molly pressed the question.
"She would be in her late twenties or thereabouts and had sandy hair." He replied with a shrug of his shoulders.
"Did she ever mention that she had a son, would you ever remember?" Molly

pressed the point.

"No, as I said she kept very much to herself, so she did. That's all we know."

"Cambridgeshire did you say?" Molly reminded them.

"No, I said she worked with us there. The last we saw of her was in Liverpool. She was looking for work in the city. She should have never gone potato hoaking. She was far too frail for the hard work. I wouldn't raise your hopes it might not be the same person."

"From your description it sounds like her, the sandy hair and the age. Indeed it could be. Whatever would she be doing so far away?" She more or less spoke to herself.

That evening she approached the vicar and told him what they had been told in Galway and sought his advice.

"Only you know what she looked like. What did you make of what they told you?"

"I'm of the opinion that it could possibly be her. What puzzles me is what is she doing in England?" She posed the question.

"There's only one way to find out and that is go there. I would suggest that you send Michael over." Bill advised.

"But he doesn't know her and anyhow where would he look?"

"He could always start with the *Peelers* and the lodging houses. Believe me everyone knows everyone in Liverpool, especially the Irish." Bill informed her.

"When do you suggest he should go and how would he get there?"

"Molly, there will be no peace in this house until you know either way. I suggest that he leaves soon as possible before the trail goes cold. He should be back in time for Christmas. There's always boats going to Liverpool from Dublin. I'll let him have some money for the journey and his keep." Bill promised.

"You're too good Bill, there's no need I have a few pounds saved."

"It's an early Christmas gift from me, so leave it at that." He insisted.

The dawn was rising in the bay when Michael approached the little ship. The gangplank had been removed and all was silent aboard. Sitting on a bollard he removed what remained of what provisions he had left.

As he ate the birds of the sea came begging for scraps. Then more and more came, hovering above his head they shook their wings. The sound of their swaking and the slapping of the keel on the seabed aroused his senses.

Looking out to sea he saw the light of the lighthouse grow dimmer as the brightness of the morning intruded. It was not yet full light but the dusk was now but a twinkle. Then above the cry of the gulls he heard voices.

Men clad in heavy clothes were coming on deck and opening the safety rail on

the boat. Six men lifted the gangplank by the holding ropes and slid it from the ship to the dockside. One went to the stern of the ship and opening the lantern quenched the light.
Michael put his foot on the gangplank and nervously climbed on to the deck.
"Do you want something son"? A weather beaten sailor asked in a strong Dublin accent.
"I'm looking for passage to Liverpool and was told that you are going there." Michael rubbed his hands together.
"Feeling the cold then. I don't blame you. Come on aboard I'm about to make breakfast." The man walked ahead of him towards the galley.
"He felt the welcoming warmth as he climbed down the raking ladder to the galley.
"So you want to get to Liverpool. Most people are going the opposite way. Getting home to be with their own folk for Christmas. Why are you going to England?"
"My mother went missing some years ago and we were informed that a woman fitting her description is in Liverpool." Michael told what he knew of his mother's disappearance.
"I hope you find her son, I really do. Now eat up it's a long journey to Liverpool."
"How much do I owe you for the fare and food?" Michael asked.
"It's not a passenger ship, I guess you can work your passage across."
There was little to do on the ship and Michael spent the daylight hours looking nostalgically out to sea. The rising swell and the mournful cry of the gulls broke through the bridle of his will. He cried letting his sorrowful tears mingle with salt sea spray. The solitude of the sea and his sudden longing to see his mother pained him beyond endurance.
"There's some grub ready in the galley." He heard the mate calling to him.
"Thanks, I'll be there in a minute." Wiping the tears from his cheeks he came below.
"Won't be long now before we dock. Made any plans as to what you are going to do?"
"I'll need to find a place to stay before I do any searching. Do you know where I might acquire clean accommodation reasonable priced?" Michael asked.
"The seamen's mission that is the best place. I'll go with you and tell them that you are a sailor." The boson promised.
"Me! Do I look like a sailor?" Michael smiled.
"How do you know what a sailor looks like? Don't worry they won't ask any questions?"

"As you don't know Liverpool you should be careful. I suggest you leave the greater part of your money with the mission." He warned as he escorted him to the mission and introduced him to the manager.

"There you are Michael. Your money is in safe hands and you have got bed and board. All you need now is to find your mother. We'll be back in Liverpool two weeks from now and if you are still here you are welcome to come aboard. Good luck and if I don't meet you again would you let the mission know how you got on. Oh yes! I hope and pray that you get your wish this Christmas and be united with your mother. Merry Christmas." With a wave he left Michael to his own devices.

A CITY OF CONTRASTS

Michael spent most of the following week making enquiries as to where Mary or May Kearney lived. He pursued relentlessly fruitless and misleading information. His search finally led him from the dock area into the city proper. He was assured that Mary Kearney worked in one of the thriving factories.
The city teemed with peoples moving hither and thither all it would seem bent on self-destruction. They paid little heed to his pathetic appeals for information. They were more concerned with their own survival.
This was a city of contrasts from the teeming slums of the dock area to the grandiose mansions of the suburbs.
Some of the main arteries in the city were cobbled. The minor roads were nothing but mud tracks filled with dung and rubble. When a cart or carriage wheel disturbed the stagnant water a stinking foul smelling concoction was released. It entered ones nostrils creating a feeling of nausea that clung to their clothing.
Narrow dark lanes led to tall factories where women and girls as young as ten years of age worked at broad benches and looms. They were indifferent to their situation of grinding poverty and an early death. They had no time for his sob story. Their own situation was far more distressing. The noise from within and without the milling factories was at times unbearable. Men smelling of stale sweat and with grimy cravats tied 'round their necks pushed heavily laden iron clad carts from one entrance to another. They ignored him when he tugged at their ragged sleeves seeking their help. This was a far cry from the homeliness of Ireland; here it was a battle for survival.
Mothers stood over long unending looms encouraging their young daughters not yet in their teens to learn her skills and to take her place at the looms when she passed on. Sons slaved under the roaring machines that refused to stop. Hurriedly they cleaned the swarf and rubbish away from the fast grinding teeth of the drums that savagely tore the cotton to shreds as it was fed into the jaws. The swarf falling beneath the rolling drum could if not removed foul up the angry monster and cost the operator her job. Fine particles of cotton entered their eyes and lungs but they like the obsequious masses above them were oblivious to the danger. Parents slaved eighteen hours day and night hoping to earn enough money to send their eldest sons to a church school where a contribution was required. Their daughters they pressed into service. Anything to take them away from the hell holes that that they worked in.
Others that life's expectation had come and passed struggled on to pay for the burial of their loved one. This sum was due to the undertaker at an agreed

weekly rate. They at least ensured that the disgrace of a pauper's grave had been avoided. The long hours working and the starvation diet justified it, for their pride remained intact. Yet as they slaved they dreaded that they too might fall ill to one or more of the pestilence surrounding them, before they had settled the debt. What would become of them? Like the sword of Damocles the debt swung in a perpetual pendulum motion. A death in a family although a tragedy and a regular occurrence became an additional millstone tied round the necks of those left behind. Their destination should they fail to meet the debt was the *'Debtors Prison'* where they would remain incarcerated until it was met in full.

There were the *'Burial Clubs'* organised by the workers themselves. In order to avoid the disgrace of being buried by the parish they would scrimp and save to buy their graves and to pay for their own funerals Their life expectancy could be read in their deep sunken eyes, drawn faces and miserable sallow skin.

Outside of the factories were the rows of tenement houses where toil worn women and girls touted for business. Their fathers and husbands deep in debt and with no money to repay even part of the debt had on the order of the court been taken to the *'Sponging Houses'* and to the *'Grate.'* There they would remain incarcerated until their debt was paid in full. Should they be in a position to bribe their turnkeys then they would be allowed to stand at the grate window and beg alms. These they would use to clear the debt and to gain their freedom. Their women folk would take in washing or scrub the houses of the gentry, anything to raise enough to have them released.

'Wash and iron only sixpence. Bed and board in clean house two shillings per week, no Irish no dogs. Piano lessons for the beginner twopence by the hour. (Success guaranteed)

House being fumigated keep clear. Dangerous building enter at your own risk. There seemed to be no services that were not covered by the notices in every window.'

On a sidecar sat a jarvey shivering in the rain. His pox ridden fatigued features denoting his miserable existence. His half starved horse with a bag that once contained a handful of oats tied over his head stood on spindly legs waiting for customers that never seem to materialise. His faithful but famished dog lay coiled up in a ball shivering to conserve heat beneath the belly of the horse. A girl of eight or nine tried to pressure passers by to purchase the matches that her younger brother had packed into boxes that he had pasted together the night before. A young woman in a ragged shawl and accompanied by two ragged barefooted children and a mangy dog walked slowly up and down the sidewalk. The woman was playing a battered accordion. The eldest child who was no more than seven years of age rattled a tin can as his mother sang...

'Underneath a gas light glitter
Stood a lonely fragile girl
Headless of the night wind bitter
That around her seemed to whirl
There are many sad and weary
In this pleasant world of our
Crying every night so bitter
Won't you buy my pretty flowers'?

Filthy black smoke belched from numerous tall stacks that stood like sentinels around the city. Like a river with many tributaries the sulphur ridden smoke tried to emulate itself yet it only succeeded in coiling and uncoiling itself round the tall stacks as they continued belching out more and more obnoxious sulphur choking fumes. In the narrow alleyways unable to escape it remained a permanent reminder of mans inhumanity to man. It deposited long slimy streaks on the cut stone façade of the factory entrances. It clung in cold black blobs like Leeches and occasionally turned into long disgusting black tears. *(Perhaps lamenting the passing of yet another slave to the looms. He thought.)*
Sounds and noises intermingled and echoed along the dark labyrinths. A canal ran in a long straight line and seemed to go on forever. In its wake it carried a vile smelling steaming yellow fluorescent soup.
Flotsam thrown from the innumerable grimy windows landed in the canal creating a steady flotilla of myriad coloured bubbles that occasionally burst releasing more noxious smells. Disgruntled slaves laboured beside the grinding carousel of life as monotonously they tried in vain to satisfy the hunger of the huge steam driven motors situated high up in the roof space.
The long unending leather belts clung precariously to the drive shaft that moved ever faster as the steam driven monster demanded more and more speed. The belts slipped and screamed in anguish trying to satisfy the hungry machines.
Engineers like so many ants raced from belt to belt carrying oilcans and bars of lanolin soap in an unending race to placate the demand. They plied on the unstoppable belts large soap sized blocks of lanolin. Holding the block to the inside of the moving belt they impregnated the sticky lotion on to it. Reluctantly at first, then with a whine the drive shaft gained in momentum. With satisfaction showing on his face the engineer moved down the line to the next stubborn insatiable monster.
Sewerage spewed out from overflowing make shift sewers and settled in the

alleyways forming cesspools of impending death. The contents bubbled and boiled as it fermented and defecated into the foul air. The great expanse of the river Mersey swallowed up the many ships plying between the great cities of the British Empire on which the sun never set. Oblivious to the cold and the smell those unable to find gainful employment or too weak to work lay along the alleyways begging for a handout. Many, far too many worn out by hours of relentless slavery and with little or no return for their labour gave up the fight and sought sanctuary in the gin palaces. Others with all hope faded and no prospects surrendered the struggle and lay under their rotting shrouds waiting for night fall when the watch would come and mercifully remove them to a paupers grave.

Gin parlours, too numerous to count flourished out of control in the grimy streets. A glass of tainted gin could be purchased for a few coppers. Women unable to pay, yet craving for a drink would sell themselves and their daughters to any man willing to oblige. Drink was the only escape from the treadmill of their miserable existence. The gin parlour was warm and inviting, friendly and dangerous.

From four o'clock in the morning to nine o'clock at night, eighteen hours of continuous drudgery, they ate and drank what little sustenance they brought with them as they worked. With life expectancy short the gin parlours offered to them a Utopia in which they could escape from their miserable existence. In their drink sodden minds the ravenous hunger, the drudgery and hopelessness was forgotten. They were trapped, victims of England's great industrial revolution.

He felt that he was wasting valuable time seeking help from those Hell bent on self-destruction.

Perhaps his mother had taken up service in one of the grand mansions he was informed.

He was directed to a tree lined suburban sprawl that was far removed from the squalor of the inner city. Here lived the shibboleths, the churchgoers, the '*Craw Thumpers,*' the upper classes. It was they who owned the vile factories and the teeming mills. There were no pools of decaying filth on their well-groomed streets. No sulphur-laden soot penetrated their grand fortress. All was quiet, sweet and tranquil, their slumber hardly disturbed. The boisterous calling of the tinkers and tradesmen, the rattle of the iron clad wheels and the raucous singing of the drunks unheard. There was order here. The birds sang in unison in the branches of the chestnut trees that stood like sentinels along the sides of the well-manicured lawns and driveways. A verbatim of gentleness was discreetly scrolled on oak panels screwed to the gates, Chestnut House- Lavender Manse-

Hawthorne Retreat. Grand names for grand houses in grand settings.
The air was crisp and clean and a gentle dusting of snow covered the manicured lawns and drives.
Retreating to a wrought iron seat in the park he sat down. Looking at the great expanding city he wondered what life had to offer.
Governess dressed in blue and white uniforms with hats to match strolled complacent along the avenues of trees now denuded of their foliage. In columns of two's their charges walked sedately before them. Their teachers in the school of elocution had no time for boisterous behaviour.
His eyes grew weary, his thoughts were of Molly and his home in Ireland.
He awoke to see a governess parking her pram at the far end of the seat on which he slept. Letting the hood down she adjusted the bedding inside the pram.
"There now, that's better." She addressed the child in the pram. Having seen that the child was comfortable she removed a feeding bottle from a large portmanteau and placing it in her own mouth sucked on the rubber teat.
"Come on now, there's a good baby." She placed the teat inside the child's mouth. When all was completed to her satisfaction she turned her attention towards Michael.
"Are you employed here young man?" She spoke without looking at him.
"Excuse me! Are you addressing me?" Michael indignantly asked.
"Of course, who else is there?" Sometimes the servants could be more audacious than their employers.
"My name is Michael Kearney and for your information I do not live in your country. I'm searching for my mother, I was informed that she worked in one of the houses."
"I'm sorry, this is a private park and you should not be sleeping in it."
"There's no notice to say that this is a private park." Michael looked for a notice.
"There is no need as this is an exclusive estate. Then we can excuse you."
"Now why should you want to make excuses for me?" He insisted.
"You're Irish and a plebeian Papist. Not used to our orderly living." She was the true bigot without knowing it and a servile servant to the aristocracy. A patriotic Victorian dedicated to the Empire and the Church of England. To them the Papist Churches in the city were more nationalistic than religious due to the large Irish influx. They lacked any morality or commitment to God. They ignored the studying the bible and genteel readings suitable for the Sabbath day. They spent their Sundays in playing their national games, blasphemous drinking and rowdy behaviour.

The people who lived on the hill were bigoted against their beggary neighbours in the teeming city. They were oblivious to the miseries, desolation and deaths of their employees. In this city he found two nations those who had and those who had not. Not alone were they ignorant or bigoted of each other, customs, breeding and feelings but they were totally indifferent. The Irish, well they tolerated them as servile slaves.

"Do you know if a Mary or May Kearney works in any of the houses?" He asked ignoring her sarcastic remark.

"Yes there was a May Kearney employed by the Burton household. She was removed some time ago to the isolation hospital." She reluctantly informed him.

"The isolation hospital! What happened to her?"

"I believe that she has consumption or some other contagious decease."

" Where do her employers live?" He asked.

"What do you want to know that for? They will not want you next or near their house. You had best inquire at the isolation hospital. I'm sure that they will be in a position to help." She sarcastically replied.

"Thank you, thank you very much. Sorry about the park." He satirically remarked and smiled.

Returning to the city he was directed to a large rambling complex. He was distracted by a large clock that took pride of place over the entrance ringing out the hour of three.

Entering a long dark vaulted corridor he approached two swing doors to his left. A notice on the door warned all visitors to take precautions. Facemasks were to be worn at all times and were not to be removed until one left the ward. The notice may as well have read, *'Abandon hope all ye who enter.'*

"What are you doing here young man?" A nurse approached him.

"Oh me!" He stuttered startled at the intrusion.

"Yes you. You are not allowed to wander round the corridors." She warned.

"I'm looking for my mother, her name is Mary Kearney. I'm informed that she is in ward fourteen. This is ward fourteen is it not?"

"Here put this on and do not remove it until you leave. Mary Kearney is in the far bed near to the window." She handed him a facemask that smelt of disinfectant.

He slowly walked down the aisle between the beds trying not to look at the patients.

Stopping at the bedside of the woman he was shocked at her wasted face. She was a woman of about thirty years of age. A wicker cage had been placed over her feet and covered with a counterpane. He looked down at the weak emaciated woman gasping for breath. Her waxen face told her story, it was weather beaten and stood out distinct and sharp in the light coming from the large window to the right of her bed. She tossed and turned in restless sleep as she battles against her inevitable demise.

"Are you Mary Kearney from Donegal?" He whispered not wishing to intrude on her dreaming. There was no response.

"Are you awake, can you hear me?" Her eyes were closed and her breathing was impaired. Slowly he turned and walked down the ward glancing back occasionally.

As he reached the door the nurse entered.

"Was she glad to see you then?" The nurse smiled.

"I think she is asleep, I'll come back later." He again looked back at the bed.

"Nonsense, she should be awake by now, follow me." Without further ado she swept down the ward.

"Come on now Mary, you have a visitor." The woman woke with a start and looked up at Michael and then at the nurse.

"This is your son, Michael. He has come to see you." The nurse informed her. Opening her eyes she looked up at the stranger standing beside her bed. Her eyes were shallow and constantly moving and searching. It was as if her mind was trying to relate to his presence. Lifting her transparent hand she shaded her eyes and looked deep into his. The long deep vertical wrinkles that were prominent on her forehead grew deeper. She let her hand fall back on the counterpane. Then opening her toothless mouth she looked away in despair.

"I don't have a son, who are you anyway?" She looked annoyed as she wiped away the bloody spittle forming on her mouth.

"I'm Michael Kearney and I believe that you are my mother." He shuffled from one foot to the other.

"I'm sorry to disappoint you but I don't have a son. Do you think I have money or something of value?" She weakly replied as she sucked in her breath. She saw him looking at her withered hands and quickly hid them under the counterpane.

"Are you in pain, is there anything I can get you?" He could see from her expression that every movement she made was agonising.

"Nothing, there is nothing that you or anyone can do. Please go and let me die in peace." Again she placed her hands on top of the counterpane. The lines on her face grew deeper and he could see the veins on her temple swell and recede. She was watching him like a hawk ready to pounce on its prey.

"You had best go, young man, I am sorry." The nurse on seeing her distressed state lay her hand on his shoulder and guided him away from the bed.

As he walked down the ward the pungent smell of chloroform seemed to fill every inch of space.

"Don't take it too hard son, you'll find your mother God willing." The nurse consoled him as they left the ward.

"Is she really that sick?" He looked back at the old woman following his every movement with her eyes.

"She's not long for this world. We had to amputate one of her legs and soon, if she lasts that long the other will have to be removed. Tubercular decease is eating her away." The nurse informed him.

"Has she no relatives?" He more or less pleaded.

"None that we can trace, then that is not surprising. Should any relatives come forward then they would become liable for the cost of her coffin and her funeral."

That night he slept a restless sleep. The vision of May Kearney haunted his every dream. Whatever pity he had for her had now turned to hatred. He wanted revenge for it was she who broke his dream.

"Why! Why did she deceive me and refuse to accept me as her son?" Again she came to him disturbing his fitful dream.

"Your other foot will have to come off, look at it." Looking down at his foot he saw his emaciated leg and the surgeon's blood covered saw. He awoke sweating and shaking.

Like a granite grave stone her image weighed heavily on his mind. This self-pity of lonely torment would last for a long while.

The chain was broken. What hope he had of finding his mother was now but a fading memory.

The sounds of the milling city brought a welcoming relief from his nightmare.

SHELIA

It was Christmas Eve and his search for his mother was proving to be a fruitless venture. Despondent and lonely he gazed out of the window of his room. His vacant expression, his pivot of emotion told of his feelings.
The thread of hope that had wound itself 'round his heart was now strangling all his dreams. He saw the milling crowds and heard the raucous laughter of the mill girls.
They were making the most of the festive season. Some had sparkling halos on their heads, more hurried home with a few presents tucked under their arms. The cold of the room ate into his young bones and made him shiver. The threatening sword of loneliness and despondency was slowly piercing his very soul.
'Happy Christmas, mother wherever you are.' He called out into the night as he heaved a sigh.
He studied his miserable room, his bed of straw and he listened to the crying children.
Rising wearily he retrieved his caubéen from the peg, opened the door and went out into the night.
Grey foam lapped the shoreline as he sat on a bollard and listened to the ship's bells.
A log of driftwood having trapped an empty drum in the river banged it monotonously as the tide lapped the quay wall. A water rat swam to the log and climbing on board sat preening itself before again diving into the bay.
The setting sun sent out long fingers of golden rays across the murky waters. A boat was making for the shore, her light high on the mast swayed gently in keeping with the boat's movement. Rising he left the docks and entered the city.
The beckoning merriment from a gin palace encouraged him to enter. He looked 'round the smoke filled room and at the welcoming large log fire. Slowly and deliberately he crossed the sawdust-covered floor and took his place beside the bar.
"What is your pleasure mister?" A buxom woman approached him.
"I'll have a whiskey if you please." Removing his caubéen he stuffed it into his pocket.
"Take a seat, I'll fetch it to you. Irish I presume?" Without waiting for his reply she went into a room at the rear of the bar.
"That will be two pence if you don't mind." A young girl placed his drink before him and held out her hand.

"Two pence, of course, yes." Reaching into the pocket of his breeches he took out the coins and gave them to her.
"On your own then, mind if I join you?" A girl speaking in a lilting Irish accent came and sat down opposite him. Her hair was rolled into a neat bun and kept in place with several decorated pins. Her clothing although showing signs of wear was clean and presentable. Her smile was warm and genuine. Her face was that of a young girl and when she smiled her rich lips and pearl white even teeth parted in a welcoming smile.
"Of course please sit down. Can I buy you a drink?" He stammered.
"Sure, I'll have a gin if you don't mind." She took her seat and smiled.
"A whiskey for me and a gin for the lady." He beckoned to the fat lady behind the bar.
" My name is Sheila, what's yours?" The girl held out her hand in greeting.
"Michael, Michael Kearney." The girl was slim and pleasant speaking and he felt relaxed in her company.
"What part of Ireland do you hail from?" He asked opening the conversation.
"I'm from the west and yourself?" She smiled with her eyes.
"I come from Donegal." He tried to avoid looking at her.
As the night wore on he found himself relaxing and enjoying the company. They sang and danced and he spent his money liberally.
"It was a lovely night Michael and I enjoyed myself. Now I must go home." She smiled beguilingly.
"Must you, I'll see you home then if I may?" He offered.
"Of course, I'm not taking you out of your way am I?" Linking arms they went out into the cold night air.
They walked down the long narrow lane past dreary houses and factories. She hummed a tune and looking up at the night sky called on him to accompany her singing.
Reaching the dock area she led him down a dreary alleyway. A single gas light flickered somewhere in the distance. Huge rambling mills lay silent awaiting their resurrection, the tall chimneys with the names of the owners ostentatiously highlighted in white brick ran the full length of the stack. In the grey light of dawn they reminded him of obelisks to a giant race long forgotten. He was apprehensive but tried not to show it. She was oblivious to the rats and vermin that scurried past them.
A mist hung over the foul smelling canal. A long row of dingy tenements had been sandwiched between the factories presumably to house the wretches that fed the insatiable machinery.
"Whatever am I doing here?" He thought.
"This is my place." Sheila stopped outside a dingy tenement building.
They stood facing each other. She leaned against the wall and rested her eyes

on his. He looked into her deep large wonderful eyes. They were silent for a moment.

"I'll be saying 'Good Night' then. Would you tell me how to get out of here?" He reached out his hand to her.

"Come inside, there's no hurry. It will soon be morning and you'll feel safer." Encouraging him inside she closed the door. Tumultuous perpetual snoring coming from a recess under the staircase made him feel uneasy. A water rat, still wet from swimming in the canal scurried down the dank steps leading to a dark cellar.

His attention was again drawn to the loud snoring coming from the recess. A drunkard sleeping off the night no doubt, he thought. As his eyes adjusted to the dim light he was surprised to see a large sow and her litter bedded down in a bed of straw.

"Come on, it's freezing." She called from the foot of the rickety staircase. He obediently followed her up the stairs to the first floor.

"This is my place." Sheila removed a large key from above the door and placed it in the lock.

"Stand there a minute, I'll fetch a candle." She instructed.

He could see her silhouette as she passed by the window before stopping by a dressing table He heard a drawer being opened. The room came to life as the flickering candle exposed the nakedness of the sparsely furnished apartment.

"Well! What do you think of it? I know it's not a palace but it's clean and tidy." She looked proudly round the room.

"It's grand, fine. Honest I like it." He smiled.

"I'm glad, do you like me?" She twirled across the floor. As she approached him she opened her arms and placing them round his neck she kissed him passionately.

She was determined to make love to him. He was taken aback and felt awkward. This was his first real encounter with a girl.

"Come on, don't just stand there." Releasing him from her arms she began undressing. He watched as she removed her garments one by one until she stood before him naked.

"Don't you want to make love to me?" She smiled as she went towards the bed.

" Do you want me to, Sheila?" He averted his eyes away from her as he undressed. He was unsure of himself and did not know how to cope with the situation.

Feeling ashamed he did not remove his shirt and on tenterhooks approached the bed.

"You're not keeping that on surely? Take it off." She demanded.
She was desperate for love but he was unsure as how he should approach her. Removing his shirt he came into the bed and lay down beside her.
She came to him unashamedly and ran her hands over his strong muscles. She took his penis in her hand and stroked it.
Unable to resist the temptation he cupped her firm breasts and explored her most intimate secrets.
His breath came in quick spasms and the palpating of his heart grew stronger. This was his first encounter with a girl, he wanted to take her. She reached her lips up to his in a lingering kiss and forcing his lips apart with her tongue she searched and probed.
He pulled her closer to him, touching her firm breasts and moulding them in his palms. He pressed his body into hers. Looking up at him she could see the dominance and savagery in his deep blue eyes.
He could no longer wait, he forced her on to her back and was clumsy in his approach.
"Not yet Michael, please wait. I want it to last." She pleaded.
"I can't Sheila, I must have you now." He panted.
She knew what he meant and opening her legs she encouraged him to mount her. "I love you Michael." She panted.
He thrust his penis deep inside her again and again and she reciprocated. Together they erupted as with a final trust they ejaculated together he filling her womb with his passionate and burning seed.
He was awkward in his lovemaking and got excited too quickly.
Crossing her legs she held on to him, her desire for him was insatiable.
"Sorry, was I alright?" He asked later not knowing what to say.
"You were great, so you were and it will get better. Now let's get some sleep." She assured him.
It was late into the morning when she awakened him.
"You didn't tell me that you were a virgin." She teased him.
"I'm sorry but...' Michael tried to cover his nakedness.
"Don't be so sensitive, relax will you. It will be better this time." She turned on her side and faced him. He looked into her deep blue eyes. Her petite lips broke into a smile. Her hair covered his face as she reached down and passionately kissed him. He rolled her sideways and reaching down pushed the bedclothes to one side.
"Go on Michael." She took a deep breath and began panting like a wild beast. Unashamed she opened her legs and invited him to take her. This time he did not hurry. She looked so precious, so mysterious. She was as savage and

perilous as the lonesome bog.

"Sheila"... He called as his rose to his knees and knelt between her legs, shaking in anticipated excitement.

She clawed his back as she encouraged him to take her, yet she did not want it to end. He continued exploring every part of her young body. Her firm strong breasts attracted his attention and he kissed them repeatedly. He licked the salty moisture from her body.

"Come on, come on." She panted like a tigress as she drew her moist hands across his body and stroked his penis.

Slowly he rose above her, she opened her thighs wider, offering her secret nectar of life. She guided his penis inside her and as a fire out of control they consumed each other. Like the pistons of the great machines he probed deeper and deeper. She responded and encouraged him by entwining her legs around his body. She forced her heaving body in time with his. She clawed at the sheets as she felt his penis grow and probe deep inside her. Her cheeks burnt as she drank the elixir of love that oozed from his sweating body. Like a probing proboscis his penis penetrated her seeking the last drop of her secret wine. He began to move quicker and she responded. She felt his penis elongate in her womb. Like leeches they clung to each other as with a shudder he ejaculated deep inside her. She felt his hot semen as in a flood of exquisiteness they climaxed. Clinging to each other and oblivious to the world around them they floated away on a bottomless tide of passion.

These were the first kisses a woman ever bestowed on him. They were to be the best of all subsequent kisses.

"I must go to work now, leave the key above the door if you go out." Again she kissed him, they were long lingering burning passionate kisses. Tearing herself reluctantly from his rapturous embrace she rose from the bed and dressed.

"I'll see you later." She blew him a kiss and opening the door was gone.

Michael lay on the bed with his hands under his head. He looked up at the bare ceiling and tried to contemplate his future. The dark outline of the miserable room was barely visible through the linen curtains that had been made from discarded flour sacks that had been dyed.

Now and again he would hear the stairs creak with the coming and going of the many tenants. He heard the sow grunt in her home beneath the stairs and knew that her litter was fighting each other for a breakfast feast on one of her many teats.

A cart trundled along the cobbled street, its ironclad wheels protesting as they became ensnared in the deep rutted holes.

"Milk! Fresh milk only one penny a quart." The cart continued on up the street.

A church bell rang out in the distance, this brought back childhood memories. Then he remembered his encounter with Sheila. He had committed a mortal sin by having sexual intercourse with her, yet somehow this did not trouble him. He remembered the old churchyard far away in the County Galway and its many Celtic Crosses.

He visualised the old yew tree and the little church that he attended with Molly. This brought back a feeling of melancholy. When would he see her again, where was his mother? Again the church bell rang out.

"God grant them peace," he heard himself praying.

"Hail Mary full of grace," his lips began whispering the customary hungry prayers for the dead. He prayed for his mother and he prayed for Molly.

His distant past rose up before him. He recalled all that happened to him in his short life. White fluffy clouds floated across a blue sky, he heard the familiar rippling waters of the little stream beside the house as it tumbled over the stepping stones. He was home again, home where he belonged…'

The bell no longer tolled, it tongue was now silent. The sun had given way to dark clouds. The waves rose higher and swallowed up the little ship tossing her high into the air before vomiting her back into the bowels of the foaming torrent.

The north winds blew violently and shrieked like the Bean-Ó-Shéidhe, this was the soothsayer's premonition of doom. He tried to escape, but where to? There was nothing out there but the boiling sea. He was puzzled as to how he came to be aboard the ship, he wanted to escape.

The waves grew higher and higher. The salty foam formed a crust on the crest of the waves. These in turn were grappled by the howling wind and were thrown violently against the superstructure of the little ship. Any that escaped being battered into oblivion leaped impetuously over one another trying to evade capture.

There was to be no escape however as the boiling seas captured them in flight and drowned them without mercy in the salty briny

The sky was foreboding and dark, the cold intense. It seemed that all was dead or dying, he was alone. He tried crying out to his God but his lips were cracked and his voice muted.

Then from the stern of the ship a form appeared, it was that of his mother. How he knew that she was his mother he did not know, someone must have told him. Who was it, Sheila perhaps?

His mother was dragging a black coffin by a rope that trailed along the deck. She was desperately trying to coil it over her shoulder to prevent it tripping her up. Her clothing was dank from the squall that clung to her as she struggled against the wind and rain trying at the same time to retain her balance. This ingenious method of balance could only be achieved from long hours of duty on the open deck in all weathers, he thought.

He called to her, he tried to approach her but every time he took a step near to her, she moved away.

Clang! Clang! Clang! Somewhere in the endless sea a bell continued its monotonous tone, warning the little ship of the imminent danger lurking beneath the waves.

Surely his mother had heard it too. If she had she seemed unaware of the danger as she continued to drag the stubborn coffin along the deck and to coil the never-ending rope at the same time.

Clang! Clang! Clang! The tone of the bell grew louder.

He shouted again and again to her, warning her of the imminent danger. The tone of the bell continued its warning cry; the ship was in dire peril. With a shuddering noise the timbers of the little ship were wrenched apart and splintered. He found himself swimming for his life, he screamed.

He grabbed at the coffin as it floated past him and held on to one of the brass handles. There was no lid on the coffin. Holding on to the side he lifted himself out of the water. As he tried to take possession of it a skeleton rose up and pushed him back into the boiling surf.

As he plunged deeper and deeper beneath the sea he looked up and saw the light receding.

He awoke in a cold sweat, his hands firmly gripping his pillow.

DECEPTION

Michael wakened to a warm ray of sunshine penetrating the room. A bird sang in the skeleton tree outside the window. he went and opened the curtains and looked out on the city. A clock in the distance showed that it was past noon. He looked down at the milling crowds and wondered what his dream meant. Filling a large floral bowl with water from a matching jug he washed himself and dressed. Locking the door behind him he placed the key above the door and went down the stairs. Opening the front door he stepped outside and was consumed in the milling crowds.

Once in the city he went to the nearest eating-house and sat by the window looking out on the street. As he sat eating two men joined him at the table.
"You don't mind us joining you?" They asked.
"Be my guest." He pointed to the vacant seats.
"You're not from Liverpool then?" One of the men on hearing his accent asked by way of conversation.
"No! I come from Ireland. He informed them.
"Ireland! Are you here looking for work?"
"No, I'm searching for my mother, I was told that she was here in Liverpool."
"There are lots of Irish girls and women here, what does she look like?"
"I don't know I never knew her, all I know is that her name is Mary Kearney."
"Mary Kearney, is that all you know about her, her name? Not a lot to go on, is it now? Did you ever hear of a woman by that name John?" He asked his companion.
"Can't say that I have, but I'm sure the priest will know, have you tried the church?"
"Do you know, I never thought of that, where might it be?"
"The nearest is Saint Jude, I should try there first, you never know you might be lucky."
"Thanks! Thanks again for your help. By the way where is it?"
"You couldn't miss it even if you were blind, go out of here and it's to your left."
"Thanks again, I'm ever so grateful. What a coincident this is; my godmother met two Irishmen in Galway who told her that my mother might be here. A lucky omen don't you think? This might be my lucky day." He shook both men's hands warmly.
"Perhaps; we wish you luck in your quest." Michael and the men parted company.

The church was nearer than he anticipated. He climbing the stone steps and taking hold of the brass latch pulled down the bolt and entered. The interior of

the church was cold and dark and his footsteps echoed throughout its vastness. Genuflecting before the high altar he took his place in a seat and knelt in silent prayer.
In a secluded and dark corner of the church a young man sat with his hands in his lap. Michael studied him for some time before approaching him.
"Excuse me, could you tell me where I might find the parish priest." He asked.
"He's not here to day, do you have a problem?" The man was young and clean shaven and spoke with a gentle voice.
"Not as such, I am looking for my mother, her name is Mary Kearney from Donegal."
"Mary Kearney, let me think for a moment. Is she a tallish woman with light brown hair, would that be a good description." The young man scratched his chin and looked deep into his eyes.
"I really wouldn't know, you see I never met my mother."
"There's a woman by that name living on the other side of the river. Would you like me to take you to her?" The young man volunteered.
"Would you please, I'd be ever so grateful."
"We would have to cross by ferry and sorry to say this but I don't have the fare." He apologised.
"Don't worry about the fare, I'll see to that there and back. If this woman is indeed my mother I'll see you right." Michael promised.
"Come on then, I'm sure that you will not be disappointed." Both men left the church and made their way to the ferry crossing.
Michael approached the ferry operator and opening his purse removed several sovereigns. "Two tickets to the other side, how much is that?" He queried holding out a handful of coins.
"You won't need all that money son, this is all you need to pay. Put that away if I were you." The operator warned him as he took a few coppers from his outstretched palm.
Leaving the ferry they went up a long incline and were soon in a labyrinth of dingy lanes and alleyways.
"Where are we going to, we must have walked miles?" Michael looked suspiciously at the sullied houses.
"Here it is, she lives on the second floor." The young man pushed open the hall door leading into an evil smelling hovel.
Michael was disorientated and apprehensive as he peered into the grimy interior.
"I doubt if anyone lives in this shamble, can't you see nobody has been here in recent times? Come on I'll pay your way back on the ferry." He was now wary of the strange young man and anxious to leave.

"You wait there, I'll go up stairs and have a look. Seeing as we came so far I'll go and see if she still lives here." The young man had his hand on the rickety banister before Michael could protest.

"Right then but don't be too long, I don't like the look of this place." Standing with his back to the street he fidgeted with his cap and felt uneasy. He couldn't hear any movement within the house and wondered what was delaying his companion.

"Anyone here, Hallo! Can you hear me?" He took a tentative step towards the staircase. "Hallo! Is there anyone here, I'm leaving." He again challenged. Hearing footsteps behind him he was about to turn round when he was pushed violently in the back. Losing his balance he tumbled down the murky stairs leading to the basement.

It was evening when he awakened to find himself lying on the dirt floor of the basement. He felt dizzy and congealed blood matted his hair.

"Good God, where am I"? He looked about him. His ears were buzzing and creating a shrill whistling noise. A hot harness held his forehead in a vice. He felt his blood throbbing convulsively in his temples. Holding his head in his hands in the hope of easing the pain he felt nauseated when he felt the flesh lifted off his scalp. Blood from a deep gash in the crown of his head seeped through his fingers. His head continued to throb and he thought it was about to burst. Holding it tightly he rocked backwards and forwards and screamed.

Rising he stumbled across the litter strewn floor towards the stairs anxious to escape from his imprisonment. As he staggered forward he felt a tearing pain in the ball of his right foot and collapsed to the floor.

He again staggered to his feet and reached out seeking some support. He lost his balance and landed back in a heap on the floor. Feeling for his foot he soon realised that his boots had been stolen together with his jacket and money. Blood was seeping from a gash in his foot. He had stepped on a broken stone jar that was now embedded deep in his foot. As he pulled the jar free fresh blood oozed from the naked wound. Tearing a sleeve from his shirt he made a makeshift bandage and wrapped it round the wound.

He sat in the stinking rubbish for some considerable time shaking from shock. As his eyes adjusted to the dim light he saw how desperate his situation was. The stairs had collapsed leaving him stranded some ten feet below the exit door. Several rats brushed past him, others were scurrying from hole to hole. He must escape but found it impossible to walk through the rubbish without footwear. Rusting tin cans, broken bottles and jagged iron was strewn across the floor. He decided that his only option was to remove his shirt and use it to sweep the debris away from his path. Slowly and deliberately he made his way

inch by inch to the foot of the staircase.
"Help! Help!" He cupped his hands and shouted. His voice echoed around the bare walls mocking him. The louder he shouted the more his head throbbed. "I must get out of here before nightfall." He spoke aloud to himself. Looking for some means of escape he saw a rusting bedstead lying against a far wall. Ignoring the pain in his foot and his nausea he succeeded in dragging it to the foot of the stairwell. Standing the bedstead on end he slowly climbed up the springs. His progress was hampered by his bandaged foot and was agonisingly slow. With a final effort he reached out for the landing. The bedstead swayed precariously as his fingers reached out to grasp the landing. It overbalanced and crashed backwards leaving him trapped under the springs, his hands were gashed and his face torn. He lay stunned for some moments. With renewed strength he lifted it and once again dragged it to the staircase. Standing it on edge he went in search of some supports to stabilise it. He found several lengths of wood and propping these on both sides of it as he once again ascended his makeshift ladder. As he grasped the landing he was glad that the bedstead remained in position. Climbing on to the head of the bed he pulled himself out of his prison. He staggered into the street and lay against the door panting. Painfully he moved along the cobbled alleyway until he reached the main thoroughfare. Seeing a horse drawn public vehicle picking up passengers he crossed the street and entered.
The passengers seeing the congealed blood and scratches on his face moved down the car away from where he was seated. The driver entered the vehicle and the conductor climbed on the back and rang the bell.
"Move on," called the driver to the horses. Slowly the vehicle moved forward. The bell rang again and the driver called on the horses to stop and looked behind to see his conductor arguing with a passenger. Leaving his seat he came round to the back of the vehicle.
"Something the matter Jack?" He looked at Michael.
"It's this drunken Paddy, look at the state of him. He claims he is the victim of an assault and wants us to take him to the ferry. Says that his money was stolen."
"How did you get in that state and why didn't you go to the police?" The driver asked.
"I told you I was attacked and had my money stolen. Now will you take me to the ferry I'll pay you when we get there?" Michael promised.
"Pay us indeed, we heard that one before. You have no money, no shoes, you're half- naked and in a filthy state. Come on off the car before we throw you off." The driver took hold of his arm.
"Nobody is going to do anything to me, do you hear me. I'll get off have no

fear." This was followed by a lot of shouting.
As he alighted two constables approached and asked what the matter was.
"This drunken Paddy would not leave when asked. He has been abusive and obstructive to my conductor and the passengers." The driver complained.
"I most certainly have not, and I left the vehicle when you insisted." Michael defended himself.
"Where are your boots and your shirt and how did you get scratched and cut. Have you been in a fight?" One constable asked suspiciously.
"It doesn't matter, forget it." Michael went to walk away.
"But it does matter, you had best come along with us." The constable placed his hand on his shoulder.
"I'm going no place, I've done nothing wrong." He brushed the constable's hand off his shoulder and went to walk away.
"Right that's it, I'm arresting you for assaulting a constable in the exercise of his duty." He was grasped on either side by the constables and frog marched to the nearest police station and incarcerated in one of the cells.
Two days later he was brought in chains before the court charged on four counts.
"Michael Kearney you are charged that on the 23rd day of May you did…
Count one assaulted a constable when exercising his duty.
Count two that you resisted arrest.
Count three that you tried to travel on public transport without paying your fare
Count four that you were drunk and disorderly.
How do you plead?" The clerk after reading out the charges asked him.
"Not guilty, Sir." Michael stood defiant in the dock of the court.
"You will address me as Your Honour young man, do you understand?" The judge demanded.
"Yes, your honour." Michael obediently replied.
"Who is representing this prisoner?" The judge asked.
"Nobody you honour." Replied the clerk.
"Very well, let's get on then." The judge sat back in his seat.
Several witnesses were called and all corroborated the charges. Finally Michael was questioned as he stood in the dock between two turnkeys.
"Mr Kearney, where do you live." The prosecutor opened the case.
"I live in Ireland." Michael replied.
"Ireland, what brought you to England, were you seeking work?"
"No! I came here searching for my mother."
"Your mother, and did you find her?"
"No I did not."
"What does your mother look like?"
"I don't know, I never met her."
"Are you telling this court that you don't know who your mother is, yet you are

looking for her in England. Surely you should be looking for her in Ireland?"
"I was informed that she was here."
"Where are you living at present?"
"No place, I'm returning to Ireland."
"So you have no fixed abode and you are going home, you tell us?"
"That's right."
"You say that you were thrown into a cellar and robbed and that is how you got your injuries."
"Yes, I was."
"Where did this assault take place?"
"In an old abandoned house. I don't know where."
You tell us that you met this stranger in a church and that he took you to a derelict house and robbed you and stole your money and boots and locked you in a cellar. Is this what you expect us to believe?"
"It's true, I swear it is."
"You don't know where this house is. You didn't go to the police and lodge a complaint, why?"
"I didn't want any trouble."
"You didn't want any trouble, why then did you assault the constable when he came to help you?"
"I never assaulted anyone."
"You don't know who your mother is, you don't know where you are living at present, you have no means of supporting yourself. You don't know where you were robbed. You never assaulted the constable and you were not drunk. It would appear Mr Kearney that all the witnesses that we have heard are, according to you liars and only you are telling the truth. Is this what you want the court to believe?" The judge intervened.
"I've told you the truth, why don't you believe me?"
"We don't believe you because the story you have told us makes no sense at all. It is the opinion of this court that you fabricated this whole story to save your own skin. As you are returning to Ireland I will be lenient with you. You will serve one calendar month in prison with hard labour. In view of the assault on the constable consider yourself lucky that I have not imposed a longer term. Take him down." The judge tiring of the case pronounced sentence.
Michael lay on his miserable bed of straw contemplating on all that happened to him since he was incarcerated inside the grim granite walls of the foreboding prison cell.
He refused to become a passive convict and accept his unjust and brutal punishment. This disobedience did not please his tormentors and he was soon brought before the prison governor.
"Prisoner Kearney whatever additional punishment I inflict on you is of your

own making. For your disruptive behaviour you will receive twenty-four lashes from the '*Cat-o-Nine-Tails*' and furthermore you will spend twenty-four hours on the treadmill. Take the prisoner away." The governor ordered.

That evening as the sun was setting he was taken from his prison cell to the whipping block where they stripped him of his clothing. Having forced a wooden block into his mouth they tied him crucifix fashion to the whipping block and proceeded with the punishment. As he lay bloodied and more dead than alive across the block his jailers rubbed brine into his open wounds. He was left there until he recovered sufficiently to walk. It was next morning before they took him to the punishment block. There he was given a bowl of rough gruel and water before he was tied to the moving *Treadmill*.

He had completed the first half of his cruel and unjust punishment. The continual bigotry and hatred of a people who neither understood his plight nor did they want to goaded him. He promised himself that he would survive with dignity their barbaric, cruel and unjust punishment.

He listened to the turnkeys as they called instructions to each other. He heard their keys rattle as they removed an unfortunate prisoner from his cell for punishment and he heard the screams. He knew who it was, it was the prisoner that had broken the handle of a pickaxe by accident that afternoon.

"Put that light out. Now!" He heard the gruff voice of a turnkey challenge.

"He quickly extinguished was remained of his tallow candle and turning over on his stomach looked out at the night sky. His sympathy lay with his fellow prisoner who was now being punished.

Beyond the bars of his cell lay freedom, freedom to roam through the mountains of his beloved land. There to spend his day listening to the thrush and the robin singing in the Hawthorne bush. They would be now in full bloom in the valley. His mind wandered back to his homeland and to the sweet meadow grasses vibrant with the chirping of the grasshopper and the droning of the bees. The clover would be a rosy red and sending out its perfume of pure nectar. His thoughts turned to Sheila and he wondered if she would remember him. His pulse rose as he remembered her twinkling mischievous eyes. She was his first love, the nectar of his life. The light slowly faded as long shadows entered his cell. The prison bars cast violet darkening shadows on the far wall. The loud hammering on his cell door by the turnkey reminded him that he was still a prisoner of her majesty and his thoughts of his homeland was all but still a dream.

FREEDOM and HOME

Having served his sentence Michael was released into the squalid outside city. He watched and waited as other ex-prisoners were met by their loved ones, then one by one they sauntered away leaving him standing alone. Looking back at the prison he picked up his bundle and left. Returning to the city he went to the Seamen's mission and withdrew a portion of his money. He looked longingly at the ships in the bay and wondered if he should return home. Memories flooded back as he climbing the long hill to the tenement where Sheila lived. Mounting the rickety stairs he stopped and listened, yes the sow and her litter were still domicile under the staircase. Reaching the landing on the floor where she lived he paused before the door. Rapping on the door he stood back and waited. There was no response, again he knocked this time louder and called her name. She must be at work in the mill he thought and was about to leave when he remembered where the key was. Reaching up he removed the key from above the door and placed it in the lock. Slowly and apprehensively he entered the room calling her name. The room was empty; removing his clothes he slumped down on the bed and was soon sleeping. It was early morning when he awakened; his hand was imprisoned under Sheila's head. He tried to remove it without disturbing her. Opening her eyes she looked up at him and smiled.

"I thought that you were never going to wake up, where have you been?" She smiled.

"It's a long story, but if you must know I've been an unwilling guest of her majesty. I missed you Sheila, how much you'll never know." Embracing her he kissed her passionately. She looked up at him, in her eyes he saw the passion that said it all. Her firm breasts were partially hidden by her long tresses. As she moved to embrace him they parted like a curtain exposing her golden brown nipples. This excited him, reaching down he held her to him and suckled them as would a babe. She encouraged him and cried out in her joy as he reached down and caressed her most intimate secret place, she reciprocated. No words were spoken as they wandered from arbour to arbour of excitement and love. He came to her, his hands, his lips searching, probing, he became bolder. She brought her legs up around him and entwined him in a vice grip encouraging him to enter her. Although he longed to satisfy himself and her, he wanted their passion to last. He made her lie down as he knelt above her. She returned his kisses, she was curious and passionate as to how her young virgin would satisfy her. With her passion reaching its climax she could wait no longer. Releasing him from her grip she opened her legs and taking his penis in her hand she guided it inside her. He no longer resisted, he let her roll over on top of him. She passionately kissed his lips, his face and his neck. She felt his penis moving deeper inside her, she moved quicker as with a cry she brought them both to the ultimate climax. Again she felt his hot seed ejaculate and enter her womb as she too climaxed intermingling their seeds of love in liquid sweetness. Tightening her arms around him she passionately kissed his lips forcing his mouth open with her tongue. Probing she drank from him as she would from a goblet of fine wine. He was intoxicated by her passionate love. A week had passed since he was released from his prison cell and he was desperately trying to break the news to her of his intention to return home. He was becoming more and more infatuated with her. Breaking the bond of love that was growing tighter by the day would not be easy. One evening as they sat at a table in the inn where they first met he looked deep into her eyes and told her of his intentions.

"Will you marry me Sheila and come home with me." He proposed to her.

"No Michael, it would not work."

"Why not? I love you Sheila and always will." He pleaded.

"I love you too Michael but listen to me, please. I knew that our love would not last. You were lonely and far from home and missing your family. Me! Well I was there to fill that vacuum and don't get me wrong I do love you and will cherish the fond memories of you." She held his hands in hers.

"No Sheila, you're wrong I love you. Please marry me." He again pleaded.

"Listen to me Michael, listen to yourself. I could never be a part of your life. You will find the girl of your dreams someplace, God willing in Ireland. When you do remember me as I will you. To night we will spend together then to morrow we must part. Please Michael I beg of you don't make our parting more sorrowful than it already is." She knew that the hills of Ireland were calling him home and she wept.

"Don't cry, please Sheila don't." He took her hand in his and held it to his breast.

"Let's go home Michael, to night will be our last night together. I want it to be special." Rising from the table she took his hand in hers. On leaving she turned and looked back.

"I'll never enter there again Michael, I want to remember always the Irish boy with the twinkling smile and curly hair who wanted me for himself." Tears filled her eyes.

He heard the clock tower strike the hour, he counted the strokes there were four. He looked down at Sheila sleeping beside him. Her tears staining her pillow, her breast heaved in a disturbed sleep. He knew that their last night together was special to them both. Reaching down he kissed her exposed nipples before he covered them with her tresses. The silence of the night frightened him and he could not sleep. Rising he went and gently opened the window. Outside all was still, a waxing moon lit up the room as myriad stars twinkled in a sullen sky. He remained at the window looking out on the city for some time. He was trying to penetrate his deep thoughts and doubts and to concentrate and make a mental summary of his being and to escape from the decision that he would have to face in a few hours time. An owl hooted from her home in the hollow of the large chestnut tree some distance away. He turned and looked towards Sheila. In her restless sleep she had tossed the covering from the bed. The moon reflected its beam on her naked breasts, before slowly disappearing behind a veil of cloud. Thick clouds gathered and without warning broke heavily. Cold sweeping rain cascaded from the night sky and wept tears on the windowpanes. He shivered in the cold of the night and closed the window. He returned to the bed and looked down at Sheila. She looked more beautiful than he ever thought possible. Her supple naked body was as slender and beautiful as the lilies of the Shannon River. Her hair cascaded across the pillow like trailing scented flowers on a bower. He could not avoid admiring the loveliness of her innocent face. As if sensing his presence she opened her eyes and smiled.

"Why are you looking at me like that?" She challenged, her eyes sparkling under long eyelashes. She made no attempt to cover her nakedness.

"Did I waken you, I'm sorry but I could not sleep?" He smiled.

"Come back to bed, you'll catch your death of cold standing there." She held her arms open and invited him to come to her. He returned to the bed and putting his arms round her waist drew her to him and kissed her inviting lips. The sorrow of parting was forgotten as he took her with a savagery that said it all. She knew that there would be no to morrow for them. The storm of the night came but they were oblivious to it. His impatience excited her and she encouraged him seeking new depths of satisfaction.

"Michael I love you." Opening her eyes wide she looked up at him offering no resistance to his demands on her body. On the contrary she too sought new ways in which to satisfy her desire to possess him. They were both aware that there would be no tomorrow.

She wanted this night to be special, she knew that the memory of it would be painful to her in the future. She loved her Irish boy and would not forget him as long as she lived.

The storm abated and the moon once again shone on their lovemaking before it too climaxed and abated. As the morning sun came peeping through the window they rose and dressed. Sheila prepared their breakfast. Little words passed between them, they knew what had to be said but it could wait just a little longer. Hand in hand they went down the long hill to the dockside and sat side by side on a bollard looking out into the waters that would soon separate them.

"Michael, don't ever forget me will you?" Instinctively she rose from the bollard and holding him close she burst into tears.

"I'll always love you Sheila and I'll never forget you. I'll remember you for your love and comfort. Don't cry Allanah, I want to see your laughter and not your tears."

He wiped the tears from her face with his kisses and felt her relax in his embrace.

"It is time for me to go. Come walk with me to the mission." He held her from him.

"Of course I'll walk with you." Together they went down the quay to the Sailor's Mission. Michael collected what money he had left in the safe keeping of the cashier.

"This is for you, Sheila I hope you will like it." He handed her a locket and chain.

"You shouldn't have." She opened the clasp and looked at the two miniatures. "It's lovely, it really is. How did you get the one of me?"

"I borrowed it from your dressing table, I hope you don't mind." He apologised.

"Mind indeed! It's wonderful, here put it on for me."

All too soon came the parting as he slowly climbed the gangplank. He stood on the deck and watched her as she waved her final goodbye. They were now divided, separated forever. Sheila climbed the hill to the head of the road and looked down at the little ship taking her lover away from her. She saw the blue emptiness of the sea and she cried. The mist of the morning mingled with her tears.

When she opened her eyes the ship was no more. Slowly she continued on up the hill.

THE AWAKENING OF A NEW DAY

Michael sat on a coil of rope on the deck of the ship and watched as the crew went about their duties. As if hypnotised by the shipmate towering over them they methodically worked like an army of ants. Looking up at the mystique of the night sky he marvelled at the power that created it. What lay beyond its infinite vastness, he wondered?
His thoughts wandered back to the incomprehensible break in his young life. Was it destiny that lured him from his native shore in search of his mother? A mother he never knew.
He thought of Sheila, his first love. Where was she now? Had she returned to the Gin Parlour? His eyes slowly closed as he was rocked to sleep by the creaking ropes and the call of the night.
He was in the field of the long pines digging beautiful potatoes and calling on Molly to bring the bucket. William Bougham the Protestant minister stood at the top of the field holding Sheila's hand calling to him.
There was a lot of noise as people came and waved to him, then they came down and began shaking him.
"Come on young man, time to go home." He looked up to see a stevedore standing above him.
"Are we there then?" He called as he looked up and saw that the ship had docked.
Picking up his portmanteau he went down the gangplank and took the road to Galway and home.
Molly was planting potatoes in the long field when he came up the old boréen.
'This has broken my dream' he mused as he opened the gate and went down the field.
She was so intent on her task that she did not notice him until he caught her around the waist.
"Michael! Michael, thank God you are back. Come up to the house and tell me all that happened. I see you didn't find your mother." She looked deep into his eyes and then began to cry.
"Please Molly, don't take on so, we knew that it might not be her. Come on, let's go up to the house. How is the minister?"
He watched her without speaking as she riddled the fire into life before she pulled the iron kettle forward over the flames.
Over tae he related most of what happened to him in Liverpool. He deliberately avoided mentioning Sheila.
"Oh Michael, I am sorry. It must have been a terrible experience for you." She sympathised with him when he told her of the cruel treatment inside an English jail.

"How is the minister? I'll go and see him if he's awake."
"Leave him be Michael. He's in great pain and can be cantankerous at times. I'll tell him that you are home when the time is right."
"Has Terry Davenny called since I left?"
"Terry! Can't keep him from the doorstep. We're getting married soon but I expect you knew that we would."
"I knew that you were walking out, but married! It never crossed my mind but I'm happy for you. You deserve all the happiness you can find and I mean that sincerely."
"Thanks Michael, I knew you would be pleased for us. Would you ever do me the honour of giving me away?"
"Molly Cullhane, I'll never give you away, but I don't mind sharing you." He promised.
"Will you stop it, Michael Kearney. You have me crying now. Before I forget it, Eugene O'Byrne, the ciscéan maker has been making inquiries as to when you are coming home."
"What is he after? As if I didn't know."
"You cannot blame him, Veronica is his only daughter and he's anxious to see her settled."
"He doesn't expect me to get married just yet surely. I have a lot of studying to catch up with." Michael grumbled.
"Studying or not, you had best get yourself over to his cottage before he decides to come here to settle the matter. You are serious about Veronica, I take it?"
"I suppose so, only I wish he would stop pestering me."
"That's not a very enthusiastic reply, you'll need to do better than that I fear." Molly insisted.
"Give me a day to settle down and I promise I'll go and see him and Veronica. Listen, there's someone banging in the backroom."
"It's Bill, He's so crippled now that he can hardly get in and out of his bed without my help. I'll tell him that you are home."
"Do you want me to help you?"
"You may as well make yourself useful and I'm sure he'll appreciate your company. Before you go in I must warn you to prepare yourself."
Anticipating the worst Michael followed her into the back room.
"What's the matter Bill? Do you want the pot? Molly asked.
"Yes please, did I hear someone else in the house?
"You did indeed, Michael is home and here to see you." She picked up the pot from under the bed and stripping the bedclothes back she gently brought his legs to the edge of the bed.

"There now!" She placed the pot between his legs and went and opened the door leading to the garden.

"Thanks Molly, that's better." Relieved he sat on the edge of the bed and waited. She removed the pot and having puffed up his pillows she settled him comfortable back in the bed.

"I'll leave you now to chat while I make a nice cup of tae." Picking up the pot she left the room.

Michael looked down at the withered face of the minister. It looked like parchment that had been folded in deep layers. His eyes were sunken deep inside his skull and were all the more obvious by the black rings around them. They looked so small that he wondered how he could possibly see.

His hands lay on top of the sheet and looked like the branches of a long dead tree. The joints were knurled and shapeless. His nostrils moved in and out as he fought for breath.

"Welcome home Michael, sit down and tell me how you fared." He raised his withered hand in a dilatory manner towards him.

Michael took the outstretched hand in his and felt its fragility. It was cold and lifeless. He tried to instil some semblance of warmth to the greeting by closing his hand in the withered hand of the minister.

With a sigh of resignation the minister retrieved his hand and lay back breathing heavily.

Michael seeing the apologetic look on his face immediately told him of his thwarted quest for his mother and his regret at having used up his money.

"Don't worry about the money, what use is it to me now? The only family I have is you and Molly. I'm not that too long for this world as you no doubt know."

Michael was lost for words and sat silently looking down at Bill wondering what to say next.

"Open the door Michael." The conversation was interrupted just in time by Molly.

"Ah! The tae, just in time would you say?" With a mischievous smile Bill looked at the inviting tray.

"You had best get your back into your studies young man." He warned him some time later.

"I'm finished studying, from now on I'm going to stay home and look after you and Molly." Michael promised.

"Is that so, well let me tell you that Molly and I can look after each other without your help, thank you. You! My young spalpeen will be taking cap and gown and I'll not hear of any refusal." The minister dictated.

"Cap and gown! Whatever do you mean?" Michael looked puzzled.
"University my boy, I want you to make me a proud old man." He seemed to perk up at his plan.
"No! That's kind of you but the cost, it's asking too much." Michael tried to refuse the generous offer.
"Michael listen to Bill. He is making this generous offer because he want's to. Accept it with gratitude and make him proud of you." Molly interrupted.
"Thank you Bill and I hope that I can do justice to your confidence in me."
"That's settled then, for a moment I thought that you were going to refuse. Now think seriously of what career you would like to follow and let me know as soon as possible. Remember you will be there for three to four years before you get your degree."
Michael went that evening to Oranmore and on to the cottage of Eugene O'Byrne. Going up the boréen he saw the old ciscéan maker busy making a basket.
"Good day to you, I've come to do the calling." Michael shuffled from one foot to the other.
"Come in Michael and welcome." He laid the basket to one side and held his hand out in greeting.
"Is Veronica about? I want her to hear what I have to say."
"Sit down and rest yourself, she won't be too long, God willing. Will you be having a drop?" A stone jug was produced from behind a pile of willows.
"No! No thank you." Michael looked with distrust at the jug of *'Potéen.'*
"You're a wise man to refuse when there's business to be discussed. Ah! Here's herself now." He pointed to the figure of a girl coming over the brow of the hillock carrying a bundle of willows on her head.
"Put them down there Veronica, there's a good girl. Michael is doing the calling and wants to talk to us both. Tell me why isn't Molly Cullhane with you? She's not sickly, I hope?"
"No She's fine thanks." Michael ran his hand round the brim of his caubéen.
"Come on then, let's hear what this proposal of yours is?" The old man put the jug to his lips and took a deep drink.
"I'm going to University on a long course, by the end of which I hope to have a degree. I would not want Veronica to feel obliged to me by waiting. I feel it only right that I tell you this." He fidgeted with his cap as he waiting for a reply.
"We appreciate your frankness in disclosing this information. Veronica has been offered a berth on a ship sailing out of Liverpool. Her Auntie Mary and her husband John were booked but John, God rest his soul has died. She asked

me if she could take Veronica in his place and I've agreed. Sure there's nothing to keep her in this forsaken land."

"This is it then, '*An American Wake*'" Michael rose to his feet. "I wish her well and may God bless and protect her in the new land." Looking across at Veronica he called the blessing on her.

"I'm afraid so Michael, it's for the best. Don't you agree? "

"Sure, I understand. There's nothing more to say. I'll bid you both good night. Good bye Veronica and I wish you well, good bye." He placed his cap on his head and lifted the latch.

"Thanks for calling Michael, I'm pleased you did. I wish you well in your studies." Veronica did not come to the door.

"Thanks! Give my regards to your daughter." With a final handshake both man and youth parted good neighbours.

A TERRIBLE TRAGEDY

With Michael away at University Molly needed all the help she could muster. The poultry and animals had to be attended, as had the demands from Bill. That welcoming help came in the form of Terry Davenny. Realising the unworkable situation she was in and her self inflicted predicament he had no alternative but to come to the aid of his fiancé.
A day seldom passed without seeing him in the fields carrying out one task after another.
"Much as I appreciate your help Terry, I feel that you are overdoing it. It's a long road here and back, take it easy for all our sakes." Molly was worried for his safety.
"Will you stop worrying, I'm grand thank God." He assured her.
"Just be careful now, do you hear me?"
"Instead of spending your energy bawling me out why don't you do something useful and put the kettle on. I'm going inside to have the 'craic' with Bill. Leaving his task, he retired from the field and went into the cottage.
"Well Bill, your looking much better to day. Any news from Michael in his fine university?" Terry took his place beside the bed.
"I had a letter from him only yesterday. He's coping very well. Finding the Latin a bit tedious though. He sends his regards to you both."
"That's good, so it is. I hope he appreciates all you are doing for him."
"Who told you that I was paying for his education. I certainly told nobody except Molly. Molly! I should have known it was she that told you."
"She did and why not? It's a fine gesture and well appreciated."
"Keep it to yourself Terry. It's of no concern to anyone what I do with my money."
"Your secrets are safe with me, you can be assured of that."
"Thanks Terry, I know that I can rely on your discretion."
"I was down the country and there seems to be a lot of talk about the failure of the potato crop." Terry changed the subject.
"Ah the potato! Ireland's currency, whatever would we do without it"?
"Sure what choice do they have? It's the only crop that yields enough to keep them alive." Terry remarked.
"True! True enough Terry, the '*Landlords Cross*' has to be set to one side come what may."
"From what I hear there will be little to give this year. The agents are already out with their battering rams." Terry disclosed this recent turn of events.
"Is it that bad now? If anyone should know then you should."
"It's pretty bad but I'd rather Molly was not told. You're lucky that you have

a diversity of crops here."

"It's not due to my husbandry I can assure you. The credit must go to you, Molly and Michael, of course. What use am I a dying cripple?" He sighed.

"Less of that now what do you think she would say if she heard such talk?"

"What talk? Is someone taking my name in vain?" Molly entered the room carrying the tray on which sat a large taepot, two mugs and a plate filled with home made soda bread.

"Thanks Molly. I was telling Terry what a God send you are, isn't that right?"

"That's the honest truth, so it is. Would I lie to you?" Terry laughed.

"Get on now the both of you and less of the sweet talk. I'm off to spancel the cow and do the milking. You'll manage on your own I've no doubt"

"Thanks! Do you need any help?" Terry was already filling a mug with tae.

"No! I can manage. You get on with whatever you are talking about."

"Would you ever prop me up on the pillows Terry? I'm a bit of a nuisance I know."

"Will you stop fishing for compliments. There how's that?" Terry lifted the old man high up in the bed and placed extra pillows under his back. He was surprised at how light he was.

"That's grand, thanks. Now can you pass me the mug of tae."

"I was telling you earlier about the potato failure. I fear it is more serious than many care to admit." Terry looked deep into the fire.

"That comes from the people putting on the poor mouth year in year out about what hardship they are suffering." Bill reminded him.

"I couldn't agree with you Bill on that score. Sure they're struggling to stay alive on a few con acres of rocky land, God help them. "There's no paltry excuses this time. There is going to be a catastrophe of epidemic proportion I fear. The problem is that the government is treating the whole matter with flippancy."

"How bad would you say it is then? If anyone can read the situation then it must be you."

"Why should it be me? What can I do about it?"

"Nobody is asking you Terry; be honest who travels this country more than you?"

"You're right at that. It first came to my notice in the town of Banagher on the Galway/Offaly border. I was coming into the town driving the heavy dray. It's a slow drag up the hill and by the time I got to the town the horses were at crawling pace. I found it strange indeed that the people ignored me. They walked past me never asking if I had any parcels or messages for them. I found this disturbing and unusual. There was a smell of sulphur in the air but I put it down to the fact that there was large pile of manure for sale in the square.

I made my deliveries and changed the horses without passing any further

remarks. I then went to the hostelry for a meal and a well-earned drink. There I got into a conversation with a local man."
"What ails you all?" I asked no longer able to stand the tense situation.
"You don't know then I take it?" He replied.
"Know! Know what? Sure I only got here to day and you could cut the atmosphere with a knife. I know that I done nothing wrong to anybody. Don't tell me that the Fenian brotherhood have caused trouble?" I more or less answered him.
"Nothing to do with the Fenians, they're a fine body of brave souls, so they are. Go out that door and sniff the air, there you'll find the answer to your question."
"Of course they are and I wouldn't take that away from them. I've been through the town. All I could smell was the rotting manure in the square." I told him.
"Come out here with me." He guided me to the door and opened it.
"Now what do you smell?" He challenged.
"Good God it cannot be, surely not?" I could not tell him what I suspected it to be.
"Yes! You know right enough what it is, now don't you? The blight, it struck yesterday without warning."
"Considering the crop is nearly ready to dig, you must have been able to salvage some of it?" I suggested.
"Save it indeed, every man woman and child went into the fields after the rains had passed and tried to save what we could. Those without forks or spades dug with their bare hands. We thought we were successful when we pulled the potatoes from the rotting stalks. Then before our eyes they turned black and were reduced to a evil smelling mass of putrid muck." He enlightened me.
"God help you all, whatever will you do?" I offered my sympathy. He looked into my face incredulously. Then picking up his cap he placed it on his head and without saying another word walked away.
"What did you expect him to say? He had no doubt lost a year's hard earned work in the space of a day." The minister confirmed.
"I had to wait in the town for a week until the goods came down from Dublin docks and the horses were rested and what I saw happening brought my temper to the boil and tears to my eyes." Terry continued relating his experiences.
Before the week had broken its back whole families were on the move. Mostly women, carrying their infants in their shawls with young barefooted children walking beside them. In their wake followed a rag tag army of old folk.
"Where are they going to?" I asked the hotelier.
"Their landlords knowing that they would not be able to meet their rents seized

their sheep and goats and milch cows before they could sell them. They have nothing left to stay for." He told me.

"Where are you going to?" I asked a band of barefooted women and children passing by the door. I thought I might be in a position to help them.

"The hunger is come on the land and the landlord has set the spleen to our cottages. We are destitute and heading out on the road to Tullamore." An ould woman of eighty years or so cried pitifully.

"Jesus help us! He took our two sheep and our goat." Another wrung her hands and cried.

"Our milch cow, Buttercup, was taken too." An innocent child intoned.

"Would you for the love of God and his blessed mother let us have a crust or two for the children?" A woman with three children pleaded.

"My man died in the garden last night, so he did. We have nothing left." She continued to plead as she walked along the road without stopping.

I went to the bakery and purchased several loaves. It was the least that I could do. As I went to hand them out the gathering stopped and stood staring at the bread.

"Here take it, it's for you." I more or less had to force the bread into their hands. Other people on seeing what I had done came forward and gave them clothing and food and vegetables. Many were crying openly. Shure in the end I was crying myself."

"God bless the folk of Banagher." The cry went up from the evicted as they crossed the old stone bridge. That was the last I saw of them. Where they went to God only knows.

Heaven help them. I prayed and me with a lump in me throat in sympathy."

"Do you think it will come this far?" Bill asked.

"There's no doubt about it. As sure as there's a God in heaven it will strike without warning." Terry confirmed.

"Well that's that. Come on out Terry and help me with the supper. You can chat all night for all I care afterwards but first let's have a morsel to eat." Molly came into the room and approached the bed.

"Terry off you go and riddle the fire. I'll see to Bill. Now who propped you up like that?" She began adjusting the pillows.

"If I could get out of this bed I'd leave it to you." Bill grumbled.

"If only I could be so lucky, what were you two talking about?" Molly asked.

"It's none of your business, it was mans talk if you must know. Ouch! There's no need to be so brutal" He protested.

"Mans talk indeed, whatever that may be. Now stop moaning and let me get on."

A MESSAGE FROM BALLISODARE

Having filled the dray Terry went and collected the team of horses and harnessed them.
"I'm off now Molly but I should be returning within the week. Tell Bill that I'll look up the minister in Stranolar should I get the chance."
"Take care on the road now and don't take any chances. Rest up if you feel tired I want you back here in one piece." She advised.
"Don't worry I'll take good care now that I have you to come back to. Tell me is there anything that you would like me to get you?"
"There's nothing that I need, thank God. Yes there is, come to think of it. When you get to Knock would get me a bottle of Holy Water from the shrine?"
"No trouble, I'll see you soon, God bless." He cracked the whip and the two horses began pulling the dray out the gate and on to the Donegal road.
On the road to Tuam he met several bands of people moving south. Many were crying,
others praying but the majority moved on as if an emptiness had overtaken them.
He knew that the Great Hunger had no respect for boundaries and that it had quickly engulfed the entire westcoast.
Periodically on his journey he saw mounted Red Coats with naked swords charge down the road scattering the miserable bands before them.
He was relieved when he reached the town of Tuam. Here he would rest the horses and indulge himself in a well-earned meal.
"Terry, I'm glad it's yourself. I was about to send a horseman to Galway to find you." The landlord of the inn approached him.
"What would you want to find me for? Has something happened?"
"Sure I don't know what it's about. We got this message from your cousin Nora in Sligo. Here read it for yourself." The proprietor handed him a letter.
"Not much information in this. Nora says that I must call in on my way to Donegal, nothing more." Terry turned the paper over and looked at the back.
"Is that it? The messenger gave me the impression that it was urgent. Why else would I be thinking of sending a messenger all the way to Galway to find you?"
He replied rather hurt by the lack of gratitude.
"Thanks for the thought John. Some people have the habit of overreacting." Terry apologised.
"Whatever, make sure you call in now. I wouldn't like them to think that I never delivered the message." John insisted.
"I'll make sure that they know you told me. Thanks again John." Terry again apologised and took his seat on the cart.
Terry continued on his journey giving little thought to the message. On the

outskirts of Claremorris he was stopped by a detachment of Red Coats.
"Where are you going to?" The officer demanded to know.
"I'm going to Donegal Town with this delivery. Is something the matter?"
"I'll ask the questions. What's your name and what good are you carrying?" He demanded.
"I'm Terry Davenny from out of Donegal. The consignment in the dray is mixed I have the list here." Producing the document he handed it to the officer.
"Park over there for now. We'll let you know when you can proceed." The officer glanced at the document before directing him into a field beside the road.
"How long will it be before I can leave? I have a long journey before me." Terry asked.
"As long as we think fit. Now get off the road." Came the abrupt reply.
Taking full advantage of the situation he released the horses from the dray and let them free in the field. Going up the boréen on foot he came to a cottage surrounded by the *'Crowbar Gang'*.
Astride a grey gelding sat the landlord's agent directing operations. A tripod has being erected in front of the cottage door.
The boreen was no longer accessible; mounted and armed Red Coats beforehand had closed it. Over their shoulders they carried naked swords ready to strike at any intruders. He joined the gathering on the small hillock and stood looking down at the crowbar gang meticulously going about their work.
"How many are there inside?" He asked a man standing mesmerised beside him.
"It's the Quinn family and their five children. They have no crop to meet their rent and taxes and no place to go to." He had heard it all before.
He noticed that this was no ordinary battering ram. The head was encased in a strong iron shield.
"I never saw one like that before, where did it come from?" He questioned.
"From his lordships forge, where else? Made by one of our own farriers you'll be pleased to hear." The bystander sarcastically remarked.
Two stout chains had been inserted inside two eyehooks. There was one to the front and one to the rear. Under the top of the tripod another large hook hung down from one of the uprights. The chains had spring-loaded clips that attached themselves to the large hook. This allowed the ram to be dismantled easily and carried from cottage to cottage. It could then be assembled quickly.
This contraption had been designed for long usage.
Slowly and deliberately the ram began its pendulum motion. Firstly gently tapping the
stout door just as a spider would its web in which a fly had been trapped. Then

having found the Achilles heel in the door they increased the momentum. The gang leader called out the time to his lackeys...'

"*A Aon, A Dá, A Aon, A Dá.*" *(One-Two)* The quisling working for the *Sacsaib Gabain (English Occupier)* called out, increasing the momentum with every stroke. These were Gaelic speaking Irishmen betraying their countrymen for the Saxon shilling.

Sweat glistened on their brows as they hauled in unison on the ropes controlling the movement of the ram.

"More weight you lazy Fenians. Put your backs into it." The agent demanded. Again the timing of the ram was increased.

"Mó Ualac" (More load) The leader screamed. Slowly the door surrendered to the assault and as it did, the crowbar gang wasted no time in entering and dragging the pathetic wretches and their children outside.

"Fetch the *Spleen*" Ordered the agent.

The lighted torch was brought forward and thrown on to the thatched roof. Immediately the cottage to become a raging inferno.

The family consisting of a father, mother and five children were driven by the Red Coats from the burning cottage.

Once order was restored the road was opened and Terry was allowed to continue on his journey.

Throughout the long night the horses hauled the dray through the countryside. Terry slept peacefully and was awakened when the horses stopped to drink before crossing the ford below Collooney.

"Come on now, I know you are tired and hungry but so am I. We're nearly home." He spoke gently to the horses to encourage them.

Rousing from a deep sleep he noticed the cottage of Nora and Brendan in the grey dawn.

"That's it then." With a sleepy yawn he flicked the reins across the backs of the horses encouraging them into a gentle trot.

Pricking up their ears the horses resumed the journey to the home of Nora in Ballisodare.

BRENDAN IS WAKED

Bruno, their faithful old sheep dog came trotting to the gate on hearing the horses hoofs in the boréen. Wagging his tail he approached the dray and began barking.
"So you're still about you old devil." Terry jumped off the dray and opening the gate led the horses inside.
"Down! Down Bruno. Let me remove the harness from the horses first." He gently chided the excited dog.
A Rooster sat on the half door of the poultry house heralding in the dawn.
'That's unusual.' He thought on seeing that the poultry had not been locked away for the night.
Having dropped the shafts of the dray and released the horses he called the dog to his side and meandered up the boréen to the cottage.
"Is that yourself Nora?" He called on seeing a silhouette outlined in the grey dawn.
"It is indeed. Thank God you are here. I thought it might be too late." Coming from round the gable end of the cottage she fell into his arms crying.
"Whatever is the matter? Pull yourself together girl."
"It's my Brendan, he's dying so he is and there's nothing that I can do." She wept uncontrollably.
"There! There now, come on let's get you into the cottage." He gentle guided her inside.
On entering the bedroom he knew instinctively on seeing the emaciated skeleton of what was once a fine man that it was only a matter of time.
"How are you feeling Brendan?" He gently called. There was no response.
Leaving the bedroom he entered the kitchen where Nora sat by the fire crying. Without disturbing her he set the kettle over the fire and proceeded to prepare the breakfast.
"Here you are Allanah, you must be brave for the both of you." He called her to the table.
"Is he going to die Terry?" She pleaded through her tears.
"He's in God's hands, so he is. Whatever happened to him?"
"Himself and Seámus Deenegan went over to Carney with a delivery of *'Poitín.'* They entered the grounds of Lissadell Manor where the exchange was to have taken place. The *'Peelers'* were waiting for them and when the boys saw them they began to run. Then out from the woods came a volley of gunfire and Brendan was shot in the chest. Somehow Seámus got him home and I sent for the doctor. He came at once and removed the bullet. He was doing fine up to two weeks ago. Then against all advice he took himself off and

ploughed the fairy meadow.
I told him that it could wait until he was a little stronger but you know how stubborn he can be. Next day he felt bad and stayed in bed. That night he got very sick and next morning I again sent for the doctor. Some kind of chest infection the doctor said. That's about all I can tell you."
"God is good, you never know. I'll see to the animals and poultry. You eat your breakfast and then try and get a little sleep." Terry comforted her.
Sometime later he returned to the cottage to find her sleeping a restless sleep in the *Leaba Suidheacan*.
Leaving her resting he went into the bedroom and called to Brendan. Terry knew that he was fighting a losing battle, it was only a matter of time. Leaving Nora sleeping he called the dog to his side and left the cottage.
Returning with the curate he gently opened the door. Nora was still sleeping a restive sleep. They entered the bedroom without disturbing her. The curate prepared Brendan before administering the last rites of the church to him.
They were kneeling beside the bed reciting the act of Contrition when they heard Nora behind them. Without interrupting their prayer she knelt and joined in the prayer.
With the last rites administered they left Brendan to his God.
"Thank you Terry, I forgot." Nora sat at the table resigned to the fate of her husband.
Late into the night she knelt by the bedside praying for her husband.
For four days and nights she kept a vigil by his bedside with little interruption. She knew that it was only a matter of time as she listened to his heavy breathing.
"Nora! Please don't you know he cannot die peacefully with another present?" Terry encouraged her to leave the room,
(It was believed that the soul of the dead would not leave the corpse as long as a mortal was present)
Early the next morning he again entered the room and knew by the silence that Brendan had died during the night.
"I'm Sorry Nora, it's over." Without replying she went into the bedroom and closed the door behind her.
Taking down his caubéen from behind the door he left the cottage. He returned some time later accompanied by the mourners. Nora was still in the bedroom. Nancy Hagerty, one of the mourners went to the bedroom and encouraged her into the kitchen.
"Sit yourself down girl there are things that have to be attended to." Gently she guided her away from the bedroom to a stool beside the kitchen fire.

Nancy sat for some time looking into the ashes and crooning to herself. Rising she prostrated herself before the fire. She covered her head with ashes before rising and sprinkling ashes on all present. Then the women mourners took their aprons in their hands and covering their faces began rocking to and fro crooning a mournful dirge out of respect for the dead.
She went to the salt barrel and taking a handful of salt she mixed it with a handful of ashes and called on Nora to open the door to her departing husband. As the door was slowly opened the women began wailing and crooning a dirge in honour of the dead. Then came the chant...'
'Ul- Lú- Lú- Ló- Ló
Over and over again and again the women crooned. Rising into a crescendo of sound one moment the next into a low murmur. As the door was thrown fully open Nancy rushed forward with her hands open in crucifix fashion preventing the demon from entering the house. Wailing in a high pitched voice she began scattering the mixture of ashes and salt before her. On reaching the threshold she challenged the evil spirit and the two great dogs of Hades that were stopping the soul of Brendan from leaving the house. Throwing the ashes to the North to the South to the East and to the West she called on those present to join her in her efforts to thwart the evil spirits. The others obliged and began banging pots and pans and wailing. Satisfied that the spirits were routed she returned to the cottage and closed the door.
Ireland had a latitudinarianism of religious dogma that was half-pagan and half-Christian.
Most of the gathering knelt on the stone floor others prostrated themselves on the dirt floor as Nancy led them into the Rosary.
The soul of Brendan had now left the house and it was considered safe to remove the corpse from the bed.
"Can we leave the arrangements for the wake with you, Terry?" Nancy took him to one side and asked.
"Of course, you see to matters here. I'll take the bucket trap to Sligo." He informed her.
"No Terry, you'll need to take the dray. How could you carry the coffin and drinks in the trap?"
"Sorry, I'm not thinking straight." He apologized.
Following his departure the cottage began filling with neighbours as the sad news was spread from mouth to mouth.
As custom demanded no words of condolence were offered within the house to the widow as she sat by the fire crooning. This would be left until after the funeral service. There was a wake to be held and this would be the time to

celebrate the good times.
Brendan was laid out under the window on a table. Two coins covered his eyes and a ribbon had been discreetly tied through his hair and under his chin. In the window sat the *'Connail Mhór'* calling on his neighbours to come and pay their last respects.
Terry returned that evening with a generous supply of whiskey, beer, tobacco and clay pipes. There was a generous supply of Poiteén in the outhouse that had been brewed by Brendan some time previously. He laid the pipes along the mantle and invited the men to join him in commemorating the good life that they had shared with Brendan in the past. There was also a generous supply of snuff for the taking. All was now ready for the waking of Brendan.
Neighbours came and having taken a pipe of Tobacco they broke the stem, shortening it and threw the surplus into the fire. Passing the corpse they stood for a moment and said a silent prayer before taking their place along the white washed wall. As the night wore on stories from Brendan's past life were again reminisced. There was soothing music and *'Sean Scéal'* to keep the mourners entertained throughout the long night. Many having to see to their own chores left early promising to return for the funeral.
As the dawn broke over an Irish Sky Terry came to the fireplace and called on Nora to come and say her last goodbyes, they were about to nail the lid on the coffin. As the lid was placed on the coffin the women again threw their aprons over their faces and began crooning. The noise of the hammer could not be heard above the incessant crooning. The purpose of this was to prevent the evil spirits from knowing that the corpse was leaving the house.
The priest and acolyte arrived some time later. An altar was arranged on the top of the coffin and the Priest called upon to celebrate the Mass for the dead.
At the Offertory Terry rose to his feet. Taking his caubéen from his pocket he approached each mourner seeking offerings (donations) for the Priest celebrating the Mass.
When the service finished Terry and three other men lifted the coffin on to their shoulders and faced the door. The Priest took up his position in front of the coffin and his acolyte stood beside him holding the bucket of holy water in which sat the aspergillum.
Nancy opened the door as the Priest retrieved the Aspergillum and blessed the coffin and the people.
Slowly the cortege wended their way up the hill to the little graveyard on the summit of the hill.
(Such wakes as this were traditional throughout Ireland. I attended such a wake in County Limerick in 1938. The Author)

THE HOMES OF DONEGAL

Terry stayed at the cottage for the rest of the week until Nora accepted that Brendan was no longer with her.
"Sorry I have to leave now Nora. The folk in Donegal Town will be waiting for their goods. I'll call in on my way back. Will you be alright?" He informed her one morning after breakfast.
"Don't fret so Terry, it was Gods will and thanks. I could not have managed without you." As the dray left the boréen he looked back and waved.
"See you in about a week or so. God bless." She stood in the boréen until the dray was on the Donegal road. With a sigh she returned to the cottage.
"Come on Bruno, there's only you and me now." The old dog snuggled his nose into her hand as if he understood.
It was raining a drizzly rain as the dray wended its way through the night. The omnipotent wind howled through the skeleton trees reaching down their claw like branches, making the horses shy. Over rough stony famine built roads and deep rutted holes the dray moved on. Terry twisted the reins this way and that doing his best to steer the dray clear and avoid an expensive loss of a wheel. The buckets slung under the rear of the dray clanged monotonously against the undercarriage, lulling him into a sleep that he did not relish. The river Glen, roared on towards ghostly Lough O'Mulligan. He saw *'One man Pass'* to his right and tried to avert his eyes away. Here it is said that the Ghost of a defrocked Friar waits at the pass for the unwary and pushes them over the cliff top to their death.
On into the night he drove accompanied by a solitary owl that kept landing on every available perch and hooting. Rounding a bend in the road he saw the outline of Killybegs, the home of the *'Spanish Lady.'* She was found buried in a bog not too far away with a fine ivory comb in her hair. She wore costly clothing and silver buckles on her dainty shoes.
It was rumoured that she was the wife of a Spanish Admiral and one of a few a survivors from the Spanish Armada that was wrecked off the Donegal coast. Those that made it ashore were robbed and killed. Fleeing from the amorous approaches of a Donegal fisherman she got lost in the bog and drowned.
The dawn was breaking when he saw before him the deep blue outline of the Blue Stack Mountains. On the shores of Donegal bay he looked out at the ruins of the Franciscan Abbey that was built for them by Red Hugh O'Donnell at his own expense. Little did he know then that it would become the final resting-place on earth for him and his wife Fingalla. The abbey left behind a treasure unsurpassed in Irish historical documents, *'The Annals of the Four Masters'.*

"It's the last resting place of the O'Donnells I dare say and my resting place for a while." He mused.
Stretching himself he jumped off the dray. Rubbing life into his cold bones he led the horses towards the field.
The lush grass was covered in a glistening frost and his feet made a crunching sound as he walked on it. A cold penetrating wind chased snow-laden clouds towards the Blue Stack Mountains. The horses shook their manes and did a *'Rinnce Fada'* down the field. Their warm breath crystallising as it mixed with the cold air that was now appreciable chillier.
A rainbow rose from Lough Derg (The Red Lake) where thousands of pilgrims come to repent their sins and hope to gain a foothold in Heaven. It traversed tranquilly across the sky until it finally rested high above Donegal Castle without touching the ground.
"I'm back and ready for a good breakfast, but first I need a hot tub." Terry banged on the door of the inn owned by Gerry and Mary Manley.
"It's yourself now, couldn't you make the noise a little easier?" He heard Gerry's wife, Mary, challenge as she drew the bolt from inside the door and opened it.
"God help me but it's nippy out there?" He retreated to the welcoming fire and lifted the tail of his coat.
"I'll make a drop of tae first, you'll have a long wait for a tub." Mary informed him.
"How is Gerry?"
"Fine and why shouldn't he be?" Mary was a bit curt in her reply.
"Just asking, I've got some goods for him."
"They should have been here a week since. He's been waiting for them if you must know." Mary grumbled.
"Well Mary, circumstances beyond my control delayed them, sorry!" He went on to explain the death of Brendan.
"Sorry Terry, it's early and I'm not thinking straight." Mary apologised.
"It's you, I might have known. Don't you ever sleep? You're welcome Terry. Did you bring anything for me?" Gerry came down the stairs scratching at his hair.
"This lot is addressed to you, I should have been here some time ago but... Ah well!"
"He found his cousin Brendan dying on his way here and has since buried him." Mary,
hoping to make amends for her previous abruptness interrupted.
"Sorry Terry, how is Nora?" Gerry apologized.
"She's fine, I'm sure she will take the reins in hand."
"Remember us to her and tell her that if ever the need arises then she won't

find Gerry and Mary Manley wanting. Isn't that so Mary?"
"Of course. Now come away from that fire and sit yourself down and have a sup of tae."
"What's the news then? I hear the famine is taking its toll and spreading." An old man in the corner by the fire asked that evening.
"The Famine, is that what you call it? It's easy to see that you've not been outside Donegal." Terry chided him.
"What would you call it when people die from starvation?" The old man questioned.
"I'll tell you if you'd care to listen. The agent of a large estate in the County Galway with the help of the Red Coats detained me on the road here. It so happened that the *Crowbar Gang* was busy demolishing a cottage on the estate for non-payment of rent. Non payment of rent indeed just an excuse. It is now the law that landlords are liable for the pauper's rates and to avoid paying it they turn them off the estates. Another reason is that they need the land for cattle. The industrial revolution in England is calling out for beef on the hoof and where betters to obtain it than from the lush grasses of Ireland. They can rear the beef cattle in Ireland and ship them over to England at a handsome profit. Root crops are easily grown in England and oats and corn can be obtained cheaply from America and Canada.
They have no use for the troublesome potato wasting valuable land that could be put to better use and so the Irish are evicted. Could you ever visualise Irishmen demolishing the cottages of their fellow countrymen for three Saxon shillings a cottage?"
"Sure they're doing it here to their own kit and kin." Grumbled another.
"I tell you I witnessed with my own eyes drays laden with Irish produce and cattle on the hoof being driven in the dead of night to the ports. From there they were loaded on to ships bound for England." Terry informed the gathering.
"Did nobody ever try to stop them?" Gerry Manly asked.
"Stop them? Will you talk some sense man? Cavalry armed to the teeth guard every shipment." Terry informed them.
"You've been lucky so far but I fear it will come here as sure as night follows day."
"Good God man, is it a '*pishogue*' you are trying to out on us?" The old man grumbled on hearing the blight mentioned.
"Not at all, I'm stating the facts as I see them. If you wish to ignore them then that's your problem." Terry warned.
"Come on now enough of that, lets have an ould song? Mary will you bring that jug of *Potéen* from the kitchen?" Gerry encouraged the gathering to change the

subject.
It was some time later that Terry brought up the subject of the disappearance of Mary Kearney.
"Do any of you know the whereabouts of Mary Kearney from Dunlogue? I've been asked to make inquiries as to her whereabouts." Terry studied their faces seeking an answer.
"Mary Kearney you say? Didn't she die in the bog?" Another scratched his chin questioningly.
"That was her mother, do you know anything at all about her daughter, Mary?"
"No! Nothing at all, God help them. They were the most unfortunate family." Gerry interrupted.
"The Kearney family you say. The last I heard of them was when their daughter left with Lord Kilgarvan of Dungloe. A real scandal it was and she only a child." Mary informed him.
"Lord Kilgarvan you say? Sure he vanished from his bankrupt estate and was never seen again. I doubt very much if Tom Kearney's daughter was with him."
"He had a bailiff who was the scourge of the estate. Now what was that fellows name?" The speaker scratched his chin.
"That was Frank McLaughlan. He was found dead by the road side wearing Lord Kilgarvan clothes having been shot off his horse."
"By God you're right. Some say he done away with his Lordship. How he got shot is a mystery."
"Whatever happened behind those walls we will never know."
"There was talk of a child somewhere along the line but then all kinds of rumours come out of these things."
"Whatever became of the housekeeper, Maura O'Reilly?" Mary asked.
"She was found dead in her bed, she died from consumption. May God have mercy on her soul."
"Will whatever happened at Cardavon Castle ever come to light, I wonder?" Another questioned.
"If anyone of you hear anything of Mary would you let me know?" Terry tiring of hearing the company going over old stories and exaggerated gossip without shedding any light on the matter asked.
Long into the night the gathering exchanged gossip and arranged to share the workload before drowning them in song and ale.

A SECRET REVEALED

Michael arrived at the university. He was dressed in his new clothes carrying all his worldly possessions in his portmanteau.
"Are you new here?" A fellow student of about sixteen years of age approached him.
He was dressed in a tight fitting suit with a bright red cravat tied round his neck. From under a slouched floppy cap two nervous brown eyes looked up at him.
"Yes, I'm new here. What about yourself?" Michael intoned
"My name is Master Seanaí Ryan and my papa is agent to Lord MacMillian." The youth held his hand out in greeting.
"Pleased to meet you, I'm Michael Kearney."
"I presume we have to approach our tutor to be directed to our quarters?" The youth looked round at the milling students.
"I wouldn't know, I've never been to university."
"Come here my good man and bring my trunk." Snapping his fingers the youth called on a porter stranding near by.
"Come on then, let's see what fate awaits us? Perhaps they will allow us to share." The young man without waiting for a reply went across the gravel drive to the main building.
The porter followed carrying the trunk on his back. Michael stood looking surprised after the audacious young gent.
"Come on Michael, whatever are you waiting for?" He called.
Although Michael was older than Seanaí he couldn't but admire his self-confidence. Here was a born leader and one that would prove a great asset to him in the future.
"You can go now." Seanaí reached into the pocket of his breeches and producing a coin
handed it to the porter before dismissing him.
Seanaí looked round the hall until he saw a grill set into the wall in an inner section.
"This is it, come on Michael." Removing his gloves he approached the grill.
"My name is Seanaí Ryan and this is my companions. His name is Michael Kearney. We are here for the new term and request that we share the same quarters."
Michael was surprised at his audacity in presuming that he wished to share a room with him. His brash approach seemed to work as without any questions being asked they were allocated a room together on the second floor. From then on it seemed that they were inseparable.

They helped each other out with their problems and shared the many hampers sent by Seanaí's parents.
Two months into their degree they were given leave of absence for a full weekend. "Michael! What are you going to do with yourself this weekend?" Seanaí asked.
"Stay here I suppose, I have no place else to go." Michael replied with a shrug of his shoulders.
"Why don't you come home with me and meet my parents? We could have a grand old time on his Lordships estate."
" I'd love to but how would we get there?"
"You leave that to me. Where there's a will there's a way."
The following afternoon a coach arrived to take them to the estate of Lord MacMillian.
"You'll like my parents, not a bit snobbish." Seanaí assured him.
They entered the estate through high security gates that were guarded on each side by a Gatekeepers cottage.
"This is our abode, what do you think of it?" Seanaí pointed out a house set in woodland some distance from the manor.
"Very cosy I must say. Nothing like that though." Michael pointed to the manor.
"We'll take a look around it before we return." He promised.
"You're welcome." Seanaí's mother came to the door.
"This is my Mom, Geraldine. Ger for short and she is the finest scone maker this side of the *Burren.*" He boasted.
"Pleased to meet you ma'am." Michael reciprocated.
"Your father is over at the manor, some business with his lordship. He offers his apologies and promises to meet you this evening." She assured them.
"Come on I'll show you to your room." Seanaí bounded up the stairs followed by Michael.
Having explored the grounds of the estate they returned to the house cold and hungry.
"Is dinner ready yet, Mom? I'm starving." Entering the kitchen Seanaí studied well-laden table.
"It's ready, I'm waiting for your father to come home." Geraldine dusted her floured hands on her apron.
"I'm here. You must be Michael, I heard a lot about you, welcome." A tall man wearing plus fours and boasting a deerstalkers cap entered the kitchen.
After dinner they retired to the sitting room.
"How is your tuition going? Still having a problem with the Latin?" Seanaí's father asked.
"Not anymore, I have a brilliant teacher in Michael here. He's good at English

and Latin and I'm good at maths, we make an excellent team. Don't we Michael?"

"Tell me Michael where do you come from?" Seanaí's father asked by way of conversation.

"I'm from Dungloe in County Donegal." He informed them.

"Dungloe! Did you ever hear of a Lord Kilgarvan of Cardavon Castle? Perhaps not, it was before your time."

"Lord Kilgarvan? Is he not the one that disappeared without a trace?" Geraldine interrupted.

"The very same and the mystery of it all is that his bailiff was found dead with a bullet in his brain wearing his lordships clothes and his horse chomping the grass beside the body."

"My mother worked for Lord Kilgarvan and she went missing many years ago and was never found. We have been looking for her since." Michael informed them.

"Would your mothers name be Mary Kearney?" Geraldine asked.

"Yes! Do you know where she is?" Michael pleaded.

"There is little that anyone knows about her except rumours. Some say she ran away with his Lordship. Others say that there was a child involved."

"John, could we change the subject? You're embarrassing Michael." His wife interrupted.

"Oh my God! Sorry." Seanaí's father suddenly realising what he was implying held his hand to his hand to his face.

"Please excuse me, I was not thinking." He again apologised.

"No need to apologise I believe you are right about the child. I am, so I'm told the illegitimate son of Lord Kilgarvan. My mother was raped by him." Michael openly admitted.

"I am sorry, we never knew. I'll fetch the afters." Geraldine feeling uneasy left the table.

"There's no need to feel embarrassed, it is best that the facts are known." Michael went on to tell of the death of his grandmother and the disappearance of his mother.

"Who are you living with now?" Geraldine entered the sitting room carrying a tray.

"I'm living with my adopted mother and a minister of the Church of Ireland. It is he who is sponsoring me at the University." Michael admitted.

"Did you know that the estate is abandoned and vacant? There are no apparent heirs to it. If you could prove what you tell us then the estate rightly belongs to you." Seanaí's father informed him.

"What would I do with an estate? It's the last thing in the world that I want." Michael shrugged away the suggestion.

"It would only be natural justice for you to claim it. If left it will go to the crown." Geraldine insisted.

"Just think of it Michael, you the lord of the manor? Wait until I tell the others." Seanaí seemed to be pleased with the news.

"You will tell no one what you were told under this roof. Don't you realise the consequences of such unfounded gossip?" His father warned.

"What harm could it do?" I'm sure he would like to claim his inheritance."

"This is Michael's business. Should he wish to disclose it then that is his prerogative? Now we'll hear no more about it." His father warned.

"Of course I'll respect his wishes. What are friends for if they cannot trust each other?" Séanaí shrugged his shoulders in resignation.

MICHAEL RETURNS ON VACATION

Hearing the sound of a coach Molly left down the bucket of food and went to the front of the house. She was surprised to see a coach and four coming up the drive.
She was pleased when she saw Michael and another scholar alight.
"Whatever are you two doing here?" She looked anxiously from one to the other.
"That's a fine greeting, I must say for the best man and his companion. This is my bosom companion, Seanaí Ryan. Seanaí meet Molly and likewise."
"I must apologise but I did not expect you so soon. Come in and welcome." She fidgeted with her apron.
"Bridal jitters I've no doubt, want to change your mind?" He laughed.
"Ah stop it, I'm having trouble trying to sort matters out on my own without you making matters worse." Molly stamped her foot in mock annoyance.
"Where is Terry then? I expected him to be here." He asked.
"He's up country and will be here in plenty of time. I hope." She added as an afterthought.
" I wouldn't be too sure of that now. Marrying Molly Cullhane could be a very expensive business and then there are the children to raise. I wouldn't blame him for getting cold feet." Michael chided her.
"Will you stop him Seanaí. Have you no influence over your companion? I'm nervous enough as it is." Molly pleaded.
"Sure he's only trying to cheer you up. I think so anyway. Are you Michael?" Seanaí joined in the friendly bantering.
"That's it gang up on me, better still go down and milk the cow and leave me to prepare the supper. If you want to eat you had better keep a civil tongue in your heads. Do you hear me?" She warned.
"See, I told you. She's a proper madam." Michael laughed.
"Get on with you, I'll have the supper ready by the time you get back."
"How is Bill keeping? I'd like to see him and introduce my friend." Michael asked.
"He's resting for now. You will have all the time in the world after supper to chat. Now will you go and see to the cow?" She insisted.
Later that evening Michael introduced Seanaí to Bill.
"We've brought our reports with us." Michael produced his reports from his valise.
"I'm glad to hear that you are both proving to be admirable students." He congratulated them having read their examination results.
"We usually have a seminar every weekend to discuss progress. It has proven to be invaluable, hasn't it Seanaí?"

"Indeed it has, I guess we would be poorer students without it." He confirmed.
"My problem is Latin, I can never seem to get it right. Still Michael seems to have mastered it."
"Tae! Who wants a cup?" Molly entered the room carrying an overladen tray of cups, scones and a large taepot.
"Talking of Latin reminds me of a tale I heard some years ago. Would you like to hear it?" Bill had another story waiting to be told to a captive audience.
"Go on then tell the story, I'll stay myself to listen. Hold on, first let me fetch another cup for myself." Molly left the room and returned shortly with the cup.
"Go ahead now, we're all ears." Molly poured herself a cup of tae and sat down.
Bill settled himself comfortable down in the pillows and began the story…'
"It all happened when the Cistercian monks of Clonmacnoise were looking for scholars to teach. They claimed to be the most talented monks in all of Ireland. They were supposed to be constrained and humble but they needed funds and so justified their arrogance.
Now it so happened that there was another order of monks in Limerick at a place called Mungret. These were of the Dominican order and they too were renowned throughout the land for their knowledge and piety. They kept themselves much to themselves and so well they could. Their monastery contained no less than six churches and there were over 1,000 learned monks available to teach willing students.
The monks from Clonmacnoise decided that they would take the rocky road to Limerick and prove that they were superior to the Limerick monks.
Once there they would challenge them to an open forum in Greek, Latin, Irish, English and French.
When the monks of Limerick heard that the monks from Clonmacnoise were coming across the Shannon to challenge them they were much perturbed. They had heard all about these arrogant monks and their boastings. They did not wish to be humiliated in public by them. But what were they to do?
They assembled in their oratory that evening and began praying for divine guidance. As they were singing the Gregorian Chant there came a clanging of the bell.
"Perhaps someone wants a Mass said for a poor departed soul." The abbot interrupted their praying and left to answer the call.
At the door stood a poor *'Bean-an-Bótar' (Woman of the road)* begging for alms.
The abbot went to the kitchen and prepared a small hamper and returning gave it to the woman.
"God bless you brother and may Heaven open up its gates to you and all the

brothers." The woman called down a blessing on the monastery.
"God bless you and thank you my daughter." The abbot replied and made the sign of the cross over her head. He looked down the road after her and found contentment and peace within himself. Had he not gained an indulgence for his community by his charitable work that evening?
Then it was as if God himself had answered his prayers as he again looked after the woman
As she slowly disappeared into the night he locked the gates and ran as fast as his legs would carry him back to the oratory.
He had a smile on his face when he entered that would do justice to a Kilkenny cat.
"Brothers! On your knees for the good Lord has answered our humble prayers." He panted. Once again he looked up at the crucified Christ and called on his brothers to follow him in an unpretentious prayer of thanks.
Obediently they knelt on the stony ground and prayed their benediction. What they were thanking God for they did not know. Yet the brother abbot told them to pray and he had to be obeyed.
"There was nobody at the gate but a poor woman of the roads." A puzzled brother reminded the abbot after they finished praying.
"A poor woman of the road she might have appeared. Yet God in his infinite wisdom has spoken to me through her manifestation this blessed night. We will not be humiliated by the monks from Clonmacnoise." Again raising his hands in salutation he called on his brothers to give thanks to the Lord.
Afterwards he disclosed his cunning plan. It was doubtful if such an insidious plot ever came from Divine providence.
The following night the monks from Clonmacnoise came outside the gates of the city of Limerick.
The night was as shadowy as a Ravens wing and they were at a loss as to know which road led to Mungret.
Coming down the road against them they perceived a gathering of women dressed in black Limerick shawls.
The abbot called on them to stop but they ignored him and continued on their journey.
Raising his crosier he can ahead of them and held it aloft.
"Do you know the road to the abbey of Mungret?" He pleaded
One of the women came close to him and looked from under her black shawl into his face. She then began explaining to them how to get there in Latin. The abbot and his followers looked open mouthed at the old crones.
Then a second pushed forward and interrupting the first began giving directions in French. She pointed to a small dirt road to their left. A third pushed the

others to one side and began directing them down a different road in fluent Greek. I tell you by now the monks were flabbergasted. They stood dumb founded as they listened to the women speaking and arguing between themselves in many tongues. They were reminded of the time when the Holy Ghost descended on the heads of the apostles and gave them the power to speak in many tongues. How! They thought was it possible for these old women to be such wonderful linguists?

It was not over yet, for a fourth woman came forward and began correcting and chastising the others in fluent Gaelic. The monks were now worried and began to converse between themselves. The women, not wishing to be outdone joined them in their conversation. It mattered little what language the Monks spoke in the women replied in that language.

Finally the monks withdrew to the safety of the city walls and began whispering between themselves.

"There is little use in us challenging the monks of Limerick." The abbot Superior warned them as he rested wearily on his crosier.

"Why is that brother Abbot?" They asked.

"If the women of Limerick are so conversed with the languages of the world and so knowledgeable, how much more do the monks of Mungret know? We would become the laughing stock of the seminaries and be humiliated throughout the world."

"What can we do then brother? We have travelled a very long road. We just cannot abandon our task." Another grumbled.

"We will return under the cover of darkness to our abbey at Clonmacnoise and never trouble or mention the monks of Limerick again. Do you hear me?" The Abbot general warned them.

They bid good night to the women of Limerick and took the rocky road back to Clonmacnoise.

The women watched as the monks passed out of the city and take the road to Clare and home. Then removing their shawls they began to laugh.

"That was a good nights work brothers. I doubt if we will ever see them again." With these parting words the monks returned to their abbey at Mungret.

That night they sang the *'Gregorian Chant'* as it had never been sung before."

"That then is the story of the *'Monks Dilemma'*." Bill lay back on his pillows and awaited the customary compliments.

THE WEDDING

As the day of the nuptials drew near, Molly went and spoke to Bill on the matter and he agreed that Terry could come and live on the farm after their marriage.

"Sure I have little choice Molly. Who would want to look after a crippled old man, or understand his ways? Only Molly Cullhane."

"Thanks Bill, I hope you will be at my wedding."

"Of course I'll be there. Where else have I to go to? I expect you have told Michael of your plans?"

"He knows that I am to marry Terry. I'm worried that it might interfere with his learning. What do you think?"

"You go and get wed one days absence from schooling won't make any difference."

"Thanks Bill, do you know I'd be lost without you. I remember the day that you took a chance on me and Michael."

"Go on, out you get and make a cup of tae for us both." He tried unsuccessfully to raise himself from his pillows.

"Here, let me help you." She came to the side of the bed and raised him into a sitting position.

"There, I told you that I needed you. Now go and do as you are asked."

The following afternoon found her in Galway bartering for a fine oak double bed with two fine Eider down mattresses. She also bought several porcelain statues and nick knack and an oil lamp.

The bed was delivered the following day and set up in the centre of her bedroom. With its canopy, fresh sheets and patchwork quilt it looked real grand. That night she slept for the first time in a double bed alone.

"Soon now my Terry will share my bed." She cheekily remarked as she stroked the vacant pillows beside hers.

She continued altering and rearranging the bridal suite. Nothing it would seem was to her satisfaction.

"No I don't like where that is. Are the curtains the right colour? It will do, like it or not, that's it." Flinging her hands up into the air she adopted a sense of despair and surrender.

"As long as we are happy, what else matters?" She again spoke to herself. Closing the door behind her she went outside to attend to her poultry.

That evening Terry arrived in a bucket trap. He was dressed in a new suit and lying across the side seat was a large trunk.

"I see you're all ready for the big day then." She came from the house and greeted him.

"Ready as I'll ever be, I'll drop the trunk here and take myself off to McQuade's. How do you like the suit?" He twirled in the lane before her.

"You'll do I suppose, I'm not marrying the suit thank God." She laughed.

"Thank you very much. Tell me has Michael arrived yet?"

"Not yet, but don't worry he'll be here. He was here with a friend not too long ago. As usual he teased me about the big mistake I am about to make."

"Come on give me a lift with this trunk." Molly helped him with the trunk into the kitchen.

"That's enough for one day. I'll take myself off and see you in church on Saturday, please God." He promised.

"Do you need me to send anyone over to see to Bill? I'm sure Jack would oblige."

"No thanks! Michael and his friend can see to him. I doubt if he will be coming to the church. Then we never know, do we?"

"Very well I'm off and if you need any help don't hesitate to ask."

"Need help from the groom before the wedding? Will you talk sense man." She laughed.

Saturday morning found Molly up early. Just because this was her wedding day it did not allow her to neglect her chores.

"What are you doing at this God forsaken hour?" Michael appeared in the kitchen.

"Come on I need your help. Oh God look at me and on my wedding day too." She studied her hessian apron and the bucket of mash on the kitchen floor.

"Will you go back to your room and get yourself ready, Seanaí and I will see to whatever needs doing." Michael promised.

"Thanks Michael, now don't forget to…"

"Will you go out of my sight, you're not needed here to day." He interrupted her.

"Seanaí get out of that bed and come and help me." He challenged.

Molly appeared in the frame of the door sometime later. She was dressed in a simple white dress and on her head was a halo of primroses and cowslips. In her hands she held a bunch of wild flowers.

"How do I look?" She fidgeted with her dress as she addressed them.

"You look real grand Molly, real grand indeed. Doesn't she Seanaí?" Michael complimented her.

"I'll be proud to walk beside such a fairy queen, so I will." Seanaí opened the door and held his arm out to her. Michael joined them as they went down the boréen to the church. Behind followed the neighbours and the musicians.

Reaching the Church they saw Terry standing up in the trap looking towards the roadway.
"Watch out for that fellow in the trap he's eyeing you something awful." Michael pointed towards him.
"Stop it will you, I'm nervous enough as it is." She chided him as she held the bunch of wild flowers close to her face.
"That's nothing to what he expects of you." Again he teased her.
"You're not helping, do you know that?"
"Ah well we're here now and there's little you can do about it." Michael entered the church with Molly holding tightly to his arm. He walked with a slow gait up the centre aisle. She wanted to get up to the rails and away as soon a possible.
"Slow down will you, you have all the time in the world to regret this day." He whispered to her.
Standing before the altar she heard the door open and the congregation whispering. Michael let go of her hand and stood to one side. She knew that Terry had replaced him but tried not to look. She felt a hand reach down and reassuringly take hers gentle in his. She knew that it was Terry, she looked up at him and smiled. There was no need to be nervous. Slowly and deliberately the Priest called on both parties to love and honour each other as long as they both should live.
"Who will give this woman in Holy Matrimony to this man?" The Priest called. Michael stepped forward and presented the gold band to Terry. Holding it between his thumb and fore finger he turned and faced Molly. A smile crossed his previous tense face. She returned his smile and held out her hand. She felt the gold band encompass her finger. The veins of which led straight to her heart was now and forever encompassed with his love. She now belonged to him.
Outside the church they paused and looked out at the villagers waiting to give them their blessings. As the gathering waved and encouraged them she turned and faced her new husband. Slowly she raised her eyes and looked deep into his. There was no need for words for in his eyes she saw love and happiness. He reached down and taking her face in his strong hands kissed her tenderly. Hand in hand they entered the bucket trap. Michael took the drivers seat and raising his whip encouraged the pony into a gentle trot.
The gathering led by the musicians followed closely behind. Soon they were at the public house of Jack McQuade. In a wicker wheelchair in front of the door sat Bill, standing beside him was Seanaí.
"Congratulations to you both and God keep you." Bill held his arms out to Molly.

"Bill! Bill thanks. You have made our day. I knew that you would come." Hugging him close she kissed him gently on the cheek.

"And you too Terry, be good to her she deserves it." Reaching out his hand he took Terry's in his and shook it warmly.

"Come in and a '*Ceád Míle Fáilte*." Bill called on Seanaí to push his chair into the house.

Along the mantle were rows upon rows of clay pipes and beside the fire a small barrel of tobacco. The table was groaning under the weight of food and a more than ample supply of stout and whiskey.

The musicians needed no encouragement to strike up and soon the *'Craic'* was in full swing with singing and dancing.

"You done us proud so you did and we'll never forget it." Terry placed his hand on Bill's shoulder.

"Forget it Terry, what are friends for? Now what about an ould comallie?"

"Quiet now if you please, the groom has consented to sing. Thank you." Jack announced.

"Well I'm not the best of singers, but I'll try." Terry took his place beside the fire.

Believe Me, IF All Those Endearing Young Charms.

Believe me, If all those endearing young charms,
Which I gaze on so fondly to- day,
Were to change by to-morrow, and fleet in my arms,
Like fairy gifts fading away,
Thou would still be adored, as this moment thou are,
Let thy loveliness fade as it will;
And around the dear ruin each wish of my heart,
Would entwine itself verdantly still.
It is not while beauty and youth are thine own,
And thy cheeks unprofaned by a tear,
That the fervor and faith of a soul can be known,
To which time will but make thee more dear!
No: The heart that truly loved never forgets,
But as true loves on to the close;
As the sunflower turns on her God, when he sets
The same look which she turned when he rose!

Thomas Moore.

There was a hush in the room as Terry finished the last notes. This was followed by loud applause.
"Now come on Molly, you'll not let him get the better of you." Michael drew Molly into the centre of the floor.
"I'll do my best but that takes some beating." She laughed.

Smiling Through
There's a little brown road winding over the hill,
To a little white cot by the sea;
There's a little green gate
At whose trellis I'll wait,
While two eyes of blue
Come smiling through at me:
There's a grey lock or two in the brown of your hair
There's some silver in mine to I see;
But in all the long years
When the clouds brought their tears,
Those two eyes of blue came smiling through at me!

And if ever I'm left in this world all alone,
I shall wait for my call patiently.
For if Heaven be kind
I shall wait there to find
Those two eyes of blue
Still smiling through at me:

Trad;

"I can you just picture the pair of them lulling their baby to sleep." Laughed Bill.
The night was closing in and Terry was anxious to be alone with his bride.
"We'll be off now and let you to enjoy the rest of the evening." Terry made his apologies and taking her by the hand stepped out into the night.
"Good luck to you both." Came the greetings as hand in hand they went down the old boréen.
She clung to his arm as the chill of the night closed in around them. In the grey dawn she saw the silhouette of the house looming up before them. As they reached the door she clung tighter to him, why she did not know.
"Are you happy Molly?" He asked as he entered the bedroom.

"You know I am." She lay her bunch of flowers on the bed and came close to him.

"Molly! You don't know how long I waited for this moment. I love you." His voice quivered as he took her in his arms. He kissed her face, her neck and opening her dress stroked her firm breasts with his rough hands. Yet he was gentle.

She drew away from him and stepping out of her dress removed her clothing and lay down on the bed.

Terry undressed and lay down beside her. She could smell his manliness as bending over her his lips met hers. These were urgent kisses, demanding trembling kisses.

"Molly I'll always love you." He whispered.

"And I'll always love you too Terry." She lay in submission beside him.

Rising above her, he reached down and suckled her breasts. She held him to her as she would a babe. She was intoxicated with her love for him. She felt her nipples stretch and stiffen in response.

As he reached down and caressed her most intimate place she opened her legs and encouraged him.

"I love you Terry, there is nothing in the whole world that I would not do for you."

Then taking his penis in her hand she caressed it and stroked it for the first time. Her breath came in short pants as she encouraged him. She felt his penis elongate in her hand. This excited her and she caressed it all the more. He was her lover, her husband.

Holding her close he opened her legs wider with his legs as she guided his manhood inside her.

As the weight of his body slowly consumed her she rose up to meet him. "I love you," she cried out as she felt his penis penetrate her.

Her arousal was awakened to the full as he stimulated her. She was audacious and moved in rhythm with him as they came to the culmination of their first intimate love. She knew that their love was sempiternal. They lay close together, bonded forever.

Terry was awakened to the clattering of a bucket in the yard. Rising from the bed he went to the window and saw Michael and Seanaí creeping around the yard. They were feeding the poultry. Smiling to himself he was about to return to the bed when Molly woke and looked round the room.

"What time is it? We must see to the animals." She looked across at him standing beside the bed exposing his nakedness and blushed.

"We can forget the animals for once, Michael and his friend seem to be managing well." He returned to the bed and took her in his arms.

"Whatever will they be thinking." She looked away as he removed the sheet covering her.
"They'll will find better things to do than worry about us. Why do you think they are here so early?" He caressed her body.
"You are happy Molly." He held her close.
"Happy as I'll ever be, I really do love you." She looked deep into his eyes.
"Take it off love". Without waiting he slipped her nightdress from her shoulders exposing her breasts.
"You're lovely, really lovely." He reached down and pressed his mouth to her nipple as he caressed her.
Smiling he lay on his back and looked across at her. Rising she slowly caressed his body. Teasing him with every movement.
"Molly! Molly my love." Placing his arms around her he pulled her over on top of him.
As his penis penetrated her she felt the most indescribable sense of enjoyment. She shamelessly began to gyrate her body in time with his. Feeling the urgency of his trusts inside her she closed her legs around his penis. She felt his hot seed enter her womb as together they brought each other to the ultimate climax. They lay in each other's arms for a long time reluctant to be separated.

A RENDEZVOUS IN GALWAY

It was one of those days when the sun began setting early far out between the jaws of Galway bay. Terry ran his scythe through the lush grass of the meadow disturbing the grasshoppers humming their mating chorus. The air was crystal clear and somewhere in the distance a Corncrake called to his mate.
He held the scythe before him with the blade facing the two old hawthorn trees growing high above the fairy fort in the marshland.
He removed the *'Strickle'* from his belt. Slowly and deliberately he began to run it over the blade stopping occasionally to glance along the edge to ensure a razor sharp finish. He looked again at the haunting hawthorn trees as he sharpened the blade.
They had, so it seemed embraced each other since time began. Then he remembered the story that Bill told him of the two hawthorns...'
The story was told that they were two lovers, she was the daughter of a poor fisherman of the *Corrib* and he was the heir to a vast estate. Their love grew from the day when out hunting he saw her collecting seaweed on the seashore. He lost his heart to her and she to him. They knew that as soon as their love for each other was discovered she would be banished from the county.
One winters evening as they walked along the shore watching the billowing clouds obliterate the blood red sun she shivered.
"Whatever is the matter, Allanah?" He asked. He listened as the breeze shook the reeds in a shallow near by.
"It's as if someone walked over my grave. *We must not wait, we must leave this place."* She gently whispered.
"Come close to me, it's cold let's go." Placing his cloak around her shoulders they left the beach and took the shore road.
Reaching the *'Cross of the Seaweed'* they heard horsemen approaching and tried to hide in the sand dunes. It was too late, for as they climbed the dunes the sand collapsed under their feet disclosing their presence.
"What is the meaning of this?" The lord of the estate demanded of his son.
The boy told him of his undying love for the peasant girl. His father listened in silent anger to his story. In a blinding rage he ordered that his son be taken back to the castle and be confined to his room.
After his son was removed he ordered his men to chase the girl into the marshland and leave her there to die.
The youth now confined to the castle began to pine for his love. Looking out the window of his room he would call her name into the night.
A faithful servant taking pity on his plight told him what happened the night

they were parted.
"Please help me to find her." He pleaded with the servant.
"You'll not find her master, for the bog has claimed her." He warned.
"I'll find her for love that rules all will guide my feet." The youth predicted.
"Then go master if you must, for there will be no peace in this place until you do. May God in his mercy guide you both." The servant departed from the room leaving the key behind him.
Donning his heavy cloak the youth left the castle and crossed into the forbidden moor.
His feet were dragged deeper and deeper into the bottomless mire. Still he struggled on, calling as a bitten would that had lost his mate. Here and there he disturbed the moorhens resting for the night.
Then from out of the night he heard her calling to him. *"Mo Leannán! Go back; Go back, you must not wait. Leave this place"* She warned him over and over again.
"Where are you '*Mo Vournéen?*' He challenged into the night air ignoring her warning.
"Mo Leannán! Mo Leannán a Vic (Lover). Go back, Go back. You must not wait. Leave this place." Again the voice in the wind warned.
"Mo Múirnín, (Darling) I'll not go from you." He called. Slowly but surely the mire consumed his body yet he continued calling to her.
The Rays of a blood red sun appeared before him and from it stepped his lover. He opened his arms to her and she to him.
The sunrays dwindled; the mire was now silent.
The *Bean-Ó-Sidhe* came to the place and cried her sorrowful lament. She remained on watch as the winter's snow hid their grave.
Hailstones played a loud tattoo above their heads but the lovers oblivious to all above and below them slept on embraced for eternity in each other's arms.
It was spring and gentle rain tears fell on the spot and formed a little pool. Two mating doves came daily and drank from it.
One day as they were collecting building materials for their nest they brought with them two twigs of hawthorn. One was pure white; the other was as red as the setting sun.
These they left beside the pool. Soon the twigs found each other and took root and became entwined.
As they grew they rose high above the bog. By nightfall the setting sun always sent its rays down on the twin trees as the gentle winds wafted the scent of the blossom skywards.
If one listens carefully in the evenings they will hear the lovers whisper…'

> *'Two hawthorns grow where we two met;*
> *It's here we lovers embrace and rest.*
> *Thread softly o'er our lonely bed*
> *Remember us as the Red Sunsets.'*

Satisfied as to the sharpness of the blade he grasped the well-balanced handles and sang in time with each swish of the blade. Hearing Molly calling he shaded his eyes from the golden ray of the sun and looked out on to the Corrib River. He was momentary distracted as an otter came from the river carrying a fine trout between her jaws. He smiled, thinking that the otter was by far a better fisherman than he was. He saw Molly standing in front of the thatched barn waving in his direction.

'Whatever does she want now and me getting into my stride?' He spoke aloud somewhat annoyed.

Placing his scythe over his shoulder he came up the meadow.

His feet disturbed the myriad insects hiding in the meadow as he climbed the hill towards the house. Swallows watched his every movement from high above him in the clear air. Swooping down they manoeuvred round him picking them up on the wing.

"Bill want's you to take him into Galway." She informed him.

"This late in the evening, will it not do to morrow? Never mind I'll harness the horse to the bucket trap. Can he manage on his own?" Without waiting for a reply he crossed the stile and called to the horse.

"Sorry to be such a nuisance Terry, I have a bit of business in Galway. You don't mind, do you?" Bill was sitting in his wicker bath chair when he returned and apologised.

"No problem, the break will do us both good. Can you manage Molly?" They lifted the bath chair with Bill inside into the well of the gig.

"Hold tight, let Terry put the straps round the handles. You know what kind of a driver he is." She held the chair forward as he secured the straps.

"Now Bill you know why I am glad to get to Galway." He laughed as he made the final adjustments to the straps.

"There's a field of hay waiting to be finished on your return, don't forget." She warned him as they left the boréen.

They came into the square in Galway and approached a narrow winding street.

"Pull in here Terry and ask someone to help you off with the chair. Then go and have a drink. The gig will not be able to get down the narrow lane." He instructed.

"Will you be able to manage on your own? I don't mind pushing the chair." Terry volunteered.

"No! I'll manage. Thanks all the same. Here my good man would you ever give us a hand?" Bill called to a passer by to help Terry down with the chair.

"Ah that's better! I'll see you back here in, say about an hour or so."

Terry returned to find Bill sitting patiently beside the gig sipping from a tankard.

"Have you been waiting long? I came back sometime ago and you were not here." He apologised.

"No! Not that long as you can see. Here go and get yourself a drink. I hate drinking alone." He held up the tankard that was three quarters filled with stout. Reaching into his purse he withdrew a florin and gave it to Terry.

"Well that's that done, take the tankards back and give my regards to the landlord." Having emptied his tankard he looked to Terry.

"Do you want to go back home now?" He asked.

"Might as well, that is unless there is something that you want to buy."

"I saw a bonnet in a shop down the road, I was thinking that Molly would appreciate it. What do you think?"

"Me! I'll tell you what she would appreciate a setting of eggs far more. Go on, away and get the bonnet."

Terry returned with a bonnet covered in feathers from tropical birds and a half veil round the brim.

"You have nice taste may she live long to wear it." Bill complimented him.

"Thanks! Now we can go home."

I doubt if I'll be seeing him again." Bill remarked on his way out of town.

"See who?" Terry asked.

"Who! The landlord of course." Bill was again being morbid.

"Whenever you want to come to Galway or elsewhere for that matter all you have to do is ask." Terry assured him.

"Give him a flick of the whip or we'll be late for our tae." Bill snuggled into the blanket and closed his eyes.

A WELCOME SURPRISE and a SAD ENCOUNTER.

"Sorry Terry but I don't feel too well, will you be able to manage?" Molly complained of stomach pains and nausea.
"Don't worry, you concentrate on getting well. You have been overdoing it, get some rest." Terry comforted her.
"I'll be well by to morrow, please God." She promised.
"Will you stop apologizing and go to bed." He insisted.
"Will you see to Bill? I know I'm asking a lot of you but…'
"I'll see to him and everything else, for pity sake get some rest and I'll bring you something to eat later." He promised.
By midday she was her old self once again and put it all down to something that she ate.
The following morning she was again feeling unwell. Terry decided to call in the doctor.
"Wait a day or two it might be nothing worth worrying about." She insisted.
"Where's Molly? I haven't seen her this last couple of days." Bill asked.
"She's not been well of late, I'm going to fetch the doctor if she is no better by to morrow. I'm worried for her." Terry explained her symptoms
"Worried for her indeed, from what you tell me you should be both congratulating yourselves." Bill chuckled.
"Congratulating ourselves, whatever do you mean?"
"I mean that from what you tell me she is with child. Now you can go and see your fine doctor. Congratulations to you both."
"Molly! Are you awake?" Terry gently called as he opened the bedroom door.
"Whatever is the matter? Has something happened to Bill?"
"No he's fine. Do you know why you are getting sick? You are going to be a mother." He reached out his arms and hugged her.
"Who told you this? I'm far to old to conceive." She felt her stomach to confirm she was not pregnant.
"Who said you're too old? Isn't that the grand news?" He chirped.
"Whatever will Bill think of me?" She again felt her stomach and smiled. "Me a mother, who would have thought it?"
"It was Bill that put two and two together and came to the conclusion that you were pregnant."
Next day she went to her doctor to satisfy herself that she was indeed pregnant.
"Bill, whatever am I to do?" She went to see him for the first time since the doctor confirmed that she was with child.
"I was about to congratulate you, don't you want a child?"

"Of course I want the child, it's about where we'll live. We can't keep imposing on you." She insisted.
"What do you mean by that? Your home is here for you and Terry and the child. I want you to stay."
"Oh Bill! What can I say? You are a saint and no mistake." She reached out and hugged him.
"Go way and get the supper ready and tell that husband of yours that from now on he will have to handle all the heavy work."
"What's that, did I hear my name mentioned in vain?" Terry entered the room.
"You did indeed. I was telling Molly that she will have to take it easy from now on."
"Bill insists that we stay here with the baby." She crossed the room and placed her hand in that of her husbands.
"What can I say Bill. You have our thanks. Here give me your hand and if ever you need me then I'm your man." Terry promised.
"Thanks Terry. Now what about a game of draughts?"
"Sorry! I'd love to Bill but I have to go over to Inismore with a Bull."
"Be careful Terry, for all our sakes, and moreso now." She pleaded.
"The bull will be spancelled on all feet and unable to move. We'll land in Killeany Bay and from there we'll go on to Cill Ronáin. I should be back in two to three days if all goes well." He promised.
"Take care of yourselves and don't you do any heavy lifting in his absence." Bill warned.
Her baby moving within her wakened her during the small hours of the morning.
"Téigim go dtí codlad mo naoidean." (Go to sleep my baby). She placed her hand on her stomach and spoke gently to her baby.
She listened to the wind rapping the branches on the windowpane. She thought of her husband somewhere out in the North Sound of Galway Bay. Her prayers were with him as she slowly succumbed to sleep.
She woke early and having prepared breakfast she went to Bills room and gently tapped on the door.
"Are you awake? " She called. There was no reply so she rapped louder.
"Bill your breakfast is ready. Are you alright?" Turning the handle she peeped around the door. He lay half out of the bed his upper body propped against a small side table.
"Bill! Oh my God. Whatever happened to you?" Going round the bed she lifted him back on the pillows.
"Whatever is the matter with you?" She placed her hand on his forehead.

"What, what is wrong?" He opened his eyes and looked up at her.
"You were hanging out of the Bed, God, I thought something had happened to you."
"It's my own fault, I remember dropping a book and reaching down to retrieve it. I must have fainted. I am sorry." He apologised.
"Thank God that's all. You had me worried. Now are you ready for a bite of breakfast?"
"Sorry! I'm feeling fine now, honest."
"You should see the doctor. Fainting like that is not natural." She warned.
"See a doctor, what do they know?" He grumbled.
"A lot more than you give them credit for, I can assure you."
He found sleep impossible that night and wondered if he should have taken her advice. He felt nauseated and isolated and put it down to his stubbornness.
"I expect that it's a punishment from God. The night will soon end and I'll feel better." He consoled himself.
He cried out for sleep, his eyes were heavy but when he began to doze off the pain would return.
He heard the cockcrow and knew that the dawn would soon give way to a new day.
Hearing the handle turning he forced himself round to face the door. Molly stood in the frame with a tray in her hand.
"Had a good night then"? She entered the room and placed the tray on the side table.
Feeling self-pity and compassion he began to weep.
She stood by the bed as if petrified, unable to cope with the situation imposed on her. Then her motherly instincts came to the fore. Her heart softened and she wept as only a woman can.
"Bill, Dear Bill is there anything that I can do?" She sobbed.
"Forgive an old man Molly but you cannot appreciate the excruciating pain I'm in."
"I'll fetch the doctor, so I will. Try and get some sleep!" She did not chide him. She understood and her heart went out to him.
"You won't ever leave me, will you?" He pleaded.
"Never! Whatever gave you that idea, where would I go to anyway?"
"I feel better now, pray for me Molly. God bless you and the child." Slowly and with the agony showing on his face he slowly turned and faced the casement window.
She looked down at the still form in the bed and discreetly left the room closing the door gently behind her. Outside she turned and faced the door, putting her

hands over her face she began to cry. Her heart was breaking, as instinctively she knew that he had run his race. Her Bill was leaving her and there was nothing that she could do about it.

She watched and waited for her husbands return. She wished him beside her to console her in her grief and she needed him to go to Galway for the doctor. She returned to the room time and time again keeping a close observation on him.

By late afternoon she heard the cart in the lane and ran from the house.

"Terry! Thank God you are home. Bill is not all that well and needs a doctor." She ran into the boréen crying and fell into his arms.

"Whatever is the matter with him?" He followed her into the house.

"Come and see for yourself." She opened the door slowly. The room was quiet; he looked towards the bed.

"Bill! It's me Terry, how are you?" He whispered.

"I'm not too good, would you help me please?" He weakly replied. Without answering they approached the bed. He followed their every movement with his eyes. They could see that he was confused and afraid. He looked up and began to cry then clutching his chest he began to tremble before he fainted.

"Fetch some water Molly." Terry went to the side of the bed and held on to him. She handed him the mug of water and stood to one side as he sprinkled a little on Bills face and tried to make him drink.

"I'll go for the doctor, can you manage here?" He let him gently down on the pillow.

"Sure, no problem. Is there anything that I can do for him when you're gone?" She asked.

"Nothing just keep him comfortable."

"He's had a seizure, a stroke. He will require a lot of attention." The doctor having examined him gave his findings. Bill's face was distorted and his left arm lay dead on the bed cover.

"Will he ever recover?" Molly asked.

"I don't know, with a man of his age it's doubtful. Still miracles do happen." The doctor confirmed his findings.

"Is there nothing that can be done?" Terry asked.

"Rest and no excitement is the cure. I'm sure he'll get plenty of that here. I'll bid you good evening." The doctor rose from the bedside and closed his portmanteau.

"Thank you doctor, I'll see you out." Terry accompanied him to his trap.

"Now don't forget should he feel any great malaise call for me at once." The doctor reminded them.

THE WILL IS READ

Bill recovered to a degree and was again able to partake in his game of draughts using his one good hand. The rest of his time he spent lying in bed looking out into the garden.
"Why don't you read a little it will help you to concentrate?" Molly suggested.
"Concentrate Molly! On what should I concentrate?"
"Oh come on, don't be so morbid. Terry will be home soon and you can have a nice game of draughts. Now eat up your supper." She adjusted his pillows and left the room.
"Evening Bill. How are you feeling?" Terry entered the room and sat down beside him.
"Molly said you'd be home early from Galway. Not too tired for a game are you?"
"Sure I never win, but go on then. This time I'm taking the blacks, I never seem to be lucky with the whites." He laid out the board across the bed.
"Right Bill my move." Terry advanced the draught.
Slowly the game moved forward with neither side gaining advantage. Terry advanced his king into a defensive corner pursued by two of Bills white kings. With a deft move Bill captured the king.
"One day I'm going to win. Fancy another game?" Terry began collecting the draughts.
"No! Thanks all the same. I'll rest now." Bill lay back on the pillows and closed his eyes.
"I don't like the look of him, shouldn't we bring in the doctor?" He asked Molly.
"Neither do I, you'd best fetch him to morrow? When he finds out there will be Hell to pay." She warned
"Whatever he might say I'm sure that the doctor will be in a better position to help him than any of us. Moreso you in your condition."
"The doctor is here to give you a check over." Molly entered the room.
"I was passing and remembered my old friend. How are you feeling to day?" The doctor queried.
"Not too good, not too good at all but then it's the will of Almighty God." Bill made a thwarted effort to raise from his bed.
"Don't exert yourself, just lie still and let me examine you."
"Not too good am I"?
"You're coming on fine, it must be all the care that Molly lavishes on you." The doctor placed his hand on his shoulder.

"She's a good soul and I could not ask for better nurses than her and Terry. Don't lie to me doctor, how long have I got?"
"How long have anyone of us got? We are all in Gods hands and you should know this better than any of us."
"I doubt if we'll ever meet again in this world." Bill shook his head slowly.
"Now there's no need to be so morbid, I'll be back in a couple of days."
"How is he doctor?" Molly asked the doctor, as he was about to leave.
"Prepare yourselves, he's very weak and it could happen at anytime."
A wailing coming from Bills room disturbed Terry's sleep in the early hours of the morning.
"Molly! Are you awake?" He called to his wife.
"What is it? Is there something the matter?" Molly awoke with a start.
"I'm sure I heard Bill calling. You stay here I'll go and see to him." Donning his trousers he went down the stairs and entered the room. His hand trembled as he looked down at Bills face. Something terrible had happened. A choking gurgle came from Bill's throat.
"How is he?" Molly came into the room and approached the bed.
"I think he is dying, will you light the lamp." Having lit the lamp she returned and held it over the bed.
"He's gone we will kneel and pray for his soul." Terry placed his hand on his open eyes and closed them. Molly began to cry aloud.
"Hush! He is now dead and God will grant him mercy for he was a good man. Remember what the doctor told us?" Terry comforted her.
"What do we do now?" Her hand holding the lamp trembled
"Give me the lamp. To morrow morning I will go and see the good doctor. Let him lie in peace this night." He placed the lamp in the window as she stood by the door.
"I wonder if Protestants have a calling from the 'Bean-Ó-Shéidhe'?" She looked down at the outline now covered over with the sheet.
" Come on love let him be." He closed the door leaving Bill alone with his God.
Molly accompanied Terry to Galway the next morning.
"This is his place." He pointed to a large brick built house near to the main square. The doctor opened the door to their knocking and invited them inside.
"What brings you here so early?" It's the minister isn't it?" The doctor confirmed.
"We're sorry to tell you but he died during the night." Terry informed him.
"Oh I am sorry, but it was to be expected."
"What do we do now? He was a Protestant you know." Terry asked.

"I know that, am I not one myself? Now go down and see the Church Of Ireland minister, better still I'll come with you. Just let me get my hat."
"Of course he will have to be buried in the churchyard here, that is unless other arrangements have been made. Did he leave any instructions?" The minister asked.
"None that we know of. We understand his wife is buried in Galway."
"Better still, now give me all the details and I will get in touch with the bishop. He will know where his wife is buried." The minister replied.
That afternoon a hearse came to the house carrying a coffin. The body of Bill was placed inside and taken to the Protestant Cathedral. They were forbidden to participate in the service, as they were Roman Catholics so they stayed outside the gate.
They watched as the coffin was placed in the grave of his late wife and closed.
"Are you Molly Davenny?" A gentleman came out from the graveyard and addressed Molly.
"I am, are you a relative of Bills? Sorry I mean the Canon." Molly apologized.
"No need to apologise, I'm sure he would like you to remember him as Bill. Would you please come to my office, I'm his solicitor. My carriage is over here."
"Sit down please." A clerk brought two chairs and placed them in front of the desk. The solicitor entered the office accompanied by two others.
"I have here the last will and testament of Canon William Conor Bougham late of Richill in the County of Armagh, Ireland." The solicitor broke the waxed seal on a red band and opened the parchment. You will witness that this is his signature and the witnesses to that signature are present in this office. Do you agree?" He held up the document for all to see. This will was drawn up on the 23 day of July of this year in my presence and that of the witnesses and signed and sealed on the same day.
It is not a very long will and I'll not keep you in suspense any longer. Briefly he leaves to one Michael Kearney the sum of £300 to be used solely for advancement of his scholarship. He also leaves him his library and his telescope.
To the dean of the Protestant Cathedral he leaves £200 for the erection of a memorial made from Connemara marble to his and his wife's memory on a wall inside the cathedral. He also leaves a bursary to be used for the education of a poor student at the discretion of the dean of the cathedral.
When all debts and expenses due have been finalized and his funeral expenses met he leaves the rest of his estate, his lands, house and assets to Molly Davenny his housekeeper to use or to dispose of, as she should wish. There is

one codicil which I do not understand and that is that she turns the curing stones on his anniversary."

"I don't understand, what does it all mean?" Molly looked from one to the other.

"It simply means that the farm and house now belong to you together with whatever sums of money and other assets are held in the bank and elsewhere. Should you wish I will pursue the matter or you could consult another in my profession to act on your behalf." The solicitor informed her.

"No I would rather leave it in your hands. Oh my God! I cannot believe he would be so kind." She burst into tears.

"He came to see me not too long ago. It was late evening and I was about to leave the office. I was more than surprised to see him. I knew from the way he expressed himself that he was not long for this world. He had no next of kin and as he held you in the highest esteem he asked my advice regarding leaving you his estate. I told him that if this was his intention then he should put it in writing."

"So that's where he went to that evening I took him to Galway." Terry remarked.

TO MOLLY A SON

Michael returned to the farm for the Christmas vacation and was greeted by Molly sitting beside the fire knitting.
"When is the happy event then? I hope that I haven't come all this way on a fools errand." He laughed.
"Your welcome Michael, let me finish this row and I'll make some tae." Ignoring his good humored chiding she put her knitting to one side.
"No! I wouldn't hear of it. You rest up and I'll make the tae." She insisted.
"Terry is down the field with the horse, would you ever give him a shout?
"Wouldn't it be wonderful if the baby was born at midnight on Christmas Eve." Michael remarked as they sat eating supper.
"That would be something as the baby is not due until the New Year." She smiled.
"Forget the doctors and their predictions. I bet that the baby will be born on Christmas Eve or Christmas day." He was adamant in his prediction.
"I'm glad that you know more than the mother and the doctors." Terry remarked.
"Will you be going to mid-night Mass, Molly?" He asked.
"No! I'll go on Christmas Day. You and Terry can go if you feel like it."
"Do you think I should? Leaving you at home alone at such a critical time is not a good idea." Terry warned.
"I'll be alright, Mary O'Brien will be calling soon. Then there's the goose to prepare. Go ahead and stop worrying."
Christmas Eve came and Michael and Terry prepared to attend midnight Mass in the Cathedral in Galway.
"Are you sure you'll be alright?" Terry stood in the doorway with his cap in his hand.
"Oh for Heavens sake will you get on and stop worrying." She gently pushed him out of the door.
The church was profusely lit with the lights from myriad wax candles. Many were set in blue globes and others in red. The golden hands of the large clock set high on foliage bound pillar slowly moved towards the bewitching hour. Michael looked up at the scroll encircling the ring of the clock. He read its message over and over again as he waited *'Would thou not watch one hour with me.'* He looked towards Terry but he seemed to have other dreams. He knew that his thoughts were not with his God but with his Molly.
The hands continued to laboriously climb up the broad face of the clock. He let out a sigh as with a final effort they embraced each other and reached out to the pinnacle of the cathedral. They had finally arrived at the bewitching hour

when Christians believed the Infant Jesus was born in a stable. A bell ringing from deep inside the presbytery called the faithful to their feet. The choirmaster pressed the keys on the great organ and the multitudinous tubes came to life uttering forth a prolonged bar of *'Silent Night'*. Then all was quiet for a moment as the notes took flight into the vastness of the cathedral. The choir situated in their loft high above the congregation took their key and began singing to celebrate the night that Jesus was born. In full voice they sang of their praise to the infant son that saved the world. It was as if the very angels were singing with them. The congregation encouraged by the euphoria of the compelling hymn of praise accompanied the choir. It was their God too and they were justified in singing his praise. Slowly the last hymn died away and the Bishop rising from his chair took his place before the high altar.

Handing his crosier to his assistant Priest he removed his mitre and lay it on a near by table. Slowly the celebration of the birth of Christ continued on into the dawn. He heard the censer rattle and watched as the thurifer filled the cathedral with aromatic clouds. Twin multi coloured clouds formed as the thurifer continued swinging the censer from side to side. Slowly and deliberately they joined together as they swirled towards the pinnacle of the high altar. Once trapped in the dome of the cathedral they spread out and formed into an arc. There was a distinct rumbling from the congregation as miraculously the arc turned into a rainbow that remained high in the dome without ever touching the ground. They watched in fear and trepidation for this was to them an omnipotent warning of things yet to come.

Unaware of the drama-taking place high above him the Bishop holding the monstrance in the folds of his chasuble moved it reverently from side to side for all the participants to adore. The rainbow encompassed it as the participants lowered their head in adoration. In a loud voice he called out...'

'Uni Trinoque Domino
Sit Sempiterna Gloria'
(To thy great name be endless praise
Immortal Godhead one in three!)

He held the monstrance higher for all to see and to adore the sacred host enclosed in the window. Returning the monstrance to the altar table he genuflected. A muffled bell sounded. The thurifer came and stood before the altar. The bishop came and added more incense to the little fire. Clang! Clang! The chains rattled as he blessed the high altar with incense before turning and blessing the congregation. As he returned the censer to the thurifer the rainbow slowly dispersed.

The deep muffled tone of the altar bell rang out once again. Beating his breast Michael lowered his head. The bishop picked up the ampoules each in turn and mixed the water and wine. Then he broke the host and prayed alone. Joining the two sections of the host he held them over the chalice. Again the muffled bell drew to the attention of the participants the solemnity of the occasion. The Infant Jesus was now present on the altar. Raising the now joined sections high above his head he called on the congregation to again pay homage to their redeemer...'

'*Ecce Agnus Dei*
Ecce qui tollit peccata mundi'
(Behold the Lamb of God.
Behold him who takes away the sins of the world)

On hearing the sacred words Michael again lowered his head and beating his breast in submission prepared himself to receive the body and blood of the risen Christ.
As he joined the congregation going to the altar rails to receive the Sacred Host the organist again struck a chord and the mighty tubes responded. This was followed by a brief pause before the voices of the choir rose in a crescendo lifting their voices once again in praise of the living God. These were permanent and sincere words of adoration and gratitude that caressed the soul. These were hymns sincere and brash and in an unadulterated adoration that reached the throne of God himself. In their exigency to reach the supernatural being they muffled the voices of veneration coming from the high altar. He stopped praying and listened for a moment as several hundred joyous voices filled the cathedral singing in unison '*Away in a Manger.*' Then he too was caught up in the euphoria. As he took his place at the altar rails to receive his communion he offered it up for the safe delivery of Molly and her child.
'Corpus Domini Nostri Jesu Christi
Custodiat animam tuam
In vitam aeternam.'
(The body of our Lord Jesus Christ`
Preserve thy soul unto life everlasting)
Feeling the sacred host on his tongue he whispered 'Amen' said a silent prayer and returning to his seat and knelt down. The service came to its conclusion and the clergy departed from the high altar leaving the choir to continue in their hymns of praise and adoration.
"Come on, we had best make a move." He nudged Terry who was in deep thought. Rising he followed Michael out of the cathedral as mellifluous music

continued to intoxicate the captive congregation. He turned and took a final glance at the ornate rose window where the rainbow had set previously. A Heavenly figure sitting on a throne looked down at him but of the rainbow there was no sighting. The tallow candles flickered to and fro in the gentle breeze. The thurifer came from a side door carrying a snuffer on a long pole. Slowly and deliberately he smothered each one leaving behind a trail of smoke where the light had been.

"It's one cold morning, I could murder a hot mug of tae." Michael feeling the chill of the early dawn wrapped his coatamore tightly around him.

"Come on, let's get a move on. Molly will be anxiously waiting our return." Terry placed the blanket round his feet and taking the reins in his hands encouraged the horse forward. They made no mention of the rainbow that had somehow manifested itself in the house of God.

When the trap finally came to a halt outside the house he handed the reins to Michael.

"See to the horse will you." He called as he ran to the house.

"See to the tae, I won't be that long." Michael called back as he removed the harness.

"We've a surprise for you." Mary O'Brien opened the door to Terry.

"Is something the matter?" Pushing past her he was more than surprised to see Molly sitting up in the bed nursing a baby.

Michael hummed to himself as he came up the meadow. On reaching the threshold he was about to enter when he heard a baby crying. Opening the door he was taken aback to see Molly sitting up in the Leaba Suidheacan holding a newborn baby in her arms.

"Come in man and look, you were right. This is your new nephew." She removed the shawl from the face of the infant and held him up towards him.

"I told you, did I not tell you? Here let me hold him." He rubbed his hands on his breeches to warm them. He reached out and taking the baby gently from her cradled him.

"Congratulations wouldn't go amiss?" Terry interrupted as he entered the room.

"God! I'm sorry. Whatever was I thinking of? Congratulations to you both."

"I knew that I should have stayed at home, anything could have happened to you and the child." Terry chastised himself.

"Nothing did happen, thank God for that. There's no need to feel so guilty. It so happened that Mary called to know if I were going to the midnight Mass and lucky for me that she did," She assured him.

"Do you think that I could have my son back Michael or would you like to nurse him?"

"Sorry! Here's your child and may he never want." He handed her the infant and reaching into the pocket of his breeches took out a sovereign and pressed it into the child's hand.

"Now you men, would you do the decent thing and pull the kettle over the coals. I've not had a drink of tae all night." She pleaded.

"Sorry love, with all the excitement I forgot." Terry placed the kettle on the crane and pulled it over the coals.

"Don't worry I'll make the tae." Mary volunteered.

"Everyone is apologizing to everyone else this morning. It must be because it's Christmas day." She addressed her child.

"Christmas day! Hold everything." Terry left the room and returned with a bottle of whiskey and four glasses. Having filled them he handed them round.

"A happy Christmas son, Thank you love for a wonderful Christmas gift. To you Mary O'Brien a special thanks. May we all, each and everyone of us prosper and live to see our children's children." Four glasses were raised above the head of the infant in the glow of the turf fire that Christmas morning.

"Now we should really celebrate." Michael having drained his glass went and picked up the bottle.

"There will be no celebration, not until the dinner is on the table. You two men can cook the goose and prepare the potatoes. As for me, I'm going to take a well-deserved rest with my son. First I want one of you to escort Mary back to her farm."

"I'll escort her back, it's the least I can do." Terry volunteered.

"You stay here with your wife, Michael can escort me. I'll call in again over the Christmas Molly." Mary put her shawl over her head and left the cottage.

"You've got our thanks Mary and be sure and call." Terry called into the night.

THE CREEPING DEATH

"It's a good day for it." Molly looked out at the early dawn. It was mid July and a soothing breeze was blowing in from the bay. Terry was called upon to make a delivery to the estate outside the village of Corafin in the County Clare. "Thank God for that, now take good care of my son Tomás and yourself come to think of it." Placing his hand in affection on the baby's head he kissed his wife and mounted the cart.
"If you get the time on your way home will you call in and see how Michael is doing at the University?" Molly requested.
"I doubt if I'll have the time, however I'll do my best if only for peace sake." He promised.
"Bless yourself now and keep away from the *'Potéen.'*" She advised as he left the boréen.
The early mist rose off the fields as he entered the town of Gort.
"Whoa! Whoa!" He halted the cart outside the hotel.
"I'm just in time then." He called as he saw the servant girl attending to breakfasts.
"Morning Terry, come in and welcome. Sit yourself down here." The landlady greeted.
"Soon as I get a bit of grub under my belt and a fresh horse I'm off to Corafin. Don't fancy coming with me, do you?" He chided her.
"With you! An ould married man. Why didn't you make the proposal before you tied the knot with another?" Sit down and eat your breakfast." She teased.
After breakfast and a rest he went to the farrier to pick up the dray.
"That's a sturdy beast, where did he come from?" he asked the farrier.
"Him! Be respectful when you address that animal. You take good care of him now, that is if you know what's good for you. He belongs to none other than the Lord of Corafin." The farrier warned.
"The Lord of Corafin indeed. What is he doing drawing my dray then?" He ran his hands over the sturdy horse's flanks.
"Your consignment is the property of the estate. You are to leave the horse with his groom and pick up a fresh horse for the return journey." The farrier instructed.
"I should have known that such a fine animal wouldn't grace my dray for long. Come on your Lordship." Terry addressed the horse and laughed.
"I'll see you when you return." The farrier waved good bye.
"Gee up your Lordship." Terry flicked the reins gently over the horses back.
"I'm not too rough on him am I, Bill?" He called over his shoulder.

Coming over the brow of the hill between the borders of Galway and Clare he came to the Churches of Kilmacduagh.

"Is it me or is it getting chilly, whoever would have expected this to happen in July?" He spoke to himself as he removed his coatamore from behind the seat and placed it over his shoulders.

The sky darkened as the morning sun was obliterated behind brazen rolling clouds. The horse sensing a change in the weather began to shy.

"Steady there, it's only a passing shower." He assured the nervous animal. The wind began to moan and from the north a dense fog came creeping out of the hills.

"God be good to me, whatever is happening?" Looking back at the advancing fog he blessed himself and hurried the horse forward seeking the nearest shelter.

Seeing an abandoned cottage he jumped off the dray and led him into the stable adjoining the cottage.

"Steady now old boy, there's nothing to be frightened of." He soothed the nervous animal and stroked his nose. Forked lightening ripped between the mountain peaks and burnt itself out on the valley floor.

"Jesus, Mary and Joseph protect me, whatever is to become of me?" He looked with apprehension out on to the valley and was surprised to see a huge rainbow manifest itself and hang high above the mountain ridge without touching the ground. As if in defiance to his prayers the heavens were ripped open. Icicles the size of canon balls were vomited over the land. They continued to cascade in a deluge until the whole valley floor was several inches deep in a bed of ice. They petered out to be replaced with driving rain and sleet. Without warning the rains ceased and the clouds parted to reveal a watery sun. The rainbow never too far away stood menacingly above the mountain range.

Venturing from the safety of his shelter he slipped on the ice covered surface. There was an uncanny silence in the air. No birds sang but a foreboding wind blew steadily from the north. It was as if the *'Bean-ó-Sidhe'* was predicting an acataleptic disaster. The acrid smell of sulphur filled the air making him cough. Feeling nauseated his stomach retched and he tried unsuccessfully to vomit. Holding on to the wall for support he ventured round to the back of the cottage. The landscape as far as the eye could see was covered in a grey fog that penetrated every pass and valley.

"We had best rest awhile until it clears." He spoke to the horse on his return. He watched as the sun's heat melted the ice. He was perturbed when the grey fog did not disperse but continued to creep slowly along the valley floor.

Taking the reins in his hands he encouraged the nervous horse forward. The fog

continued its slow crawl across the valley floor to his left. On reaching the bridge outside the town he came to an old *'Round Tower.'*
The acrid smell in the air was stronger now and the horse sensed it. Opening and closing his nostrils he sniffed the air as his eyes rolled in his head. Then in a state of confused panic he bolted towards the village.
"Whoa! Whoa! Stop you brute." Holding on to the winkers he tried in vain to sooth the nervous animal. Failing to calm him he was dragged down the road. The dray swayed from side to side shifting its load. He was obliged to release his grip on the winkers and found himself left sprawled in the centre of the road. The horse continued on his charge and only halted when a stone wall confronted him.
"I can't blame you old man, I don't understand it myself." Having regained his composure he comforted the animal. Shaking from his ordeal he tied the horse securely to a tree. This would give the frightened animal ample time to calm down.
"God in heaven, what's that smell?" Placing his cravat over his nose and mouth he walked down the high street. There was little if any sign of life. A few hens wandered up and down the street but nothing else. It was as if the people had deserted the place in a hurry. Where had all the people got to he wondered? He found his answer when he came to the Church. From inside he could hear sorrowful crying mixed with prayers of supplication. The church was filled to capacity with men women and children. Women held their infants up before the altar and openly cried and pleaded to the crucified Christ to take pity on them.
"Have mercy on our children, you died on the cross to save them. Do not desert them now." The traumatized people prayed their supplications. The stench filled the church but they were oblivious to it. They were clinging to their one hope of salvation, their crucified Christ.
"The crop, you must go now and try to save what you can." He saw the priest standing aloft in his pulpit pleading with the villagers.
"The storm, it has passed. I'm going to save my potatoes. Come on all of you" A man rose from his seat and running from the church encouraged the others to follow him.
Soon the whole congregation was on the move. Through the fog and mire, like a plague of locust they descended on their potato patches and began hooking the ground.
"Look! Will you look at what was once a fine crop of potatoes?" An old man held up a stinking stalk in one hand for all to see.
"Mine are safe, mine are fine." A delighted husband called hysterically. Joining hands with his wife they danced round their patch. Then before they could put

the slán back into the ground brown spots began to manifest themselves on the healthy stalks. They looked with incredulity as their crop collapsed before their eyes. The woman stopped celebrating and stared in silence at the poor ould man standing dumb in the centre of his patch still holding the rotting stalk.

"It's all your fault, you and your tainted potatoes." The woman suddenly turned on the old man and began chastising him.

"It's not my fault, look, I lost everything." He held up the putrid stalk that dripped a foul smelling liquid to confirm his misfortune.

"You...' You done this to us, you were always jealous of our crop. We will be evicted to starve on the hillside and it will be your entire fault. You...You!" The woman screamed as she picked up the slán and struck the old man across the temple with it.

Bleeding heavily from the inflicted wound he fell forward into the putrid slime. Holding his hand to his temple he felt the blood oozing from between his fingers.

"May God forgive you, Arlene Duff." He looked up at her with supplicant eyes. "You have killed me for sure." He held up a handful of slimy earth mixed with his blood.

"What's the matter with you Arlene? Poor ould Tom is not to blame. He never harmed a soul. It's the cursed *'Blight'.*" Her husband Mike rushed forward to assist the old man.

"I'm sorry Tom, I'm sure that she meant you no harm you." Mike apologized.

"I know that and I forgive her. It's the blight, its back with a vengeance. I'll not live through it." He staggered from the slime and collapsed against the stone wall and lay still.

"It's not the blight, it's the *'Curse of Christ'.* Look! Will you look at the rainbow, it will not touch the cursed ground, so it won't." Facing the rainbow Arlene opened her hands wide and dropped to her knees. The others followed and all began praying aloud.

A young mother holding her infant close to her breast looked out at the desolation manifesting itself and began to shiver. Opening her dress she brought her child to her and began breast feeding it. Why she did not know.

"Mo Chúsla! Mo Chúsla!" Disorientated and in a deep trance she rocked her child to and fro. She spoke to her infant in her native tongue assuring him that she would protect him and not to be afraid.

"What is happening, Father?" The people gathered round their pastor seeking a logical explanation for the phenomenon.

"It's the will of Almighty God." Came the pretentious reply.

"What have we done to deserve this? Look at us, will you take pity on our

children and ask God to show us his mercy?" They pleaded.
"Go back to your homes, God is indeed merciful, he will provide." This was the only comfort that the puzzled priest could offer.
The people stood in their small potato patches unsure as to the outcome. They were reluctant to leave what had once been their salvation. Small groups gathered and looked with incredulity at the devastation still manifesting itself. The sky again darkened and the rainbow moved higher into the sky. A piercing cold wind rose, this was followed by a deluge drenching the land and the people. The women threw their shawls over their heads and prostrating themselves in the slime began a funeral dirge.

'Ul-Lú-Lú-Ló-Ló'

The sorrowful lament echoed through the valley and was answered by others in adjoining villages. The dogs of the village on hearing the lament began to howl like the Bean-Ó- Sídhe. This added to the already eerie atmosphere.
Covering their faces in the cursed slime the women pleaded with their God to show them compassion. Their pastor stood in the mire with his hands clasped in supplicant prayer. Their pitiful crying echoed throughout the mountain range and on to the sea.
As nigh came down a mystique came upon the land. Myriad's of croaking frogs took possession of the potato patches and sat croaking their own lament. This added to the fears of the superstitious people. Like Zombies they came from their hovels and stood looking in fear and trepidation as the army of frogs continued to multiply.
"What does it mean, Father?" They fearfully asked.
Unable to elucidate he opened his breviary and began praying aloud in Latin.
"They've been driven out by the cold." Terry informed them.
"Why then did they not come out in the past? This is a curse from Heaven." The terrified people cried out.
"Father! It is your duty to stay with us until the cock crows. The Devil is about this night and it befalls on you to protect us." An old woman foretold. Logic and rationality was now being replaced by superstition.
Unable to convince them as to the reason why the frogs left the swamp Terry departed leaving them arguing between themselves as to the reason why. These were very frightened superstitious people and who could blame them? There was no rational or reasonable explanation for what was happening.
Tired out from his traumatic experience he decided to rest and wait until the following morning before continuing on his journey. Seeking refuge in an abandoned cottage he let the horse loose into an adjoining field and returning to the cottage settled down to a restless sleep.

ON THE ROAD TO COROFIN

After a night disturbed by the pathetic crying of the people of Kilmacduagh he was glad to see the dawn. Rising wearily he went into the field and harnessed the horse.
"Come on old fellow, I hope you had a better nights sleep that I had?" He stroked the horses nose.
Going down the muddied road he was surprised when he saw villagers still in their potato patches digging with their bare hands hoping against hope to find a few edible potatoes. He knew that they must have spent the night on the hopeless venture and he felt sorry for their plight. There was nothing he could do to help them.
He was tired and hungry and regretted not taking the hamper that Molly offered him.
Halting outside the Church he sought out the priest.
"I'm going to Corofin and will bring to the notice of the authorities the plight of the people of Kilmacduagh." He promised.
"Thank you and may God go with you my son." The weary priest blessed him.
As he continued on his journey he was surprised and shocked at the speed the fog was travelling. It continued moving over the land destroying the potato crop in its path. He witnessed families standing knee deep in the fog trying desperately to waft it away from the stalks. Their pitiful wailing followed him as he continued on his journey. He knew that there was little hope of help for the people of Kilmacduagh.
The rain, the acrid smell and the fog was with him at every turn of the road. There was nothing on earth or in heaven so it seemed that could stop the vile progress of this curse. Like a tidal wave it moved south ably assisted by a constant moaning wind. Day again turned to night as dark foreboding clouds swept low over the land.
This was mid-summer, but where was the song of the birds, the rabbits and the hares and the call of the bitten?" This evil phenomenon was now affecting him. Something dreadful was taking place in Ireland that he could not rationally explain. He was now frightened for the welfare of his family.
On reaching Corofin he was surprised to see the local supply store under attack.
"We know you have supplies, let us have some." Demanded the riotous mob.
Seeing the dray enter the square they ran toward it and tore off the covering.
"Did you bring us supplies?" A man brandishing a shillelagh demanded to know.

"No! These are good for the estate." Unable to escape he sat on the high sprung seat and let them rifle the contents.

As the mob were leaving with their loot mounted peelers suddenly surrounded them. They were ordered to return the stolen goods and line up in the square.

"I presume that these are the good for my estate?" The commanding officer asked.

"Yes Sir! I had problems getting this far and have not eaten since I left Galway." Terry informed him.

"Galway! Has the blight struck there yet?"

"Not that I know of, the first I knew about it was when I reached the village of Kilmacduagh. Terry informed him.

"Take the dray into the square and then go and have something to eat. Afterwards take the supplies to my estate and have the horse changed. Have you a family?" the officer asked.

"Yes Sir, I have a wife and child." Terry informed him.

"Then I suggest that you take yourself away from here as soon as possible. These poor wretches are suspicious of any strangers." He warned.

"The people of Kilmacduagh are in desperate need of help, Sir." Terry pleaded.

"They'll have to wait and suffer like the rest until a relief agency is set up. Stop and tell them that if you dare. Sergeant get this man a dry coat and a meal." The officer returned to his troops leaving his sergeant in command.

"Here you are my man, try this for size." Terry was given a police coat with a waterproof cape attached.

"Thanks! That's grand. He gratefully accepted the warm coat and entered the hostelry accompanied by the sergeant.

"Set up two meals as soon as you can, please." Ordered the sergeant.

"I feel sorry for the poor wretches, they lost everything in the blight and now they face eviction from their hovels." The sergeant looked out at the sullen gathering.

"I thought we had seen the last of the blight in '46. It seemed to have petered out then." Terry remarked.

"We should have know better, look at the fields yonder. Did you ever witness the like?" Through the fog a phosphorus glow hovered.

"What in God's name can it be?" Terry joined him at the window.

"You've never seen the blight then?"

"I've witnessed the blight but I've never seen fields glowing before, that's uncanny and frightening."

"I've little doubt but that there's a rational explanation for it. Still, try telling that to the poor superstitious wretches. Do you know I hate my job." The sergeant turned his back to the window.

"Superstition and fear of the unknown is indeed a terrible curse, but then…" Shrugging his shoulders in resignation he too turned his back on the street.

"Your meal is ready, not a lot but the best I could muster under the circumstances." Their host apologized.

"We're grateful, it's kind of you and thanks." They took their places at the table and sat down.

"I'll send a troop to escort you from his Lordships estate. They'll see you safely out of the village. Beyond that you're on your own. I suggest that you pull the cover back off the dray. The villagers will see that you are not carrying goods will not molest you. Good luck to you. Believe me you'll need it." The sergeant suggested.

The villagers watched the dray with suspicion as it left. Terry lifted his whip in friendly greeting. The people scowled back at him suspecting him to be a lackey of the landlord.

He didn't feel any animosity towards them; rather did he feel for their anguish. He would have liked to leave the dray and explain to them that he was just a drayman doing a job. Discretion being the better part of valor and remembering the advice of the sergeant he drove on. He was relieved when once again he was alone and in open countryside.

Nearing the Round tower at Kilgarvan he was surprised to see blazing fires in every potato patch. The horse shied as a number of men and boys came through the hedge dragging branches. These they threw on the fires and ran back to collect more. They returned with bundles of gorse and bracken, anything combustible and fed the fires.

"Whatever are you doing?" Terry jumped from the sprung seat and approached the participants.

"We are burning the fog, look!" They pointed to the watery sun peeping from the sullen clouds.

"I told them in Corofin of your plight here. It seems that nothing can be done until the relief arrives from Galway or Limerick. I am sorry." He tried to explain to them.

"Thank you but we are winning, look for yourself?" As if in answer to their efforts the clouds dispersed and a watery sun broke through.

"Good bye and good luck." Terry returned to his seat. There would be little use in explaining the futility of burning fires in the hope of dispersing the fog. If anything it would only intensify it.

He did not look back as slowly and deliberately the horse dragged the stubborn dray towards Galway and home.

THE LETTER IS DELIVERED

That Autumn was the coldest in living memory or so the elders claimed. To add to their misery the rain fell on the cursed land without respite. There was little if any food in the country as most had been exported to England. Although the government of the day was aware of the catastrophic situation in Ireland she still insisted on exporting cereals and animals to feed her own people. What was left in Ireland was tied up in warehouses and guarded day and night. The Irish nation would be left to starve culminating in judicial murder.
Molly stood before the window with her infant son in her arms looking out at the bleak landscape. It was a dark night with little to see. In the distance she could hear the little stream meandering its way to the sea. The silvery blue mist that brought the cursed blight to her land continued to hover over the abandoned fields. It was the only thing that could be seen. The long protruding branch of the old oak tree swept backwards and forwards in a sweeping monotonous motion. Ably assisted by the wind that blew continuously it splashed the rain from the roof and in doing so created a mournful dirge. She tightened her shawl round her child and shivered, yes it was getting colder. Jack Frost was slowly turning the rain on the windowpanes into intricate patterned webs. She turned her back to the window as the wind continued lamenting.
"Perhaps he too is cold and wants in from the night," she mused on hearing the cracking of the frost on the windowpanes. She smiled at her absent-minded remark.
Placing her child in the cradle she moved it nearer to the heat and took down her spinning wheel. She drew long threads of sheep's wool through her fingers and began rocking the cradle with her foot. Slowly and deliberately she fed the spindle as she hummed a lullaby. The candle waved to and fro in time with the motion of the wheel. When the occasional wool fiber strayed into its flame it ensnared it. Consuming it in its flame it dispersed its charred remains towards the open chimney. Her eyes grew heavy...
Molly took the flower from Mary and threw it high into the air. She searched the sky looking as to where it went. She was startled when it landed with a crash beside her. She awakened with a start and looked down beside her chair. Her spindle had fallen from her lap as she slept. The night was dark and silent; how long she had slept she did not know. There was now a distinct chill to the room. The fire was all but a burning glow as the last of the burnt embers fell into the grate. Rising she went to the ciscéan and retrieved several sods of turf and fed the hungry fire.

"We have to go to the University to morrow, please God." She spoke aloud.
"Wha! What did you say?" Terry wakened from his slumber and looked questioningly at his wife.
"Were you sleeping? I said that we have to go to Galway to morrow. It's Michael's graduation ceremony, now don't tell me you forgot?"
"I haven't forgotten, pity Bill will not be here to witness it. God but it's got cold." Rising he stretched himself and rubbed his hands over his shoulders.
"I hope the weather breaks in time." She looked towards the window now covered in a thick layer of ice.
"God is good, it will mend. Anyhow I can cover the cart and make it more comfortable." He assured her.
"We'll have a bowl of warm gruel and make an early night of it. We'll need to be away first light." Molly pushed the crook over the flames.
"Come on shift yourself, we have a long day before us." She nudged Terry awake the following morning.
"What's it like out there?" Rising he went to the window and drawing the curtain looked out at a bleak landscape. The frost of the previous night was now replaced with a drizzling rain.
Molly picked up the bucket of pounded mash and mixed it with the nettles that she had boiled the previous evening. Lighting the lantern she wended her way to the rear of the house. She could hear the cacophony coming from the coop as the hens fought each other for a place beside the door. The fields were still covered in the fluorescent fog that was omnipresent throughout the west and south. It rolled about in a cabalistic and awful dance of death. It's light flashed as it formed a dome before bursting and releasing obnoxious foul smelling gases. It crawled through the dry stone walls seeking new fields to contaminate. The putrid smell of sulphur filled her lungs; long streams of rotting stalks vomited their way down the drills leaving a fluorescent trail of slime behind. It gurgled as it moved from side to side in a devilish dance of death.
Tightening her shawl round her she said a silent prayer and hastened on her way. Opening the barn door she was greeted by the hungry hens demanding their food.
Although her flock had been decimated by the *'Great Blight'* she still had enough to stave off the hunger.
She was unaware that the hens were helping themselves to the contents of the bucket as she studied the skyline. The trees still hung out their branches to dry in the shadow of the dawn. Had God finally abandoned this cursed land, she thought? She was frightened and prayed for the sun to send its warmth on the bleak landscape. Unknown to her the sun was rising slowly and the shadows

were shrinking. She was aroused from her dreaming when she saw the bucket of mash rolling down the field with the hens in hot pursuit. Quickly she retrieved it and scattered the contents on the ground. She returned to the coop and collected what few eggs there were.

Back at the house she was pleased when she saw Terry preparing the breakfast. "There weren't too many eggs and it's still raining. I'm wondering if we should go." She looked with apprehension at the black clouds sweeping in from the Ocean.

"It will clear, I feel it in my bones." He tried to assure her.

"In your bones indeed, I hope that you are right this time." She was far from convinced when she saw the rain creeping under the half door.

"Come on eat your gruel, there's plenty time yet before we leave. By that time the storm will have blown itself out." Unconcerned he called her to the table. She ate her meal, cleaned the house and sat down beside the fire awaiting the fine weather promised by her husband. As the needles clicked and clanked she swung the cradle with her foot. She hummed an ould Irish lullaby to sooth her infant son.

"Time to get ready, see I told you so." He looked out at the miserable morning; at least the storm had abated.

"Not all that encouraging, is it? Will you shut the door." She wafted the reek coming from the chimney away from the cot.

"The rains have let up at least that's a blessing. I'll go and harness the horse. That is if I can catch him." He added as an afterthought. The cunning horse had a habit of hiding whenever he saw anyone approaching carrying the winkers.

When he returned she was busy adjusting her flowered hat on her head. It was the same one that he had purchased for her in Galway.

"There now I'm ready for the road." She smiled into the mirror.

"Here tuck this round your feet." He brought a blanket from the house and presented it to her.

"That's a bit better, come on then before I change my mind." She settled the baby comfortable in the straw ciscéan beside her feet.

"This is the place" He pointed to the imposing gates leading to the university proper.

"Wonder where we'll find Michael? She looked at the milling crowd moving hither and thither like so many ants.

"He'll be on the look out for us and will know where we are, don't worry." Terry looked into the crowd hoping to catch a glimpse of Michael.

"That's him, look over there to your left. Cooee! Cooee!" She stood up in the

cart and began waving and calling.
"Don't embarrass him, you sound like a pigeon." He chided her.
"Don't refer to me as a pigeon and I'll let you know I'm no embarrassment. There I told you, he's seen us." She stepped off the cart and adjusted her flowered hat.
"So you made it then? I was fearful that the weather would spoil the day." Michael delighted with their presence greeted them.
"Well Mick are you going to introduce us?" A tall young gentleman approached them.
"Of course! This is Mr and Mrs. Ryan, Seanaí's parents and this is my mother and her husband Terry."
Pleased to meet you both, Michael has told us so much about you that we feel as if we already know you both. Did he mention that you are invited to dinner at our home following the ceremony?"
"Gosh! With all the excitement I really did forget, I'm so sorry." Seanaí apologized.
"It's too good of you and then there's the baby." Molly reminded them.
"Ah yes! Mick told us all about the unexpected Christmas gift. He also told us that he predicted the day and the hour. I found that hard to swallow, still you will come. Won't you, please?" He pleaded.
"Of course we'll come and thank you. We heard of the help you gave Michael and we are grateful." Molly assured them.
"It was reciprocal I can assure you, reciprocal! We shared our talents such as they are, isn't that so Mick?"
"Come on there's the bell calling assembly." He warned.
The graduates took their places in the seats reserved for them at the front of the stage. Parents and invited guests took the seats behind them.
A door to the rear of the stage opened and the gathering came to their feet. Tutors, principles and teachers took their places behind a long table and sat down. On it were displayed piles of coveted diplomas each one tied neatly with a ribbon of different colour to denote subjects passed in order of merit.
"If only his mother and Bill were here to witness this day." Molly wiped a tear from her eye as Michael proudly walked up the steps and held out his hand to receive the coveted diploma from the principle.
"They'll know and be proud. Not alone of Michael but of you too Molly. You deserve a lot of credit." Terry squeezed her hand to assure her that she was appreciated.
"I hope so Terry and I pray that God brings him the prize he wishes for most, his mother."

They stood for some time chatting on the lawn and were about to leave when a Priest approached them.
"Excuse me, which one of you is Michael Kearney?" He asked.
"That's me, is there something that I can do for you, Father?"
"This letter was placed in my charge some time ago. I was instructed to find you and deliver it to you personally." He removed a letter from inside his coat and handed it to him.
"A letter! Now who would be sending me a letter?" He questioned.
"I am not at liberty to divulge this information. Suffice to say that the letter is self-explanatory. That is all I can tell you. Now if you'll excuse me I'll wish you good day and may God bless you. Congratulations son, I hope you'll put your knowledge to good use." Lifting his hat in salutation he walked away and was lost in the milling crowds.
"We had best be going, dinner will be about ready." Seanaí's mother informed them.
Michael placed the letter in the pocket of his coatamore and joined the others.

THE LETTER IS READ

"Now that you are finished with your studies, what are your plans?" Molly asked as they sat round the fire chatting that evening.

"Plans! I'll take a break first and help on the farm. Come the New Year I'll go to the city and seek my fortune as they say." Michael informed them.

"There's not a lot to be done on the farm at present but there are a lot of stone walls waiting to be rebuilt. The rest I fear will have to wait until the cursed blight leaves the land, if ever." Terry added as an afterthought.

"I often wonder if it will ever leave this cursed land. Four years, four long disastrous years. In God's name how long more must we suffer? Does anyone care anymore?" Molly picked up her son and hugging him to her breast began to cry.

"Don't, please don't upset yourself. Remember that this is Michael's big day. Come on show us your diploma, we never saw one, did we Molly?" Terry diplomatically changed the subject.

Michael reached into the pocket of his coatamore and retrieved the certificate. As he did so the letter fell to the floor.

"What's that Michael?" Terry picked up the letter that had fallen heavily from his pocket. As it hit the floor it made a loud metallic noise.

"Why it's the letter from the Priest. I wonder what it is all about?" He handed the letter to Michael.

"There's only one way to find out and that is to open it." Molly looked suspiciously at the envelope.

"Can't be that important, still here goes." Michael opened the envelope and withdrew the contents.

"It's a long letter, some four pages in all and there's also this large key. See!" He held the key up before them.

"It's from, ah yes here it is. It's from a Maura O'Reilly, whoever she might be?" He searched for a signature on the last page.

"Michael! Don't you know who she is?" Molly looked worried.

"No why should I? Oh my God, that Maura O'Reilly. She knows my mother." Michael returned to the letter.

"Read the letter, come on read it. She would not write unless she had some information regarding your mother." Molly laid the baby in the cradle and went to his side.

"Yes here it is, she states that she and…' Stopping he continued reading the letter in silence.

"Come on, tell us what she says." Molly anxious to find out what the letter contained pleaded.

"Good God! Jesus, Mary and Joseph, it cannot be true, it cannot." He glanced rapidly through the pages and then dropped the lot to the floor.

"What is it Michael? Tell us what happened?" She looked in surprise as the pages fluttered to the floor.

"My Mother is dead, murdered by that bitch. I was right all along but you wouldn't listen, would you?" Michael began pacing the floor.

"What are you talking about, who murdered your mother?" Molly began picking up the pages.

"Do you want me to read it Michael?" Terry took the letter from his wife.

"Please do! I cannot make any sense of it." Michael bit his knuckles.

Terry read the letter aloud slowly and deliberately. His hand shook as he divulged the gory details of Mary's rape that culminated in her brutal murder. On finishing it he stood silently for some time his head bowed.

"She says in her letter that she is dying and asks for your forgiveness. In all probability she is long dead by now. This key is the key to the vault where your mother is entombed. I know how you must feel Michael, God but I'm sorry." Terry apologized.

Laying his hand on the shoulder of his friend he stood beside him in an act of solidarity and friendship.

"Thanks Terry, you're a good friend so you are, and you too Molly. His eyes filled with tears.

There was a silence in the room for a time then Michael looked towards them and spoke.

"How could that murderer have the audacity to write to me from her death bed and ask me to forgive her for murdering my mother? How could she be so insensitive? For all I care she can rot in Hell." He again began pacing the floor in an agitated state.

"There's nothing that you can do for her now, it's for the better that you discovered the truth no matter how painful." Molly tried to console him.

"I'll go at once to Cardavon Castle and reclaim the body of my mother. I know that she cannot rest peacefully sealed inside the vault with a family of murderers."

"I'll come with you Michael. It's best that you have company on the road." Terry volunteered.

"No! I'm going on this pilgrimage alone. I am all that she has left in this world. As her only son it is my duty to carry her to the family grave and to say the hungry prayers over her." He went to the window and looked out on the bleak landscape.

"As you wish, I'm going as far as Sligo to morrow and would appreciate your company." Terry requested.

"Thanks! I didn't mean to be so rude. You've done so much for me that my conduct just now is in inexcusable. I'm not thinking straight at the present. I'll be glad of the company. Sorry!" He apologized.

"Oh Michael! Michael Allanah my heart goes out to you. Won't you please let me accompany you?" Molly pleaded.

"No Molly, your duty is here with your son. You done all you could do for mother and me; thanks all the same. Your prayers would do more good than taking the rocky road to Dungloe with me. Remember what happened to grandmother? Worrying for your welfare would not help the situation. I know that you mean well and I thank you, but I'm sure you'll understand." Michael consoled her.

That night as she lay on her pillow her mind wandered in tender solitude. She could hear the deep sleeping of her husband. His breast heaved slowly as he took deep restful breaths.

Covering her face with her hands she burst into tears. Like a coiled spring releasing its tension she let all her pent up emotions flow. Her tears wet her pillow for now all the praying the hoping and the disappointments were over. That letter dashed her hopes. The emptiness left behind she would find hard to fill.

She listened to the crying wind and the spattering of the snow as it caressed the windowpanes. The main door rattled as if someone was seeking entrance. She cast her mind back to the night of the tossing of the cup.

The happenings of that night were not a coincidence, they portended ill fortune. Perhaps it was the spirit of Mary that had returned to warn her. Her restless dreaming was disturbed as senseless visions floated by her.

'A tragedy always presses hardest on the hearts of those you love.'

A HAZARDOUS JOURNEY

Molly rose wearily from her bed and thanked her God for the dawn. She busied herself in the kitchen preparing food for the two men.

"Did you sleep at all Molly? I couldn't but help hear you crying." Terry sympathized with her.

"Well enough under the circumstances, I prayed that Michael would make it safely to Dungloe and you too." She replied.

"Sure will you not be worrying about us, God is good; we'll be just grand so we will." He consoled her.

"He didn't take care of his grandmother, now did he?" She remembered her dream and the rattling of the latch.

"The weather is on the mend and the snow is melting. It's going to be fine weather for the journey" Ignoring her comments he opened the door and looked out at the grey dawn.

"Do you need any help with the horse?" Michael joined him in the doorway.

"Thanks! If he sees the least sign of snow when I open the door he will do a '*Rinnce Fada*' down the long field and it will take the devil himself to capture him."

"Off you go then, your breakfast will be on the table by the time you get him harnessed." Molly called from the kitchen.

"Come on we don't want to leave too late." They crossed the yard to the stable.

"There you are old man, had a good sleep did you?" The horse was not one to be fooled by Terry's sweet talk. Sniffing the air he cocked his ears forward and looked towards the door. Michael had the exit covered leaving the animal no alternative but to submit. As they led the horse to the front of the house he continued to protest.

"Look here, you have to earn your keep the same as the rest of us. Now stop all this nonsense." Terry backed the stubborn horse between the shafts of the cart.

"What are you bladdering about, I can't hear you?" Molly shouted.

"I'm talking to the horse, he's playing me up so he is." He called back.

"I never seem to have that trouble with him. He understands me fine." She sarcastically remarked.

"He's the only one that does, who'd be brave enough to argue with you less alone a horse." He softly replied.

"Did you say something? Oh come inside your breakfast is getting cold."

"That was as fine a meal as I ever put under my belt, thanks love. Have you

prepared the provisions for the journey? Where has Michael got to?" Terry picked up his bundle.
"Be with you in a minute just packing a few essentials." Michael emerged from his bedroom carrying a satchel over his shoulder.
"We'll be away now Molly and don't fret, I'll be home in a day or two. All going well Michael should be back in a week." Terry promised.
Molly blessed the men, the cart and the horse with Holy water as they set out on their journey. The weather was fine as they took the road north and most of the snow had gone. The omnipotent yellow fog however persisted in the decaying and putrefying fields. The fields that once echoed to the laughter of children were now the graveyards to a dying race.
"We'll change horses at Ballyhaunis and again at Collooney. That way we should make good time." Terry broke the silence.
"Won't that take you out of the way of the grotto at Knock?" Michael reminded him.
"Knock! What would we be doing going there of all places?" Terry asked.
"Didn't Molly tell you to get her a bottle of holy water from the well?" Michael reminded him.
"She keeps on about that well. Shure there's no well at Knock and anyhow she has a cupboard filled with holy water." He grumbled.
"There's Ballyhaunis ahead we're making grand time. I hope the new horse is as strong and willing as this one." Michael nodded on seeing the outline of the town.
"Hallo Terry, nice to see a smiling face." The farrier greeted them.
"Good to see you Tom, this is my friend Michael Kearney from out of Donegal."
"Pleased to meet you, I'm sure." The farrier held out his hand in greeting.
"Before you let the old boy here into the field would you take a look at her rear left hoof. His shoe is working loose I fear." Terry informed him.
"No problem Terry, you leave that to me. Do you see the speckled beast yonder? I would take her if I were you. She's a fine strong willing animal and you won't regret it." He pointed to a mare calmly chewing the grass in the field.
"Thanks Tom, we'll have a bite to eat and be on our way. I'll leave the mare at Collooney, I want to make Sligo before the night settles in."
"That should be no problem as long as the weather holds. I'm told that the weather is a bit on the rough side above Gurteen." The farrier disclosed.
"Coming off the lakes I've no doubt. It's been bad all over this recent while."
"Come on Michael you can finish your grub on the cart." Terry sat impatiently

on the high sprung seat waiting.
"Looks like snow ahead, hope that it frizzles out." A flurry of snow greeted them on the outskirts of the town, As they journeyed deeper into open countryside the wind gained in strength. The drifting snow obliterated all before them.
"Can't see a thing in this storm." Terry tried to look into the distance.
"I'll lead the horses until it clears." Michael dismounted from the cart and taking the horse by the blinkers encouraged her forward. He stumbled into hidden holes in the rough road taking the mare with him. The cart was in constant danger of losing a wheel or sliding into the open ditch.
"Best you walk ahead and keep a sharp lookout for any hidden pot holes, I'll lead the mare." Terry instructed.
"Now then old girl don't be feared I'll guide you." He stroked the nose of the animal gently to sooth her. The snow continued to fall and more time was lost clearing it from under the wheels. The wind drove the snow directly into their faces making their journey all the more hazardous. The mare was now growing tired and restless from constantly having to drag the heavy cart out of the mire. Day gave way to night and they were still many miles from their goal.
"We cannot go on, we'll need to find some kind of shelter. The mare has done all she can and so have we. We'll die out here unless we find shelter." Terry alarmed at the deteriorating situation soothed the sweating mare.
"You stay with her, I'll go ahead on foot and see if I can find a shelter." Without waiting for a reply he went over the hill and out of sight. The storm eased and a watery moon peeped out momentarily from behind the sullen clouds. It was enough for not far away he saw the outline of a cottage. Returning to the cart he told Michael the good news.
"You take her head and I'll encourage her from behind. Once we get over the brow it will be all down hill." Going to the rear of the cart he took hold of the shafts and called on Michael to encourage the mare forward. Once more the mare dug her heels into the rough ground as slowly the cart was pushed and pulled out of the deep rut. On reaching the cottage Terry left the cart and struggling to the door banged on it hard. The door opened and by the light coming from the turf fire he saw an elderly gentleman in a long nightshirt standing in the doorframe.
"What are you doing out on such a night. Will you come in and warm yourselves?" The old man held the door open in greeting.
"This night is neither fit for man or beast." Terry took the liberty of removing several sods of turf from the creel and placed them on the fire.
"Where do you hail from? Why! You're Terry Davenny and who is this

gentleman?" He looked knowingly as Terry removed his slouched hat.
"This is Michael Kearney from Dungloe in Donegal. Can I put the mare in your barn? The poor beast would not last the night in that storm." Terry pleaded.
"You do that and welcome, I'll make a pot of gruel for you both." The old man placed the pot on the crane and pulled it over the fire. The door creaked and drifting snow swept across the dirt floor as Terry returned.
"That's a fine warm stable, she should be comfortable in there." Terry dusted the snow from his trousers with his cap.
"Come in and close the door. You must be frozen with the cold, come nearer the fire and warm yourself and you too." He encouraged them to partake of the heat.
"The gruel won't be that long cooking, I put it in soak ready for the morning." Removing the lid from the pot he stirred the contents.
"A little salt and it should be ready." Having added enough salt to his satisfaction he stirred the pot and took it to the table.
Terry rose early next morning from his makeshift bed beside the fire and looked across at the old man lying in his bed of straw. Michael lay in the opposite corner covered in several hessian sacks. A strange silence prevailed both inside and outside the cottage. He could hear the old man grumbling in his dreams and the deep breathing of Michael. This was not the silence of the countryside. This was a foreboding uncanny silence that he could not fathom.
Dismissing it as a figment of his imagination he riddled the fire and filled the grate with fresh turf.
"Time to hit the road, Michael." He called.
"What time is it, has the storm passed"? Discarding the cumbersome sacks that irritated his skin Michael rose and approached the fire.
"I've put the kettle over the coals, best we have something warm to drink before we leave. Will you go and harness the mare?" Terry continued preparing their meal.
"The storm has passed, is there a slán in the cottage?" Michael looked at the wall of snow piled against the stable door.
"Here you'd best have something to eat before you start snow clearing." Terry invited.
"Would you like a drop of tae?" Terry noticed that the old man was awake.
"Thanks! You'll be anxious to be on your ways I have no doubt." He took the procured mug and embracing it with both hands appreciated its warmth.
"We'll be saying 'Good Bye' then and thanks for your generosity. We won't forget you in our prayers." Leaving the old man sitting on his bed of straw they opened the door and went out into the cold dawn.

THE HOMES OF DONEGAL

"Thank God that we made it, we owe our lives to that old man and this mare." Terry remarked as he drove the cart through the gates of the depositary.
"Take good care of her and see that she has a feed of good sweet hay and a warm bed. She's worth a million." He told the boy leading the mare away to pastures new.
"This is where we part company Michael. Are you sure that you want to go on alone? I don't mind accompanying you." Terry offered as they stood beside the cart discussing strategy.
"Thanks Terry; it is much appreciated but I waited a long time for this moment. I would rather be alone if you don't mind."
"I understand and may God guide your feet." With a shaking of their hands Michael slung his bundle over his shoulder. Terry stood watching as he took the long walk by the bay and joined the rocky road to Donegal and home.
Looking at the flat surface of *'Benbulben Mountain'* Michael recalled some of the enchanting stories told to him by Molly. Someplace within the mountain was the entrance to *'Tír-na-nÓg'* she told him. His uncle together with his dog 'Óisin' had found that entrance many years ago. They would never to return she had predicted.
The story is told that Óisin was born out of a union between Finn maCumhal and Queen Sadbh...'
When out hunting one day they heard the steady canter of a horse. They stopped and waited to see who was trespassing in their woods. From the trees came a great white charger and astride his back was a maiden of great beauty. By her attire and rich gold and silver adornments they knew that she was a lady of standing. Her hair was as yellow as gold and entwined with gold and diamonds. Her deep blue eyes sparkled like the jewels of the lake.
Her steed was magnificent and the like was never seen in Érin before. His harness was of pure gold and his shoes were made of silver.
"Who are you and where have you come from?" Finn took hold of the reins and addressed her.
"Great and noble King, I come from afar in the western seas. I am the Princess Niamh, the daughter of the king of *'Tír-na-nÓg.'* " She proudly replied.
"We know not of this place that you speak of, what brings you to the land of Erin?" He questioned.
"I have come to claim the hand of your son, **Óisin.** Many suitors have fought for my hand and lost but none other than **Óisin** do I love." She assured him.
Óisin flattered by these words of endearment stepped forward and taking her

delicate hand in his faced his father.

"Father! Of all the princesses in Érin and all the princesses in the far seas and beyond I choose but this fair maiden." He vowed.

"That then is your '*Geasa*'. We must be away so say good bye to you kit and kin and take her to you." They held a great feast that night in the forest in their honour. Towards dawn the great Finn McComhal rose from the long table and in great sorrow addressed his son.

"We will never see you again my son. Come let us embrace for now it is time to leave the land of Érin. Remember your Fenian brothers and me your father." Father and son embraced. The princess then invited him to join her on the back of the great stallion.

Finn and the Fianna raised great laminations when they saw the great steed move like the wind towards the western seas for they knew that they would never see Óisin again. As they traveled over land and sea they witnessed many wonderful sights. Óisin was fascinated by all that he saw and brought it to the attention of princess Niamh.

"What you see on our travels Óisin are but trivialities. In Tír-na-nÓg you will witness many wonders far beyond your comprehension." She promised.

After several days and nights they approached a great palace glistening in the rays of the setting sun. A palace so beautiful that it surpassed any that he had ever seen before.

"Who owns such a splendid palace and where might we be?" He asked.

"We are in the '*Land of Virtues.*' A vicious giant named '*Formor of the Blows*' rules it. His intended queen is the daughter of the king of the '*Land of Life.*' She was captured by him and is held captive. She put a '*Geisha*' on him promising that he could never ask her hand in marriage until she could find a champion that could beat him in battle. She remains in bondage for many the years as no champion has ever beaten him. Many have tried and lost their lives in the effort." Princess Niamh informed him.

"I have no fear of this giant and I'll be the queens champion or die in my efforts." Proud Óisin promised.

Princess Niamh reluctantly agreed, yet she feared that the giant would slay her lover. Keeping true to his promise they approached the palace. The queen on hearing Óisin's offer to be her champion prepared a great feast of finest mead and choice foods. Having eaten their fill they sat on thrones of gold and listened as the princess through her tears told her story…

"I love my country and my father and mother but I cannot return for the giant holds me in bondage." She wept.

"I will be your champion and challenge the giant '*Formor*' I will do you

honour or die attempting same." Óisin again pledged.
The ground shook and looking up they saw the giant enter the palace grounds. On one shoulder he carried a great Irish elk and in the other a giant club. Seeing Óisin sitting on his throne next to the princess he flew into a rage. Throwing the great Elk at him he charged forward uttering such a challenge that the very walls of the palace shook.
Óisin came from the throne and stepped to one side as the great elk landed on the throne crushing it.
Drawing his sword he fearlessly attacked the giant. The fight continued without respite for three days and three nights during which time they neither ate nor drank.
On the morning of the fourth day Óisin was so weak from loss of blood that he knew it was only a matter of time to his demise, still he valiantly struggled on. He saw the princesses weeping and clinging to each other in great fear and he felt shamed. Should he now fail then both princesses would become slaves to the giant.
Taking his sword in his right arm he called on the Gods to surge what remained of his Fenian blood through his right arm in a final effort to kill the monster. The giant seeing his weakened state rushed forward intent on inflicting a mortal blow on his body.
Óisin saw him coming and raising his sword he called on the Celtic Gods to come to his aid. As he raised his sword it was struck by lightening and his strength returned to his right arm. With a mighty slash from his sword he cut off the giants head. He saw the princesses running towards him then all went black.
He awakened some days later to find his wounds covered in precious balms and healing. They stayed at the palace until Óisin was strong enough to continue the journey. Finally they mounted the great white stallion and bade farewell to the princess.
On they traveled through tempest and storm, sunshine and showers looking neither to the right or left.
As night gave way to morning he awakened to see before him a sight that took his breath away. Before them he saw a palace that sparkled like the rainbow. There were flower gardens by the score and the scent coming from the trees and flowers filled the air. Water gushed and sparkled from a thousand fountains. Birds sang sweetly as animals roamed freely in the fertile lands. This was indeed the land of youth.
"What land is this?" He asked fascinated by all he saw.
"This is my land, the land of *'Tír-na-nÓg.'* Whatsoever you seek you will find

here." She promised. He heard the blowing of trumpets and saw the waving of banners as a great host came to greet the return of their princess with her betrothal.

They held the *Caitim Feastá Aois agus Fléad* (The feast of age instituted by Mannanan Mac Lir. All that partook of the festival would be free from sickness, decay and old age so long as they remained in Tír-na-nÓg.) The king's trumpeters blew their trumpets calling the noisy assembly to order. Then the King rose from his throne and spoke…'

"This is Óisin, son of the great Finnian warrior, Finn Mac Cumhal. My daughter Niamh of the golden hair traveled throughout the land of Érin in her search for him. I now give her to him and welcome him to *'Tír-na-nÓg.'* They were joined together by the chief druid and went to live in a palace by *Loc-an-Iomramain*. (Lake of Voyage)

They lived in joy and contentment for three score years or so Óisin thought. Niamh sitting by a pool one day called on the lute players to play the music of the Fianna to please her husband. As he listened a longing came over him to visit his father and companions. He disclosed his feelings to her and together they went and consulted with the king. The king granted him permission but warned him not to walk on *'Talab-na-hÉireann'*. (The land of Ireland)

Niamh then went and consulted with the great druid as to the meaning for his longing. She was told that it was only natural and that he should go. However should he put a foot on Talab-na-hÉireann then he would age three hundred years and never return to Tír-na-nÓg he warned.

"The land of Érin is no longer the land that you knew and left so very long ago. Your father, the great Finn McComhal and your race are long gone. The land is now occupied by a different race of people. I know that you will never be content until you see this for yourself so go. Take the great white steed Óisin, he will take you to the green isle of Érin.

Remember that you must not dismount from the back of the great steed for if you do you will age three hundred years and die. That is the period of time that you have spent in Tír-na-nÓg." May the God's protect you." She warned.

Thrice she warned him of the outcome should he fail to follow her instructions. Promising to do as she asked he embraced her and mounting the great white steed left for *'Talab na hÉireann.'*

There was a great sorrow in the palace as they watched the great steed gallop off into the mist.

The great horse came out from the mist on the shore of *'Muir Nicht'* now known as the Irish Sea. He traveled through the clouds over mountains and valleys until he came to

'Connail Gavra.'
The great steed took him the length and breath of the land in search of his Father Finn and his companions but there was no trace of them.
One day when passing through *'Slieve Crot'* (The Galtee Mhór Mountains) in the county now known as Tipperary he espied a gathering of little people. They were mounted on little ponies not much bigger than they were. Apprehensively they approached this giant of a warrior mounted on the great white steed.
"Fear me not for I come in peace." Óisin assured them.
"Who are you and what brings you to our fair land?" Their leader challenged.
"I am Óisin, the son of Finn and I've come seeking the whereabouts of my people."
"Yes! We have heard in song and story of the great Fianna and of Finn Mac Cumhal but they lived a long, long time ago. The race has long since died out. His son, Óisin was taken to *'Tír-na-nÓg'* from where he can never return." They told him.
On hearing this he was heavy hearted and leaving them in peace he took the highway east. It was here that his father's palace stood beside the river **Dodder** in the valley of *'Glenasmole.'* He found the ruined palace now covered in ivy and slowly decaying. He heart was heavy and he wished to dismount and kiss the valley floor but knew that he could not.
Returning to the valley he had recently vacated he again met up with the little people. They were trying unsuccessfully to lift a great flat stone.
"Oh mighty warrior would you please raise the great stone, several of our companions are trapped beneath it." They pleaded. Reaching down he took hold of the stone and lifting it he pitched it several perches away. *(This stone can be seen to this day buried in the rushes beside the river Dodder.)*
As he straightened up in the saddle the golden girth broke and he fell heavily to the ground. The great steed feeling the burden leaving his back reared up shook his mane and galloped off into the mist, just as the Druid foretold he would.
A sorrowful change came over the great warrior as he lay on the ground. Gone was the handsome young prince. All his strength was gone and he became a withered old man, blind and feeble and three hundred years of age.
The little people took him to the ruins of his father's palace and lay him down.
"I am about to die and when I do would you bury me beside my father and companions, the Fianna." He pleaded.
And so *'Óisin'* the last of the Fianna was buried in the valley of *'Glenasmole'*. This was the story that Molly told him as a boy.'
It was late evening when he came upon Bundoran town. He listened to the

ocean pounding the deserted beach with large round stones. It rolled them on to the roadway and on its return claimed them back only to fling them once again onto the beach. He stood watching the fluorescent creatures of the sea appear and disappear like so many twinkling stars. Suddenly he became aware that the sulphur smell was no longer in the air. Turning he looked deep into the night towards the barren Leitrim border. All was serene they must have left the cursed blight behind them on the Galway road.

Sitting on a resting stone outside a derelict cottage he looked long and hard into the abandoned vegetable plot. It had been created from a piece of barren ground that was considered neither good for man or beast by the avaricious landlord. This he presumed had been tended to and cultivated in the stubborn soiless bare rocks by the hands of a couple long gone. The potato ridges ran close to the shoreline and had been constructed with earth brought laboriously in their hands and mixed with seaweed and spread on the barren rocky bed. This poor garden probably produced enough potatoes to keep starvation from their door. That was until the cursed blight struck it down turning their last vestige of survival to tears of despair. Now abandoned they remained clinging stubbornly to the rocky shore as obscene monuments of mans inhumanity to man.

Having secured a shakedown in a barn for the night he rose refreshed. Humping his bundle on his back he took the road towards Donegal town. He looked apprehensively at the looming heights of '*The Blue Stack Mountains.*' These were the last obstacles that barred his way to '*Glenties*' and home. Heaving a deep sigh he looked down at his tattered boots. They were nothing now but a hindrance to his progress. Abandoning them by the roadside he continued on into the mountain barefooted.

On reaching Donegal Town he bargained for a pair of stout boots. They would serve him well on the final lap of his journey.

Behind the '*Derryveagh Mountains*' was situated the cottage of his grandparents. The reality of his closeness to it encouraged him to hasten his steps. Day and night he forced marched his aching limbs through the mountain gap. As the grey dawn broke over an Irish sky he conquered the peak of '*Slí Ulaidh*'. Below him he saw his past life spread out before his eyes. It was all too much to see and bear; he had traveled half way across Ireland to be with the ghost of his mother, a mother that he never knew.

"I'm home! Mother its me, Michael your son." He shouted into the mist. His echo vibrated from peak to peak until it finally faded out on the valley floor.

Headlong he dashed down the mountain path to the boréen where the old abandoned thatched cottage stood waiting his return. The boréen was now obstructed with fallen rocks, briars and heather. As he hastened to the door he heard a cock crowing some distance away and the calling of a church bell. He looked towards *'Crohy Head'* and saw a rainbow surrounding the sunrise as it rose slowly from far out in the Atlantic Ocean. He did not wait to see if it would touch the ground. It was too much to bear. The trauma of the hazardous journey and the prospect of finding his mother was too much. Rushing headlong into the old cottage he fell on the dirt floor and began weeping. "Mother" I'm here. I promised you that I would find you." Picking up a handful of earth he let it slowly run through his fingers. This was the soil that his mother had walked all those years ago. Exhausted both in body and spirit he succumbed to sleep on the mud floor.

HOME TO DUNGLOE

He awoke lying on the dirt floor of his grandparent's cottage. The night was as dark as a raven's wing and a foreboding storm made its presence known to him.
This was a night of evil, a Devil's night; he was going on his final pilgrimage to bring peace to the tormented soul of his mother. He knew that his lordships damned spirit was now in league with the Devil and trying to prevent him from reaching his goal. A stalwart power in the form of his mother's spirit was guiding him and no power on this earth or beyond would prevent him. Rising he tightened his coatamore round his shoulders and left the cottage. His efforts to reach the castle were thwarted by the evil spirit of Lord Kilgarvan at every turn in the long unyielding road. He would not release Mary's spirit from his evil spell. She was his in death as she was in life.
Death came from the sky as rain and piercing sleet from the north penetrated his coatamore and saturated his very soul. The wind shrieked like the cry of the '*Bean-ó-Shéidhe*' through the barren landscape. The sky continued to cry and there was an omnipotent force about the land. Did a cold death await him before he could accomplish his mission? He thought. Guided and protected by the spirit of his mother he struggled on.
As he passed along the shore of '*Lake Craghy*' he saw the foam washing the stones. The sky was dark and foreboding. The foam formed itself into large fluffy clouds before floating away on the wind trying to escape from the storm. Yet there was to be no escape as they were mercilessly captured by the howling wind and dashed back against the rocks. There they impinged themselves on others about to take flight. As one they joined forces and once again rose above the tempest leaping over each other in their effort to escape. Some reached freedom but were soon ensnared in the damp moss that seemed to form a bastion around the lake and were savagely consumed. Evil presence tried to tear his cloak from him and push him into the forbidden lake.
He cried out for help above the roar of the tempest to the spirit of his mother for guidance. Then storm eased and he saw the reek of the smoke in the distance and smelt the welcoming tang of a turf fire. He was safe at last from the demons of the night.
He had arrived tired and weary in the village of Dungloe in the highlands of Donegal. There he would find a warm fire and a shake down in the *Leaba Suidheacan*.
He awoke next morning to the unrelenting crowing of a rooster in full voice. Refreshed and after a generous breakfast prepared by his jovial host he left the

hostelry and set out to climb the hill leading to the ruined estate of the late Lord Kilgarvan.

As he rounded a bend in the old boréen he saw silhouetted in the morning light the grim outline of the castle. Nostalgic tears clouded his eyes and a lump rose in his throat. He hesitated for a moment in order to regain his composure and contemplate as to what lay ahead of him.

His dreaming was disturbed by the cackle of a corncrake calling. Slowly he continued on his quest. There was now no need to hurry. He had waited in anticipation most of his young life for this moment. It was not the sight of the castle that made him emotional; it was the shock and reality of standing where his life began. He was not searching for his family and friends for they were long dead. He had come to exorcise a ghost. A ghost that he knew he would find within the grim walls of Cardavon castle.

He reached the imposing portcullis of Renaissance feature. An ornate gate prevented one entering the cobbled courtyards, of which there were two. One was situated to the south and one to the North. He could see what was once a magnificent axial approach through a series of gateways.

Two cottages stood like sentinels guarding the entrance to the castle. There was one to the right and one to the left. The remnants of drapes hung from the broken windows like shrouds on a corpse. He paused and looked up at the family crest emblazoned on a block of granite. It formed a purloin that ran the full length of the archway. Ivy, of that there was abundance snaked out long tendrils consuming all before them. It was slowly and deliberately obliterating the family motto, which was an obscenity to his eyes. Two stalwart unicorns held an unfurled stone ribbon between them on which the family motto had been chiselled deep into its very heart with Irish blood...'

'FACTA NON VERBA'
(Deeds before words)

These superfluous words were to him as meaningless to day as the day when they were when first commissioned by the first Lord Kilgarvan three hundred years previously.

It was under this archway that one was required to stop and state their business before being allowed into the courtyard.

This was no longer necessary, for now the two huge iron gates that once guarded the entrance so constructively in the past had been flung open and left to the elements. One was half buried in the undergrowth. The cotters and their families upon whom the task was incumbent to open and close the gates had long since departed. All that now obstructed the trespasser was a tangled mass of briars growing through the cobbles of the deserted courtyard.

He passed through the imposing dark archway; the bulls eye windows, of which there were two, were now obliterated by encroaching ivy. Barn owls had now commandeered the recesses to rear their young. He listened as the irons on his boots echoed their message. Centre over the archway stood an ornate cupola that was built of red brick with bulging cushions of stone every six courses. A bell that in the past regimented the smooth running of the estate now hung mute. Its great tongue hanging like a rotting corpse on a long blighted chain was now silent. He passed on into the light of day and found the castle proper standing defiantly before him.

The castle itself was an aristocratic castellated residence made from dressed granite. It was a handsome Gothic castle with classical undertones. The mantle of which totally masking the antiquity of the core. It having its foundations firmly embedded in the ruins of a long forgotten Cistercian monastery.

It barley twisted ornate chimneys which in the past belched out the sweet aroma of burning turf now had new residents, in the form of a large rookery of noisy crows. He looked up at the great oak door with its square headed bolts embedded into the timbers to give it strength. These were now a rust coloured brown and weeping. The door hung precariously on one rotting hinge. Slowly like an apprehensive stoat he approached the semi-circle of the granite steps leading to the balustrade encircling the great castle. A three bay fascia of convex windows looked out onto a panoramic view of the open countryside. This was a building that must have inspired the spiritual touch of a genius. It was indeed a gem among houses. The sense of euphoria that the owner must have felt on seeing its magnificence for the first time surely defies imagination. It was the custom for carriages arriving along the drive to stop under the portcullis, rather than entering the courtyard. Visitors were obliged to alight from their carriages and cross the courtyard on foot to the door of the castle. Gentlemen were required to walk bareheaded to the door. Ladies were constrained to walk haughty with their umbrellas folded.

It was obligatory on male servants to remove their caubéens and walk backwards into the courtyard. Women servants were indulged to walk humbly with their eyes downcast. All this pomp and ceremony came about on strict instructions from the first Lord. The custom was prevalent in England and he saw no reason as to why it should not apply to Ireland.

The purpose of this pomp and ceremony was to encourage visitors to appreciate the panoramic view of the magnificence of his castle and the grandeur of its surroundings. That is with the exception of the servants who were considered of a lower caste and not worthy to look at the castle direct. The vanity of the Kilgarvan's does not need a humble pen to relate.

The steps were covered in weeds and briars and an abatis of rotting branches obstructed his passage. He would not be denied, for having come this far he had no intention of abandoning his mission. In trepidation he took his first punitive steps avoiding what obstructions he could.

Reluctantly the thorns and weeds surrendered to his determined efforts as slowly he climbed the steps. On reaching the patio he again paused and looked into the dark interior of the great hall. Was the evil spirit of Lord Kilgarvan at this moment planning his demise? Was his late lordship in his damned death determined to deny him his ultimate goal? Taking a deep breath he pushed the door aside. The door collapsed in a cloud of dust and noise that vibrated through the endless house. He was now standing in an abyss that seemed to be interminable. Looking down he saw the black and white chequered marble floor of the great hall under his feet. He made to examine the spot where he stood for rough marks; old traditions do die-hard.

There was nobody there now to chastise him for his intrusion, he smiled. Before him stood the central saloon which was supported on four black marble columns. This led one into the great hall that in turn led one to an ornate imposing horseshoe style staircase. It's grandeur and size overawed him. A central glass dome took pride of place high up in the roof. This to allow light into the hall and saloon and was the *piece de résistance.* Here was a house that had struggled out of the chrysalis of mediaevalism.

He was distracted by several black rats knawing their way through the house. On hearing his intrusion into their domain they quickly scurried through a door leading to the basement. There they vanished into its dark recesses leaving their squeak of warning behind them.

He moved deeper into the interior and listened. He could hear ghostly mummerings and feel his blood pulsating through his ears. The mournful cry of the wind calling, forever calling and searching echoed throughout the house. Was it the wind or more likely the ghost of his mother welcoming her son home? He felt that he was being swallowed up in its vastness. He looked apprehensively from left to right and back again. He shivered for he felt that someone or something was watching him. He studied the half open doors of the many rooms, in which room was his stalker lurking; he thought?

The rooms were in darkness for the windows had been secured by heavy wooden security shutters against intruders. Did he see them move? Was his stalker now watching him from the dark interior?

Would he see his lordship seated at a table playing a never-ending game of cards with the demons from Hell? His mind was in turmoil and racing with the fantasies from his not too distant childhood.

Putting his childish fears to one side he approached the staircase to his left. He tried unsuccessfully to avoid looking at the open doors. With sweating palm he gripped the balustrade. Although he did not wish to do so he found himself compelled to look up at the long whispering gallery that occupied the full length of the first floor. He envisaged his lordship dressed in a smoking jacket standing haughtily holding the rail and looking down at him questioning his intrusion. He dismissed this as a figment of his imagination and forced his reluctant feet to slowly climb the staircase. His footsteps echoed their arrival on the naked treads.

On reaching the first floor he stood looking down at the great hall that he had so recently vacated. It stood vast and bare, like a mausoleum awaiting its first coffin.

His daydreaming was interrupted as two pigeons flew out from a bedroom to his right and perched on the rail. Turning he looked at the open door that seemed to invite him to enter. On hesitant steps he approached and pushed it fully open.

"My God, this is it!" He placed his hand over his mouth and cried out. A curious pigeon cocked its head to one side. His blood, the blood that he inherited from the very soul of the castle raced through his veins. He could feel his heart pumping faster and faster. His ears were throbbing.

"Run! Run!" A voice warned. Yet he would not run for there was also a soothing presence in the room, the spirit of his mother.

Regaining his composure he went deeper into the room. His eyes were now focused on a long servant call pull that swung lazily in the breeze over where he anticipated the bed once stood. He could envisage it being rung and rung again urgently without any response. He heard his mother's death screams and the drunken laughter of Lord Kilgarvan. He came to standing in the bare room. The floor was covered in bird droppings, several panes of glass were missing allowing the wild life free access. The cords on the top sash had rotted away and the sash lay smashed on the floor.

On the window ledges were several rough bird nests that had long since been abandoned? A hungry rat ran along the skirting board with a dead bird clamped in its jaws.

He looked up at the foliage bound cornice and then at the matching centre rose where once the chandelier hung. Trapped as if in a time warp he stood transfixed and a foreboding came over him. In fancy he could see the large bed in which his mother was murdered all those years ago. He again heard her screams echoing throughout the castle. He could feel the lash of the riding crop as it tore flesh from bone. And yes! He could see Maura O'Reilly with a sneer on her face as she held his mother's arms in a vice like grip as her master satisfied his sadistic lust for her. He clenched his fingers into the palms of his hands trying to absorb the hurt. He felt the pain of the stigmata as blood seeped from his self inflicted wounds. Slowly he opened his palm and looked down at the blood stained wounds. Droplets fell on to the bare boards. Was his lordships ghost now punishing him too? His own flesh and blood.

Then a voice from the grave spoke gently to him...'

"Remember what I am telling you Michael mo cúshla. Remember long after I am no more where and how it all came about..."

"There was a servant pull cord in the room that matched the drapes and the ceiling was decorated with a foliage bound centre piece that matched the railings. A large lake can be seen from the window of the bedroom, and in the distance lies a spinney from where the deer came accompanied by their fawns."

The ghost of his mother spoke to him from her tomb in the crypt situated some distance from the main house.

He approached the window and looked out past the crumbling stone balustrade and on over the Ha Ha. There were several ornate follies in the abandoned park and on a hill some distance away stood a prominent obelisk to commemorate the wedding of the first Lord and Lady. He remembered the story that Molly told him of her ladyship sitting under its canopy with her eyeglass to her eye watching the servants. Any found slacking in their duties would be summary dismissed. Perhaps his mother told her did it matter?

This was the room in which he was conceived and where his life began all those years ago...'

Retreating down the stairs he left the mansion and crossed the courtyard to where the family mausoleum was situated in a secluded silent garden. He paused and looked down at the ironclad door that had been put in place to deter grave robbers. The steps were now covered in moss and briars a sure sign that the place had remained undisturbed for many years. Taking the key from his pocket he handled it fondly before making tentative steps down to the vault door.

Placing the key in the lock he turned it and after several attempts the bolt surrendered. Slowly he pulled the door open and placed a large stone against it. This to stop the door springing closed and trapping him, another device to deter robbers. The crypt once closed could not be opened from the inside. Before him situated on the far wall was a centre apse. An altar on which a crucifix and two candlesticks stood took centre place. On this altar he

presumed the last service to the departed would be held, but not for his mother. He looked along the rows of slate beds; some were vacant awaiting the next coffin. Large oak coffins occupied several of the beds. Below each emblazoned on a brass plague was the name of the occupant. Slowly he walked deeper into the crypt studying the names as he went. It would appear that the male members of the family were buried to the right and the females to the left.
'*Lady Agata Cornwall-Kilgarvan.*' The name flashed before his eyes. He ran his hand along the nameplate time and time again. He began to sweat and shake, why he did not know. Leaving the crypt he stood outside for some considerable time. It was now that he wished that he had accepted Terry's offer to accompany him. He remembered his dream of his mother lying in the narrow room and of the man demanding he left.
Returning he again approached the coffin and studied it. Why he wondered was he drawn to this coffin and not to one of the others? Deliberately he removed the brass thumbscrews one by one.
'Why; he thought were there so many'? He counted them as he lay them to one side there were twenty-four in all. With the last screw removed he took hold of the heavy lid and lifting it free he placed it against the wall.
Slowly he turned to face the coffin, what would he find inside? He closed his eyes and having said a hungry prayer he blessed himself. Taking a deep breath he opened his eyes and looked inside. Although he hoped to find the body of his mother he was shocked by what met his eyes. The coffin contained two mummified bodies one on top of the other. The lower torso of the body on top was covered in a blanket. Her hands were facing upwards and her mouth was open wide in a silent scream. He shrank away from the open coffin and the grim spectacle within. Then as he looked at the scratches and embedded fingernails on the underside of the coffin lid the reality of what happened struck home. His mother was not dead when they locked her in the coffin but in a deep coma. She had regained consciousness inside the locked coffin and scratched the lid in a vain attempt to escape and to draw attention to her desperate situation. What agony must she have suffered as her lungs starved of oxygen slowly collapsed before mercifully she succumbed to death?
"Oh God! The murdering bastards they buried my poor mother alive." He screams echoed round the tomb.
Now drained of all emotion he stood back and looked in on the bodies. This was all that was left of his mother; a withered mummy dressed in torn rags. She had sacrificed her life to save him.
"That is why you came to me in my dreams. You were pleading with me to come and save you. Please forgive me Mother I never knew." He cried.

The trauma was now past the cup was drained. Slowly and silently he replaced the lid, locked the crypt and left the estate.

He went to the village of Dungloe and disclosed his findings to the authorities and sought immediate permission to remove the body of his mother and have her interred in the family grave at *'Crohy Head'*.

Later he led the cortege that took his mothers remains to the little graveyard overlooking the wild Atlantic Ocean. Looking out into the unending waters he hoped to see a rainbow but there was none. He listened to the noises of the waves as they pounded the shore. A 'Pookaún' nosed its way round the headland and he heard the crew singing the lament of *'The Maid who lived On the Rill.'* They sang in unison as they harvested the seaweed from the shoreline. He looked down at them and waved, they waved back. He wondered if they were aware that he was burying his mother that day, still it did not matter.

"You can rest in peace now mother, you have no further use for rainbows." His mission accomplished he placed his caubéen on his head and without looking back took the road back to Galway and home.

THE AMERICAN WAKE

"Thank God you are back." Molly looked up from her stool beside the fire as the latch lifted and Michael stood in the doorframe.
"Yes! I'm back. Mother is finally at rest with her kit and kin." Removing his caubéen he retreated to the fireplace.
"Sit yourself down, you must be tired out. I'll get you something to eat." She placed the kettle over the coals.
"They buried my mother alive." He more or less whispered to himself.
"Oh no! Jesus, Mary and Joseph help us all, not that." Molly let the taepot drop to the floor where it smashed to smithereens.
"That's what the bastards done, they buried her alive." He repeated showing little emotion.
"How in God's name could they?" Molly ran from the kitchen crying.
Later she returned to the kitchen where Michael was still sitting looking deep into the fire. She prepared a meal and placed it before him without speaking.
"That was grand, thanks Molly, much appreciated. How is the baby doing?" He thanked her on finishing his meal.
"He's fine thanks. Do you want to go and have a rest now?"
"No! Don't worry for me, I'm alright thanks. I really am." He took his place beside the fire and again sat looking into the flames.
"How did you get on then, did you bury your mother, God rest her soul?"
"She's at rest now and I have concluded my business in Donegal. I've no reason to return there again." There was tension in his voice.
"Is there something the matter, what happened regarding the estate?" She questioned.
"The estate! The letter from Maura O'Reilly and other facts that came to light were accepted. It would appear that I am now the owner of Cardavon Castle and lands."
"You're now a rich man so you are. You can settle down and take a wife at your ease."
"Where! In the castle, are you thinking straight? My mother was butchered and murdered in that castle defending my right to life. I doubt it very much." Rising from his stool he began pacing the floor in a state of agitation.
"Blood money, blood money. That's all it is." He spate the words out.
"What happened about the murder of your mother?" She pressed him for answers.
"There was the usual cover up with a finding of murder by person or persons unknown. There was no mention of Lord Kilgarvan's involvement. His naked

body was dredged from the lake and confirmed as suicide."
"I'm proud of you Michael, you done your duty and lifted a heavy burden from all our shoulders. Are you sure that you would not like to rest now?" She pressed.
"No! I'm fine thanks, just leave me be. The estate has been signed over to me and if there are no objections then I'll dispose of it lot stock and barrel." He waited for her reaction.
"Good for you, you can now plan ahead." She agreed.
"I met Eugene O'Byrne on my way here, Veronica is back from the States. I'm going to see them this evening."
"Whatever for?" Molly asked.
There are outstanding matters that concern us both to settle. I'll be sure to let you know of the outcome."
"What do you mean concern us both, what has it got to do with me?" Molly looked worried.
"No! Not you Molly. This is between me and Eugene O'Byrne."
"Don't be too hasty now Michael remember you have just buried your mother under trying circumstances. Give yourself time to settle down? She advised.
"Hasty! What do you mean hasty? I know mother is dead and buried. It was I who buried her; don't forget. You and Terry have a comfortable home here and I have my ill-gotten estate. What more could we ask for?" Like a snake about to strike he turned on her.
"Sorry Michael, I was only trying to be helpful. Whatever has happened to you, you've changed?" She was worried by his abrupt tone of voice.
"Please accept my apologies I didn't mean to upset you. I told you that I would tell you what I decide this evening. Now would you please leave it at that?" He insisted.
"Alright Michael, we'll let the matter rest for now. You'll tell us in your own good time I'm sure." She tried to calm the tense situation.
Michael left the house shortly afterwards promising to tell them all on his return.
"Terry, Michael is back and is not his usual self, he had some terrible news. His mother did not die in the castle as the letter stated. He told me that she was buried alive in a coffin in the crypt. There's something strange in his behavior that I just cannot fathom." She confided in her husband that evening.
"Oh no! You didn't leave him go out on his own?" Terry went to the half door and looked down the road.
"There was nothing that I could do to stop him." Molly wrung her hands.
"Never mind I expect he wants to be alone for now. Sure that's only to be

expected considering the trauma he has gone through. Finding his mother like that and the trauma of the funeral. What do you expect of him? He'll come round in his own good time, now what about my supper?" Terry dismissed her concern.

It was late evening and there was still no sign of Michael and Molly was worried.

"I wonder where he is and if he's alright? I hope to God that nothing has happened to him." She paced the floor and occasionally opened the door and looked out into the night.

"Will you come and sit down for God's sake. He's a grown man and knows what he's doing." Terry rose from the fire and closed the door.

It was sometime later that they heard footsteps in the boreén.

"Now remember don't press him to tell us anything. If he wishes to disclose any information let him do so in his own time. I'm warning you for your own good." Terry cautioned.

"You look frozen, here come and take my stool. There's a pot of gruel over the coals. Would you like a bowl?" Molly smiled benignly as Michael entered the house.

"It's cold and a bowl of your gruel would not go amiss." Michael rubbed his hands together before sitting down.

Terry looked at his wife and signaled to her that she should remain quiet.

"We had a long discourse, myself, Eugene O'Byrne and his daughter Veronica." Michael paused before continuing eating his gruel.

"Good for you, whatever you decided will have our full support." Terry assured him.

"You may not be so pleased when you hear what we planned." He corrected him.

"What are your plans then?" Molly unable to contain herself asked.

"I'm going to sell the estate and emigrate." There came a gasp from Molly.

"No Michael, you mustn't, you are now a rich man. Think of what you are doing?" She pleaded.

"Saying! Doing! Don't you understand, I told you that I'm selling the shagging lot? How could I live on land that's tainted with the blood of my mother?" He nosily threw his spoon on to the table.

"But what will you do and where will you go to?" She pressed for answers.

"Molly will you sit down. I warned you to leave Michael to make his own decisions." Terry intervened.

"That's right Terry, you tell her. It's nobody's business but mine. For your information if you let me finish I'm going to America and Veronica is coming as my wife."

"You and Veronica. Oh Michael please forgive me. I am really glad for you and may God be with you both." Full of contrite she ran to him and hugged him.

"It will be the *'American Wake'* then for all of us. We'll miss you and if at anytime you need help you need look no further." Terry held out his hand that was gratefully accepted.

"Just think of it, in America there's land that stretches far beyond the rainbow that is going for less than £1 per acre. Better still where all men are equal and rightly so under the laws of man and God. Where no man has to doff his cap in submission to an arrogant landlord. The land will be mine, mine to sow and reap, as I feel fit without being dictated to by an arrogant landlord. What I grow with my own hands I will keep and I'll no longer have to put aside the *'Landlord's Cross'*. Sorry! I got carried away and feel like I'm making a speech of sorts." He apologized.

"It's no speech Michael. It's but a fact of life. It's a dream in the making and we are proud of you." Molly began to cry.

"I'll be beholding to you for as long as there's life in my body. No spoken words of mine can express how I feel." He gratefully acknowledged their help.

"Veronica and I will be wed this coming weekend in Galway. We would appreciate it if you were the best man Terry and Veronica would like you, Molly to escort her to the altar. We'll sail on the tide the following week for America. I'll not bless the ship that takes us away from Ireland. I'll always hold her in my affections. I'll leave my curse behind on the landlords and their lackeys that deprived me of a fond mother's blessing and her tears. Sorry! There I go again making speeches." He apologized once more.

"Don't take bad blood with you to the new land Michael, it could fall on you." Terry warned.

"We have planned to build our home on the praries and call it *'Derryveagh Heights.'* I know mother would appreciate that. Our children, should God bless us with any will be named after members of our families and you too. Perhaps one-day uncle Seán will return from the mountain. If he should would you tell him that there is a *'Céad Míle Fáilte'* awaiting him at *'Derryveagh Heights.'* His eyes filled as he looked out into the night.

The wedding was a grand affair and lasted long into the dawn.

As they stood on the quayside bidding their fond farewells Michael placed his portmanteau on a bollard and opened the hasps.

"Look what I'm taking with me to the new land, Molly? Removing a linen cloth he showed her a handful of earth.

"Whatever is it?" Molly asked.

"It's a handful of clay from the family grave and look here." From round his neck he produced a little bag.

"That's your *'Caul'*. Oh Michael, Michael allanah. Oh God in heaven protect my child." Falling to her knees she wept openly on the quayside.

There were many tears of fond farewells as the ship in full sail passed through a rainbow that formed a huge bower from *'Spiddal Head'* to *'Black Head'* without ever touching the ground.

"Look Terry, do you see who's following their ship?" A school of dolphins leaping and singing followed in the wake of the ship.

"No Molly they are not going with them, they are saying their fond farewells, They will return to *'Crohy Head'* to await the day when once again *'TheRainbows touch the ground of Ireland.'* Terry promised

"When will that be?" She looked out at the little ship now no more than a dot on the horizon.

"Very soon, very soon mo cúshla." He gently squeezed her hand as the ship slowly faded into the setting rays of the rainbow.

Dear Reader

You have now read my account of my mother's life and death and I leave the verdict to your indulgence.

I'll not see my native land again nor will I say a humble prayer beside my parent's grave, This sorrow and regret I'll carry with me to my grave. This heavy burden was not of my making for like so many before me and so many yet unborn we must leave our native shores. My shackles I have broken, I am no longer a bonded slave to my usurper and freedom is now mine. The period of struggle and conflict I have set aside. Yet I am thankful to my God for giving me the opportunity and gift to walk through the heather and wild flowers of my native Donegal.

I still hear the babbling brook and the wild calling of the bitten. I see my parents, my brothers and sister standing on top of the Blue Stack Mountains as the rainbow once again touches our native soil. How I wish that I could be there with them to witness such a sight. I pray to God to once again give me the privilege to walk through the primroses and cowslips and to shake the fairy bells of the bluebells and feel the morning dew on my bare feet. Alas! it is all but a dream for the story is told and the book is closed.

I hope and pray that the rainbow has returned to my native shore and that it stretches from barren Ben Bulbeen to the far shores of Malin Bay. That my land is free and her chains of steel are replaced with chains of flowers. That the long sorrowful days and nights have come to a close but I know not for I am far away and alone. Would that God granted me this last wish.

I wish you good luck and if fortune befalls you may you die in Ireland. I leave you with the following verse.

> "Deem not the just by Heaven forgot!
> Though life its common gifts deny, -
> Though, with crushed and bleeding heart,
> And spurned of man, he goes to die!
> For God hath marked each sorrowful day,
> And numbered every bitter tear;
> And heaven's long years of bliss, shall pay
> For all his children suffer here."

Michael Kearney. AD. 1865

On the shores of America.

GLOSSARY

ACT OF CONTRITION
Atonement to God for forgiveness for ones sins. Usually made after confession with a promise to amend ones life style. Should the penitent be unable to participate in the act, I.E. Dying or dead, the Act of Contrition is said into the right ear.

ARAN SWEATERS
Each family had their own design (pattern) for their Aran Sweaters. Fisherfolk would only ever wear that pattern. Should an accident happen in which the wearer was beyond recognition then the sweater was used as proof of identification.

ARAN SWEATER PRAYERS.
The sweaters were knitted within the confines of the fishermen's cottages. They were knitted by both sexes of the family. As they knitted they invoked their prayers and blessings into the sweaters. When finished they would take them to the church to be blessed. One prayer that was never omitted was 'The Act of Contrition.' These prayers and blessings were then passed on to the wearer.
(I understand that this custom was also carried out in the Islands of Scotland)

BEAN-Ó-SÍDHE STILES
All Irish stiles are guarded by a Bean-ó- Sidhe or other spirit after midnight and should not be crossed after this hour. Stiles were avoided on the feast of Samain (Halloween). The feast of the dead. It is then that the departed souls use them to return to visit their folks. Under no circumstances should you impede the departed on their journey. They were also used as meeting places by courting couples. There were many different designs of stiles all served the same purpose, to allow access to pedestrians and deter animals. Some were zig-jaged. Squeeze stiles with an eye to the bottom, not used where small animals grazed as the animal could be squeezed and killed trying to cross it. Bench stiles with a crossed bench and a hurdle over. Laddered stiles, by far the easier to cross, not used where sheep grazed, as they could climb them.

BOYS DRESSED IN GIRLS CLOTHING.
In the 18th /19th/ 20th Centuries it was believed that the fairies would steal healthy boys from the house and replace them with their own sick boys. In order to thwart them the boys were dressed in girls clothing and a piece of iron in the shape of the cross was placed round their necks.

BRATACH BRÍDEAC (Cloth bride)
A female seeking the intercession of Saint Bridget tore a piece of unwashed cloth from her clothing and brought it to Tobar Bhride and rinsed it in the holy water. It was then left all day on a bush or beside the well. As night fell it was believed that Saint Bridget came and touched the cloth. It was then removed under the cover of darkness and either sewn into the clothing of the penitent or placed under her tick. This relic was confined to women. Saint Bridget would grant their wish and protect them.
Also worn by Virgins to protect them from the Tally Man. (See Tally women)

BUTTER MAKING
*Butter making was a very mysterious and secretive operation and fraught with danger. If the milk did not separate then it was a **Pishog** that had been put on it by the fairies during the churning. Neighbours were not welcome during churning but should they call then they were obliged to take a turn on the crank or help with the dash and saying a prayer. This not to remove the **Good Luck** from the butter. In parts of Munster a sprinkling of salt was laid across the threshold to prevent the fairies entering and stealing the butter. This also informed neighbours that churning was taking place and that they should desist from entering the cottage. Most churns had an old horseshoe nailed to the bottom to ward off evil. A piece of the **Rowan Tree** was also incorporated in the making of the churn to deter the fairies.*

CAIPÍN LÁSA AGUS BONAEÓG (White lace cap and collar)
Worn by country girls/women after they wed to denote that they were spoken for.

CAUL or veil.
Membranous bag enclosing the foetus, sometimes enveloping the head of the infant is known as the Caul. When this happens it is considered a lucky omen by many. Some mothers place the caul in a small pouch and tie it around the infant's neck as a charm against being burnt to death or drowning.

CAVE OF SHELLS
The starving Irish of the great hunger (1845-1850) did not know of the potential dangers of eating 'Dulse' 'shellfish', 'limpets and seaweed as their sole means of survival. Having eaten their fill they lay down and died. The skeletons of those who died are still found in the many caves dotted along the West Coast of Ireland, the piles of shells beside them marking their graves.

CLUICEAC CAINTEÓIR (Frolicsome satirist)
Played games and tricks at funerals and entertained the mourners. Irish wakes were jolly affairs and morbid though it may appear to some were looked forward to. There was no disrespect meant to the dead. A wake usually lasted three days, longer should a relative on his way to the funeral be delayed on his/her journey. See **'Dare You Ripple My Pond'**.

COERCION BILL
*As the 'Great Hunger' took its toll on the Irish nation the people demanded relief from England. Instead of sending food, more troops were sent to quell any revolt. Then another Coercion Bill was passed. There was but one objection and that from William Smith O' Brien. The bill was extreme in its entirety. Strict curfew was imposed from sunrise to sunset. Anyone picked up out of doors faced deportation for a period of seven years. Possession of firearms or any weapon brought immediate hanging. (***See Cry the Cursed Land***)*

COGRAIM DUINE
Whispering secret people, weird folk, men and women who arrived unannounced whenever an animal was sick. It was said that they could bargain with the fairies. They would spirit the sick animal away from the farm to a secluded spot. There they would break the spell on the animal and cure it. It is documented that on one occasion a farmer curious as to know what the **Duine Cograim** *was doing to his animal followed him and spied on him. He reported back that the whisperer and the animal were in deep conversation with the fairies. Next morning the farmer was found dead in his bed.*

CONACRE
This was a contract giving the right to occupy. The rent amounted to approximately £14 per acre per annum, Far in excess of the value of the produce from the land. The occupier would be granted permission to build a hovel on the land. If the crop was successful then the tenant just about survived. Should it fail then they starved.

CRANNÓGS
It is believed that these island dwellings were first occupied in about 540.A.D. Carbon dating on the trees used to build these dwellings come from that date. The reason given as to why the people abandoned the land and took to living on these man made islands is as follows...
An active volcano known as **Krakatao** *on the island of* **Java** *in the* **Sundai Islands** *blew itself asunder about this time. Yellow ash from the volcano*

obliterated the warming rays of the sun plunging the earth into a mini ice age, Crops failed and starvation and death followed. The Irish believed that the great God **Lug** had put a curse on their land and abandoned it in favor of living on water. They lived on what fish they could catch and other edible foods until the sun God once again returned to the earth. To day **Krakato Junior** is kept under close scrutiny as it is expanding at an alarming rate.

CUCKOO FARMER
Irish farmers went to the fields the day after Good Friday to begin the sowing. They would start the day with a prayer in the 'Name of the Father and of the Son and of The Holy Ghost'. They would give the horse or ass a handful of corn and cover the rump with ashes from **Ash Wednesday** *as atonement for their sins. All sowing had to be completed before the first of May. May was a fairy month and the calling of the Cuckoo. Any farmer found sowing after this would be shamed and humiliated. He would also be blamed for any failure of the crops of his neighbours in that he upset the fairies. He would be branded for his idleness a* **Cuckoo Farmer**

CUIREACT AN SASACNAC RÍ (Pig Knave of the English king)
The carrier of the pole bearing a pig's bladder on St Stephen's day was known as The Pig knave. It was on him that malevolence was inflicted at the Festival of the Wren. See **Straw Boys.**

CURRAGH
A canvas covered boat painted on the outside with pitch or tar to make it watertight.

CURSING GAP (Bearna na mallacht)
Off the road outside Carron or Callon, in the county Clare lies **'The Cursing gap'***. This gap together with the cursing stones should be approached with extreme caution. To execute your curse you should walk nine times at sunset in an anti clockwise direction around the stones and through the gap. Turn the stones in the direction you think your victim can be located. Repeat the following curse...*
"May the nine sows of Hell skutter on him/her and curse him/her to damnation" (Note the number nine again) The story is told that...
A widow woman evicted from her cottage by Marie Rhua (Red Mary) from Leamaneagh castle (The O'Briens of Thomond) went to the cursing gap where she uttered her curse to the stones...
"May Marie Rhua die roaring with her legs in the air"

Shortly afterwards as Marie Rhua was out hunting her horse for no apparent reason took fright and bolted. Her long red flowing hair got caught in a thorn bush and she was dragged from the saddle. She was left trapped hanging upside down for a day and a night before she was found. She had died in agony with her legs in the air screaming for help that never came. She was found next day ensnared in the bush upside down.
(Unless you know how to reverse the stones you should avoid them)

DIARMUID and GRAINNE beds (DOLMENS)
Large megalithic monuments found throughout Ireland comprising of a large sloping capstone standing on three supporting upright stone legs. These were magical places as well as burial plots. Young maidens would slide down the capstones hoping to see their future husbands in their dreams. Young runaway lovers always spent their first night sleeping under the capstone. Thus the corrupt name of Diarmuid and Grainne beds. The **Celts** believed that the spirits of the dead could be reincarnated in their off springs through the women-hence their belief that all their God's were born to human mothers. Pregnant women would sit on the capstone hoping that the Gods would ease the birth of their offspring's. Another reason given was that should the child be still born then the spirit would of the infant would be reincarnated into the next born.
Should you visit a **Dolmen** you should toss a small round pebble onto the capstone. If it remains in place then good luck will follow you... But beware if the stone should roll down the surface and land on the ground. The most impressive Dolmen in Ireland is at **Ballymascanlon** in **County Louth.** The most mystical are to be found in the countryside around **Lough Gur** in **County Limerick.** (See *'In the glow of theTurf Fire'* By the author)

DOOMSDAY BELL
The Church bell was only rung outside church services when a disaster occurred.
This to call the people together to hear the news. Thus **Doomsday bell.**
At a man's funeral services the bell is rung in series of three notes then a pause.
At a woman's funeral service the bell is rung in a series of two notes then a pause.

DROICHEAD COISE
A removable footbridge spanning a river or stream in order to gain access from one part of a farm to another was known as Droichead Coise. Many of these bridges which were no more than a plank of wood were placed over streams where the evil fairies, Bean-O-Shéidhes and damned souls were known to traverse. Should a person encounter one of these and God forbid

they should. In order to escape they would place the plank over the stream and cross to the other side. The bridge would then be drawn across behind them leaving the evil one stranded. Evil spirits will not cross running water. Most were footbridges but when the land was required for ploughing it would be widened enough to take a cart.

FAIRY STONES
*Before any building could commence permission had to be sought from the fairies. Stones were borrowed from a fairy fort or fairy stream and used to disclose fairy paths. They should always be returned to where they came from. See **placing the stones.***

FEAR BRÉIGE
***Scarecrow** made from old clothing to make it look like a person. Used to frighten birds off crops. It would be moved daily to different locations to try and fool the birds. Robins had a habit of building their nests in the pockets. It was also claimed that the 'Good Folk' (The dead) would borrow them and go and visit the homes of their people.*

FEAR (GRASSES)
Féar Féarcaorach Pasture Grass. Féar Capaill Meadow grass. Féar Garbh Coarse Grass. Féar Gorta. Hungry Grass or mountain grass. It was believed that should one step on the Féar Gorta then an unnatural craving for food came upon one. Most farmers carried a piece of scone in their pockets that they ate as a cure. Féar Gaoil. Quitch Grass or fairy grass, a course grass with travelling roots not welcome in any meadow. Fairies would plant this in a meadow if the household upset them.

FIELD OF BLOOD (See relish cakes)

FINGER OF TOBACCO
A measure of tobacco from the knuckle of the index finger to the tip.

FREE MASONRY (Gobhan Saór)
The Gobhan Saór or Free Smith was well known in Irish mythology. When excavating the foundations of 'Baals Bridge' in Limerick the following inscription was uncovered....
      ' Upon this level... By the square
      I will strive to live, with love and care'.
Freemasonry was in vogue in Limerick as early as the $15^{th}/16^{th}$ century. Freemasonry was not confined to the Protestant religion. Daniel O'Connell

was a Freemason and a member of the Catholic Limerick branch. He was also a landlord extracting rack rent from his starving captive tenants in Caherciveen in County Kerry.

FUNERALS AND THE DEVIL

The coffins of the dead were carried on the shoulders of their immediate family to their graves. The devil would follow the funeral hoping to steal the soul of the departed. Three steps behind the cortège a relative with his coat on back to front would walk. The cortège would take the longest route to the graveyard, at the crossroads it would take a turn to the east away from the graveyard. The cortège would then turn round leaving the relative with his coat back to front walking on alone to the west. The devil would think that he was still following the funeral leaving it to make it safely to the graveyard.

FURROW or furrow-in-length (Furlong)

The most convenient length of a furrow was about 250 yards. The length was roughly calculated by walking a horse drawn plough down an average field and turning him comfortable at the end.

GENTLEMAN WHO PAID THE RENT

The gentleman who paid the rent was the hog or in some cases the sow. Should one be lucky enough to own a hog they could take it to the sow of a neighbour for mating. In return for allowing his hog to service the sow he would be rewarded accordingly when the sow gave birth. This payment was made in the form of a bonbh (Piglet) or two according to the size of the litter. These he would raise and when the bailiff came calling for his rent the tenant would pay him in kind with a pig or two. Thus 'The gentleman who pays the rent'

GREGORY. WILLIAM HENRY (Quarter acre clause)

William Henry Gregory member of the British parliament (Dublin) brought in the Poor Law Amendment act of 1847. Small holders starving to death were forced to surrender without compensation all their land in excess of a quarter acre before they would receive any relief. (A small bowl of watery soup for each person) Those who refused to part with any of their land were allowed to starve to death. Family owning even one inch of land above this would not be deemed to be destitute nor could they claim relief or enter the workhouse. This act was brought in with the sole purpose of driving the Irish off their land. (See **'Dare You Ripple my Pond)**

GLEN COLUMCILLE

Situated in a glen north of Donegal bay. In the glen is a shrine to saint Columcille. Pilgrims go there to atone for their sins or to seek his intervention. A pilgrimage is made to his shrine such as Lough Derg, Knock, Doon Well etc;

GOMBEEN MEN
Racketeers who exact a very high interest rate on a loan or sell goods to the poor at exhorborant prices and interest.

GUARDIAN OF THE GRAVEYARD (Bárda an Tamhlacht0
Guardian of the graveyard is the task given to the most recent corpse entering the graveyard. The spirit of the corpse has to stand guard at the gate awaiting the next spirit to arrive in a corpse. The spirit cannot leave for the **Astral World** *until another enters and takes its place. The task is then handed over to the new arrival and only then can the spirit leave.*

If two funerals were entering the graveyard at the same time then there would be a dash as to who should get to the graveyard first. Mourners would not wish to see the ghosts of their loved ones wailing at the gate awaiting another funeral. It was believed that as the souls rested in Limbo within the confines of an unguarded graveyard, evil spirits would be in a position to steal them away to the underworld. Placing a guard on the graveyard prevented this from happening.

HA HA
Colonel Robert Dormer of **Rousham Park Steeple Aston Oxfordshire** *began the transformation of the gardens at Rousham in about 1719. He commissioned Charles Bridgeman, the Royal gardener, to draw up plans for his new gardens. Bridgeman created the* **Ha-Ha** *making the invisible but essential division between pasture and garden.*

HANGING GAEL
Tenants unable to meet their rent and taxes in any one year could with the permission of their landlords hold their dues over until the following season. The tenant in the meantime could not leave his landlord until the debt and profits were duly met.
Therefore the tenant had the debt due and the power of the landlord hanging over him. He became a bonded serf; Thus **'The Hanging Gael.'** *(See* **'Cry the Cursed Land')**

HEDGE SCHOOLS

Following the ratification of the ignominious Treaty of Limerick in 1697 to the satisfaction, welfare and safety of his Majesty's loyal Protestant subjects in the kingdom of Ireland there followed a number of barbarous Statutes. These were passed into law between 1695-1727.

Not taking the sacraments according to the Anglican Rite excluded one from state offices and parliament. This act excluding Catholics from taking any part in the government of their country. An act in 1710 brought about the most brutal breaking of the Treaty of Limerick.

IRISH CATHOLICS could not sit in Parliament.
IRISH CATHOLICS could not bear arms.
IRISH CATHOLICS could not own a horse valued over £5. If a Protestant wanted a horse belonging to a Catholic then he could take it on payment of a pittance.
IRISH CATHOLICS could not become apprentices.
IRISH CATHOLICS could not own land
IRISH Catholics could not be commissioned into His majesty's forces.
IRISH CATHOLICS could not be educated.
IRISH CATHOLICS could not be sent abroad to be educated
IRISH CATHOLICS could not vote
IRISH CATHOLICS who changed their faith could put their families out of their homes and take full possession. Nicknamed **Soupers, Jumpers, Perverts.**
CATHOLIC clergy were banished from the land by an act of 1703.
These are just a handful of the cruel laws imposed on the indigenous population.
Schools known as hedge schools were secretly established by learned clerics and scholars to teach the deprived Catholics. This to overcome this anomaly.
'Faith of our fathers living still in spite of dungeon, fire and sword'

HOLY WELLS

In ancient Ireland wells were sacred and guarded by spirits, Druids would visit these wells and call on the spirits to perform cures on the sick. When Christianity came to Ireland it gave the names of saints to the wells. Some that were visited by saints became shrines and the water from these wells could only be used to cure or bless. To use this water to cook with or wash would bring disaster on the household. It was believed that water from these wells would never boil.

KEEP HOLES

Keep holes can be seen on each side of fireplace in Irish cottages. The one on the left belonged to the woman of the house where she kept her knitting and odds and sods. The one to the right was owned by the man of the house where he kept his cre duideen, tobac and the family bible. When a wife became a widow she moved to the right. This meant that she now had the right to sit at the right side of the fire.

KERRYMAN'S TABLE
In Ireland churns of milk were left in recesses near to the farm. They usually had a slate table or bench. The full churns were placed there to be collected by the creameries for pasteurising and butter making. That evening the empty churns were then returned to the recess for collection by the smallholder. As this was some distance from his home he would take a packed lunch. Sitting at the table he would eat his lunch, smoke his cré duídín and have the 'Craic' with his neighbours or perhaps a game of '45. (Irish card game) Thus the name.

LANDLORDS CROSS
The marking out of a percentage of the tenant's crop by the landlord's agents to meet the demands for rent and taxes. Many tenants starved to death as the landlords cross of food lay awaiting collection. To tamper with it in any way would result in eviction or deportation.

LAZY BEDS
Ridges approximately two feet six inches wide into which potatoes are set. (Grown) The potatoes are laid in a staggered pattern on top of the grass. The bed is then built up from the upturned sods taken from the trenches formed on each side. The beds always follow the slope of the field to avoid flooding. When the young shoots appear the **Earthing up** takes place. The young shoots are covered again with earth from the trench to protect them from frost and to ensure a heavy cropping.

LIOS
An immense and atmospherical ring of stone surrounded by trees. It stands on one of the most important sites of prehistoric Ireland at Lough Gur in the County of Limerick. Here the Neolithic Irish race built their villages some five thousand years ago. Here you will also find their wedge-shaped megalithic tombs, ring cairns and standing stones. The Lios was constructed in a ring shape marked out with ten huge stones weighing many tons. One opposing pair was aligned on the moons minimum midsummer's setting. Mud was taken in woven baskets from the lake and piled between the Lios. Massed Lunar ceremonies were held within the Lios. (Baetyls. Egg shaped stones known or believed to have sexual significance have also been found)

LYKE WAKE
A corpse found alone would be guarded over pending the arrival of the family This to deter evil spirits from stealing the soul and to let the dead know that they were remembered and being attended to. A corpse was never left alone until it was interred in the soil. (Not to be confused with the three day wake)

ORANGE TOAST/ ORANGE PEEL
*Following dinner in the Houses of Parliament it was traditional to drink '**The Orange Toast**'. The tradition was for the parliamentarians to stand on their chairs charge their glasses and placing one leg on the dining table raise their glasses and call the toast.*
"To the Pious, glorious and immortal memory of William of Orange, William the Third." *This annoyed the Catholics and moreso Daniel O'Connell and the Duke of Leinster. (The royal clan Fitzgeralds) The duke sickened by the antics of Robert Peel at the dinners gave him the nickname '**Orange Peel**'.*
Many say that the exposing of ones bare right leg at freemason initiation ceremonies originated from this practice.

PAUPERS SUN
*The landed gentry who had settled along the West Coast of Ireland would invite their guests to come and sit by the coast and watch **THEIR** setting sun. The Irish were denied this privilege. However much they watched the setting sun they could never own it. Nor could they stop the Irish from seeing it. The sun set over Ireland would always belong to the nation. Thus the setting sun became known as the '**Pauper's Sun.**' God's gift to be shared by rich and poor alike.*
'To sit beside a turf fire in a cabin and watch the sun go down in Galway Bay'

PLACING THE STONES

Before attempting to build a house the builder consulted with the fairies in the form of placing fairy stones in the field. The stones were brought from fairy forts, fairy fields or fairy streams. The stones would be placed on the four corners one on top of the other if the stones were not disturbed or removed by mystical powers then it was not a fairy field and building could take place. The stones had to be returned from whence they came. To ignore the fairy warning brought grave consequences. The house may be tumbled the first born ghosted away to Tír -na-nÓg

POOR MAN'S GENERATOR

In 1847 England appointed Chef Soyer to open his so-called model soup kitchens in Phoenix Park Dublin. An elaborate kitchen was set up and the gentry were invited to sit and observe the starving people for the sum of £5. This went towards the purchase of the ingredients. (The head of one ox minus the tongue, 28 lbs. turnips, 3lbs onions, 7lbs carrots, 20lbs pea meal, 14lbs Indian corn. This would be put into a pot containing 30+ gallons of water and boiled. This he claimed would be sufficient to sustain 500 persons for a day. One quarter pint per person.)

The starving would queue up outside the large tent and when the bell rang they would be allowed into the tent. There they would sit on the long benches provided. Quarter pint bowls with a chained spoon attached to the table would be filled with the watery soup. When the bell rang for the second time each person would rise and leave on the opposite side. On leaving was given a hard tack army biscuit the residue of rations from the French wars as they left. The next in line came in behind them and took their places and so on. Colonel Douglas, a relief inspector when asked what he thought of this vile mixture which was giving the people bowel trouble remarked...

"We have done all we can the rest we must leave to God". The Churches also maintained that Ireland's problems were the will of God.

Mr Bishop a relief worker reported that the soup for the starving now known as 'POOR SOUP' was killing as many people as the hunger was...

"It runs through them offering no nourishment." He remarked.

Chef Soyer saw that his recipe was of no value gave up the task and returned to his restaurant in fashionable London.

'Beware!
The horns of the bull
The puck of the goat
The heel of the horse

And the smile of the English'

PRAYER STICK
Sticks that had one decade of the Rosary notched on one side and five notches on the other side. This to allow the pilgrim to say and count the five decades of the rosary. Pilgrims left them beside holy wells for use by others.

QUARTER DAY
The day when the bailiff called for the landlords rent, usually every three months. See HANGING GAEL.

RACK RENT
Exorbitant rent demanded for a piece of land.

RELISH CAKE or famine cake
Cattle owners bled their healthy cattle and mixed the blood with wild mushrooms, cabbage, turnips etc; it was then made into cakes and fried over a fire until dry. This they stored and used throughout the great hunger. The blood letter, a man capable of bleeding an animal without killing it usually was appointed to carry out this task. His commission was 10% of the blood. Where he bled the animal became known as the **'Field of Blood'**. *One such field can be seen on the roundabout at Castleconnell in Limerick.*

RESTING STONE
A flat stone set into the wall outside a cottage as a seat. Some seats sat on a stone leg. Others had a flat stone set behind them as a backrest. (Can be seen to this day outside older cottages)
'The stone outside Dan Murphy's door'

RIBBON MEN/WHITE BOYS
Irish agrarian society whose members wore a white ribbon on their sleeves when raiding landlords estates/ White boys wore white frocks. All originated in Limerick/Cork and Clare.

ROCKED IN THE POT
Illegitimate children were frowned upon and brought shame on the household. When callers came to the house the child would sometimes be hidden in the big iron pot out of view. When the matchmaker came to make the match he/she would ask if the son/daughter had been 'Rocked in the pot.' **(See 'In the Glow of the Turf Fire')**

RUNDALE
Land held in Rundale consisted of approximately 150 Irish acres. This was rented from a landlord by a number of stewards in common tenancy. Each tenant would receive a piece of good land and an equal piece of poor land. The rents were set so high that it was impossible to survive less alone meet the exorbitant rent.

SAINT COLUMBA
West of Letterkenny lies three lakes, Gartan, Akibbon and Macally. Of there three Gratan is the most famous for it was on its shore that Saint Columba was born in 521.A.D. Columba was one of the great Irish saints that would not accept dogmatic rule from Rome. On his mother's side he was descendant from the Royal House of Leinster and on his father's side from Niall of the Nine Hostages. When still a young boy he trained under Saint Finian at Strangford He was ordained in a monastery at Glasnevin when he was twenty-five years of age. He returned to Derry where he founded his first of many monasteries. This earned him the title of Columbkille (Columba of the Chapels) He had a fierce tempter that caused him a lot of problems. He was in constant conflict with Diarmid, the High King of Ireland.
He wrote his own version of the New Testament and this brought him in direct conflict with the Church and State. He fought many battles over this and was finally defeated and excommunicated. With twelve of his loyal disciples he sailed away from Ireland in 563.a.d. and landed on the island of Iona where he established a monastery. Many more followed all committed to his interruption of the New Testament. He died on Iona in 597.A.D.

SAINT BRÍDGET'S FEAST DAY
Traditionally the feast of Saint Bridget falls on the second day of February. It marks the beginning of the farming year. In olden times the girls in the family carrying effigies of the Saint known as Brídeogs and St, Brídget's crosses would assemble in the field to *'turn the first sod'* and say special prayers invoking her blessing on the land and hoping for a generous harvest.

SCALP
Earth removed to a depth of six feet or thereabout by an evicted tenant. This was roofed over with sods of grass to conceal it from the land lords agents. In these burrows evicted families eked out a miserable existence.
Not to be confused with a *'Scalpeén'* which was constructed inside a

demolished cottage. When discovered the occupants were horsewhipped and deported.

SETTLED BEDS (LEABA SUIDHEACHAN)
Common in all Irish country houses up until the twentieth century. It was used by day as a settee. At night it was opened out into a bed and became a refuge for stranded travellers. There was always a 'Cead Mile fáilte' in Irish houses for those in need.

STRAW BOYS
Boys and men covered themselves in a straw suit on the feast of Saint Stephen and joined the wren boys for the burial of the wren. They also turned up at weddings much to the amusement of the guests. In the south west of Ireland Limerick/Kerry/ Clare and Cork the straw boys would carry wooden swords. Some would be appointed to carry a pig's bladder tied to a pole. The carriers of the bladder represented English knights. When they had gathered enough customers the Irish knights (Straw men) would attack the English knights who carried the bladder and after a short skirmish kill them. Then a collection would be made for the burial of the wren. Actually the money was used to buy drink and food for the festival. Nobody wanted to be the carrier of the bladder as they received the worst wounds and could never win. Lots had to be drawn for the unwelcome task. *(See 'Tears on my Pillow')*

STIPALLÁN
A heavy pole drawn across a gap in a field to deter large animals from wandering. Used in place of a gate where sheep and cattle shared the same fields. Sheep could only pass unhindered under the gap to get to the next field. Sometimes known as Stick-in-the-Gap.

SOLD THE PASS.
Comes from the siege of Limerick when Robert Adam betrayed the Irish at the pass of Cratlow to the forces of Oliver Cromwell. 1690-1692

TALLY WOMAN/ TALLY STICKS
Táille Bata (Tally Stick) was a stick scored with matching notches for items held on account. The stick was split lengthways in half and each party, the debtor and the creditor held a half each. When the debt was honoured the two pieces were brought together and destroyed in the presence of both parties, thus honouring the debt. In the case of the girl, the parents were allowed the freedom to build a hovel and struggle to make a living on their half acre of poor land provided by their master (The landlord). In part payment of rent,

should he so desire he would take a daughter of his choice as a tally woman? The girl would be taken to the bedchamber of the landlord to satisfy his every desire. Should the girl become pregnant then she would be removed as far away as possible from the estate and married off to a tenant or servant of a fellow landlord in another county. The servant would be forced to swear on oath that the child was theirs. The landlord would not accept the child and no claim on the estate would be entertained. Once the tally woman left the estate then it was deemed that the contract had been fulfilled. Families were large and the Irish were not allowed to own their own land, therefore their options were few if any. They could refuse and be evicted from the land and forced into the mountains where in most cases they would die from cold and hunger. The landlord should he so desire could still claim the daughter making their resistance a futile gesture. This feudal and barbaric system of slavery was prevalent throughout Ireland before and during the nineteenth century...

TASMANIANS
They were a single aboriginal race of friendly stone aged people. They were the indigenous population of Tasmania. (Not to be confused with the Aboriginals of Australia) Within a generation, the English invaders greedy for their land had annihilated all of them, not one remained. They were shot, poisoned and raped to extinction. The last Tasmanian was a woman named Truganini and she followed her people into oblivion on the 8th May 1876 in the town of Hobart. The same method was used in Australia but failed. Even in death the last of the Tasmanian's found no peace in their native soil. Their bodies were exhumed in the dead of night and removed to London for exhibition. The white settlers wanted their bodies as a macabre exhibition for their museums in Tasmania and London.

'*The she-oaks wail in the autumn gale,*
And the sad mists shadowy rise
O'er the wild swamps stream,
Where the curlew screams
As the queen of the dead tribe dies.
What has become of Cihuapan?
Quantintecomtzin brave?
And Conahuatzin mighty man?
Where are they? In the grave!
Their names remain, but they are fled,
Forever numbered with the dead.'

TITHE LAW
Catholics were obliged to pay1/10 of their miserable income to the Anglican

Church. This like many laws of the period was indefensible. The Protestant Church who owned in excess of five million acres of fertile Irish land demanded and collected this draconian rent from impoverished Catholics. This to add to the coffers of the Protestant Clergyman who was paid in excess of £10,000 per annum.

TRIMMINS
Special family prayers said outside the Rosary for personal and special intentions

VAN DIEMEN'S LAND (TASMANIA)
Tasmania was known as Van Diemen's land until 1856. It is an island in the Bass Straits and was part of the British Empire. The British used it as a penal colony. It is now part of the Commonwealth of Australia. The British wiped out the indigenous population. See **Tasmanian's**.